Kuunmong

The Cloud Dream of the Nine

石橋奇緣

THE FAIRIES ON THE BRIDGE

Kuunmong

The Cloud Dream of the Nine

A KOREAN NOVEL:
A STORY OF THE TIMES OF THE TANGS OF CHINA
ABOUT 840 AD

By Kim Manjung

Translated by James Scarth Gale

INTRODUCTION BY
Susanna Fessler

WITH AN INTERPRETATIVE ESSAY BY
Francisca Cho

ORIGINAL INTRODUCTION BY
Elspet Keith Robertson Scott

KURODAHAN PRESS
2003

Originally published by Daniel O'Connor, 1922
at the Westminster Press, London

NS-KR0001L5
ISBN 978-4-902075-03-8

KURODAHAN PRESS
KURODAHAN.COM

Contents

The Novel

Appendix

INTRODUCTION

THE *Cloud Dream of the Nine* (*Kuunmong* 九雲夢) is a seventeenth century Korean novel set in ninth century China. On the surface it is an entertaining tale of a young man who travels through two lifetimes accompanied by eight beautiful maidens; at its core, it is philosophical novel about Buddhism and Confucianism. The author, Kim Manjung, wrote the novel while in exile, reputedly to console his mother. The result has pleased thousands of readers in the following ages.

THE LITERARY CONTEXT OF THE NOVEL

Literature in Korea has complex past. As in most traditions, Korean literature began with verse in its many and varied forms. The earliest verse dates to the Three Kingdom period (roughly the fourth through the seventh centuries), although much has been lost and in many cases the only extant remnant of a work is its title. This early verse was composed before the Koreans had developed their own writing system, and was written using the writing system developed in China, but with Korean syntax. The Chinese language also played a role, and was used by educated Koreans for both official communications and for various other forms of literature. Although Korean and Chinese are not in the same language family, this convention persisted. It was not unlike the convention of using Latin as an official language throughout medieval Europe. Later, when the Korean script (hangul) was developed, there was a distinct division between works composed in Korean and works composed in Chinese.

The use of Korean script emerged largely in the seventeenth century, which is when Kim Manjung (1637–1692) wrote *The Cloud Dream of the Nine*. Scholars long thought that *The Cloud Dream of the Nine* was initially composed in Korean and later translated into Chinese. However, in the late twentieth century the discovery of an early eighteenth century Chinese version of the text and subsequent studies concluded that it is likely Kim Manjung composed this work first in Chinese, and that it was later translated into Korean. Consequently, some scholars hail this work as the first great Korean novel; others decry that it is not really Korean at all, being composed in Chinese and set in China. It is useful to note that Kim was not the only author composing works of this nature; there are hundreds of other works from this time composed both in Korean and Chinese.

Regardless of the linguistic taxonomy of the novel itself, it was clearly part of an active age of development in Korean literature. The growth of a literate readership during Kim's time helped spur a production and distribution of literature that was unprecedented. Prose was coming into its own in Korea, as it was in the West. (Kim's contemporaries in Europe included Molière, Locke, and Defoe.) And, although verse continued to be composed in the centuries that followed, prose has largely taken over as the most popular form of literature in modern Korea.

THE PHILOSOPHICAL CONTEXT OF THE NOVEL

The Cloud Dream of the Nine reflects the philosophical and literary values of Kim Manjung's time and earlier ages, both in Korea and in China. Kim was a product of *yangban* ("two orders") culture, the society that resulted from the complex Sinicized bureaucratic structure of the Yi (Chosŏn) Dynasty. Briefly, *yangban* culture followed the Confucian example of requiring civil service examinations of the elite in order to place them in the hierarchy of the government and, by extension, society. Kim Manjung, a bureaucrat, did not fare well in this system, and he died in political exile. Nonetheless, the importance of Confucian values – benevolence, propriety, filial piety, loyalty, righteousness, and reciprocity – were deeply instilled in the author and his contemporaries.

Confucianism is in essence an ethical system, one that does not attempt to explain the metaphysical nature of the world – or that it defers usually to Taoism. Confucianism is based on what are known as the "Five Classics" and "Four Books," historical and literary texts of ancient China. Confucianism holds that one is duty-bound to obey the structures of society; the system mandates inequalities – men are superior to women, elders are superior to juniors. These inequalities are in the interest of maintaining a natural harmony, not in the interest of political tyranny. Most importantly, the reward for societal obedience is a peaceful, balanced, and just life in this life. That is, there is little or no concern with an afterlife, or a subsequent existence. Confucianism was and is profoundly influential throughout East Asia, and is largely the tradition behind what is currently termed "Asian values."

At the same time that Confucianism ordered society in Korea, Buddhism was the predominant religion. Whereas Confucianism stressed proper behavior in a current world, Buddhism focused beyond this life to lives before and after. That is, Buddhism holds that one's life is but one of an almost infinite number of lives in a cycle of death and rebirth. The petty concerns of this life are insignificant when put in the context of the larger whole. Concern with and focus on prosaic, mundane issues cloud one's ability to see beyond this life, and an inability to see beyond this life dooms one to the continuous, meaningless cycle. Escape from this cycle can only come from dedication to the Buddhist teachings. This dedication requires that one jettison the creature comforts of luxuriant living and the emotional ties to family and friends. Although this is a great demand, the Buddhist scriptures emphasize (as does Kim Manjung when he quotes them) that "all is illusion" and clinging to this illusion is in vain.

Thus Confucianism and Buddhism presented two conflicting philosophical approaches for the seventeenth century Korean author, as they did for the ninth century Chinese characters in this work. Kim Manjung's novel asks the ageless question: what is the meaning of life? In this sense, although the author and characters are thousands of miles and hundreds of years away from our own time, they are faced with a common human conundrum that transcends time and space.

A reader from the Judeo-Christian or Muslim tradition might still be puzzled by Kim's presentation of the question. However, it is important to remember not only that Buddhist and Confucian values differ from other traditions, but also that Kim Manjung has created a caricature of these values in his work. The Buddhist hero, Yang Song-jin, is a monk who lives in a miserable cell, eats meager fare, and spends most of his time in prayer. The Confucian hero, So-yoo, passes all bureaucratic examinations with ease, wins military campaigns with a word, indulges happily in liquor with abandon, and easily finds himself with eight wives / concubines. Kim Manjung purposely gives the reader an example of the extreme in both cases, and although this is arguably a didactic novel, it is unlikely that the reader is meant to identify directly with either character. Much ink has been spilt on the unrealistic nature of these characters and the consequent poor value of the novel, but I believe the reader really need not concern himself with this. In the end this lack of verisimilitude is of little consequence; one can easily suspend disbelief and indulge in the adventure, as one does when watching a contemporary Hollywood film. In other words, the modern reader should not walk away from this novel in disbelief at the behavior of the characters, but rather should look beyond their surface behavior to the values that drive them. It is there that the message of the work lies. The entertaining flourishes are merely a sweet indulgence to help the more serious question take hold.

THE CULTURAL CONTEXT OF THE NOVEL

Modern readers of this novel are often surprised by the behavior of the characters. A few points one should keep in mind while reading are as follows: First, polygamy was an accepted practice in Tang China, and was not an indication of lasciviousness. Therefore, although So-yoo's eight mates are seen as excessive by the end of the novel, his initial desire to have more than one mate is quite acceptable. Second, heavy consumption of alcohol was common, in part due to Taoist ideas about inaction and alchemy. Thus, when the characters partake in drink we are not necessarily meant to think poorly of them. Third, fraternization between the unmarried sexes, at least in the upper class, was restricted to such an extent that potential lovers often courted through words alone, usually poetry. Thus, the ability to compose good poetry was highly valued. Finally, propriety was paramount, particularly in the Confucian sense. The characters debate at length such issues as which woman should be considered first or second wife, not because they are petty but because proper positions were seen as necessary if social harmony were to be maintained.

INTRODUCTION

THE HISTORICAL CONTEXT OF THE NOVEL

This novel is set in the early ninth century in China. The country at that time was unified, although its borders were smaller and differed significantly from what they are to-day. There was a central bureaucracy, headed by the Emperor, whose dynasty (the Tang) had been in place since AD 618.

In the eighth and ninth centuries the Chinese faced the expansion of Tibetan forces (often referred to as proto-Tibetan or Turfan) from the west; these forces were formidable, and briefly managed to take the capital city of Chang An in 763. It is no surprise, therefore, that Kim Manjung makes the Tibetan forces the major foe for his hero, So-yoo, the general of the emperor's army. One should note, however, that "Tibet" is a loose concept here, and is not the same as the geo-political entity of to-day. In sum "Tibet" here means the area to the west of Tang China, what is northwest China to-day.

The government rank system reached its maturity under the Tang. We are told of So-yoo's promotions to Chief Minister, Minister of State, and Chief Commissioner and Minister of War, none of which mean much to the uninitiated reader. Short of drawing charts here it is difficult to convey the prestige that each promotion brought, but the reader can rest assured that each promotion was noteworthy and indicative of So-yoo's exclusive and elite position in the bureaucracy.

It would seem that Kim Manjung did not model his characters on any real historical figures, but the setting he chose – minus the magical dream sequences – resembles what we know about Tang China.

THE CLOUD DREAM OF THE NINE TO-DAY

The Cloud Dream of the Nine remains popular and can be found in print to-day in Korea (in both the hangul and Chinese versions). Like classical literature in other traditions, though, it is not a bestseller.

This translation, by Rev. James S. Gale, was originally published in 1922 by Daniel O'Connor at the Westminster Press. Gale (1863–1937) was a Canadian who resided for over thirty years in Korea as a Christian missionary. His translation is relatively complete and accurate, although there are some exceptions to this rule (see below). In 1974 Richard Rutt published an English translation titled *A Nine Cloud Dream* (Seoul: Royal Asiatic Society Korea Branch), and in 1973 a consortium of translators from Ewha Womens University in Seoul published an English version also titled *The Nine Cloud Dream*. The only other language into which the work has been published is Mandarin Chinese. Until this reprint, however, all of these translations remained obscure, held by only a few dozen libraries around the world.

Although Gale's translation is very readable, the reader should note that he often took liberties with the poems in order to make them rhyme in English. The original form of the poetry follows Chinese poesy, which has its own set of complex rules, few if any of which can be easily conveyed in English. Gale also chose to transliterate the characters' names in Korean, even though the action takes place in China. Rutt, on the other hand, chooses the Chinese transliteration. For example, Gale writes "So-yoo" where Rutt writes "Shao-yu" for the characters 少游. Also, in the tradition of early translations from Asian literature, Gale omits certain short passages at his discretion. For example, when Kim Manjung quotes a short passage from the Diamond Sutra in the last scene, Gale omits it. In the end none of this much changes the content of the book. Gale's translation is in the spirit of the original, and continues to bring this classic to a western audience.

Susanna Fessler
University at Albany

DREAM TALE AND MEANING:
A literary analysis of Kuunmong

COMPARING KUUNMONG AND THE MODERN NOVEL

T HE *Cloud Dream of the Nine* is a pre-modern Asian novel, and as such, does not conform to the model of the novel as it formed in the modern West. For contemporary readers, both Western and Asian, the cultural challenge of Kim Manjung's *(literary name:* Sŏp'o) work lies not in its remote historical setting – which happens to be ninth century China – but rather in its literary qualities, which reflect the world of seventeenth century Korea.

To begin, the characters of the novel exhibit nothing in the way of psychological depth or evolution. They are instead highly idealized, being more representative of social archetypes than of unique and individual personae. So-yoo, the main character of the frame tale, or the dream sequence that comprises the bulk of the novel, is the archetypal scholar, handsome and gifted, who lives out the idealized path of success in the Imperial examinations that determined political careers in Tang China. His eight wives and concubines are all beautiful, accomplished, and remarkably generous in their willingness to share their paragon of a husband between them. The life of So-yoo offers a most wishful vision of reality set on the Confucian model, which is dominated by a male perspective, as well as optimism in the perfectibility of secular life. The fact that this vision is ultimately rejected, via the monk Song-jin's "awakening" from this dream, conveys the author Sŏp'o's own disillusionment with romantic Confucianism and lends greater depth to his work than supplied by the surface features of his main characters.

From the perspective of literary origins, the tale of So-yoo participates in the genre of narratives originating from Tang China known as the *quanqi,* or "transmitting the marvelous," and a particular subset of this genre known as the *caizi-jiaren*, or "talented scholar–beautiful maiden"story. Most broadly speaking, the dominant feature of *quanqi* is its lack of realism and its favoring of the fantastic. Its tales are populated by fox-fairies, ghosts, magical beasts and dream journeys to other worlds. Didactic commentary usually concludes the tales. These elements of fable comprise the second major departure of *The Cloud Dream of the Nine* from the contemporary novel. Sŏp'o's departure from historical realism is compounded by yet another literary practice common to his time, which is the use of the Buddhist concept of karma as a way of forging links between major characters. Karma was a popular mechanism for romantic tales, in particular: such stories reveal that in a prior life, the lovers had an encounter that necessitates completing their romantic destiny in the present life/tale.

In *The Cloud Dream of the Nine*, this previous encounter is narrated in the outer tale of the Buddhist novice Song-jin, whose celibacy is disturbed by his chance meeting with the eight fairy girls of Queen Wee. The frame tale of So-yoo is, in fact, Song-jin's dream realization of his previous temptation, and his final enlightenment is contingent upon the lesson of the illusoriness of life that he learns as a result of dreaming. From the perspective of plot, the karmic device offers a handy explanation of So-yoo's chance encounters with his eight lovers and the ready ease of his romantic successes. There is no specificity or emotional realism in these romances, and they function more in fulfillment of a stock literary mechanism than as the central interest of the novel.

RELIGIOUS AND LITERARY MEANING IN KUUNMONG

Given the pre-modern qualities of our work, appreciation of the meaning of *The Cloud Dream of the Nine* first entails understanding the political context of its author, and the general historical significance of the novel in East Asia. As a scholar official, Sŏp'o was officially a Confucian, and thus aligned with an ideology that privileged historical narratives as vehicles of moral instruction, and which frowned upon fictive narratives as instruments of social corruption. Hence for Sŏp'o to write a work of fiction, particularly one which trumps the idealized Confucian life with the Buddhist verdict that such a life is ultimately illusory and wanting, is an act of private rebellion. Sŏp'o wrote the present novel in 1687, during one of his many political exiles, and only five years before his death at the age of fifty-five. His career, like that of his fictional protagonist So-yoo, conformed to the ideal model, placing on top of the state examinations at the age of twenty-eight, followed by prestigious political appointments. But like many a political minister, Sŏp'o suffered repeated reversals of fortune, playing victim to a system of court factionalism in which monarchical whim and marriage alliances could change careers overnight.

In this environment, literature – particularly the creative literature of fiction and poetry – functioned as vehicles of political complaint. Poetry functioned as a public as well as private practice – that is, poetic composition was a part of official state events, and poetic talent was the prerogative of the public man. Fiction, on the other hand, was a purely private enterprise, to be shared with close friends and family rather than created for public consumption. *The Cloud Dream of the Nine*, for example, did not achieve its literary status and broad circulation until the nineteenth century. The private nature of fiction hence made it the safest medium of political criticism, and the novels of seventeenth and eighteenth century Korea frequently voice the discontent of the socially dispossessed.

The particular interest afforded by Sŏp'o's literary work is that it speaks from within the ranks of the most socially and politically privileged. In this respect, Sŏp'o's novel differs from, say, Ho Kyun's (1569–1618) *Hong Kiltong*, which speaks for the second sons dispossessed of wealth and office in the Korean practice of primogeniture; or the much loved narrative of Chunhyang, which depicts the powerlessness of the low class of courtesans known as *kisaeng*. Sŏp'o's view from the top of the social hierarchy is representative of many a scholar-official in traditional China and Korea, and their special brand of discontent is enacted through the conflicting ideologies of Confucianism and Buddhism. The tale of the Buddhist monk Song-jin and the Confucian minister So-yoo, who are but one person, is a literary mirroring of men like Sŏp'o, who were juxtapositions of a public Confucian identity ultimately at war with a private Buddhist self.

The curriculum of the educated gentleman unofficially included Buddhist texts, and Sŏp'o's nonfictional writings attest to first hand knowledge of and reflection upon such classics as the *Lotus Sutra*, the *Platform Sutra*, and the *Vimalakīrtinirdeśa Sutra*. Sŏp'o's brand of Buddhism was Mahāyāna, particularly Sŏn Buddhism, or the Korean version of Chan/ Zen. Of particular relevance is the Sŏn tendency to depict all phenomenal reality as ultimately insubstantial projections of the mind. The goal of religious meditation is to understand this nature of the world – that it is temporary and empty of innate characteristics, so that one can become detached from it. From a literary perspective, the Buddhist lesson that life is the imaginative play of the mind, much like a dream, could not help but be applied to the nature of fiction itself. And unlike the Confucian sensibility, which ranked history both morally and ontologically above creative literature, the Buddhist worldview suggested little difference between the putatively "real" nature of life versus the "unreal" nature of worlds created by the imagination. Furthermore, if life and art are phenomenally equal, the value of art for exploring the nature of "reality" can be affirmed. Art and fiction, in other words, can function philosophically and speak of truth.

THE DREAM TALE

Sŏp'o chose to realize his philosophical practice of fiction through the literary device of the dream tale. Generally speaking, this is a frame tale in which the protagonist, always a male, harbors "visions of grandeur"and then dreams a dream in which he attains maximal success. Upon awakening from the dream, he realizes that this long life was lived in a comparatively brief dream, and abandons his ambitions, realizing their vanity. Such tales can also be found outside Asia in European and Arabic sources. In China, the dream tale surfaces as early as the Six Dynasties (fourth-sixth centuries), in Gan Bao's *Soushenji* ("Record of Spirits"), and is most common to the Tang era. These dream narratives capitalize primarily on the conceit of the didactic function of the dream. The brief dream stands in for life itself, and the dreamer is spared the necessity of living out his vain ambitions in "real" life.

The Cloud Dream of the Nine, as a much later entity, exhibits the influence of Indian and Chinese Daoist metaphysical thought. In this respect, Sŏp'o's work is in the same category as Cao Xueqin's eighteenth century novel, *Dream of the Red Chamber*, which is undoubtedly the culmination of the dream tale genre, both in terms of literary magnificence and length. In East Asia, the didactic observation that life is nothing more than a dream is commonly attributed to Buddhist and Daoist teachings, without much discrimination between the two. Perhaps the most famous source of this adage on the Daoist side is the philosopher Zhuangzi's butterfly dream, which is recounted by Song-jin's own Buddhist master after Song-jin awakens from his dream: Zhuangzi recounts dreaming that he is a butterfly, and after awakening, he is not quite sure whether the butterfly is the dream, or if the butterfly is dreaming that he is Zhuangzi. In other words, Zhuangzi is not sure why his waking self as Zhuangzi is any more real and substantial than his butterfly incarnation. His point goes beyond the idea that dreams have the power to edify. Instead, it is a metaphysical inquiry about the nature of ultimate reality itself, suggesting very pointedly that the distinction between dream and reality is ultimately insubstantial.

Similarly, in Indian philosophy, the concept of *māyā*, or "illusion," is predicated not upon a distinction between illusion and reality, but rather on the more radical contention that the perception of anything at all is illusory. Consider the following story from the *Yogavāsistha*: King Lavana is visited by a magician and made to dream that he is an untouchable. When the king wakes up, he goes in search of the place in his dream and discovers the village in which he lived as an untouchable, as well as the people he knew there. The dream that turns out to be real is an inverse telling of the philosophy that everything is illusion. The point is to nullify any distinction between greater or lesser degrees of reality. In the early Chinese Daoist source known as the *Liezi*, dreams are again used to convey this lesson. One tale, for example, concludes that the slave who dreams every night that he is a rich man leads a life equivalent to the rich man who suffers every night the dream that he is a slave.

When Song-jin awakens from his dream of his long and successful life as So-yoo, he and his master ponder the meaning of the dream. Clearly recognizable in this conversation is the variegated history of the dream tale. Is dreaming a form of edifying vicarious experience? Does it stand in for life itself, implying that life is illusory, or might it be that illusion, like literature, is how life is composed? The virtue of literature, in contrast to philosophy proper, is that multiple interpretations can be simultaneously held and appreciated.

CONCLUSION

Sŏp'o's personal and literary lives reflect an ideological conflict at the heart of East Asian culture. Confucianism trained on the contours of social reality, and was absolute in its demands of filial piety, familial duty, and political loyalty. Buddhism and Daoism, on the other hand, contested the hardness of this reality. They did so not only by negating ordinary life and ambitions as vainglorious, but by inviting one to create possibilities for life shaped by the poetic imagination. Hence it is no surprise that Sŏp'o, and so many other men of his culture, turned to fiction and poetry for more than pleasant diversions. To be sure, from our perspective, much of this literature employs stock conceits and images that were repeatedly utilized by authors through time. Premodern Asian fiction did not know the ideal of individual genius. But in a world where identity was a highly fixed entity, creative literature was a way of imagining the self and actualizing the idea that more than one option was possible.

Francisca Cho
Georgetown University

THE CLOUD DREAM OF THE NINE

KUUNMONG

九雲夢 • 구운몽

BY KIM MANJUNG

金萬重 • 김만중

LIST OF PRINCIPAL CHARACTERS
(IN ORDER OF APPEARANCE)

Song-jin   *the hero of the story, later called...*
性眞 • 성진
Yang So-yoo   *also called the Master, the Hallim, the*
楊少游 • 양소유   *Minister, the General, & Prince Wee*

Chin See (Phoenix)   *daughter of a government*
秦彩鳳 • 진채봉   *commissioner, later a servant*

Kay See (Moonlight)   *entertainer*
桂蟾月 • 계섬월

Cheung See (Jewel)   *daughter of Justice Cheung,*
鄭瓊貝 • 정경패   *later Princess Yong-yang (Blossom)*

Ka Choon-oon (Cloudlet)   *her servant and companion*
賈春雲 • 가춘운

Princess Nan-yang (Orchid)   *daughter of the Empress Dowager,*
李簫和 • 이소화   *also known as Yi See & Yi So-wha*

Chok Kyong-Hong (Wildgoose)   *close friend of Moonlight, entertainer*
狄驚鴻 • 적경홍

Sim Hyo-yon (Swallow)   *assassin sent to kill So-yoo,*
沈梟烟 • 심효연   *and entertainer*

Pak Neung-pa (White-cap)   *daughter of the Dragon King,*
白凌波 • 백능파   *later an entertainer*

CHAPTER I
THE TRANSMIGRATION OF SONG-JIN

T HERE are five noted mountains in East Asia. The peak near
the Yellow Sea is called Tai-san, Great Mountain; the peak
to the west, Wha-san, Flowery Mountain; the peak to the south,
Hyong-san, Mountain of the Scales; the peak to the north, Hang-
san, Eternal Mountain; while the peak in the centre is called
Soong-san, Exalted Mountain. The Mountain of the Scales, the
loftiest of the five peaks, lies to the south of the Tong-jong River,
and on the other three sides is circled by the Sang-gang, so that
it stands high, uplifted as if receiving adoration from the surrounding summits. There are in all seventy-two peaks that shoot
up and point their spear-tops to the sky. Some are sheer cut and
precipitous and block the clouds in their course, startling the
world with the wonder of their formation. Stores of good luck
and fortune abide under their shadows.

The highest peaks among the seventy-two are called Spirit of
the South, Red Canopy, Pillars of Heaven, Rock Treasure-house
and Lotus Peak, five in all. They are sky-tipped and majestic in
appearance, with clouds on their faces and mists around their
feet, and are charged with divine influences.[1] When the day is
other than clear they are shrouded completely from human view.

In ancient days, when Ha-oo restrained the deluge that came
upon the earth,[2] he placed a memorial stone on one of these
mountain tops, on which was recorded his many wonderful

---

1   *The worship of the hills.* This religion of the East finds its origin in a passage of the
"Book of History" which reads, "King Soon (2255–2205 BC) offered sacrifice to God, to the
six Honourable Ones, to the hills and streams, and to the multitude of spirits." Since that
far-away time mountains have been regarded as divinities, presiding over the fortunes of
the State and the welfare of the King, and as such have had prayers and sacrifices constantly
offered to them.

2   *Deluge.* In the "Book of History" there is an account of a deluge that lasted for nine
years, from which the people were saved by the might of Ha-oo (2205–2197 BC).

deeds. The stone was divinely inscribed in cloud characters, and, while many ages have passed, these characters are clear cut as ever.

In the days of Chin See-wang,[3] a woman of the genii, named Queen Wee, who became a Taoist by divine command, came with a company of angelic boys and fairy girls and settled in these mountains, so that she was called Queen Wee of the Southern Peak.

It is impossible to relate all the strange and wonderful things that have been associated with these mountain fastnesses.

In the days of the Tang dynasty a noted priest came hither from India, and being captivated by the beauty of the hills built a monastery on Lotus Peak. There he preached the doctrines of the Buddha, taught his disciples, and put an end to fearsome demons and foul spirits, so that the name of Gautama grew great in influence, and people bowed before it and believed, saying that God had again visited the earth. The rich and honourable shared of their abundance, the poor gave their labour, and so they built a wide and spacious temple. It was deeply secluded and quiet, with a thousand and one beautiful views encircling it, and a majesty and impressiveness of mountain scenery for background that was unsurpassed.

This preacher of the Buddha had brought with him a volume of the Diamond Sutra, which he expounded so clearly that they called him Master of the Six Temptations and the Great Teacher of the Yook-kwan. Among the five or six hundred disciples that followed him there were some thirty well versed in the teaching, and far advanced. One, the youngest of them, was called Song-jin, Without Guile. His face was fair and beautiful to see and the light of his expression was like running water. He was barely twenty, and yet he had mastered the three Sacred Books. In wisdom and quickness of perception he surpassed all the others, so that the Master greatly loved him and intended later to make him his successor.

---

3   *Chin See-wang.* (221–209 BC). This is the king who built the Great Wall of China; he is likewise famed for having destroyed all the libraries and literature of the kingdom, saying that it was a source of pride and contention, and of no service to the State. For this his unblessed name has been handed down through the centuries as *keul-e to jok,* the "thief of literature."

As the Teacher expounded the doctrine to his disciples, the Dragon King himself, from the Tong-jong Sea, used to come in the person of an old man dressed in white clothes to listen and learn. On a certain day the Teacher assembled his pupils and said to them: "I am now an old man and frail in body, and it is thirteen years and more since I have been outside the mountain gates. Who among you will go for me to the Palace of the Waters and pay my respects to the Dragon King?" At once Song-jin volunteered. The Teacher, greatly pleased at this, had him fitted out in a new cassock, gave him his ringed staff of the gods, and he set off briskly towards the world of Tong-jong.

Just at this moment the priest who guarded the main entrance to the monastery came to say that the noble Lady of the Southern Peak had sent eight fairy messengers to call, and that they were now waiting before the gate. The Master gave command that they be admitted, and they tripped across the threshold in modest order, circling about three times and then bowing and scattering the blossoms of the genii. They knelt reverently and gave their message from the Lady, saying: "The noble Teacher lives on the west side of the mountain and I on the east. While the distance is not great, and we are comparatively near as neighbours, still I am of humble birth and am so busily occupied that I have never come even once to the sacred temple to hear the doctrine. I have no wisdom of my own to keep me in touch with the good, but now I am sending my serving maidens to pay my respects, and at the same time to offer to your Excellency flowers of Paradise and fairy fruits, along with some other gifts of silk, which I sincerely trust you will accept as a token of my earnest heart."

Each then made her presentation of flowers and treasures to the Master. These he received and passed on to his disciples, who had them placed as offerings before the Buddha. With much bowing and folding of the hands, according to the required ceremony, he replied: "What merit has an old man like me, I pray, to have such gifts as these presented to him?"

He gave liberally to the eight maidens in return and they set off lightly on their way.

They passed out through the mountain gate hand in hand, talking as they went. Said they: "These divine mountains of the south, being of one range and having the same streams encircling them, once upon a time were all within our own boundaries, but since the setting up of the temple of the Great Teacher certain limitations have shut us off from freedom so that we have not seen the beautiful places that were once our own. Now by the good fortune of our Lady's commands we are here in this valley at this lovely season of the year. It is early in the day. Let us take the occasion to go up to the heights and have a breath of the sweet air of Lotus Peak, dip our kerchiefs in the limpid water, sing a verse or two and awaken our souls to the joy of life. On returning home we shall be the praise and envy of all our sisters. Let us do this."

They set off, on their way looking down with wonder at the rushing water, walking skilfully along the giddy ridges and following the streams. At last, on this happy day of the third moon they found themselves on the stone bridge that spanned the torrent.

All the flowers were in bloom; the streams beneath them sparkled with silvery brightness. There hung a tent-work of flowers and leaves like a silken canopy. The birds vied with each other in the beautiful notes of their singing. The soft breezes awakened glad and happy memories, while the beauty of the scene held them spellbound.

Thus were the eight fairy messengers charmed as they sat in delight on the bridge looking down at the wonderful mirror of the streams that met and sparkled in a crystal pool below. Their delicate eyebrows and glowing bright faces shone forth, reflected in the water as if seen in a famous picture from a master's hand. They were so entranced that they had no thought of going till the sun began to descend toward the western hills and the day to darken.

At this moment Song-jin crossed the Tong-jong River and entered the Water Palace of the Dragon King. His Majesty was greatly delighted at his coming, stepped outside the gates to meet him, took him by the hand, led him in and bid him share his throne.

Song-jin made his obeisance and gave his message from the Master.

The King in response bowed low and ordered a feast of welcome to be prepared, at which were fruits and dainties of the fairies in abundance, and of such flavour as the dwellers in the hills alone know. The Dragon King himself passed the glass and urged him to drink. Song-jin several times refused, saying: "Wine is a drink that upsets and maddens the soul, and is therefore strictly forbidden by the Buddha, so your humble servant must not partake."

But the Dragon King replied: "I am aware that among the five things forbidden by Gautama wine is one, but the wine that I offer is different altogether from the maddening kind that men drink. It represses the passions and quiets the soul. You will not mistrust my sincerity in offering it I am sure."

Song-jin, moved by this kindness, could not any longer refuse, and he drank three glasses. He then spoke his greeting and came forth from the Water Palace, riding on the wind and sailing directly for Lotus Peak.

When he had landed at the base of the hill the influence of the wine was already manifest in his face and a feeling of dizziness possessed him, so that he reprimanded himself, saying: "If my honoured Master sees me with this inflamed expression how startled he will be and how soundly he will chide me."

He sat down by the bank of the stream, put off his outer garments, placed them on the clean sand and dipped his hands in the limpid water. Thus he sat bathing his hot face, when suddenly a strange and mysterious fragrance was borne toward him, not the perfume of orchid or musk nor that of any special flower, but something wholly new and not experienced before. The soul of passion and uncleanness seemed dissipated by its presence, and a purity indescribable seemed to remain. He said to himself: "What wonderful flowers are these by the side of this brook that such sweet perfume should come floating on its wavelets? I will go and see from whence it comes."

He dressed carefully, followed the course of the stream upwards, and found the eight fairies seated on the stone bridge so that they met suddenly face to face, he and they.

Song-jin laid aside his pilgrim's staff and made a deep, low bow, saying: "Ladies of the Fairies' Paradise, hear what a poor priest has to say. I am a disciple of the Master Yook-kwan and live on Lotus Peak. Just now I am returning from a mission beyond the mountains on which he sent me. This stone bridge is very narrow, and you goddesses being seated upon it block the way; will you not kindly take your lotus footsteps hence and let me pass?"

5

The fairies bowed in return and said: "We attendants who wait on Queen Wee are on our return from carrying a message of goodwill to the Master of the Temple, and have stopped here for a little to rest. We have heard that it is written in the Book of Ceremony concerning the law of the road that man goes to the left and woman to the right. Now as this bridge is a very narrow one, and we are already seated here, it would seem more fitting that you should avoid it altogether, and cross by some other way."

Song-jin said in reply: "But the water of the stream is deep, and there is no other way. Where do you suggest that your humble servant should go?"

The fairies replied: "It is said that the great Talma[4] came across the ocean on a leaf. Now if you are a disciple of the Teacher Yook-kwan and have learned the doctrine from him, naturally you will have learned to do some such wonderful thing. There surely will be no difficulty for you to cross this narrow stream instead of standing here and disputing with us girls about the way."

Song-jin laughed and said: "I see by your ladyships' behaviour that you ask that I pay some price or other for the right to cross, but I have no money, for I am only a poor priest. I have, however, eight jewels which I will present to you if you will kindly permit me to pass by."

At this he threw the peach blossom that he carried in his hand before them and it became four couplets of red flowers, and these again were transformed into eight jewels that filled the place with sparkling light, shooting up to heaven.

The fairies each picked up one; then they looked toward Song-jin, laughed in a delighted way, arose, mounted the winds and sailed off through the air.

Song-jin stood at the head of the bridge and watched them for a long time till they were lost in the clouds and the sweet fragrance had melted away. In loneliness, as though he had failed of his highest hopes, he came back to the temple and gave his message from the Dragon King to the Master.

The Master reprimanded him for his late return, and Song-jin said: "The Dragon King treated me so liberally, sir, and his

---

4   *Talma*. He was the 28th, or last of the Indian patriarchs, Boddhidarma.

urgent request to stay was so impossible to refuse, that I have been delayed beyond the time."

The Master gave no direct reply, but simply said: "Go away and rest."

Song-jin went back to his little hut of meditation while the evening shadows closed down upon the day. Since meeting with the eight fairies his ears had been ringing with sweet voices, and though he tried to forget their beautiful faces and graceful forms he could not succeed. However much he endeavoured to rein in his thoughts he found it impossible. His mind was as that of a person half insane or half intoxicated. He pulled himself together, however, and knelt reverently, saying: "If a man study diligently the Confucian Classics and then grow up to meet a king like Yo or Soon, he can either become a general to go abroad, or be a minister of state at home. He can dress in silk and carry a seal of office at his belt; can bow before the king; can dispense favours among the people; can look on beautiful things with the eyes and hear delightful sounds with the ears. He can have his fill of glory in this life, and can leave a reputation for generations to come; but we Buddhists have only our little dish of rice and flask of water. Many dry books are there for us to learn, and our beads to say over till we are old and grey. It may be high and praiseworthy from the point of view of religion, but the vacant longings that it never satisfies are too deep to mention. Even though one gets to understand all the laws of the Mahayana revelation, though one proclaims the same and finds oneself exalted to the place of sage and teacher, when once the spirit and soul dissipate into smoke and nothingness, who will ever know that a person called Song-jin once lived upon this earth?"

So his thoughts wandered. He tried to sleep but sleep refused to come. The hours grew late. Sometimes he closed his eyes for a little, but the eight fairies persistently appeared before him in a row and drove sleep far away. Then he suddenly realised that the great purpose of Buddhism was to correct the thoughts and the heart. "I have been a Buddhist for ten years," said he, "and I had well-nigh succeeded in getting done with the world till this deceitful mind of mine got itself tangled up to the damage of my soul."

He burned incense, knelt, called in all his thoughts, counted his beads, recalled to his consciousness the thousand Buddhas that could help him, when suddenly one of the temple boys came to his window and spoke, saying: "Elder brother, are you asleep? The Master is calling you."

Song-jin, in alarm, said to himself: "His calling me in this unusual way in the middle of the night can only mean something serious."

He went along with the boy to the Audience Hall of the Buddha, where the chief had assembled all the priests of the temple and was sitting in solemn silence. His appearance was one to inspire fear and question. The light of the candles shone brilliantly. He spoke with great care, but with severe intonation.

"Song-jin, do you know how you have sinned?"

Song-jin, who was bowed low, kneeling before the dais, replied: "I have now been a disciple of the Master for ten years and more, and have never disobeyed any command or any order concerning acts of worship in which I have had a part. I am dark and ignorant I know, and so am not aware of how I have offended."

The Master said: "There are three things that must be exercised in the ordering of one's acts, namely, the body, the mind, and the soul. You went to the Dragon King and drank wine, did you not? Again, on your way back by the stone bridge you had a long and frivolous conversation with the messengers of Queen Wee. You gave them each a flower and made jokes and light talk. Since coming back, too, you have not put these recollections from your mind and heart, but instead have allowed yourself to be entangled with worldly delights; you have been thinking of riches and honour with all the other temptations of the earth, and have turned with loathing from the doctrine of the Buddha. Thus your three degrees of attainment have all fallen from you in a single hour. You can remain here no longer."

Song-jin, overcome to tears, prayed for forgiveness. He said: "Great Master, I am indeed a sinner. Still my breaking the rule regarding drink was because the king so forced and compelled me; and my talking with the fairies was only because I asked of them the way. I had had no such intention in my heart. Why am I thus condemned? I will go back to my cell, and though evil thoughts assail me I will keep my spirit awake against them and overcome their madness, so that a true mind will assuredly return. I will bite my hands and I will repent of the wrong I have done, and my heart will be restored. It tells in Confucianism how one can thus return to the right way. As I have sinned will my revered Father not give me a flogging and set me right? This is what I understand to be the teaching of the Buddha. Why should you drive me away from all possibility of reformation? I came to you when I was only twelve years of age, gave up my parents and relatives, cut my hair and took the vows of a priest, and ever since have lived dependent on you. It is just as though you had begotten me and brought me up, and our love is as between an only son and a father. My cell is the special meeting place of the monastery, and my hopes are all here. Where shall I go?"

The Master said: "You desire to go and that is what makes me send you off. If you did not desire to go who would ever think of sending you? You ask 'Where shall I go?' I answer 'To the place where you desire to go.'"

He then shouted: "Hither, Yellow Turban Guards!" Suddenly the commander of the guard dropped from mid-air, bowed low and received his orders.

The Master said: "Arrest this guilty man, take him to Hades, hand him over to the King of Youma and then come back to me."

When Song-jin heard this his spirit seemed to depart from him, his eyes streamed over with tears, he fell forward and cried out: "Father, father, please hear me, listen to what I have to say. In olden days the great teacher Aron entered the house of a harlot and had intercourse with her, and so broke all the laws of the Buddha. Still the divine Sokka did not condemn him, but took him in hand and showed him more clearly the way. I am guilty of a lack of care, but still as compared with Aron I am surely less at fault. Why do you send me thus to Hell?"

The Teacher replied: "Even though Aron fell into sin, still his mind was repentant; you, on the other hand, have had but one sight of these seductive things and have lost all your heart to them. Your thoughts are now turned to a life of pleasure and your mouth waters for the riches and honours of the world. If we compare you with Aron you are worse by far. You cannot escape the sorrow and distresses that lie before you."

Still Song-jin cried for mercy, and had no thought of going, so that the stern Teacher comforted him finally, saying: "While your mind remains unpurified even though you are here in the mountains, you cannot attain to the truth; but if you never forget it and hold fast you may mix with the dust and impurities of the way, and your return is safe and sure. If you ever desire to come back here I will go and bring you. Depart now without doubt or question."

There being no help for it, Song-jin made a low bow before the Master, said good-bye to his priest companions, and went along with the constables of Hell past the Look-out Pavilion till he came to the outer walls, where the guards at the gate asked the cause of his coming.

The constables replied: "At the order of the Teacher Yook-kwan we have arrested this guilty man and brought him."

The soldier guards then opened the gates for them. The constables reached the inner enclosure and announced why Song-jin had been arrested. The King of Hades had him brought in and then spoke to him in the following way: "Honoured Master, although you live in the Nam-ak Hills under Lotus Peak, your name is already on the incense table before the great King Chee-jang.[5] I have said to myself that hereafter when you are exalted to the throne of the lotus all living creatures of the earth will be greatly blessed thereby. For what possible cause are you arrested and brought here thus in disgrace?"

Song-jin, in confusion and shame of face, did not reply for a long time. At last he said: "I met the fairy maidens of Queen Wee on the stone bridge of Nam-ak and failed to restrain my thoughts about them. Thus I sinned against my Master and now I await the commands of your Majesty."

The King of Hades sent a message by those who waited on him to King Chee-jang that ran thus: "The Teacher Yook-kwan of Nam-ak has sent me one of his disciples under arrest by his Yellow Turban constables in order that we may decide here in Hell as to his guilt. As he is different from ordinary offenders I am asking counsel of your High Majesty."

King Chee-jang replied: "A man who would be perfect has his journey to make, and his return, in order to accomplish all things

5   *Chee-jang.* The God of the Buddhists, who has supreme charge of all earthly things, and under whose commands the King of Hades is supposed to act.

in accord with his own will and purpose. He cannot escape it, so there is no use to discuss the matter."

Just as the King of Hades was about to decide, two devil soldiers announced that the Yellow Turban guards, by command of Master Yook-kwan, had brought eight more offenders, who were outside the gate waiting. When Song-jin heard this he was greatly alarmed.

The King then ordered them in, when, behold, all the eight fairies of Nam-ak came haltingly over the threshold, and knelt down in the court. The King spoke, saying: "You fairy maidens of Nam-ak, listen to me. Fairy folk live in the most beautiful worlds that are known, and have joys and delights beyond measure. How is it that you have come to such a place as this?"

The eight in great shame and confusion made reply: "We were ordered by Queen Wee to go and make inquiry of the Teacher Yook-kwan as to his health and welfare. On our way back we met with his disciple Song-jin, and because we talked with him the Teacher said that we had defiled the sacred precincts of the hills, and he wrote and asked that we be sent to the place of the dead. All our hopes and prayers are with your Majesty. Pray have mercy upon us and let us go once again into the world of the living."

The King of Hades then called nine messengers who appeared before him. He ordered them in a low voice, saying: "Take these nine and get them back as soon as possible into the world of the living."

Scarcely had he finished when a great wind arose and whirled about, carried off the nine into space, drove them asunder, and sent them into the four corners of the earth. Song-jin, following his leader, was borne along by the wind, tossed and whisked through endless space till he seemed at last to land on solid ground. Then the tempest calmed down. Song-jin gathered his scattered senses, and found himself shut in by a range of hills with the waters of a clear, beautiful stream running by. He also saw inside a bamboo paling and between the shady branches of the trees glimpses of thatched roofs, a dozen or more. Two or three people were standing and talking together. They said in his hearing: "The hermit Yang's wife, now over fifty years of age, is to give birth to a child, a marvellous thing indeed! We have expected it now for some time, but no infant's voice is yet heard, a somewhat anxious circumstance."

Song-jin said to himself: "I am to be born again among men, for now that I behold myself I have no body, but am a spirit only. My body I left on Lotus Peak, where it has already been cremated, and because I was so young I had no disciples to take my saree [6] and safeguard them."

Thinking thus over his past his mind was distressed, when a messenger appeared and waved his hand to him to come, saying: "This is So-joo township of Hoi-nam county, of the Tang Kingdom, and this is the home of the hermit Yang. He is your father, and his wife Yoo See is your mother. You are destined from a former existence to be a son in this home. Go in quickly and do not lose the favourable moment."

At once he went in, and there the hermit sat with his reed hat on his head and a rough hempen coat wrapped about him. He had before him a brazier on which he was preparing some medicinal drink, the fragrance of which filled the house. In the room, indistinctly, there were heard accents of suffering. The messenger urged him on, saying, "Go in quickly now," but as Song-jin still hesitated and delayed, the messenger pushed him from behind and Song-jin fell to the ground, when suddenly he lost consciousness, seeming to pass into some great convulsion of nature. He called, saying, "Save me, save me!" but the sounds stuck fast in his throat and failed to find expression, so that they became the cries of a little child only. The attendants quickly informed the hermit that his wife had borne him a beautiful son. He took the medicinal drink that he had prepared, went close up to her and they looked at each other with happy faces.

When Song-jin was hungry milk was given him, and when his wants were satisfied he ceased to cry. When first born his little mind still recollected the happenings on Lotus Peak, but when he grew older and learned to know of the love of his parents the things of his former existence faded away, so that he forgot them altogether.

---

6   *Saree.* These are relics that are said to spring forth from the body of a faithful Buddhist, usually during cremation. They are guarded with great care, oftentimes having monumental stones placed over them; sometimes again they are swallowed by devoted disciples.

When the hermit saw how handsome he was and well gifted he stroked his little brow, saying: "This child has indeed come from heaven to sojourn among us," so he called his name So-yoo, Little Visitor, while the special name given him was Chollee, Thousands of Miles.

Time that goes like running water saw him grow as in the space of a moment to ten years of age. His face was like the jade-stone and his eyes like the stars of the morning. His strength was firm and his mind pure and bright, showing him to be indeed a Superior Man. The hermit said to his wife: "I am originally not a man of this world, but because I was united to you I have remained long among the dust of this mortal way. My friends of the genii who live on Mount Pong-nai [7] have sent me many messages asking that I come. On account of your labour and sorrow, however, I have refused, but now that God has blessed us and given us a gifted son superior to others in his attainments, on whom you can rely and by whom in your old age you will assuredly see riches and honour, I shall delay no longer to go."

On a certain day a number of the genii came to escort him on his way. They rode some on the white deer, some on the blue heron, sailing off toward the distant hills. Though one or two letters came at intervals from the blue sky, no traces of the hermit were ever seen on earth again.

---

7   *Pong-nai Hills.* One of the fabled abodes of the genii, supposed to belong to some celestial island in the Eastern Sea. The story of it dates from 250 BC. The fairy inhabitants of the place are said to live on gems found on the sea-shore. The elixir of life is also dug from its enchanted slopes.

CHAPTER II
A GLIMPSE OF CHIN SEE

THE Hermit Yang left the world while the mother and son remained and lived together.

Already before So-yoo (Song-jin) was in his teens he manifested extraordinary attractiveness and ability. The governor of his county called him the Marvellous Lad, and recommended him to the Court. But So-yoo on account of his mother declined all favours. When he was fifteen or thereabouts, with his frank and handsome face, he was said to resemble Panak[8] of ancient China. His physical strength, too, was unrivalled, and his skill in the classics and composition was excellent. In astronomy and geomancy he was well trained, while in military knowledge, such as tossing the spear and fencing with the short sword, he was indeed a great wonder. Nothing could stand before him. In his former existence he had been a man of refined tastes, so his mind was clear and his heart kindly disposed and liberal. He deftly solved the mysteries of life as one would split the bamboo. Different altogether was he from the common run of men.

Said he one day to his mother: "When my father went up to heaven he entrusted the reputation and honour of his home to me, and yet here we are so poor that you are compelled to toil and struggle. To live here like a mere watch-dog or a turtle that drags its tail and makes no effort to rise in the world means that we shall be blotted out as a family. I shall never comfort your heart, and shall fail of the trust that my father has imposed in me. I hear just now that Government Examinations are to be held and that they are open to any candidate of the empire. May I not leave you for a little and try my skill?"

While Yoo See, his mother, had no desire to restrain this good

---

8   *Panak.* A youth of great beauty who lived in the time of the Chin Kingdom, AD 300.

purpose on the part of her son, she feared for the long journey that he would have to take. However, since his spirit was awake and anxious to go she gave her consent. Selling what few treasures she had she provided means for the journey.

He then bade her good-bye, and with a limping donkey and a little serving-boy to accompany him, he set out on the way. The views of mountain and stream by which he passed were specially fine, and since the opening of the examination was still somewhat distant, he lingered as he went along looking at points of interest and seeking out old landmarks and records.

At a certain place as he went by he saw a neat and tidy house surrounded by a beautiful grove of shady willow trees. A blue line of smoke, like silken rolls unwinding, rose skyward. In a retired part of the enclosure he saw a picturesque pavilion with a beautifully kept approach. He slowed up his beast and went near to enjoy the prospect. The encircling boughs and leaves barely permitted him to make out through their shade a wonderful fairy world.

So-yoo pushed aside the intervening greenery and lingered for a time, unwilling to go. He sighed and said: "In our world of Cho there are many pretty groves, but none that I ever saw so lovely as this."

He rapidly composed and wrote a poem, which ran:

> "Willows[9] hung like woven green,
> Veiling all the view between,
> Planted by some fairy free,
> Sheltering her and calling me.
> Willows, greenest of the green,
> Brushing by her silken screen,
> Speak by every waving wand,
> Of an unseen fairy hand."

When he had jotted this down he sang it out with a rich, clear voice, the notes of which resounded like the clink of silver or

9   *Willows.* Before the capital of ancient China there was a grove of willows where people said their farewells and where expressions of sorrow at departure were spoken; hence the willow became the token of special love. It is the first tree, too, of springtime to announce by its blush of green the happy season.

the echoing tones of crystal. It was heard in the top storey of the pavilion, where a beautiful maiden was having a midday siesta. She awoke with a start, pushed aside the armrest on which she leaned, and sat up. She then opened the embroidered shade and looked out through the painted railing here and there. Whence came this singing? Suddenly her eyes met those of So-yoo, while her hair, like a tumbled cloud, rested soft and warm upon her temples. The long jade pin that held the plaits together had been pushed aside till it showed slantwise through her tresses. Her sleepy eyelids were still somewhat weighted, and her expression was as though she had just emerged from dream-land. Rouge and cosmetics had vanished under the unceremonious hand of sleep, and her natural beauty was unveiled, a beauty impossible to picture and such as no painting has ever portrayed.

The two looked at each other with a fixed and startled expression, but said not a word. So-yoo had sent his boy ahead to order his affairs at the inn, and now he suddenly returned to announce that it had been so done. The maiden looked straight at So-yoo for a moment, and then suddenly recollected herself, closed the blind and disappeared from view. A suggestion of sweet fragrance was borne to him on the breeze.

So-yoo regretted at first that the boy had disturbed him by his announcement. And now that the blind had closed it was as though a thousand miles of the Yangtze had cut him off from all his expectations. So he went on his way, looking back at times to see, but the silken window was made fast and did not again open. He reached the inn with a sense of loss and home-sickness upon him, and with his mind mixed and confused.

The family name of the maiden was Chin, and her given name Chabong. She was the daughter of a Government Commissioner, and had lost her mother early in life. No brothers or sisters had she ever had, and now she had attained to the age when girls do up their hair, but she was still unmarried.

The Commissioner had gone up to the capital on official business, and so the daughter was alone when she thus unexpectedly met the eyes of So-yoo. His handsome face and manly bearing attracted her wonderfully. Hearing, too, the verses that he sang she was carried away with admiration for his skill as a scholar, and thus she thought to herself:

"The woman's lot in life is to follow her husband. Her glory or her shame, her experiences for the span of life are wrapped up in her lord and master. For this reason Princess Tak-moon, although a widow, followed General Sa-ma. I am yet an unmarried girl and dislike dreadfully to become my own go-between and propose marriage, but it is said that in ancient times courtiers chose their own king, so I shall make inquiry concerning this gentleman and find his name and place of residence. I must do so at once and not wait till my father's return, for who knows whither he may have gone in the meantime, or where I may search for him in the four quarters of the earth."

She unclasped a roll of satin paper, wrote a verse or two and gave it to her nurse, saying: "Take this letter to the city guest-hall and give it to the gentleman who rode past here on the little donkey and sang the Willow Song as he went by. Let him know that my purpose is to find the one that is destined for me, and on whom I may depend. Know forsooth that this is a very important matter and one that forbids your acting in a light or frivolous way. The gentleman is handsome as the gods; his eyebrows are like the loftiest touches of a picture, and his form among common men is like the phoenix among feathered fowls. See him now for yourself and give him this letter."

The nurse replied "I shall be careful to do just as you have commanded, but what shall I say if your father should inquire later?"

"I shall see to that myself," said Chin See, "so do not be anxious."

The nurse then left, but returned again in a little to ask: "What shall I do if the gentleman is already married or engaged?"

On hearing this the maiden thought for a moment and then replied: "If that unfortunately be so I shall not object to become his secondary wife. He is young, but whether he is married or not, who can tell?"

The nurse then went to the guest-hall and asked for the gentleman who had sung the Willow Song. Just at that moment So-yoo stepped out of the entrance into the court, and there he met the old dame who came bearing the message. He responded at once and said: "Your humble servant, madam, is responsible for the Willow Song. Why do you ask me?"

When the nurse saw his handsome face she no longer doubted

his being the one in question, and softly said: "We cannot speak here."

So-yoo, wondering, led her into the guest-house, and when they were seated quietly he asked why she had come.

"Will your Excellency," said she in answer, "please tell me where you sang the Willow Song?"

So-yoo replied: "I am from a far distant part of the country and have come for the first time into the neighbourhood of the capital. The beauty of it delights my soul. To-day at noon as I was passing along the main highway I saw to the north of the road a little pavilion with a grove of green willows, exquisitely beautiful. I could not restrain my joy, and so wrote a verse or two which I sang, but why does your excellent ladyship ask concerning that?"

The nurse replied: "Did your Excellency meet anyone at that time, or come face to face with any stranger?"

So-yoo made answer: "Your servant came face to face with a beautiful fairy, who looked down upon him from the pavilion by the way. Her lovely features I see still and the fragrance of her presence has filled the world."

The nurse went on: "I shall speak directly to the point. The house you mention is the home of my master, Commissioner Chin, and the lady you refer to is his daughter. From childhood she has been pure of heart and gifted in mind and soul, with a wonderful talent for knowing people. She saw your Excellency but once and for a moment, yet her desire is to entrust herself to you for ever; but the Commissioner is away from home in the capital and he must needs return before any decision can be arrived at. Most important is the matter, however, and in the meantime your Excellency may be far enough away like the floating seaweed on the drift, or the autumn leaves in the wind that blows. Fearing she might never again find you, she has sent me to say that the destiny of life is the all important subject, while the diffidence of the moment and the fear to speak of it are but a passing unpleasantness. Thus has she, contrary to good form and her bringing up, written this letter and ordered me, her old servant, to ask your excellent name and place of residence."

When So-yoo heard this he was greatly interested, as his countenance showed. He thanked her, and said: "My name is Yang So-yoo, and my home is in the land of Cho. I am young and not yet married. Only my aged mother is alive, and while the marriage question is one that will need inquiry on the part of both our clans, still consent to the contract may be given even here and now, and so for my part I consent at once, and swear it by the long green hills of Wha-san and the endless reaches of the Wee-soo River."

The nurse, delighted at her success, took a letter from her sleeve, gave it to So-yoo, who tore it open and found a poem which read:

> *"Willows waving by the way,*
> *Bade my lord his course to stay,*
> *He, alas, has failed to ken,*
> *Draws his whip and rides again."*

When So-yoo had read the verse and noted its brightness and freshness, he praised it, saying: "No ancient sage ever wrote more sweetly." Then he unrolled a sheet of watered paper and wrote his reply thus:

> *"Willow catkins soft and dear,*
> *Bid thy soul to never fear,*
> *Ever may they bind us true,*
> *You to me, and me to you."*

The nurse received it, placed it in her bosom, and went out through the main gateway of the guest-hall, but So-yoo called her again, saying: "The young lady is a native of Chin, while I belong to Cho. Once we separate, a thousand miles come between us. With hills and streams and the windings of the way, it will be difficult indeed to get messages back and forth. We have no go-between to make proof of our contract, so I would like to go by moonlight and see my lady's beautiful face. What think you? In her letter there is some such suggestion, is there not? Please ask her."

The nurse consented, and on her return gave the message to the maiden. "Master Yang has sworn by the Lotus Hills and the long stretches of the river that he will be your companion. He praised your composition most highly, and wrote a reply which I have brought you." She then handed it to the lady.

The maiden received the letter, read it, and her face lighted up with joy.

Again the nurse went on to say: "Master Yang has asked if it would be agreeable to you to have him come quietly by moonlight and write another message which you could enjoy together."

Her answer was: "It is not good form for a young man and a young woman to meet before marriage. I am promised to him, it is true, and that makes a difference. If we meet at night, however, it might cause unseemly rumour, and also my father would reprimand me for it. Let us wait till noon to-morrow and meet in the great hall and there seal our happy contract. Go and tell him, will you?"

The nurse went once again to the inn and told the young master what had been said.

He expressed his regret and made reply: "The lady's pure heart and right ordered words put me to shame." Several times he urged upon the nurse that there should be no failure in their plans, and so she left.

While Master Yang slept in the guest-house his thoughts were agitated and on the wing, so that he did not rest well. He got up and waited for the crowing of the cock, impatient at the length of the long spring night. Suddenly the morning star began to dawn and the awakening drums to beat. He called his boy and ordered him to feed the donkey. At this point an unexpected inrush of mounted troops greeted the city with all the clamour that goes with an army rabble. Like a great river they went thundering by, hurrying in from the west. In fear he hastily gathered up his effects and looked out into the street, where the whole place seemed filled with armed men and fleeing people. The confusion was indescribable, and the earth rang with the thunders of it, while the wailing of the citizens shook the very sky.

He asked someone standing by what it meant, and was told that it was the rebel Koo Sa-ryong[10] who had risen against the Government and proclaimed himself Emperor. His Majesty was away on a visit of inspection in Yang-joo, and so the whole capital was in a state of hopeless confusion, with the rebels everywhere

10 *Koo Sa-ryong.* He was a noted rebel who attacked the State during the period of the Tangs, AD 840.

robbing the homes of the people. There was word, too, that they had locked the gates of the city so that no one could escape, and were enlisting by force rich and poor, every man who could bear arms.

Master Yang, in a state of fear and bewilderment, got hold of his boy and hastened away with the donkey toward the south mountain, that stood just in front, hoping to hide himself among the rocks or in some cave. He looked up and saw on the highest peak a little thatched house that seemed to hang in the shadows of the clouds, with the voices of cranes echoing about it. Thinking it the home of some dweller in the city, he went to it, picking his way, when suddenly he was confronted by a Taoist genius who, seated on his mat, saw the young man coming toward him. He got up, greeted him, and asked: "Are you making your escape from the confusion of the city, and are you indeed the son of the hermit Yang who lived in Hoiram county?"

So-yoo gave a sudden start of surprise, bowed low, broke out into expressions of wonder, and said in reply: "I am indeed the son of the hermit Yang. Since the departure of my father I have lived with my old mother. I am dull and slow of intellect and have learned next to nothing, and yet presumptuously thinking that I might have some chance to pass the examination, I came as far as Wha-eum when this rebellion blocked my way. In trying to make my escape I entered these mountain recesses and have been so fortunate as to meet your Excellency. God has helped me to such a meeting I know. I have not heard of my father for so long, and as time has gone by my soul waits more impatiently than ever for news from him. As I hear your words I am sure you have definite knowledge of him. I pray you, lord of the fairies, do not withhold anything, but give a son the greatest comfort that can come to him. In what height does my father dwell, please, and how is he in health?"

The fairy master smiled and said in reply: "Your father and I have just had a game of draughts together on Cha-gak mountain peak, and only said good-bye a little time ago; but I cannot tell you where he has gone. His face is not changed a whit, nor has his hair grown grey, so you do not need to be anxious about him."

Yang replied in tears, saying: "I wish the noble teacher would help me just once to meet my father."

But the master smilingly replied: "The love between son and father is great, but still mortals and the genii are of two different orders. I should like to help you, but it is impossible. The hills where the genii live are distant, and their ten provinces wide and far-reaching, so that it is impossible to know just where your father dwells. Now that you are here, stay for a time, and when the way opens again it will be all right for you to go."

Though Yang heard that his father was well, still the fact that the teacher had no intention of bringing about a meeting beclouded his hopes; tears rained from his eyes and his soul was in deep distress. However, the holy man comforted him, saying: "To meet and to part is one of life's common experiences; also to part and to meet again. Why do you cry over the inevitable?"

Then Yang brushed his tears away, thanked him and sat down. The teacher pointed to a harp hanging on the wall and asked: "Can you play that instrument?"

Yang replied: "I have some ear for music but have never had a teacher, and so do not have a practised hand."

The genius then had the harp brought, gave it to Yang and told him to try.

Yang took it, placed it on his knees and played a tune called "The Wind in the Pines."

The teacher, delighted, said: "You have skill and are really worth teaching." He then took the harp himself and taught him in succession four different selections. The music of it was entrancing, and such as no mortal had ever listened to before. Yang was by nature a skilful hand at the harp and had a well-trained mind, so that when he once caught the spirit of it he was master of the mystery.

The genius sage, seeing this, was delighted, brought out also his jade flute, and after playing a tune taught it to Yang, saying: "Even among the ancients it was rare indeed that two should meet who are masters of music. Now I present this harp to you and this jade flute. You will find use for them later on. Guard them safely and remember what I have told you."

Yang received them, bowed low and spoke his thanks. "Your humble servant's good fortune in thus meeting the lord of the genii is due to my excellent father. He has led the way for me, and you are my father's friend. How could I serve you other than as I serve him? I long to devote my life to you as your disciple."

The teacher smiled and said in reply: "The glory and honour of the world lie before you and are urging you on. There is no withstanding their power. It would never do for you to spend your time here in the hills with me. Your world differs from mine, and you were not intended for my disciple. Still your earnest thought I shall remember, and I here present you with the book 'Paing cho-pang' in order that you may not forget my love for you. If you once master this law, though you may not attain to earthly immortality, still old age will be long deferred."

Yang again arose, bowed low and received it, saying: "The great teacher has said that I am to enjoy riches and honour. I would like to ask about my other prospects. I have just decided to arrange marriage with the daughter of a gentleman of Wha-eum county, but have been caught by this rebellion and compelled to fly for my life, without definitely deciding. Will this wedding turn out propitious or not?"

The teacher laughed loudly, saying: "Marriage is a matter hidden in mystery and one must not talk lightly of God's plans. Still several beautiful women are destined for you, and so you have no need specially for this daughter of Wha-eum."

Yang knelt and received this word and then went with the teacher to the guest-room, where they spent the night. Before the day dawned the genius awoke Yang and said: "The way is now clear for you to go, and the examination is postponed till the coming spring. Your mother will be anxiously waiting. Hasten back to her and quiet her faithful heart." He gave him also money for the way.

Yang, after saying a hundred thanks, set out on his journey, his harp with him, his flute, and his sacred book. As he left the place the sadness of departure was borne in upon his heart, so that he turned to look back just once more, but already the house and the genius were gone and only the day remained with the white clouds sailing by, fresh and clean.

When Yang entered the hills the willows were in bloom and the catkins not yet fallen; and now in a single night the chrysanthemums were all aglow. He asked concerning this, and was told that it was the eighth moon of autumn. He went to seek the inn where he had stayed, but it had passed through a war meanwhile and was not the same at all. The whole world seemed changed, in fact. A great crowd of candidates was gathered and he asked about the rebellion. They said that soldiers had been enlisted from all the provinces and that the rebels had been put down, that the emperor had returned to the capital, and that the examination had been postponed till the next spring.

Yang went to see the home of Commissioner Chin, but only the faded willows greeted him, as they trembled in the wind and frost. Not a trace was there left of its former beauty. The ornamented pavilion and the whitened walls were but dust and ashes. Stones, blackened with smoke, and broken tiles lay heaped up in the vacated enclosure, while the surrounding village was all in ruins. There were no sounds of domestic life, no animals or birds. Yang mourned over the transitory nature of life's affairs, and how a happy agreement had ended in desolation. He caught the willow branches in his hands, and turning toward the evening sky sang over the Willow Song that the maiden Chin See had written. His tears fell and his heart was indescribably sad. There was no one from whom he could inquire concerning the catastrophe, so he came back to the inn and asked of the inn-master: "Can you tell me what has become of the family of Commissioner Chin?"

The inn-master twisted a wry face, saying: "Has not your Excellency heard what became of them? The Commissioner, it seems, went up to the capital on official business while his daughter and servants remained at home. It turned out later, after peace was restored, that Chin had been in league with the rebels, and so he was arrested and beheaded. The daughter was taken to the capital. Some say that she too was condemned; some that she had become a *yamen* slave, and only this morning, seeing a crowd of prisoners passing the door, I asked who they were and where they were going, and was told that they were slaves bound for Yong-nam, and someone added that among them was Chin See, the Commissioner's daughter."

Yang heard this, and was again cut deep with sorrow. He remarked: "The master of the South Hill said that marriage with Chin See would be like groping blindly in the night. She is dead, I suppose, and there will be no longer any possibility of inquiry." So he packed up his baggage and started for his native province.

During this time, Yoo See, his mother, had heard of the war and of the attack made on the capital, and fearing lest her son should be in danger, she called on God with all her heart, and prayed till her face grew thin and her form poor and emaciated. It seemed as though she could not physically long endure it. Beholding her son return safe and sound, she clasped him to her bosom, and wept as for one who had been dead and come to life again, so transported was she with joy.

In their talks together the fading year departed. Winter went its way and the spring came round, and Yang once again made preparation for departure to attend the examination.

Yoo See said: "Last year you experienced all sorts of danger on your way, so that my soul still trembles as I think of it. You are young yet, and there is plenty of time for fame and fortune. Still I must not forbid your going as your wish is mine also. This Soojoo county is too narrow and isolated for a scholar's world. No one here is socially your equal, or with ability or bringing-up sufficient for your companionship. You are now eighteen, and it is high time that you decide lest you lose life's fairest opportunity. In the Taoist Kwan (Temple) of the capital I have a cousin, the priestess Too-ryon. She has been a guide to the world of the fairy for many a year, and yet she is still alive. Her appearance is commanding and her wisdom very great, I am told. She is acquainted with all the noted families, too, and the nobility. If you give her a letter from me she will treat you like a son, and will certainly assist you in your selection of a helpmeet. Bear this in mind," said she, and wrote the letter.

So-yoo, hearing what his mother had said, told of his meeting with Chin See of Wha-eum, and at once his face clouded over with sorrow. Yoo See sighed and said: "Even though Chin See was so beautiful she was evidently not destined for you. It is unlikely that a child of such confusion and disaster could live. Even though she be not dead, it would be very difficult to find her. Leave off vain thoughts of her, I pray, and seek a wife elsewhere. Comfort your mother and do as she desires."

The young man bade her farewell and started on his way. He reached Nakyang,[11] and a sudden storm of rain overtaking him, he made his escape into a wine shop that stood outside the South

11   *Nakyang.* This city lies south of the Yellow River, not far from the great elbow where the stream turns east, and its name to-day is Ho-nan. The capital mentioned in the story is modern Si-an, or Si-ngan, that lies about 250 miles directly west.

Gate, where he purchased a drink. He inquired of the master, saying: "This is fairly good wine, but have you no better?"

The host said: "I have none other than this. If you desire the best, however, you will find it sold at the inn at the head of the Chon-jin Bridge. It is called 'Nakyang Springtime.' One measure of it costs a thousand cash. The flavour is very good indeed, but the price is high."

Yang thought for a moment and said: "Nakyang has been the home of the Emperor since ancient time, a very busy and splendid city, such as the world looks on as supreme. I went last year by another road and so did not see its sights. I shall stop this time to look through it."

CHAPTER III
THE MEETING WITH KAY SEE

M ASTER SO-YOO bade his servant pay for the drink and rode off on his donkey towards Chon-jin Bridge. When he passed within the city walls he was struck by the beauty of the surrounding scenery, and the crowds of people confirmed the reports he had heard of its being a very busy world. The Nakyang River flowed across the city like a strip of white silk, and Chon-jin Bridge spanned its rippling wavelets with archways bearing down at the extreme ends as a rainbow drinks the water, or like a green dragon with bent back. The red ridges of the housetops rose high above the city, their blue tiles reflecting back the rays of the sun. Their grateful shadows fell upon the perfumed way. To So-yoo the city seemed the metropolis of all the world. Hastening forward till he reached the Chon-jin Pavilion, So-yoo stopped in front of it, where many finely caparisoned horses were tied, grooms and servants bustling about amid noise and confusion. So-yoo looked up, and from the upper storey of the pagoda came sounds of music that filled the air, while the fragrance from rich dresses and silken robes was wafted on the breeze.

The young master, thinking that the governor of Hanam must be giving a feast, sent his boy to inquire. He discovered that the young literati of the city had brought certain dancing girls with them and were planning an evening's amusement. So-yoo, somewhat under the influence of wine, with his spirit awake to youthful adventure, dismounted from his donkey and went inside the hall. He found there a dozen or so of young men with a score of pretty girls sitting gracefully about on the silken matting, with dainty tables of food and drink placed before them. Laughter and jesting went on in merry and hilarious tones. All the dresses were of the finest fabrics and their appearance very striking.

Master Yang said: "I am a humble literatus from a remote prov-

THE CHON-JIN PAVILION

ince on my way to take part in the Government examination, and when passing here heard the sound of sweet music. My foolish heart, unable to go by without a greeting, has set aside all ceremony and come in as an uninvited guest. Please forgive me, noble gentlemen."

Noting Yang's handsome face, intelligent bearing, and well-measured words, they arose with one accord and responded to his salutation, giving him a place beside them, each announcing his name. Among them was a certain student No, who said: "Brother Yang, since you are a scholar on your way to the examination, though not an invited guest, you are welcome, and may take part in the entertainment for the day. We are delighted to have so distinguished a visitor, and you have no reason in the world to apologise."

Yang's reply was: "I see by your gathering that it is not one at which to eat and drink only, but one where verses are written, and where a man may try his skill of hand at the character. For such an ignoramus as I from the obscure confines of Cho to push my way in here to a seat among you and to a part in the feast is a very rash and impudent thing."

Seeing how humble Yang was, and how apparently unsophisticated, they all felt for him an undisguised condescension, and said in reply: "Brother Yang, your suggestion that we have a trial of skill at the character is very good, but since you are the late comer we will let you off if you so desire. You may write or not just as you please. Have a drink with us and a pleasant time." So they urged him, passing the glass and calling on the dancing-girls to sing.

Yang looked at the dancers assembled and saw that all twenty of them were persons of striking appearance. Among them was one specially noticeable, who sat in a lady-like and modest way, neither playing nor talking. Her face was very beautiful and her form was most graceful, such as few on earth could rival. She might have been likened to the merciful goddess Kwan-se-eum, who sits aloft in her silken picture. Yang felt his mind moved by her presence, and forgot all about the feasting and the drink. She also looked straight at him, and by her expression seemed to pass him a message of recognition. He also saw that there were many compositions in verse piled up before her, so he said to the gentlemen: "I presume that these compositions are by your excellencies; I would like permission to read them."

Before they could reply the dancer herself arose, brought them and placed them before him.

He looked them over, one by one. Among them were some fair compositions of an average grade, but nothing striking or of special excellence. He said to himself: "I used to hear that the gifted literati of Nakyang were masters at the pen, but seeing these I count that a false report." He gave back the compositions to the fair lady, made a bow to the gentlemen and said: "A humble countryman like myself never had a chance to read the writings of the capital before. Now by good fortune I have had the opportunity and my heart has been made glad."

The various guests had by this time become quite exhilarated. They laughed in reply: "Brother, you have thought only of the beauty of the composition you do not know what beauty of reward goes with it."

Yang made answer: "I have already had special proof of your kindness, and in the passing of the glass have been permitted to become an intimate and sworn friend. Why don't you also tell me what this beauty of reward is of which you speak?"

They laughed again and said: "Why should we not? There is an old saying that the wisdom of Nakyang is very great, and that if in the Government examination our candidate does not come off the winner he surely will have second place. We all here are sharers in the matter of literary reputation, and so cannot act as our own judges. But yonder fair dancer's family name is Kay Som-wol and her given name is Moonlight. She is not only the first singer and dancer of this East Capital, she is a master hand at the pen, and knows by intuition as the gods do. All the scholars of Nakyang consult her as to the probabilities of the examination. She decides and they pass or fail like the fittings of the tally. Never is there a mistake in her estimate. Thus have we each given over to her our compositions to have her point out their defects, to pronounce on that which specially meets her approval, and to sing it over for us with the harp. She is our judge, and we await her unerring verdict. Kay See's name is the same as that of the famous cinnamon tree of the moon, and she will indicate for us the next successful candidate. Won't you try your hand as well, and is not this a glorious opportunity?"

Master No said: "There is beyond this, too, a still more interesting fact, namely, that the one whose composition she selects and sings will have Kay See for his fair companion. We are all friends here and hopeful candidates. Brother Yang, you are a man as well as we, and appreciate the joys and delights of life. Will you not accept the invitation and be a competitor in this trial of skill?"

Yang replied: "I have not written for so long a time, I really do not know what I can do. Has not Kay See sung you the winner's verses yet?"

Master Wang replied: "The fair lady has not once struck the harp or opened her cherry lips. Her pearly teeth have not parted, nor has a single note greeted our ears. We have evidently not written up to her demands, so her heart is unmoved and weighed down for shame of us."

"Your humble servant," said Yang, "is from the distant land of Cho and though I have written verses I am an outsider, and am afraid to venture on a contest with you honourable gentlemen."

Wang, however, shouted out: "The Master Yang is prettier than a girl – why is it that he fails in the spirit of a gallant knight? The Sage says: 'If it is a question of good to be done, step not aside even for your teacher,' and again, 'It is the duty of the Superior Man[12] to do his best.' I doubt not that Master Yang is no hand at the pen. If he were, why should he be so modest concerning this small venture?"

Now although Yang had modestly desired to decline this unexpected invitation, when he beheld the fair dancer Kay See he was all awake to the occasion. There was no power now to restrain him, so he caught up a sheet of paper that lay on the matting, selected a pen and wrote three stanzas. His writing was like a boat on the sea scudding before the wind, or like a thirsty horse making straight for a stream of water. The various guests caught the spirit of the composition so strong and swift, and seeing how the characters crowded forth from his pen like flying magic, were all startled and turned pale.

12 *Superior Man.* This is a translation of the term *koon-ja*, which means a man of superior virtue. Learning and training play their part, but goodness is the *sine qua non* for this great master. His superior, again, in the scale of immortals is the "Sage," or holy man.

Yang then threw down the pen, and said to the guests: "I ought to ask the opinion of you gentlemen first, but to-day as Kay See is judge and as the time allowed is passing, with your kind permission I'll hand it directly to her."

The verses read:

> "*The man from Cho moves west and enters Chin,*
> *He sees the wine pavilion and boldly steps within,*
> *Now who shall pluck the flower from the tree within the moon,*
> *And claim the winner's honour and the fairy's magic tune?*
> *The catkins of the willow they float o'er Chon-jin's stream,*
> *The gem-wrought shades of many ply close out the sun between;*
> *Our ears awake to hear a song of special gift and grace,*
> *Our eyes behold in silken scenes a gifted fairy's face.*
> *The flowers of spring are filled with awe and drop their heads for*
> *   shame,*
> *They sense her song, they feel her step, the fragrance of her name;*
> *The passing shadows stay their course, unwilled to steal away,*
> *The lighted halls of gladsomeness proclaim my winning day.*"

For a moment Moonlight let her awakened vision rest on the composition, and then her clear voice broke forth into singing sweet and compelling. The cranes stepped forth into the city commons to cheer her, and the phoenixes made their responses. Flutes lost their charm, and the harp its store of sweet melody. The hearers were intoxicated by the music, and all faces turned pale. Out of contempt they had compelled Yang to write, but now when his composition had become the song that Moonlight sang, their joy gave place to envy, and they looked at each other speechless with dismay. To think of giving Moonlight over to this unknown stranger roused rebellious feelings. Their desire was to break the agreement, but such an act of dishonour was hard to suggest, so they sat gagged and dazed looking at each other.

Yang saw their ominous faces, and at once got up and made his farewell: "All unexpectedly I have met with so kindly a welcome from you gentlemen, and have boldly taken part in this happy contest. I have eaten and drunk of your hospitality, for which I thank you most heartily. Having still a long way to go I cannot spend more time with you as I would like, but must now take my departure. Let us meet again at the winner's festival on the close of the Government[13] examination," so he quickly took his leave, none of the guests detaining him.

When he had passed outside of the pavilion and was about to mount his donkey, Moonlight came suddenly out and said to him: "On the south side of the road you will see a house enclosed by a white wall with cherry blossoms lining the way; that's my home. Go there, please, and wait for me. I shall come at once." He nodded and started off in the direction indicated.

Moonlight re-entered the pavilion and said to the guests: "You gentlemen have highly honoured me, and have permitted me to sing a song by which my destined one is made known. What is your wish in the matter?"

They could not hide their feelings of disgust, and said in reply: "Yang is an outsider and not one of ourselves; you are not called upon to concern yourself with him." They talked and discussed, and said this and that, but came to no conclusion.

Moonlight, with determination written on her pretty face, replied: "I have no confidence in people who break faith. You have plenty of music here, please continue to enjoy yourselves. Kindly excuse me, I am feeling unwell, and so cannot stay until the end." She arose and went slowly out. Because of the agreement that had been made, and also by reason of her quiet dignity, they dared not say a word.

In the meantime Yang had gone to his inn, packed up his baggage and started in the darkness for Moonlight's home. She had already arrived, had put in order the entry hall, lighted the lamps and was waiting. He tied his donkey to a cherry tree and rapped at the double-panelled gate. At the sound she slipped on her light shoes and came out quickly. "You left before I did," said she, "but I am here ahead of you – how does this happen?"

Yang replied: "The host awaits the guest, not the guest the host. I had no heart to be late, but 'my horse is slow,' as the old saying runs."

They met with great delight as those destined for each other. She passed him the glass of welcome and bade him sing. His voice was sweet and such as to awaken and captivate the soul.

13 *Examinations.* According to the old laws of China the official examinations were held only in the years of the intercalary moon, but special examinations might be held at other times with the permission of His Majesty.

She said: "I am yours from to-day, and shall tell you my whole heart in the hope that you will condescend to take pity on me. I am originally from So-joo. My father was a secretary of that county, but unfortunately he fell ill and died away from home. Because we were poor, and his station far distant, he was buried without the required forms. Having lost his protecting arm, my step-mother sold me as a dancing-girl for one hundred *yang*. I accepted the disgrace, stifled my resentful soul, and did my best to be faithful, praying to God, who has had pity on me, so that to-day I have met my lord and can look again upon the light of sun and moon. Before the approaches of my home is the main roadway that leads to the market square. There is no cessation to the sound of traffic that passes day and night. None come or go without resting there. Thus for four or five years I have had a chance to study thousands of passers-by, and yet never has one passed by who is equal to my master. We have met and now my hopes are realised. Unworthy as I am, I would gladly become your serving-maid to prepare your food and do your bidding. What is your thought toward me, please?"

Yang comforted her with many kind words and expressions of appreciation: "I am drawn to you," said he, "as truly and as deeply as you are drawn to me, but I am only a poor scholar with an old mother depending on me. I should like nothing better than to grow old with you as husband and wife, but I am not yet sure of my mother's wishes, and I am afraid you would be unwilling to have her choose you as my secondary wife, with some unknown stranger to take first place. Even though you had no objection to it yourself, I am sure there is no one your superior or even your equal. This is my perplexity."

Moonlight said in reply: "Why do you say so? There is no one in the world just now equal to thee, my master. I need not say to you that you are to win the first place in the coming examination, and in a little you are to carry the seal of a minister of state, and the insignia of a great general's authority. All the world will desire to follow you; who am I that I should expect to have you to myself? Please, my lord, when you are married to some maiden of high degree and you receive your mother under your faithful care, kindly remember me. Assuredly I shall keep myself pure for thee only, and shall be at thy commands alone."

"Some time ago," said Yang, "I went through Wha-joo city and caught by chance a passing glimpse of one, Commissioner Chin's daughter. Her beauty and her talents were not unlike those of yourself. Now, alas, she is gone, not to be seen again I fear. Where would you suggest then that I find your equal or superior?"

"The person you refer to," said Moonlight, "is undoubtedly the daughter of Commissioner Chin, whose name is Cha-bong. When he was formerly magistrate of our county his daughter and I were bosom friends. She is a surpassing mystery of loveliness, like Princess Tak-moon.[14] But there is no use in thinking of her; let your thoughts go elsewhere, I pray you."

Yang said: "It is an old understanding that not many special marvels of beauty are born into the world at one and the same time. Now we have the maiden Moonlight and Chin See, two who have known and seen each other. I am afraid that the powers of heaven and earth are exhausted and that no more such are living."

Moonlight laughed, and said: "Your words are like those of the tadpole in the well. I'll tell you who there are among us dancing girls of special beauty. There are said to be three, Sim Oh-kyon, the Swallow, who lives in Kang-nam; Chok Kyong-hong the Wildgoose who lives in Ha-pook; and Kay Som-wol, Moonlight of Nakyang. I am Moonlight, and though I have won a name out of all proportion to my merits, Swallow and Wildgoose are truly the greatest beauties living. Why do you say that there are no more such in the world?"

Yang answered: "My opinion is that those two are unfairly and unjustly given a place and name equal to yours."

Moonlight replied: "Ok-kyon, Swallow, lives so far away from me that I have never met her, but all who have come from the south are unstinted in their praises. I am sure she has no unfair reputation. Wildgoose I know and love like a sister. I'll tell you about her. She is the daughter of the Yang clan of Pa-joo, who

14 *Princess Tak-moon.* The daughter of a great Croesus of China, 150 BC, she has become associated with the most famous of all historic scandals. Through the influence of his skill upon the lute, she became enamoured of the scholar and poet, Sa-ma Sang-yo, and, contrary to all the laws that govern widows and keep them exclusively to the memory of their late husband, she eloped with him. Her name is universally associated to-day with the delights and charms of sweet music.

lost her parents early in life and lived with her aunt. From her girlhood days a rumour went forth through all the north land of her beauty, so that thousands of golden *yang* were offered for her. Go-betweens crowded her gateway like a swarm of bees. Wildgoose spoke to her aunt about it, and had them driven away. Said they to the aunt: 'Your pretty niece has driven us away and will consent to no one. What sort of person does she desire in order to be satisfied? Does she want to be wife of a minister, or of a provincial governor, or is she to be given to some noted literatus or writer of renown?

"Wildgoose replied for herself, saying: 'If there be as in the days of the Chin Kingdom someone like Sa An-sok, I'll follow him and be the companion of a minister of state; or if as in the days of the Three Kingdoms someone like Choo Kong-keun, I'll follow him and be the wife of a noted governor; or if there be someone like Yee Tai-baik,[15] doctor of the Hallim, great in letters, I'll follow him; or if he be like Sa Ma-chang, who sang the phoenix song in the days of Han Moo-je,[16] I'll follow him. Where my heart goes I will go, but who can tell in advance where this shall be?'

"Then the various go-betweens laughed loudly and took their departure. Wildgoose said to herself: 'How could an imprisoned girl from an obscure part of the country with no experience of the world ever be expected to select a noted lord for husband? But a dancer like me is one who shares the festal season with the rare and gifted, and talks to them face to face. She even opens the door to princes and nobles. She learns to distinguish the high-born from the mediocre, and becomes an expert in assaying human worth. She can sense the bamboo from the Tai, or jade ornaments from Namjon; how should she be anxious about whom to choose?' So she yielded herself up as a dancing-girl in order that she might attach herself to one great and

15   *Yi Tai-baik.* The most famous of China's poets. He lived from AD 699 to 762, in the Tang Kingdom, a hundred years or so before the time of this story. He claimed, as this story depicts, that he was one of the genii, exiled for a period to this dusty, troubled world.

16   *Han Moo-je.* Died 87 BC. He is one of the most famous Emperors of China. At first he was a great lover of Confucian literature, but later this love waned and he became a devotee of Taoism. He is said to have visited the famous Western Queen Mother, So Wang-mo, who kept her court of paradise on the tops of the Kuen-luen Mountains. She also visited him, and this has become the most famous incident in the life of this Emperor, who reigned for over fifty years.

renowned, but in all these years she has found nothing but an empty reputation.

"Last year the noted literati from the twelve counties of Shantung north of the river held a great feast in the capital and had dancing and music. At this time Wildgoose sang the Yea-sang Kok (The Rainbow Robes of the Fairy). She was like the wild bird itself in grace of motion and matchless beauty. All the dancers of the day dropped their heads before her. When the feast was over she went away by herself to the top of Tong-jak Tower, walked back and forth under the light of the moon, thinking over the writings of the ancient sages, her heart full of loneliness and sorrow, sighing to herself over past events that had broken in upon her fragrant way. All who saw her revered her grace and gazed with wonder at her loveliness. When Wildgoose and I played together in the Sang-kok Monastery and told our hopes one to the other, she said to me: 'If we two meet a master whom we like let's recommend each other. As we serve the same husband we shall pass our happy days without faults or failings.'

"I agreed, and now that I have met with my destined lord I naturally think of Wildgoose, who is at present in the palace of the governor of Shantung. Alas, as the ancients said, there are many devils to interfere with what is sweet and good. The wives of the governor are surrounded with riches and honour, but this is not what Wildgoose wishes." And Moonlight sighed and added: "Would that I could meet my fairest companion and tell her."

Yang said in reply: "There are many gifted ones among the dancers, and yet why should a daughter of the gentry have to take a second place to them?"

Moonlight answered: "Among those I know there is no one who equals Chin See. How could I dare propose a name to my lord not her equal? Still I have frequently heard the people of the capital say that there is no one like Justice Cheung's daughter. For beauty of face and nobility of heart she is regarded as first of all. I have not seen her myself, but there is no question that her name is well won. When my lord reaches the capital please think of this. Seek her out if possible, and learn if this be so."

But the time had come to part, and Moonlight said in haste: "You must not stay longer. The various guests were fiercely angry with you and will be so still. There may be danger; go quickly, please. We shall meet and have many happy days together, why should I be sad?"

The master spoke his greetings: "Your words are like gold and jewels to me, and shall be written on my heart," and in tears they parted.

CHAPTER IV
IN THE GUISE OF A PRIESTESS

YANG now made his way from Nakyang to the western capital, found a lodging-house and disposed of his baggage. Learning that the day set for the examination was still distant, he called the host and inquired of him about his mother's cousin. He was told that she resided outside the South Gate. So he prepared something in the way of a present and went to find her. She was now a little over sixty years of age, was held in great respect, and was the head of the Taoist sect of women.

The master appeared before her with due ceremony and gave his mother's letter, while the priestess inquired about his health, and with evident emotion said: "It is twenty years and more since your mother and I parted, and now here is a young man of the second generation, so handsome and strong. Surely time goes by like galloping horses or swift running water. I am an old woman now and am tired of living in the noise and confusion of the capital. I was just on the point of going off to the hills, where I could meet some sage and give my mind to non-earthly things, but now I find in my sister's letter a commission that she has for me, so I must stay and carry it out on your behalf."

Yang's appearance was most attractive, and his young countenance like that of the gods. The priestess realised that it would be very difficult indeed to find a fitting mate for him from the homes of the gentry. Still she would try. "Come and see me often in your moments of leisure," said she.

Yang's answer was: "Your humble nephew belongs to a family that is poor and unknown, with only his aged mother left to him. He is now nearing twenty, and living in an unfrequented part of the country had no chance to find a companion. In these straits, and with the question of food and clothing added, he had to remember first the law of faithfulness to his mother. Between

IN THE GUISE OF A PRIESTESS

fears and hopes he has come to solicit help from his excellent aunt, and she has so kindly consented to assist him that he is very grateful indeed. There are no words by which he can express this." He said good-bye and withdrew.

The time for the examination drew gradually nearer, but now that a question of marriage had arisen, his desire for fame and literary distinction little by little declined. A few days later he went again to see his aunt.

The priestess met him laughingly, and said: "There is a maiden of whom I have thought whose beauty and intelligence are a match indeed for the young master; but her family is terribly proud and exclusive, with dukes and barons and ministers of state and so forth in its train for generations. I fear this family is quite unapproachable. If you could but win the first place in the examination you might think of this as a possibility. Otherwise I fear there is no hope. My advice to you is not to come visiting me so often, but to spend your efforts in the way of preparation so as to win the first place of honour when the examination takes place."

Yang asked: "To whose home do you refer?"

"Just outside the Chong-yung Gate," said she, "is Justice Cheung's house. That is the one I refer to. Before it is an approach-way ornamented with red arrows. This Justice has a daughter who is a veritable fairy, evidently some angelic visitor to the earth."

Yang then thought of what Moonlight had told him, and said to himself: "How is it that this girl is praised so highly?" Then he asked of the priestess, "My honoured aunt, did you ever see this daughter of Cheung?"

"See her? Of course I've seen her, and she is indeed an angel from heaven. No words can express how wonderful she is."

The young master then said: "I don't like to boast, but I am sure I shall win first place in the examination as easily as drawing my hand from my pocket. Don't be anxious on that score, please. But I have had one foolish wish all my life, and that is not to ask in marriage one whom I have never seen. Please, excellent aunt, take pity on me and help me to see what the lady is like?"

The priestess replied: "How could you ever hope to see this daughter of a high minister of state?[17] You do not trust what I say?"

---

17 *The Division of the Sexes.* This custom has been strictly observed in Korea up to the

He replied: "How could I ever doubt your words? But still we each have our own likes and dislikes. Your eyes could never be just the same as mine."

"There is no such danger," said she. "Even children know that the phoenix and the unicorn mean good luck, and the lowest classes in the world understand that the blue sky and the bright sun are exalted and glorious. A man who has any eyes at all would know that Cha-do was a beauty."

Yang returned home unsatisfied in heart, and next day went once more, greatly desiring to obtain his aunt's definite permission. The priestess met him and laughingly said: "You have come early to-day; you must have some special news to tell me."

Yang smiled and made reply: "Only by seeing Justice Cheung's daughter can your humble servant rid himself of his doubts and fears. Think once again, please, of my mother's commission and my earnest desire, and tell me some plan by which I can look upon her face. If you will only do this I will thank you for such kind favour by a never ending gratitude."

The priestess shook her head, saying: "That's a very difficult thing indeed." She thought for a time and then asked: "You are so highly accomplished otherwise, have you ever had leisure in your studies for music?"

Yang replied: "Your humble nephew once met a great teacher of the genii, and took from him a special course, and so knows something of the Five Notes and the Six Accords of the gamut."

The priestess then said to him: "Justice Cheung's home is a very large one, and has five successive gates of entrance. It is a long way into the inner quarters, and the walls about are high and forbidding. Without wings to fly, there is no possible way of entrance. The Justice himself follows the Books of Rites and Poetry carefully and conforms his household in every particular to their teachings, so that members of the former never come here to offer incense, nor do they seek sacrifice in the Buddhist temples. The Feast of Lanterns[18] of the first moon, and the celebration on

present time, and forbids not only acquaintance but even the seeing of women and girls by members of the male sex. According to the law of Confucius, brothers and sisters were divided at seven years of age, the girls to abide thereafter in the inner quarters,while the boys were to live their lives outside this enclosure.

18   *The Feast of Lanterns.* Held as a prayer to the first full moon of the year. One of the

the Kok River[19] of the third have no attractions for them. How could an outsider ever expect to gain entrance to such a family? I have thought of a plan, however, but do not know whether you would care to try it."

Yang replied: "If it be a matter of seeing the maiden Cheung, I'll go up to heaven or down into Hades; I'll carry fire on my back or walk on the water, if you just say the word."

The priestess made answer: "Justice Cheung is now advanced in years, is in poor health, and has little interest in the affairs of state. His chief delight is in sight-seeing and in hearing music. His wife, Choi See, is extravagantly fond of the harp, and the daughter being so quick and intelligent and able to grasp the thought of any and every question, has acquired a thorough knowledge of the ancient masters. A single hearing and she understands at once a player's excellences or defects. The mother, Choi See, likes to hear something new, and constantly calls people to play for her, keeping her daughter at hand to comment and to listen. Thus she delights her old age with the charm of music. My idea is this, that since you understand how to play, you should practise some special selections and then wait till the last day of the third moon, the birthday of No-ja. They always send a servant on that day from Cheung's house with candles to burn in the temple here. You might take advantage of this opportunity to dress as a Taoist priestess and play so that the servant could hear you, and the servant will assuredly take the news of it to her mistress. The lady, when she learns this, will unquestionably call you. In this way you might gain admission. As for seeing or not seeing the daughter, that depends on the decrees of fate, of which I am not the master. Apart from this I have no other suggestion to offer." She added also: "Your face is quite like a girl's, and you have no beard. Priestesses, too, do not do up their hair as other girls do, or cover their ears with it. I see nothing difficult in the matter of your disguise."

Yang, greatly delighted, took his departure. He counted over on

great sacrificial seasons of the Far East.

19   *Kok Kang.* In the year AD 785 King Tok-jong, on the first day of the second Moon, called his ministers and made them come to the Kok Kang Pavilion and write for him. The commemoration of this event has become a festival for the literati, and is called the Kok Kang Assembly.

his fingers the days that must elapse before the end of the month.

Justice Cheung, it seems, had no other child but this daughter. When she was born the mother, Choi See, half unconscious, saw a fairy angel come down from heaven and drop a sparkling gem into the room before her. Then it was that the child was born. She was called Kyong-pai, Gem-Treasure, and grew up little by little, more and more beautiful, more and more graceful, more and more gifted, so that none from ancient times was ever like her. Her parents greatly loved her and sought someone to be a fitting husband, but as yet none had been found to suit them. She was sixteen now and yet no marriage had been arranged.

On a certain day Choi See called her nurse, old Chon, and said: "To-day is the anniversary of the great teacher No-ja. Take four candles and go to the Taoist temple and give them to the priestess Too-ryon. Take these cloth gifts as well and refreshments, and present them with my kindest greetings."

Old Chon took her orders, entered a little palanquin and went to the temple. The priestess received the candles and lit them before No-ja's portrait. She said a hundred thanks and made her bow for the presents; treated Chon royally and sent her on her way rejoicing.

Meantime, in the guise of a young priestess, Master Yang had come into the temple, tuned his harp and had begun to play. Just as the old nurse had said good-bye and was about to step into the chair, she suddenly heard the sound of music from before the portrait in the main hall. Lovely music it was, clear and sweet, such as belongs beyond the clouds. Chon, ordering the chair to wait for a moment, inclined her head and listened.

She turned to the priestess Too-ryon and said: "While I have waited on the lady Cheung I have heard sweet music, but never in my life have I heard anything like this. It is wonderful. Who is playing?"

The priestess replied: "Recently a young acolyte from Cho has come to visit me, desiring greatly to see the capital. It is she who plays. Certainly her powers of execution are wonderful, but I am not a musician myself, and cannot well distinguish one part from the other. Still I am sure after what you say that she must be very gifted indeed."

Chon said: "If the lady Cheung knows of this she will certainly invite her. Ask her to stay for a little, please."

The priestess replied: "Very well, I'll do so." So she sent her on her way and then she told Master Yang what old Chon had said. Yang was delighted, and awaited impatiently his summons to the house of Cheung.

On her return the old nurse said to the lady Cheung: "In the Taoist Temple there is a young priestess who plays the harp as I have never heard it played in my life; it is the most wonderful playing in the world."

The lady Cheung replied: "I wish I could hear her." The following day she sent a closed chair and a servant to the temple bearing a message to the teacher Too-ryon, saying: "Even though the young priestess should not wish to come, please use your kind offices to have her visit me."

The priestess then said to Yang before the servant: "This high and noble lady invites you; you must not refuse to go."

"It is not fitting," said Yang, "that one born of the low classes in a distant part of the country should go into the presence of nobility, and yet how can I refuse to do what your ladyship commands?"

So he donned the robe and hat of a priestess, took his harp and went forth. Truly he was as startling in appearance and as sweet as the ancient favourites of China. The servant of the Cheungs was beside herself with joy.

Master Yang, in the closed chair, safely reached Cheung's. The servant then led the way into the inner quarters. The lady Cheung, with dignified but kindly countenance, was seated in the main hall.

The musician bowed twice before the step-way, and then the lady ordered her to be seated, saying: "My servant went yesterday to the temple and was so fortunate as to hear the music of the gods. She returned and expressed a wish that I might hear it so. Now indeed I realise what the saying means that the beautiful presence of the genii drives all worldly thoughts from the soul."

The young priestess arose from her seat. "Your humble servant," said she, "is from the land of Cho, and is making a hasty journey like a passing cloud. Because of my slight attainments in music your ladyship has called me to play before you. How could I ever have dreamed of such an honour?"

The lady Cheung told the servant to place the harp in order. She touched. it lightly herself, saying: "This is a beautiful instrument indeed."

The young priestess answered: "It is made of o-dong wood that has dried for a hundred years on the Yong-moon mountain. Its fibre is close knit and hard like metal or marble. It was a gift to me that I never could have purchased with money."

As they talked together the shades of the afternoon began to fall upon the white stone entry, but still there was no sign of the daughter.

The musician, in a state of great inward impatience and doubt, said to the lady: "Though your servant knows many ancient tunes and prefers them to the modern, I play them only, but do not know their names or history. I have heard the priestess in the temple say that your excellent daughter's knowledge of music is equal to that of the famous Sa-kwan. I should like to have her hear and comment concerning my poor efforts."

The lady then sent a servant to call the daughter. In a little the embroidered door slid open and a breath of sweet fragrance issued forth. The maiden came sweetly out and sat down beside her mother. The musician arose, made two bows and slightly lifted his eyes to see, and lo, it was as when the first rays of the morning bursts upon one, or as when the fresh bloom of the lotus shows above the water. His mind was all in a daze, his spirit intoxicated so that he dared not look. He was sitting at a distance where he had difficulty in seeing, so he said to the lady: "I should like to hear more clearly what the young mistress says. The hall is so large and her voice so soft that I cannot catch the words."

The lady then told one of the servants to bring the priestess's cushion up closer. The servant did so and arranged the seat just in front of the lady Cheung and to the right of the young mistress, and adjusted it so that they could not look straight at each other. Yang was disturbed by this, but did not dare to suggest a second change. The servant then placed the incense table in front and brought incense. Then Yang, the pretended priestess, touched the strings of his harp and began with the tune, "The Feathery Robes of the Fairy."

The young lady said: "Oh, how beautiful! This is proof indeed of the happy world of Tang Myong days. The maiden's playing is beyond human conception, but, alas, it is said of this tune that the

O-yang barbarian with the sound of the drum came thundering in, shaking the earth and drowning out the notes of the 'Feathery Robes.' This is a tune associated with wild war, and though wonderful in its power it has fearsome associations connected with it; try another, please."

Yang played again. Then the young mistress said: "This is a beautiful tune too, but it suggests a wild, reckless life that rushes to extremes. King Hoo-joo of China enjoyed this tune to the undoing of his kingdom, and its name to-day is famous, 'The Garden of Green Gems and Trees.' The saying runs: 'Even though you were to meet Hoo-joo in Hades it would be out of place to ask him about Green Gems and Trees.' This is a tune that caused the loss of a kingdom, and is one not to be honoured. Won't you play another?"

Yang played another tune. Then the young lady remarked: "This tune is sad, glad, sweet and tender. It is the tune of Cha Moon-heui, who was caught in a war and carried off by the barbarian. Cho-cho gave a fabulous ransom for her and had her brought home. When she bade good-bye to her half-barbarian sons Cha Moon-heui wrote this tune. It is said, 'The barbarians on hearing it dropped their tears upon the grass, while the minister from Han was melted by the strains of it.' It is a very beautiful tune, and yet she is a woman who forsook her virtue. Why should we talk of it? Try another, please."

Then Yang played again. The young mistress said: "This is 'The Distant Barbarian,' written by Wang So-gun.[20] Wang So-gun thought of her former king and longed for her native land. She put into her song her lost country, and a wail of sorrow over the portrait that was her undoing. She herself had said: 'Who will write a tune that will move the hearts of the people for a thousand years as they think of me?' Still it is born of life with the barbarian and is a half-foreign tune, and not just what we should call correct. Have you another?"

---

20 *Wang So-gun.* This marvellous woman, by her beauty, brought on in the year 33 BC a war between the fierce barbarian Huns of the north and China Proper. She was finally captured and carried away, but rather than yield herself to her savage conqueror, she plunged into the Amur River and was drowned. Her tomb on the bank is said to be marked by undying verdure. The history of Wang So-gun forms the basis of a drama, translated by Sir John Davis, and entitled "The Sorrows of Han."

Yang then tried another. Then the young lady's expression changed, and she said: "It is long since I heard this tune. You are surely not an inhabitant of the earth. This calls up the history of a great and wonderful man who had fallen on evil days and had given up all thought of worldly things. His faithful heart was bewildered over the mystery of life, and he wrote this tune called 'The Hill of the Wide Tomb.' As he was beheaded in the East market he looked at the setting sun and sang it, adding the words 'Alas, alas, will anyone ever desire to learn it? I have kept it to myself; now I grieve that there is no chance to pass it on.' You must indeed have met the spirit of the Buddha Sok-ya to have learnt it."

Yang, kneeling as he was, replied: "The young mistress's wisdom is unequalled by any other on earth. I learned this from a great teacher, and his words were indeed the very words of your ladyship."

He played still another. Then Cheung See said "Enough, enough, 'tis the sadness of the autumn. The brown hills are bare and craggy, the waters of the river wide and far across. The footprints of the fairy are seen upon the dust of earth. This is the tune of the 'Water Fairy.' My priestess musician has all the knowledge of a hundred generations."

The young master played again, while the lady adjusted her dress and knelt circumspectly, saying: "This is the supreme expression of all music. The Sage alights on an evil world, travels through all parts of it, desiring to help the distressed and the needy. If not Confucius, who ever would have written a song like this? It is no other than 'The Fragrant Orchid.' The thought runs: 'He travelled through all the nine provinces and found no place in which to rest his heart.' Is this not so?"

Yang, kneeling, cast more incense on the fire, then played again, whereupon the young lady said: "Refined and beautiful is 'The Fragrant Orchid' as it came from the mind of the great Sage, who sorrowed over the world and desired to save it; but there is a strain of hopelessness in it. In the song, however, all is bright and happy like the opening buds of May, free and gladsome; there are no words by which to tell it. This is the famous tune of the 'Nam-hoon Palace of King Soon.' Concerning it, it is written: 'The south wind is warm and sweet and bears away on its wings the sorrows of the world.' This is lovely, and fills one's heart to overflowing. Even though you know others I have no desire to hear them."

Yang bowed and said in reply: "Your humble servant has heard that you must play nine before the spirit of God comes down. I have already played eight; one still remains, which, with your kind permission, I will play." He straightened the bridge of the harp, tuned it once again, and began.

The music seemed far distant at first, miles away, awakening a sense of delight and calling the soul in a fast and lively way. The flowers in the court opened out at the sound of it; the swallows in pairs swung through their delightful dancings; the orioles sang in chorus to each other. The young mistress dropped her head, closed her eyes, and sat silent for a moment till the part was reached which tells how the phoenix came back to his native land, gliding across the wide expanse of sea looking for his mate.

The young mistress opened her eyes and looked once straight at the priestess. Then she bent her head as though to adjust her dress. The red blushes mounted to her cheeks and drove even the paler colour from her brow, until she looked like one who was red with wine. She quietly arose and went into her own room.

Yang gave a start of surprise, pushed away his harp, got up, looked straight before him towards the place where the young lady had gone. His spirit seemed to leave him, and his soul to die away, so that he stood like a porcelain image. Her ladyship told him to be seated, asking: "What was it that you played just now?"

Yang replied: "I got this tune from my teacher, but do not know what its name is. I should like the young lady kindly to tell me." But though they waited long she did not reappear. The lady Cheung then asked the cause from the servant, who returned to say that her young mistress had been exposed to the draught somewhat and was feeling unwell, so that she would not be able to rejoin them.

In doubt whether he had been discovered or not Yang felt uncomfortable, and did not dare to stay longer. He arose and made a courteous bow to the lady Cheung, saying: "I am so sorry to hear that the young mistress is feeling unwell. I am afraid I may have upset her by some lack of good form on my part. Your ladyship will be anxious, too. May I ask leave to go?"

The lady gave money and silk by way of reward, but the priestess refused it. "Though I know something of music I have studied it only as a pastime," said she, "and must not accept these rich presents." She then bowed her thanks, went down the stone steps and was gone.

The lady made anxious inquiry about her daughter but found that there was nothing serious the matter.

Later Cheung See entered her mother's room and asked of the servant there: "How is Cloudlet feeling to-day?"

The servant replied: "She is better. Finding that your ladyship was enjoying the music, she got up and made her toilet."

Now Cloudlet's family name was Ka and her birthplace was So-ho. Her father had come up to the capital, and was a secretary in one of the offices of the ministry. He had proved himself a faithful servant to Chief Justice Cheung, and shortly after his death, when Cloudlet was about thirteen years of age, the Justice and his wife took pity on the orphan and made her a member of their family and the playmate of their daughter. There was a difference of a month only between the ages of the two girls.

Every line and feature of Cloudlet's face was a model of comeliness. She was the equal of the young mistress in literature, in penmanship, and in embroidery, and she was treated in every way like a sister, and one whom the young lady would scarcely let go out of her sight. Though there was the relationship between the two of mistress and maid, they loved each other as only bosom friends do. Cloudlet's name originally was Cho-oon, a Cloud from Cho, but her young mistress was so in love with her beauty that she borrowed an expression from the writings of Han Toi-jee which says, "Beauty is like a cloud of springtime," and called her instead Choon-oon, "Spring Cloud," and so all the members of the family called her familiarly, Cloudlet.

Cloudlet inquired of the young mistress, saying: "The servants were all excited about the visitor, telling me that the priestess who played the harp was like a fairy and that her execution was most wonderful. Your praising her so made me anxious to forget my little ailments and get a glimpse too. Why has she left so suddenly?"

The young lady blushed, and said hesitatingly in reply: "Cloudlet, my dear, you know how I have been as careful of my behaviour as the Book of Rites requires; and how I have guarded my thoughts as the pearls and jewels of my life; that my feet have never ventured outside the middle gates; and that in conversation I have not even met my friends. Would you believe it, I have been deceived and have had put upon me a disgrace that will never be wiped out. How shall I bear it or lift up my face again to the light of day?"

Cloudlet was greatly alarmed and asked: "What do you mean?"

The young lady replied: "I did really say of the priestess who came just now that she was very, very beautiful, and her playing simply marvellous." Then she hesitated and did not finish what she was about to say.

Cloudlet made answer: "But what of that?"

The young lady replied: "The priestess began by playing the 'Feathery Mantle,' and then went on playing one by one, till she came to 'King Soon's Palace.' They were all in keeping, each selection following the other, so I asked her to stop there. She said, however, that she had one more that she would like to play. It was none other than the tune by which General Sa-ma fascinated the heart of Princess Tak-moon, the song of the phoenix seeking his mate. I was in doubt the minute I heard this, and so looked closely at her face, and assuredly it was not a girl's face at all. Some cunning fellow, wanting to see me, has pushed his way in here in disguise. I am so sorry for one thing; if only you, Cloudlet, had been well enough to have shared in this, and had seen him, you would have detected the disguise at once. I, an unmarried girl of the inner quarters, have sat for two full hours face to face with a strange man unblushingly talking to him. Did anyone ever hear of such a thing in the world before? I cannot tell this even to my mother. If I hadn't you to whom I could unburden my heart, what should I do?"

Cloudlet laughed and said in reply: "Even though you are an unmarried girl why shouldn't you hear the tune of General Sa-ma looking for his mate? The young mistress is mistaken and has seen a snake's shadow in her glass of wine."

The young lady replied: "Not so, there is a law that governs the selection of tunes. If there was no meaning in the search of the phoenix for his mate, why should it have been played last of all? While there are those among women who are delicate and refined, there are also those who are coarse and ugly, but I never saw anyone just like this person before, so beautiful and yet so commanding. I have a conviction now that the examination is close at hand and candidates are gathering, that some one among them has heard a false rumour of me, and has taken this way to spy out and see my face."

Cloudlet said: "If this priestess be really a man, and her face so beautiful, her manner so free and fresh, and her knowledge of music so astounding, one can only conclude that she is a most wonderfully gifted person. How do you know that it may not be General Sa-ma himself?

The lady replied: "Even though it be Sa-ma Sang-yo I certainly am not Princess Tak-moon."

"But," said Cloudlet, "your ladyship must not talk nonsense. Princess Tak-moon was a widow and you are an unmarried girl. Princess Tak-moon followed her lord intentionally. You have heard it without being responsible in any way, or being influenced. How can you compare yourself with Tak-moon Koon?"

So the two laughed and talked together for the rest of the day.

Some time later, when the young lady was seated with her mother, Justice Cheung came into the room with the announcement of the successful candidates. He gave it to his wife, saying: "We have not yet made arrangements for the marriage of our daughter, and I had intended to make a selection from this company of successful scholars. However, I find that the winner is not of the capital, but is a certain Yang So-yoo from Hoi-nam. His age is eighteen, and every one is loud in his praises, saying that he has ability of the first order. I hear also that he is remarkably handsome, with commanding presence for so young a man, altogether a person who has before him a great career. They say he is not yet married. I should think he would be a very suitable person for a son-in-law."

The lady replied: "To hear of him is one thing; to see him may be quite another. Even though others praise him you cannot trust to that. After you have seen and met him, let us talk the matter over."

The Justice replied: "That's a very easy thing."

CHAPTER V
AMONG THE FAIRIES

WHEN the daughter heard what her father had to say, she hurried into her room and said to Cloudlet: "The priestess who came here to play the harp was from Cho; her age was eighteen or thereabouts. Now Hoi-nam is the same as Cho, and the age corresponds. I have more suspicion than ever of this priestess. If the winner is the same as she, he will undoubtedly come to see my father. Now I want you to take note of his coming and obtain a careful view of him."

Cloudlet replied: "I did not see the other person who came, and so even though I see this one face to face how should I recognise him? I think it would be much better if your ladyship would peep through a chink and see him for yourself." Thus they laughed and talked together.

Yang So-yoo had passed both the Hoi[21] and the Chon examinations, winning the highest place of all. He was recorded a *hallim*,[22] a master of literary rank, and his name shook the city. All the nobility and the peers who had marriageable daughters strove together in their applications through go-betweens, but Yang declined them all. He went instead to Secretary Kwon of the Board of Education, and made proposals of marriage with the house of Justice Cheung, asking a letter of introduction. This the secretary readily gave.

Yang received it, placed it in his sleeve, and went at once to Justice Cheung's and sent in his card.

Cheung, seeing that it was the card of the winner, said to his wife: "The champion of the *kwago* has come to see us."

---

21   *The Hoi Examination.* This is the second regular examination taken by those who have passed the first. The Chon is a special examination taken before the Emperor.

22   *Hallim.* The term hallim means a member of the college of literature, a literary senator.

He was at once shown into the guest-room. His head was crowned with the victor's wreath of flowers. Government musicians followed in his train, singing his praises.

He bowed to the Justice and made his salutation. Exceedingly handsome, modest and respectful in his manner, he so impressed the Justice that he looked on with open-mouthed wonder. The whole house, with the exception of the daughter, was in a state of excitement, anxious to catch a glimpse of him.

Cloudlet inquired of one of the lady's attendants: "I understand from the conversation of the master and mistress that the priestess who came the other day and played the harp is a cousin of the gentleman who has won the honours. Do you see any marks of resemblance?"

The attendant caught at the suggestion at once, saying: "Really now that must be true. They resemble each other wonderfully in looks and manner. However could two cousins be as much alike as they?"

At this Cloudlet hurried to the apartment of the young lady and said: "There is no mistake, your ladyship is correct."

The young mistress replied: "Go again and hear what he says and come and tell me."

Cloudlet went, and after a long time returned to say: "On our master's proposing marriage, the winner Yang bowed very low, and said: 'Your humble servant has heard many reports of your daughter's excellence, of how gifted and beautiful she is, and so boldly and presumptuously had set his hopes high upon her. For this reason I went this morning to Secretary Kwon and asked a letter of introduction, which he wrote and kindly gave me. Now, however, since I see how far inferior my family is to yours, I find we should be ill-mated like bright clouds and muddy water, or like the phoenix with a common crow bird. Such being the case I had not thought of presenting the introduction, which is still in my sleeve pocket, too ashamed and afraid was I.'

"He then gave it to the Justice, who, after reading it with a very agreeable countenance, ordered wine and refreshments to be brought."

The young lady gave a start of alarm, saying: "No one ought ever to decide marriage in this light and hasty way. Why has my father made such a reckless decision?"

Before she had finished speaking a servant came to call her to her mother.

She went at once and the mother said to her: "Yang So-yoo is the winner of the examination, and his praises are in everyone's mouth. Your father has just decided on his marriage with you, so we two old folks will have a place of support and will no longer be anxious or troubled."

The daughter replied: "I have just learned from the servant that Master Yang's face is like that of the priestess who came the other day to play the harp. Is that so?"

The mother said: "The servant is quite right about that. The priestess musician was like a very goddess, and I quite fell in love with her beauty. Her looks have been constantly in my mind so that I wished to call her again just to see her, but I have not had the opportunity. Now that I see Master Yang he is indeed the very image of the priestess. You will know by that how wonderfully handsome he is."

The daughter replied: "Master Yang is very handsome I know, but I dislike him and so am opposed to the marriage."

"Really," exclaimed the mother, "this is a startling thing to say. You have been brought up within our women's enclosure, while Master Yang has lived in Hoi-nam. You have had no conceivable way of knowing each other – what possible dislike can you have for him?"

The daughter replied: "I am very much ashamed to say why, or to speak of it, and so I have not told you before, but the priestess who came to play the harp the other day is none other than the famous Master Yang. Disguised as a Taoist acolyte he found his way in here and played in order to see me. I was completely taken in by his cunning ruse, and so sat two full hours face to face with him. How can you possibly say that I have no reason to dislike him?"

The mother felt a sudden shock of surprise that rendered her speechless.

In the meantime Justice Cheung had dismissed Yang, and now came into the inner quarters. Delight and satisfaction were written over his broad countenance. He said to his daughter: "Kyong-pai, Jewel, you have truly mounted the dragon in a way that's wonderful."

But the mother told Justice Cheung what her daughter had said, and then the Justice himself made fresh inquiry. When he learned that Master Yang had played the Phoenix Tune in her presence he gave a great laugh, saying: "Well, Yang is indeed a wonder! In olden times Wang Yoo-hak dressed as a musician and played the flute in Princess Peace's Palace, and later became the winner of the *kwago* (examination). This is a story handed down, famous till to-day. Master Yang, too, in order to win his pretty bride, dressed as a woman. It would prove him to be a very bright fellow. For a joke of this kind why should you say you dislike him? On the other hand, you saw only a Taoist priestess; you did not see Master Yang at all. You are not responsible for the fact that he made a very pretty girl musician, and your part is not to be compared with that of Princess Tak-moon who peeped through the hanging shades. What reason have you to harbour dislikes?"

The daughter said: "I have nothing to be ashamed of in my heart, but to allow myself to be taken in thus makes me so angry I could almost die."

The Justice laughed again: "This is not a matter for your old father to know anything about. Later on you can question Yang about it yourself."

The lady Cheung asked: "What time have you fixed for the wedding?"

The Justice answered: "The gifts are to be sent at once, but we must wait till autumn for the wedding ceremony, so as to have his mother present. After she comes we can decide the day."

"Since matters stand thus," said the mother, "there is no hurry as to the exact time." So they chose a day, received the gifts, and invited Yang to their home. They had him live in a special pavilion in the park. He fulfilled all the respectful requirements of a son-in-law, served them well, and they loved him as their very own.

On a certain day Cheung See, while passing Cloudlet's room, saw that she was embroidering a pair of shoes, but fanned to sleep by the soft days of early summer, she had placed her embroidery frame for her pillow and was deep in dreamland. The young mistress went quietly in to admire the beautiful work. She sighed over its matchless stitches, and as she thought of the loving hands that worked them, she noticed a sheet of paper with writing on it lying under the frame. She opened it and read a verse or two written as a tribute to her shoes. It read:

"Pretty shoes, you've won the rarest gem for mate,
Step by step you must attend her all the way,
Except when lights are out, and silence holds the silken chamber;
Then you'll be left beneath the ivory couch forgotten."

The lady read this through, and said to herself: "No hand can write like Cloudlet's. It grows more and more skilful. The embroidered shoes she makes herself, and the rare gem is me, dear girl. Till now she and I have never been separated. By and by when I marry she speaks of being pushed aside. She loves me truly." Then she sighed and said: "She would like to share the same home and the same husband. Evidently this is the wish of her heart."

Fearing to disturb her in her happy dreams Cheung See softly withdrew and went into her mother's room. There her mother was busy with the servants, overseeing meals for the young master. Jewel said: "Since Master Yang came here to live, you, mother, have had much anxiety on his behalf, seeing to his clothes and his food and the directing of his servants. I am afraid that you are worn out. These are duties that rightly fall to me. Not only should I dislike to do them, however, but there is no precedent or warrant in the law of ceremony for a betrothed girl to serve her master. Cloudlet, however, is experienced in all kinds of work. I should like if you would appoint her to the guest chamber in the park, and have her see to what pertains to Master Yang. It would lessen at least some of your many responsibilities."

The mother replied: "Cloudlet with her marked ability and her wonderful attractiveness can do anything well, but Cloudlet's father was our most faithful attendant, and she herself is superior to the ordinary maid. For this reason, your father, who thinks so much of her, desires a special choice of husband and that she may have her own home. Is not this the plan?"

The daughter replied: "Her wish, I find, is to be with me always and never to leave."

"But when you are married," said the mother, "she could not go with you as an ordinary servant. Her station and attainments are far superior to that. The only way open to you in accord with ancient rites would be to have her attend as the master's second-ary wife."

The daughter answered: "Master Yang is now eighteen, a scholar of daring spirit who even ventured into the inner quarters of a minister's home and made sport of his unmarried daughter. How can you expect such a man to be satisfied with only one wife? Later, when he becomes a minister of state and gets ten thousand bales of rice as salary, how many Cloudlets will he not have to bear him company?"

At this point Justice Cheung came in, and his wife said: "This girl wants Cloudlet to be given to the young master to care for him, but I think otherwise. To appoint a secondary wife before the first marriage takes place is something I am quite opposed to."

The Justice answered: "Cloudlet is equal to our daughter in ability and also in beauty of face. Their love for each other is so great that they will have to be together always and must never be parted. They are destined for the same home, so to send Cloudlet ahead will really make no difference. Even a young man devoid of love for women, being thus alone, would find but poor companionship in his solitary candle, how much more one so full of life as Yang! To send her at once and have her see that he is well looked after would be very good indeed; and yet to do so before the first ceremony comes off would seem somewhat incongruous. Might it not cause complications for his first wedding? What do you think?"

The daughter replied: "I have a plan, however, by means of which Cloudlet may wipe out the disgrace that I have suffered."

The Justice asked: "What plan, pray? Come, tell me about it."

"With the help of my cousin," said the daughter, "I wish to carry out a little plan that will rid me of my mortification over what he has done to me."

The Justice laughed unrestrainedly. "That is a plan," said he.

Among the many nephews of the Justice was one known familiarly as Thirteen, a fine young fellow, with honest heart and clear head, jolly and full of fun. He had become a special friend of the young master and was most intimate with him.

The daughter returned to her own room and said to Cloudlet: "Cloudlet, I have been with you ever since the hair grew on our brows together. We have always loved each other since the days when we fought with flower buds. Now I have had my wedding gifts sent to me, and you too are of a marriageable age. You have no doubt thought of being married. I wonder who you have thought of for a husband?"

Cloudlet replied: "I have been specially loved by you, my dearest mistress, and you have always been partial to me. Never can I repay a thousandth part of what you have done. If I could but hold your dressing mirror for you for ever I should be satisfied."

"I have always known your faithful heart," said Jewel, "and now I want to propose something to you. You know that Master Yang made a ninny of me when he played the harp in our inner compound. I am put to confusion by it for ever. Only by you, Cloudlet, can I ever hope to wipe out the disgrace. Now I must tell you; we have a summer pavilion, you know, in a secluded part of South Mountain not far from the capital. Its surroundings and views are beautiful, like a world of the fairies. We could prepare a marriage chamber there, and get my cousin Thirteen to lead Master Yang into the mystery of it. If we do this he will never again attempt a disguise or to deceive anyone with his harp; and I shall have wiped out the memory of those hours that we sat face to face. I am only desirous that you, Cloudlet, will not mind taking your part in it."

Cloudlet said in reply: "How could I think of crossing your dear wishes, and yet on the other hand how could I ever again dare to look Master Yang in the face?"

The young mistress made answer: "One who has played a joke upon another never feels as bad when put to shame as one who has simply had the joke put upon him."

Cloudlet laughed and said: "Well then, even though I die I'll go through with it and do just as you say."

In spite of Master Yang's turn in office with the business it involved, he had abundant leisure and many days free. He would then pay visits to friends or have a time of amusement in some summer pavilion or go for jaunts on his donkey to see the willows in bloom. On a certain day his friend Thirteen said to him: "There is a quiet spot in the hills to the south of the city where the view is unsurpassed; let's go there, brother, you and I, to satisfy our longings for the beautiful."

Master Yang replied: "Happy thought! That's just what I should like to do."

Then they made ready refreshments, dispensed with their servants as far as possible, and went three or four miles into the hills where the green grass clothed the mountain sides and the forest trees bent over the rippling water. The lovely views of hill and valley calmed all thoughts of the dusty world.

Master Yang and Thirteen sat on the bank of the stream and sang songs together, for the time was the opening days of summer. Flowers were all about them in abundance, adding to each other's beauty. Suddenly a bud came floating down the stream. The master saw it and repeated the lines:

> *"Spring is dear, fairy buds upon the water*
> *Now appear,*
> *Saying 'Garden of the fairies, here!'"*

"This river comes from Cha-gak Peak," remarked Thirteen. "I have heard it said that at the time the flowers bloom and when the moon is bright you can hear the music of the fairies among the clouds, but my affinities in the fairy world are all lacking, so that I have never found myself among them. To-day with my honoured brother I would like just once to set foot in the city where they live, see their wing prints, and peep in at the windows on these angel dwellers.'

The young master, being by nature a lover of the wonderful, heard this with delight, saying: "If there are no fairies of course there are none, but if there are, surely they will be here. Let us put our dress in order and go to see if we can find them."

Just at this moment a servant from Thirteen's home, all wet with perspiration and panting for breath, came to say: "The master's lady has been suddenly taken ill and I have come to call you."

Then Thirteen reluctantly arose and said: "I wanted so much to go with you into the region of the genii and enjoy ourselves, but my wife is ill, and so my chance for meeting the fairies is ended. It is only another proof of what I said, that I have no affinity with fairies." He then mounted his donkey and rode hurriedly away.

Master Yang was thus left alone. He was not yet satisfied with what he had seen. He followed up the stream into the enclosing hills. The babbling waters were clear and bright and the green peaks encircled him solemnly about. No dust was there here of the common world. His mind was exalted and refreshed by the majesty of it as he stood alone on the bank of the stream or walked slowly on.

Just then there came floating by on the water a leaf of the cinnamon tree with a couplet of verse written on it. He had his serving-boy fish it out and bring it to him. The writing said:

"The fairy's woolly dog barks from amid the clouds,
For he knows that Master Yang is on the way."

Greatly astonished, he said: "How could there by any possibility be people living on these mountains, and why should any living person ever write such a thing as this?" So he pushed aside the creeping vines and made his impatient way over rocks and stones.

His boy said to him: "The day is late, sir, and the road precipitous. There is no place ahead at which to put up for the night; please let us go back to the city."

The master, however, paid no attention but pushed on for another ten or eight *li*, till the rising moon was seen over the skyline of the eastern hills. By its light he followed his way through the shadows of the trees and crossed the stream. The frightened birds uttered cries of alarm, and monkeys and other eerie night creatures voiced their fears. The stars seemed to rock back and forth over the wavy tips of the tree-tops, and the dewdrops gathered on all the needles of the pine. He realised that deep night had fallen and that no trace of human habitation was anywhere to be seen. Neither was there any place of shelter. He thought that perhaps a Buddhist temple might be nigh at hand or a nunnery, but there was none. Just at the moment of his deepest bewilderment he suddenly saw a maiden of sixteen or so dressed in fairy green, washing something by the side of the stream.

Being alarmed by the stranger she arose quickly and called out: "My lady, the Master is coming."

Yang hearing this was beside himself with astonishment; He went on a few steps farther but the way seemed blocked before him, till unexpectedly he saw a small pavilion standing directly by the side of the stream, deeply secluded, hidden away in the recesses of the hills – just such a place as fairies were wont to choose to live in.

THE POEM BY THE WAY: AMONG THE FAIRIES

A lady dressed in red then appeared in the moonlight, standing alone below a peach tree. She bowed gracefully, saying: "Why has the Master been so long in coming?"

So-yoo in fear and wonder looked carefully at her and saw that the lady was dressed in a red outer coat with a jade hairpin through her hair, an ornamented belt about her waist, and a phoenix-tail fan in her hand. She was beautiful seemingly beyond all human realisation. In deepest reverence he made obeisance, saying: "Your humble servant is only a common dweller of the earth, and never before in all his life had a moonlight meeting like this. Why do you say that I have been late in coming?"

The maiden then ascended the steps of the pavilion and invited him to follow. Awe-struck, he obeyed her, and when they had seated themselves, each on a separate mat, she called to her maid, saying: "The Master has come a long way; I am sure he is hungry; bring tea and refreshments."

The servant withdrew and in a little while brought in a jewelled table, dishes and cups. Into a blue crystal cup she poured the red wine of the fairies, the taste of which was sweet and refreshing, while the aroma from it filled the room. One glass, and he was alive with exhilaration. Said he: "Even though this mountain is isolated it is under heaven. Why is it that my fairy ladyship has left the Lake of Gems and her companions of the crystal city and come down to dwell in such a humble place as this?"

The fairy gave a long sigh of regret, saying: "If I were to tell you of the past only sorrow would result from it. I am one of the waiting maids of the Western Queen Mother[23] and your lordship is an officer of the Red Palace where God dwells. Once when God had prepared a banquet in honour of the Western Mother, and there were many officers of the genii present, your lordship thoughtlessly singled me out, and tossed me some fruit of the fairies in a playful way. For this you were severely punished and driven through transmigration into this world of woe. I, fortu-

---

23   So Wang-mo (Western Queen Mother). A great divinity of Taoism, who is supposed to dwell in her paradise on the tops of the Kuen-luen Mountains, Tibet. For thousands of years she has been regarded as the chief of the genii, and kings and emperors have become immortalised from having had audience with her. She dwells by the "Lake of Gems," near whose border grow the peach trees of the fairies. Anyone eating of this fruit will live for ever. The gentle messengers who carry her despatches are the "azure pigeons" mentioned so often in Far Eastern stories.

nately, was more lightly dealt with and simply sent into exile, so here I am. Since my lord has found his place among men and has been blinded by the dust of mortality, he has forgotten all about his past existence, but my exile is nearly over and I am to return again to the Lake of Gems. Before going I wanted just once to see you and renew the love of the past, so I asked for an extension of my term, knowing that you would come. I have waited long, however. At last, through much trouble, you have come to me and we can unite again the love that was lost."

But scarcely had they had a chance to express their love or recall the awakened secrets of the past, when the birds of the mountains began to twitter in the branches of the trees, and the silken blinds to lighten. The fairy said to the Master: "I must not detain you longer. To-day is my appointed time of return to heaven. When the officer of the genii, at the command of God, comes with flags and banners to meet me, if he should find you here we should be accounted guilty. Please make haste and escape. If you are true to your first love we shall have opportunities to meet again." Then she wrote for him a farewell verse on a piece of silk which ran thus:

> *"Since we have met, all heaven is filled with flowers,*
> *Now that we part, each bud is fallen to earth again.*
> *The joys of spring are but a passing dream,*
> *Wide waters block the way far as infinity."*

When the Master had read this he was overcome with regret at the thought of their parting, so he tore off a piece of his silken sleeve and wrote a verse which ran:

> *"The winds of heaven blow through the green stone flute,*
> *Wide-winged the white clouds lift and sail away.*
> *Another night shall mark our gladful meeting,*
> *E'en though wild rains should block our destined way."*

The maiden received it, and said: "The moon has set behind the Tree of Gems; hasten away! On all my flight to heaven I shall have this verse by which to see your face." So she placed it in the folds of her robe and then urgently pressed him: "The time is passing, Master, please make haste."

The Master raised his hands, said his regretful good-bye and was gone. He had scarcely passed beyond the shadowed circle of the grove when he looked back, but there was only the green of the mountains that seemed piled one upon the other till they touched the white clouds in companies. He realised then that he had had a dream of the Lake of Gems and thus he came back home.

But his mind was all confused and his heart had lost its joy. He sat alone thinking to himself: "Even though the fairy did tell me that the time had come for her return from exile, how could she tell the very moment, or that it was to-day? If I had only waited a little or hidden myself in some secluded corner and seen the fairies and their meeting, I would have come back home in triumph. Why did I make this fatal blunder and come away so quickly?" So he expressed his regrets over and over as he failed to sleep the night through. With these vain thoughts upon him he greeted the dawn, arose, took his servant, and went once more to where he had met the fairy. The plum blossoms seemed to mock him and the passing stream to babble in confusion. Nothing greeted him but an empty pavilion. All the fragrance of the place had vanished. The Master leaned over the deserted railing, looked up in sadness, and sighed as he gazed at the grey clouds, saying: "Fairy maiden, you have ridden away on yonder cloud and are in audience before Heaven's high King. Now, however, that the very shadow of the fairy has vanished what's the use of sighing?"

So he came down from the pavilion. Standing by the peach tree where first he met her he said to himself: "These flowers will know my depths of sorrow."

When the evening shadows began to lengthen he returned home.

Some days later Thirteen came to Master Yang and said "The other day on account of my wife's illness we failed in our outing together. My regret over that disappointment is still with me, and now though the plums and the peaches are past and the long stretch of the willows is in bloom, let us take half a day away, you and I, to see the butterflies dance and hear the orioles sing."

Master Yang answered: "The green sward with the willows is prettier even than the flowers."

So the two went together outside the gates of the city across the wide plain to the green wood. They sat upon the grass and made counting points of flowers to reckon up the drinks they had taken. Just above them was an old grave on an elevated ridge. Artemisia weeds grew over it, the fresh sod had fallen away, and there were bunches of spear grass and other green tufts mixed together, while a few weakly-looking flowers strove for life.

Master Yang, awakened from the dejection caused by the wine he had drunk, pointed to the grave, saying: "The good and the good-for-nothing, the honourable and the mean, in a hundred years will all have turned to heaped up mounds of clay. This was the regret of Prince Maing-sang long, long ago. Shall we not drink and be merry while we may?"

Thirteen replied: "Brother, you evidently don't know whose grave this is. This is the grave of Chang-yo, who died unmarried. Her beauty was the praise and admiration of all the world in which she lived, and so she was called Chang Yo-wha, the Beautiful Flower. She died at the age of about twenty and was buried here. Later generations took pity on her and planted these willows to comfort her sorrowful soul and to mark the place. Supposing we, too, pour out a glass by way of oblation to her lovely spirit?"

The young Master, being by nature kind-hearted, readily said in reply: "Good brother, your words are most becoming." So they went together to the front of the grave and there poured out the glass of wine. Each likewise wrote a verse to comfort her in her loneliness.

The Master's words ran thus:

> "The beauty of your form o'erturned the State,
> Your radiant soul has mounted high to Heaven;
> The forest birds have learned the music of your way,
> The flowers have donned the silken robes you wore.
> Upon your grave the green of springtime rests,
> The smoke hangs o'er the long deserted height,
> The old songs from the streams that bore you hence,
> When shall we hear them sung?"

The scholar Thirteen's words ran thus:

"I ask where was the beautiful land,
And of whose house were you the joy,
Now all is waste and desolate,
With death and silence everywhere.
The grass takes on the tints of spring,
The fragrance of the past rests with the flowers,
We call the sweet soul but she does not come,
Only the flocks of crows now come and go."

They read over together what they had written and again poured out an offering. Thirteen then walked round the back of the grave, when unexpectedly in an opening where the sod had fallen away, he found a piece of white silk on which something was written. He read it over, saying: "What busy-body, I wonder, wrote this, and placed it on Chang-yo's grave?"

Master Yang asked for it, and lo! it was the piece he had torn from his sleeve on which was the verse he had written for the fairy. He was astounded at it, and greatly alarmed, saying to himself: "The beautiful woman whom I met the other day is evidently Chang-yo's spirit." Perspiration broke out on his back and his hair stood on end. He could scarcely control himself, and then again he tried to dismiss his fears by saying: "Her beauty is so perfect, her love so real. Fairies too have their divinely appointed mates; devils and disembodied spirits have theirs, I suppose. What difference is there, I wonder, between a fairy and a disembodied spirit?"

Thirteen at that moment arose, and while he turned away the Master took advantage of the occasion to pour out another glass of spirit before the grave, saying as a prayer: "Though the living and the dead are separated the one from the other, there is no division in love; I pray that your beautiful spirit will accept of my devotion and condescend to visit me again this night so that we can renew the love that was broken off."

When he had done so he returned home with his friend Thirteen, and that night he waited all alone in the park pavilion chamber. He leaned upon his pillow and thought with unspeakable longing of the beautiful vision.

The light of the moon shone through the screen and the shadows of the trees crossed the window casements. All was quiet till a faint sound was heard, and later gentle footsteps were audible. The Master opened the door and looked, and there was the fairy whom he had met on Cha-gak Peak. Delighted in heart, he sprang over the threshold, took her white soft hands in his, and tried to lead her into the room, but she declined, saying: "The Master knows now my place of dwelling, and does he not dislike me for it? I wanted to tell you everything when we first met, but I was afraid I would frighten you, and so I made believe that I was a fairy. Your love is so dear that my soul has a second time returned to me, and my decaying bones are again clothed with flesh. To-day also your lordship came to my grave and poured out a libation and offered me condolences written in verse. Thus have you comforted my soul that never had a master. I cannot sufficiently express my thanks when I think of what you have done, and so have come to-night to say my word of gratitude. How dare I again have my dead body touch the form of my lord?"

But the Master took her gently by the arm and said: "A man is a fool who is afraid of spirits. If a man dies he becomes a spirit, and if a spirit lives it becomes a man. A man who fears a spirit is an idiot; and a spirit who runs away from a living man is a foolish spirit. They all come from one and the same source. Why should we make a difference or divide the living from the dead? My thought is thus, and my love is thus. Why do you resist me?"

The maiden replied: "How could I ever resist your kindness or refuse your love? But you love me because of my dark eyebrows and red cheeks, and these are not true, only make-believe. They are all part of a great trick to get into touch with one who is living. If the Master really wishes to know my face, it is but a few bones with the green ivy creeping through its openings. How can your lordship ever wish to come into contact with anything so unclean?"

"The Buddha says: 'A man's body is but froth on the water, or a gust of wind, all a make-believe,'" he said. "Who can say that it is anything, or who can say that it is nothing at all?" So he led her into the room.

Later as they sat talking, "Let's meet every night," said he, "and let nothing keep us apart."

The maiden replied: "Dead spirits and living people are different, and yet love can bind even these together."

He loved her from the depths of his heart, and apparently his love was reciprocated. When the sound of the morning bells was heard she disappeared among the flowers. He remained leaning over the armrest as he saw her go. "Let's meet again to-night" was his farewell greeting, but she said nothing in reply and was gone.

CLOUDLET'S MEETING WITH WILDGOOSE

CHAPTER VI
IT IS CLOUDLET

AFTER meeting with the fairy, Yang no longer kept company with his friends nor received guests. He lived quite by himself in the park pavilion and gave his thoughts to this one thing only. When night came he waited for her footsteps, and while day dragged on its way he waited again for the night. He hoped to persuade her to more frequent visits, but she refused to come often. Thus his mind became more and more consumed with thoughts of her.

Some time later two persons came to visit him by the side entrance of the park. He noticed that the one in front was his friend Thirteen, while the other was a stranger whom he saw for the first time. Thirteen presented the stranger to Master Yang. "This is Professor Too Chin-in," said he, "from the Temple of the Absolute. He is as well versed in physiognomy and fortune-telling as were the ancients. He would like to read your Excellency's face, for which purpose he has come at great effort."

Yang received him with open-handed welcome. "I have heard your honourable name for a long time," said he, "but we have never met before. Our coming thus face to face is beyond my highest hopes and expectations. Have you ever read our friend Thirteen's fortune? What do you think of it, pray?"

Thirteen replied for himself, saying: "The professor read my face and greatly praised it. 'Within three years,' said he, 'you will pass the examination and become a magistrate of the Eight Districts.' This satisfies me and I know it will come to pass. Brother Yang, you try once and have him read yours."

"A good man," said Yang, "never asks about the blessings he has in store, but only of the troubles that await him, and now you must tell me the whole truth."

After Professor Too had examined him for a long time, he

said: "Your eyebrows are different from those of anyone I have ever seen. You have almond eyes that are set slantwise across the cheek-bones. They indicate that you are to rise to the rank of a minister of state. Your complexion is as though powdered with rouge, and your face is round like a gem. Your name will assuredly be known far and wide. Across your temples and over your face are indications of great power. Your name, as a military officer, will encompass the Four Seas. You will be made a peer when three thousand miles away, and no blemish will ever tarnish your fair name. One danger only I see, a strange and undreamed of one. If you had not met me I am afraid you might have come to an untimely end."

"A man's good luck," said Yang, "or evil fortune all pertain to himself if they pertain to anything. Sickness I accept as something that I cannot of myself escape. Are there any signs that I am to fall seriously ill?"

Professor Too replied: "What I refer to is a wholly unexpected evil. A bluish colour is evident on your upper brow, and an unpropitious expression has got itself fastened on to the rims of your eyelids. Have you any serving man or maid in your employ whose origin you are doubtful of?"

The Master thought in his heart of the spirit Chang-yo, and guessed that this must be due to her, but he suppressed his feelings and replied without a quaver: "There is no such person as you suggest."

Then Too said further: "Have you passed an old grave or anything of the kind that has upset you or given you a fright? Or have you had any intercourse with disembodied spirits in your dreams?"

"I know nothing of that kind," said the Master.

Here Thirteen broke in to say: "Professor Too's words never miss the mark to the fraction of a hair. Think well, Yang, please," but Yang made no reply.

The Professor then went on: "A mortal has his being from the yang or positive principle in nature, while a spirit has its from the negative or eum. As it is impossible to change day for night or night for day, so the difference between the two remains for ever fixed, like that of fire and water. Now that I see your Excellency's face, I can read that some spirit has got its hold upon your body,

74

and that in a few days it will get into your bones, in which case I fear that nothing can save your life. When this comes to pass please do not complain against me or say that I did not tell you."

Master Yang thought to himself: "Even though Too's words are true, still Chang-yo and I have long had to do with each other, and have sworn a solemn oath to live and die together. Our love increases day by day, why should she do me harm? Yang Won of Cho met a fairy and they were married and shared the same home, and Nyoo Chon had for wife a disembodied spirit, and they had children. If such things happened in the past, why should I be specially alarmed?" So he said to the Professor: "A man's length of life and good or evil fortune are all decreed and appointed for him when he is born. I have proofs already of becoming a great general and minister of state, with riches and honour to my name; how could an evil spirit upset such a fortune as this?"

Too replied "The shortening of life rests with yourself; the lengthening of life rests also with yourself. But this is no concern of mine." So he gave his sleeves a shake and was gone, the Master no longer urging him to stay.

Thirteen comforted him, saying: "Brother Yang, you are by nature a lucky man. The gods are on your side, why should you fear any spirit? This contemptible fellow likes to upset people with his miserable fortune-tellings and sleight-of-hand."

So they drank together, spent the day happily and then parted. In the evening the Master, recovered from the effects of the wine, burnt incense and sat in silence waiting impatiently for Chang-yo to come. The night passed on into the morning watches, and there were no signs of her. He beat the table with impatient hand, saying: "The day is beginning to dawn and yet there is no Chang-yo." He put out the lights and tried to sleep, when suddenly he heard someone crying outside his window, and then a voice speaking which was no other than Chang-yo's. She was saying: "The Master wears upon his head a demoniacal charm, placed there by this woeful professor. I dare not approach him. I know it was not accepted of your own free will, but still it is done now, and it indicates that our destiny is finished, and this dire creature has found his delight. My one wish is that the dear Master may be protected safe and sound from all harm. I say my last and final farewell."

Yang gave a great start of alarm, opened the door to see, but

there was no trace of her. A piece of folded paper only remained
on the doorstep. This he opened and read. Two verses that she
had written on it ran thus

> *"To fill our lot as God intends,*
> *We rode the gilded clouds together,*
> *You poured the fragrant wine as friends,*
> *Before my grave upon the heather.*
> *Ere you had time my heart to see,*
> *We're parted wide as gods and men,*
> *I have no fault to find with thee,*
> *But with a man called three and ten."*

The Master read it over in a state of woeful astonishment. He felt
his head and there under his topknot was, sure enough, a charm
against spirits. He roared out against it: "This miserable demon
of a creature has upset my plans," so he tore it all to pieces and
flew into a towering rage. He again took up Chang-yo's letter,
read if through, and suddenly recollected, saying: "This word
'three and ten' indicates that her resentment is directed against
Thirteen. He's at the back of this, and while his part may not be
the wicked one that Too's is, he has interfered with what is good.
The rascal! I'll give him a piece of my mind when I meet him."
Then following the rhyme characters of Chang-yo's verses, he
wrote a reply and put it in his pocket, saying: "I have written my
answer, but by whom shall I send it?"
It ran thus:

> *"You mount the speeding wind,*
> *You ride upon the cloud;*
> *Don't tell my soul you dwell*
> *In the gruesome, secret shroud.*
> *The hundred flowers that blow,*
> *The moonlight soft and clear,*
> *Are born of you, where will you go,*
> *My soul, my life, my dear?"*

He waited till the morning and then went to pay a call on
Thirteen, but Thirteen had gone for a walk and was not to be

seen. On three successive days he went again and again, looking for him but failed each time to find him. Even the very shadow of Thirteen seemed to have disappeared. He visited Cha-gak Pavilion in the hope of meeting Chang-yo, but he found that it was a difficult thing to meet a disembodied spirit at will. There was no one to whom he could unburden his heart. Filled with distress, little by little his sleep failed him and his desire for food fell away.

Justice Cheung and his wife took note of this and in their anxiety prepared special dainties, had him called, and while they talked and partook together the Justice said: "Why is it, Yang my son, that your face looks so thin and worn these days?"

Yang replied: "Thirteen and I have been drinking too much. I expect that is the cause."

Just at this point Thirteen came in and Yang, with anger in his eye, gave him a side glance but said nothing. Thirteen spoke. "Brother, is it because you are so taken up with affairs of state that you seem disturbed in heart? Are you homesick or feeling unwell? What is the reason, I wonder, for your dejected looks and unhappy frame of mind?"

Yang made an indefinite answer: "A man who is away from home, knocking about in strange places, would he not be so?"

The Justice then remarked: "I hear the servants say that you have been seen talking to some pretty girl in the park pavilion. Is that so?"

Yang replied: "The park is enclosed, how could anyone get in there? The person who said that is crazy."

"Brother," said Thirteen, "with all your experience of men and affairs, why do you blush and act so like a bashful girl? Although you sent off Too with such dispatch, I can still see by your face that there is something you have concealed. I was afraid that you would get yourself bemused and not see the danger ahead, and so I, unknown to you, placed Too Jin's charm against evils under your topknot. You were the worse for drink and unaware of what I did. That night I hid myself in the park and took note of what passed, and, sure enough, some female spirit came and cried outside your window and then said her good-bye. She cleared the wall at a bound and was gone. I know by this that Too Jin's words were true, and so my faithfulness has saved you. You have not thanked me for it, however, but on the other hand have seemed angry. What do you mean by such conduct?"

Yang could no longer conceal the matter, and so said to the Justice: "Your unworthy son's experience is indeed a very strange and remarkable one. I shall tell my honourable father all about it." And so he told him everything. He said finally: "I know that Thirteen has done what he did in my interests, but still the girl Chang-yo, even though you say she is a disembodied spirit, is firm and substantial in form, and by no means a piece of nothingness. Her heart is true and honest, and not at all of evil or deceptive make-up. She would never, never do one a wrong. Though I am a contemptible creature, still I am a man and could not be so taken in by a devil. Thirteen, by his misplaced charm, has broken into Chang-yo's life with me, and so I cannot but feel resentment toward him."

The Justice clapped his hands and gave a great laugh: "Yang, my boy," said he, "your taste and elegance are equal to that of Song-ok.[24] You have already called up the fairies; how can you fail to know the law by which it is done? I am not joking now when I say to you that when I was young I met a holy man, and I learned from him the law by which spirits are called up, and I shall now for the sake of my son-in-law call forth Chang-yo, have her forgive your sin, and comfort your troubled heart. I wonder if this would suit you?"

"You are making sport of me," said Yang. "Even though Song-ok called up the spirit of Lady Yoo, the law by which he did so has been lost for many generations; I cannot believe what you say."

Then Thirteen broke in: "Brother Yang called up the spirit of Chang-yo without making a single effort, and I drove her away by means of one small charm. When we think of this it surely proves that there is such a thing as calling up spirits; why do you lack faith so?"

At this moment the Justice struck the screen behind him with his fan and called: "Chang-yo, where are you?"

Immediately a maiden stepped forth, her face all sunshine and wreathed in smiles. She tripped gently forth and went and stood behind the lady Cheung.

---

24   *Song Ok.* He was a great poet of the fourth century BC. His teacher was Kool-won, who was drowned in the Myok-na River. Song Ok, by supernatural power, called up the dead spirit of his teacher and talked with him.

Yang gave one glance at her, and lo! it was Chang-yo. He was in a state of inexpressible astonishment and entirely unable to understand.

The Justice and Thirteen looked at him in a questioning way, and asked: "Is this a spirit or a living person? How can it come forth thus into the broad light of day?"

The Justice and the lady Cheung laughed gently, while Thirteen simply rolled in fits of merriment. All the servants likewise were convulsed with laughter.

The Justice then went on: "Now I'll tell you, my son, how it all came about. This girl is neither a disembodied spirit nor a fairy, but Ka See, who was brought up in our home and whose name is Choon-oon or Cloudlet. We thought of you living by yourself in the park pavilion, so lonely, and sent this girl, telling her to see to your home and to comfort you. This was a kind thought on the part of us two old people. But the young folks came in at this point and arranged a practical joke that has gone beyond all bounds and limits, and put you to no end of discomfort, and yet a laughable enough joke in its way."

Thirteen, at last getting himself under control, said: "Your meeting the fairy twice was a favour accorded you by me. You have not been thankful to me as a go-between, but have, on the other hand, treated me as an enemy. Evidently you are a man with no gratitude of heart."

Here Yang laughed and said: "My father it was who sent her to me, and Thirteen it was who played the trick between us; what possible favour have I to thank him for?"

Thirteen replied: "I am unmoved by your reprimand for the joke. The whole plan of it, and the directions for the carrying of it out, belong to another person. I bear only the smallest part in the blame."

Then Yang laughingly looked at the Justice and said: "Can it be true, did you, my father, play this joke on me?"

The Justice said: "By no means. I am already an old, grey-headed man. Why should I indulge in the sport of children? You have made a mistake in so thinking."

Then Master Yang looked at Thirteen and said: "If you are not at the back of it I'd like to know who is?"

Thirteen made answer: "The sage says, 'What comes forth

from me returns to me again.' Think, brother, where this could come from. Who did you once play a trick upon and deceive? If a man can become a woman, why can't a woman become a fairy, or again a fairy become a disembodied spirit? What is there so strange about it?"

Then it was that the Master understood. He laughed and said to the Justice: "I see it now, I see it now. I played a trick once upon the young lady of this house and she has never forgotten it."

The Justice and his wife both laughed, but said nothing in reply.

Master Yang then turned to Cloudlet and said: "Cloudlet, you are indeed a bright and clever girl, but for you to undertake, first of all, to deceive the man you intend to serve, is hardly the law that governs husband and wife, is it?"

Cloudlet knelt down and made her reply: "Your humble servant heard only the general's orders, not the commands of her king."

Yang sighed and said: "In olden times fairies in the morning were clouds and in the evening they became rain, but, Cloudlet, you became a fairy in the morning and a disembodied spirit in the evening. Though clouds and rain differ they were one and the same fairy, and though the fairy I saw and the spirit differed they were one and the same Cloudlet,[25] Yang Wang understood it to be one and the same fairy in the trick of the rain and the clouds. I, too, understood it to be Cloudlet now, so why talk about fairy or spirit? Still when Yang Wang saw a cloud he didn't call it a cloud but a fairy, and when he saw the rain he did not call it the rain but his fairy. I, when I met a fairy, did not call her Cloudlet but a fairy, and when I met a spirit I did not call it Cloudlet but a spirit, which shows that I have not yet attained to Yang Wang; and also that Cloudlet's power to change is not equal to that of the ancient fairy. I have heard it said that a powerful general has no poor soldiers. Since the soldier is such as this, I can only guess at the nature of the general whom I have not seen."

All joined in the universal merry-making, more refreshments were brought in, and they spent the day in feasting.

Cloudlet, a new person in the company, sat on the mat and took part. When night had fallen she carried a lantern and went with

25   *Cho Yang-wang* (650 BC). He met a fairy from Moo-san Mountains and lived with her. Her way of going and coming was by becoming rain in the evening and visiting him, and by becoming a cloud in the morning and so sailing away.

her lord to the Park Pavilion. He, hilarious from wine, took her by the hand and jokingly said: "Are you truly a fairy or a spirit?" Again he added: "Not a fairy, and not a spirit, but a living person. If I can love a fairy thus, and even a spirit, how much more a living person. You are not a fairy, and you are not a spirit; but she who made you a fairy, and again she who made you a spirit, surely possesses the law by which we turn to fairies and spirits, and will she say that I am but a common man of earth and not want to keep company with me? And will she call this park where I live the dusty world of men, and not wish to see me? If she can change you into a fairy or into a spirit, can't I do just the same and change you too? If I turn you into a fairy shall I turn you into Han-ja who lives in the moon, or if I turn you into a spirit shall it not be into Chin-chin of Nam-ak that I turn you?"

Cloudlet replied: "Your dishonourable wife has done a bold and terrible thing, and my sins of deception are without number. Please, my master, will you ever forgive me?"

The Master replied: "Even when you changed into a spirit I did not dislike you. How could I now bear any fault in mind toward you, my Cloudlet?"

She arose and bowed her thanks.

After Yang Hallim had won his honours he entered the office of the graduates, where he had his official duties assigned him. Till the present he had not yet visited his mother, whom he greatly desired to see and bring up to the capital, so that she might be present at his wedding; but just at this juncture a mighty event happened that changed all his plans. The Tibetans arose in revolt and marched into the western part of the kingdom. The three governors also of the territory north of the river, in league with their stronger neighbour, arose likewise, calling themselves the Kings of Yon, Cho and Wee. The Emperor, in a state of anxiety, discussed the whole situation with his ministers and made preparation to send troops to put them down, but the various officials could not agree on a plan of action, till at last the graduate Yang So-yoo stepped forth and said: "In olden times Han Moo-je summoned the king of southern Wol, and remonstrated with him. Let your Majesty do the same. Have an imperial order written out and reason with these men. If after that they do not yield, then let troops go against them with all the force possible."

The Emperor, pleased with this, commanded So-yoo immediately to write out such an order. So-yoo bowed low, took the pen as commanded, and wrote it.

Delighted with him, the Emperor said: "The form is splendid and preserves our dignity, at the same time demonstrating our favour. So reasonable is it, too, that the foolish rebels will be won over I am sure."

Thus was it sent to the three armies in insurrection. Cho and Wee at once laid aside their claims to kingship, submitted, and sent humble memorials confessing their sins. Along with these came ten thousand horses and a thousand rolls of silk as tribute. Only the King of Yon refused. His district was far distant from the capital, and he had under his command many well-trained troops.

The Emperor announced that the submission of Cho and Wee was due entirely to the merits of Yang So-yoo, and he wrote out the following edict:

"About a hundred years ago the three districts to the north of the river, each separated by wide stretches of territory, and trusting in its trained forces, raised an insurrection. The Emperor, Tok-chong, marshalled an army of a hundred thousand men and ordered his two best generals to the front. But they failed entirely to obtain the required submission. Now, however, by one word, written by Yang So-yoo, we have brought two armies of rebellion to terms, in which not a single soldier was killed or a person injured. The power of the Emperor has been demonstrated to a distance of ten thousand *li*. We view this with deepest gratitude, and send herewith five thousand rolls of silk and fifty horses to express our highest favour."

He desired to raise his rank, but Yang So-yoo went into the imperial presence, thanked his Majesty, and declined the favour, saying: "The striking off of a draft of an imperial order is the duty of a minister; the submission of the two armies is due to your imperial prestige. What merit have I ever won to receive such bountiful gifts as these? There remains still one army unyielded. I regret that I have not been able to draw the sword and wipe out this disgrace. How could your humble subject receive promotion with pleasure under such circumstances? My office now is sufficiently high to display any merits that I have. Nothing would be gained by its being higher. As victory or defeat are not dependent on the number of troops engaged, I wish that I might have a single company of soldiers, and with the backing of your imperial presence go out to settle the matter with Yon for life or death. Thus would I make some little return for the ten thousand favours that your Majesty has conferred upon me."

The Emperor gladly welcomed the suggestion, and asked the opinion of the ministers assembled. They replied: "Three armies in league with each other were against us, and now two have submitted. Mad little Yon will be like a piece of meat ready for the boiling pot, or an ant caught in a hole. Before the imperial troops he will be but a dried twig, or a decayed piece of wood ready to be broken. Let the imperial army try all other means before striking. Let Yang So-yoo be put in command, to try his skill for better or for worse. If after that Yon does not yield, then make the attack."

The Emperor, deeming this wise, ordered Yang So-yoo to start for Yon with all the insignia of power, flags, drums and battle-axes, but his commands were to use persuasion first. So Yang So-yoo set out on his way after having said good-bye to Justice Cheung.

On parting, the Justice said to him: "Men are wicked in these far distant places, and rebellion against the state is a matter of everyday occurrence. I feel that you, a scholar, are going into danger. If some unforeseen misfortune should overtake you, it would not only be your old father-in-law who would be left desolate, but the whole house. I am old and out of the question, so I no longer have a share in the affairs of state. My desire is to send a memorial objecting to your going."

"Please do not do that," said Yang in reply, "and don't be over anxious. These far-off peoples sometimes take advantage of a disturbed state of affairs in the government to rise up, but with the Emperor so great and powerful, and the Government so enlightened, there is no such fear. Also the two states of Cho and Wee have yielded. Why should we be anxious about the little isolated kingdom of Yon?"

"The Emperor's commands," said the Justice, "are supreme, and the matter is already decided, so I have nothing more to say. Only be careful of yourself, and let not His Imperial Majesty have any cause for shame."

The lady of the house wept over his going, and in parting said:

"Since we have won so noble a son we have tasted the joys and delights of old age. Alas for my feelings now as you start off for this distant region! To go and return quickly is my one wish for you."

Yang withdrew, betook himself to the park pavilion, and made ready for his journey. Cloudlet shed pearly tears over him, saying: "When my lord went daily to his duties in the palace, your humble wife loved to rise early, make neat his room, bring dress and official robes; while you looked on with kindly eyes upon her, and delayed your steps as though you found it hard to go. Now you are starting for a thousand miles distant. What word of love could answer under such a circumstance as this?"

The Hallim replied laughing: "The man of affairs who enters upon a mighty question of the state, impelled by the commands of his Emperor, thinks naught of life or death. All the minor affairs of the day disappear from his vision. You, Cloudlet, bear up bravely now. Don't be anxious or mar your pretty face. Serve your mistress well and in a little, if all goes right, I'll finish what I have to do, win great renown, and come back with flying colours and a gold seal like a grain measure hanging at my belt. Be patient and wait for me."

He passed through the gate, mounted his palanquin, and was gone. When he reached the city of Nakyang he found once more the old landmarks. On his last journey he had been but a youngster in his teens, in his student's dress, riding a hobbling donkey.

A few years only had passed and here he was with the banners and spears of office going before him, and he seated in a four-horse palanquin. The magistrate of Nakyang hastily repaired the roads, while the governor of the south of the river respectfully assisted him on his way. The glory of his progress lightened the world, while the vanguard of his march shook the towns like an earthquake. Country folk struggled for a place to see, and the passers by in the street shouted out their acclamations. So great was his splendour as he passed along.

General Yang got his boy servant to make inquiry first of all as to any news of Moonlight. He went to her home and inquired but the entrance gates were locked, and the upper pavilion closely curtained; only the cherry blossoms were in bloom, smiling over the wall. He asked the neighbours, and they answered that

Moonlight had left the place a year and more ago. Some gentleman, they said, who was on his way to a distant part of the country had become betrothed to her, and after that she pretended to be ill, received no guests, went to no official feasts, and declined everything. A little later, in a fit of insanity, she threw away her jewels and head ornaments, donned the garb of a Taoist priestess, and went visiting the temples in the mountains. She never came back and no one knew where she had gone.

The boy returned and told his master, and Yang, who had been happy in the high expectation of seeing her, fell into a fit of gloom and sadness. He passed her home and thought of the happy experiences gone by, and with disappointed feelings went to a public guest-house. Their mysterious meeting had now faded away into the distance, leaving him sleepless.

The governor sent him a score of dancing-girls to entertain him, all women of note in their world. As they sat about in their pretty dresses he recognised among them some who had been present at the Bridge Pavilion. They vied with each other in their attempts to please and win his attention, but he would have nothing to do with any of them.

He composed these two verses and wrote them on the wall:

> "The rain sweeps by the Bridge Kiosk,
>> And o'er the catkins fresh and green,
> Its music calls me through the dusk,
>> Back to its flowery silken scene;
> Behold me now dressed out in state,
>> Returned to greet my chosen one,
> But I have come, alas, too late,
>> And she, who stirred my heart, is gone."

When he had finished, he tossed aside his pen, mounted his palanquin and rode away, while all the dancing folk seeing him thus leave untouched by their influence held down their heads in shame.

The dancing-girls copied the verses and gave them to the governor, and he scolded them soundly. "If you had won General Yang's attention your names would have been enhanced a hundred-fold," he said. "But with all your finery you did not even win a glance from him, and have caused Nakyang to lose face."

He asked them who the General meant by his reference, and when he learned who it was, he advertised for Moonlight far and wide in the hope of finding her before the General's return.

Yang finally reached the land of Yon. The people living in that distant region had never dreamed of the power or splendour of the capital. Now when they beheld Yang Hallim he seemed like the fabled unicorn that steps down upon the earth, or the phoenix that appears among the clouds. They jostled each other to get close round his palanquin, and blocked his way in their desire to see.

The General in his power of execution was like the swift thunder, and in his readiness to bestow favour like the spring rain; so that these rude people were overcome by his presence, danced and sang with delight, and said to one another: "His divine Majesty the Emperor, will indeed spare us."

When Yang met the King of Yon he spoke so boldly of the power and prestige of His Majesty; praised the attitude of the Government, and explained so fully the difference between submission and opposition, assistance and resistance, that his words were as irresistible as the lift of the sea, or the falling of autumn frosts. The King of Yon, greatly moved and impressed, was won over. He bowed down to the earth and confessed his faults, saying: "We, in this benighted district, are so far away from the great centre of things, and so out of touch with imperial blessings and favours, that we dared to offer resistance to the state. We have made light of life, and have been ignorant whence our blessings and favours come. And now having heard the convincing words of your Excellency, I see that I have done a great wrong. No more shall such mad thoughts possess me, but I shall sincerely do the part of a loyal and faithful subject. Please, on your return, make my statement for me and let this tributary land find peace instead of war; and blessing and life instead of calamity. This indeed would be for me more than I could expect."

A great feast was held in the palace of Yon, and the General was offered when he left a hundred talents of gold and ten of the finest horses as tribute presents.

Yang bowed, but did not receive them, setting out empty-handed on his way westward toward home. In ten days or so he passed

Hantan, the old capital of Cho, when suddenly a beautiful lad, riding a superb horse, appeared just in front of him. He had heard the calls of the General's out-runners and had dismounted, standing respectfully by the side of the way.

The General looked at him and said: "Yonder horse that that young man rides is a Persian steed, surely."

As he advanced closer the young rider appeared strangely beautiful, as an opening flower, or the returning circle of the moon. His graceful form, with the light that seemed to emanate from him, dazzled the eyes of the onlooker.

"In all my travels," said Yang, "I never before saw so handsome a youth as yonder lad. One glimpse of his beautiful face would tell of his gifts and graces. He said to the servants: "Invite him to follow us, will you?"

When the General had retired to his lodgings for the night, the young man appeared before the door and was invited in. Yang at once fell a captive to his spell, and said: "Your handsome face has wholly won my heart. I wish to take you with me, and so sent for you. My one fear has been that you might not respond or wish to follow. Now that you have come I am greatly delighted and want to know who you are and your honourable name."

The young man made answer: "Your humble servant is from the north land, and my surname is Chok, and given-name, Paiknan. I have been brought up in an exiled country, have had no special friends or teachers to guide me, and so my learning is of a very shallow nature, attaining to proficiency neither in the character, nor in the handling of the sword. My heart only is right adjusted, and means to stand by its friends, or if need be die for them. Your Excellency's journey through the north, where all have been equally impressed by your commanding presence and unexampled favour, has awakened my heart in admiration to a point that knows no bounds. Forgetful of my low birth and ignorance, I desired to attach myself to your lordship, to be your faithful bird of the morning or watchdog of the night. Now your Excellency, taking note of this wish of mine, has condescended to call me, and has done me such an honour as I had never dreamed. Assuredly the great teacher's kindness bestowed upon a humble pupil is mine to-day."

Yang, greatly delighted, made reply: "The ancients said, 'A

similar sound makes like echo, and like strength does a similar deed.' A beautiful fulfilment of this is evident in the fact that our hearts agree."

From this time on Master Chok rode bridle by bridle in company with the General and lived and dined with him. They admired the beauties of nature together, delighted themselves under the soft rays of the moon, and forgot all about the hardships of the way.

Again the cavalcade arrived at Nakyang and crossed the Chonjin Bridge. Old remembrances came crowding back on Yang, and he said: "Now that Moonlight is a so-called priestess, my heart condemns me when I think of her wandering over the hills in order to fulfil her vow, and to wait for my return. Already I have gone by once with the insignia of battle-axes and banners accompanying me, but she was nowhere to be seen. So all our plans have come to naught, as men's plans do. How can I be other than sad? If Moonlight knew of my coming she would not fail to meet me, but her sweet face is not here. I expect that if she is not to be found in the Taoist Temple, she will be somewhere among the Buddhist priestesses. How can I send word to her? Alas, if we do not meet this time, how much of life may pass before we ever meet again?"

Just then he raised his eyes toward the distance and there he saw a young woman with a gem screen hanging before her, leaning gently on the railing of a neighbouring pavilion, evidently watching the chariots and the horses go by. It was Moonlight.

Yang, pent up with heart longings and desire to see her face to face, caught sight of her lovely expression which took a fresh and new grip upon him. He drove hastily by and the two looked their messages of lively recognition each toward the other.

When he reached the guest-house Moonlight was already there, having come by a short and ready road. She saw him dismount from the chariot and tripped forth to meet him. First she bowed low. She then accompanied him into the guest-room, where, in her joy of soul, she took hold of the border of his robes and told how happy she was after the sorrows of the year that had gone. Her tears flowed faster than her words. She bowed again and congratulated him upon his safe return. All that had happened during the long interval since they had said good-bye was told.

"When you left me," said she, "I was invited to the gatherings of the princes, and feasts of the nobility. Invitations came from north, south, east and west, till I was wearied out. At last I cut off my hair with my own hands to escape dishonour, and then pretended that I was smitten with a dangerous illness. I threw away all my pretty ornaments, put on the dress of a priestess, made my escape from the busy city and went and lived in the mountains. From the guests who came to visit the temples, and from others of the city and the capital who were studying Taoism, I learned news of your lordship. Early last spring I heard that you had memorialised the Emperor and had gone forth as his special envoy. I knew that you passed the city, but the distance was too great for me to return. All I could do was to look toward the distant kingdom of Yon and let my tears fall. The magistrate, knowing that I had become a priestess because of you, showed me what you had written on the walls of the monastery, saying: 'General Yang, with direct orders from His Majesty the Emperor, came by this way. Many dancing-girls welcomed his coming, but because his lordship did not see you, he was greatly disappointed and would have nothing to do with any of them. In his disappointment he wrote this on the wall and left. How was it that you of all others should be off there in the hills and so cause my entertainment of the envoy to be a failure?'

"And thus desirous of showing you all respect, he apologised for his hard treatment in the past, earnestly desiring me to come back to my home in the city to await your return. I was delighted to do so. Then it was that I first realised that I, an insignificant woman, had a certain value attaching to my person. I waited alone in the Chon-jin Pavilion hoping for your coming. Will not the many dancing-girls of the city and the crowds of the streets, every one of them, envy my place of honour and the glory that comes to me?

"I have already learned that you won the *kwago* (examination), and that you were made a *hallim* (a literary senator), but I have wondered whether you were married or not."

Yang replied: "I am already engaged to the daughter of Justice Cheung, but the ceremony has not yet been celebrated. The superior attainments of the lady are already known to me, and she is exactly what you foretold. My pretty go-between has loaded me with obligations greater than the mountains of Tai."

They renewed their former happy acquaintance and he tarried

for several days. Because of Moonlight's presence the young man Chok did not call. Once the servant-boy came in in great alarm to say to the master: "Your humble servant has noticed that the young gentleman Chok is not a good man. I saw him in the women's quarters joking and playing with Moonlight. Moonlight is in the service of your lordship, how could she be treated thus familiarly?

The Hallim made reply: "Master Chok would never do such a thing as this, and I have all confidence in Moonlight too; you have been mistaken."

The boy was very angry and went out. In a little he came again and spoke: "Your lordship said that my report was nonsense. The two now are holding hands and enjoying themselves together. If you will please come out and see for yourself you will know whether my story is correct or not."

Yang went out and looked toward the servants' quarters, and there the two were leaning over the wall talking and laughing together, fondling each other's hands and having a very amusing time.

Desiring to hear what they were saying, Yang went closer, but master Chok hearing the sound of footfalls took alarm and ran away. Moonlight looked back at the master, and an unexpected blush of shame covered her face.

Yang asked gently: "Moonlight, my dear, are you specially acquainted with master Chok?"

Moonlight replied: "We are not relatives, he and I, but I dearly love his sister and we were talking about her. I am, as you know, only a dancing-girl, so that my eyes and ears are steeped in the ways of the world, and I am not afraid of men. By holding hands and jesting, and whispering as I have done, I have raised a doubt in my kind master's mind. My shame is so great for it that I really desire to die."

Yang said: "I have no doubts of you at all, so do not be in the least disturbed."

He thought to himself: "Chok is a young man, and his being caught thus by me will make him feel ashamed. I must call him and assure him that I am not disturbed." So he sent for his boy to come, but he was nowhere to be found. With great regret he said: "In olden time King Cho-jang made them all break off their hat-strings in order to quiet their fears; now I, in my aimless peering about, have disappointed my friend and have lost me my lovely scholar. What shall I do about it?" He made the servants seek high and low, inside and outside the walls for Chok.

That night he talked over the past with Moonlight and said how they were indeed destined for each other. They drank and were happy till the hours grew late. Then they put out the lights and slept. When the east began to lighten he awoke and saw Moonlight doing up her hair before the mirror. He looked at her with tenderest interest and then gave a start and looked again. The delicate eyebrows, the bright eyes, the wavy hair like a cloud over the temples, the rosy-tinted cheeks, the lithe graceful form, the white complexion – all were Moonlight's, and yet it was not she.

Alarm and doubt overcame him so that he dared not speak.

THE STORK DANCE: THE PALACE MAIDS IN WAITING

CHAPTER VII
THE IMPERIAL SON-IN-LAW

W HEN Yang had looked again carefully and had made sure that it really was not Moonlight, he asked: "Maiden, who are you?"

She replied: "Your servant was originally from Pa-ju. My surname is Chok and my given name is Kyong-hong, or Wildgoose. When I was young, Moonlight and I became covenanted sisters, and because of this close bond of union, she said to me last night: "I am feeling unwell and cannot wait on the Master. Take my place, please, and save me from a reprimand. Thus at the request of Moonlight I came boldly into your lordship's room."

Before she had done speaking, Moonlight herself opened the sliding door and came softly in. She said: "Your lordship has won a new and wonderful person to yourself, and I congratulate you. You will remember that I recommended Chok Kyong-hong when we were in the North River District. Is she not equal to my recommendation?"

"She is sweet in face and reputation," replied he. He looked at her again and behold she was like the young scholar Chok in every feature. By way of inquiry the Master remarked: "The young literatus Chok must be some relative of yours; have you a brother? I regret to say that I saw Chok yesterday acting in a way very improper. Where is he now do you suppose?"

Wildgoose said in reply: "I have no brothers or sisters."

Then the Master looked at her for a moment and suddenly guessed the whole game that had been played upon him. He laughed and said: "The one who followed me from the side of the way near Hantan was the maiden Chok; and the one who talked across the wall with Moonlight was Chok See also. I wonder how you dared to deceive me in such a disguise."

Then Wildgoose answered: "How could I ever have ventured to

do such a thing were it not that I have had born in me one great and indomitable longing that has possessed me all my life – to attach myself to some renowned hero or superior lord. When the King of Yon learned my name and bought me for a heaped-up bag of jewels, he fed me on the daintiest fare and dressed me in the rarest silk. And yet I had no delight in it but was in distress, like a parrot bird behind cage bars, grieving out its days and longing to shake its wings and fly away. The other day when the King of Yon invited you to his feast, I spied on you through the screen chinks, and you were the man that my heart bounded forth to follow. But the palace has nine gateways of approach, how could I safely pass these? The journey on which you had entered was a thousand miles long, how could I escape and follow for so great a distance? I thought over a hundred ways and means, and then hit on a plan, but I dared not put it into execution at the time of your departure. Had I done so the King of Yon would have sent his runners out to arrest me. When you had been gone ten days or more, I secretly took one of the King's fast horses and sped forth on my way, overtaking you at Han-tan and making myself known to your lordship. I should have told you at once who I was, but there are so many eavesdroppers about, that I did not dare to speak; so I made myself a deceiver and am guilty of great sin. I wore a man's dress in order to escape those who might attempt to arrest me. What I did last night was done at the earnest request of Moonlight. Even if you graciously overlook these many faults of mine, the longer I live the more I shall look with amazement on my having been so bold. If your lordship will kindly forgive and forget my wrongdoing and overlook my poor and humble birth; if you will permit me to find shelter under your wide-spreading tree where I may build my little nest, Moonlight and I will live together, and after the Master is married to some noble lady, she and I will come to your home and speak our good wishes and congratulations."

General Yang said in reply: "My fairest maid, not even Chi-pool the famous dancer was your equal. Not only have you highly esteemed the attainments of this poor prince of Wee, but you desire to follow him for good. How can he remember any fault of yours?"

Then Wildgoose thanked him, and Moonlight said: "Now that

Chok See has waited on my lord as well as I, I thank thee on her behalf." And thus they bowed repeatedly.

Next morning by break of day the General was ready to depart, and said to the two: "There are many who spy and eavesdrop on a long journey, so we may not go together, but as soon as I have completed the marriage awaiting me, you must both come." Thus he resumed his way.

Once more he reached the capital and reported at the Palace. At this time, too, a letter of submission arrived from the King of Yon, with quantities of tribute, gold, silver, silks, etc. The Emperor, greatly delighted at his success, comforted Yang after the long hardships of the way; congratulated him, and proposed to make him a tributary prince as reward; but Yang, alarmed at this too high favour, bowed low before the throne, asking earnestly to be permitted to decline.

The Emperor, charmed with his modesty, yielded to his wishes and made him only a chief minister as well as Director of the Hallim (College of Literature), besides giving him great rewards. He caused him to be most lavishly honoured by the State, so that history scarcely presents a case of one so markedly distinguished.

After his return, Yang went to pay his respects to the home of Justice Cheung. He and the lady Cheung greeted him with special joy, congratulated him on his high attainments and honour, and were delighted at his being made a minister, so that the whole house was filled with rejoicing.

Yang then went to his quarters in the park pavilion, once more met Cloudlet and renewed the happy relationship with her that had been broken off by his departure.

The Emperor was greatly delighted with the rising fame of Yang So-yoo. He frequently summoned him to the inner palace to talk about history and the Classics, as well as other subjects, so that the days went by imperceptibly.

One evening Yang was detained till late in the presence of the Emperor. On his return to his official quarters, the moon shone softly and his feelings of happiness were so great that sleep refused to come. He went alone up into the upper pavilion, and there leaned on the balustrade and looked out upon the scene so softly gilded by the shining moon. Suddenly he heard on the gently passing breeze the notes of a flute, far off, as though from among the clouds, coming nearer and nearer. He could not distinguish the tune, but the sweetness was such as is not heard among mortals.

Minister Yang then called one of the secretaries of the Hallim and asked him, saying: "Does this music come from outside the palace, or is there someone within the enclosure who is playing?"

The secretary said he did not know. The minister then ordered wine to be brought, and when he had taken a glass or two he called for his flute on which he began to play. The sound of it went up to heaven, and soft tinted clouds came out to listen; the phoenix birds called to each other, and two blue storks came flying from the palace and danced to the music; while all the secretaries looked on in wonder, saying: "Wang Ja-jin[26] has come down to earth to share our joys and sorrows."

The Empress Dowager had two sons and one daughter; the Emperor, Prince Wol, and Princess Nan-yang or Orchid. When Orchid was born, a fairy had come down from heaven to the Empress in a dream, and had placed a jewel in her bosom. Such was the princess. When she was grown up she was graceful in form as a flower and all her ways were according to the highest measure of the genii. No marks of earth were there upon her. Marvellously skilled was she, too, in the character, in needlework and embroidery. The Empress loved her better than all others.

Among the tribute paid at this time there was a white stone flute from the western empire of Rome. The form of it was very beautiful, and the Empress ordered the court musicians to try it, but they failed and no sound was forth-coming. In a dream one night the princess met a fairy and learned from her how to play it. After waking she tried this flute of the far west and the tones

---

26 *Wang Ja-jin.* A man of the time of Han Myong-je (AD 58), who became one of the genii. He was a magistrate of a far distant county, and yet he came the first day of every month to pay his devotions to the Emperor. His Majesty, amazed at his coming thus over so impossible a distance, had an officer commissioned to watch and find out how he came. This official, when the time came for Ja-jin's arrival, was on the look-out and saw two ducks flying toward the capital. He caught them in a net, when suddenly they changed into a pair of shoes. The shoes, on being examined, turned out to be a pair that the Emperor had given to Ja-jin. When the time of Ja-jin's departure from the earth came, a green stone coffin descended from heaven. Ja-jin, seeing it, said that God was calling him. He then bathed and took his place in the coffin; the lid arose of itself and covered the top. A grave was found made without human hands just outside the city, where he is said to be buried.

were exceeding sweet, agreeing in harmony with the laws of the *eum-rul* (Chinese music).

The Empress Dowager and the Emperor were greatly astonished at this, but no outsiders knew anything of it. At one time when she played the storks gathered in front of the audience hall and danced to the music.

The Empress said to the Emperor: "In ancient days Prince Chin-mok's daughter, Nong-ok,[27] played beautifully on the crystal flute, and now Orchid plays no less marvellously. Nong-ok found her destined husband by this matchless music of hers. May it be so with Orchid, and may we thus happily settle the question of her marriage." Though Nan-yang was grown up she had not yet been betrothed.

On this night, Orchid, inspired by the soft light of the moonbeams, played till the storks danced before her, and when she had finished they flew away to the office of the Hallim and danced there likewise; so it became reported throughout the palace that the storks had danced to the music of General Yang. The Emperor heard it, and marvelled as he thought to himself: "The Princess's destiny evidently rests with this man."

He then reported to the Empress Dowager, saying, "General Yang's age is about the same as that of Princess Orchid, and there is no one in the Court his equal in handsome bearing or ability. Never again can we expect to find his like if we search the whole wide realm."

The Empress laughed, and said: "Orchid's marriage has not yet been decided upon, and I have been somewhat anxious about it. Now that I hear this, I am sure that Yang So-yoo is God's appointed mate for her; still, I must have a look at him before I decide finally."

"That will be very easy," said the Emperor in reply. "I shall summon Yang one of these days to one of my private audiences, have a talk with him on some literary subject, and then you can peep through the screen and see what kind of man he is."

The Empress was greatly delighted and so the matter rested.

Princess Orchid's special name was So-wha, so called because

---

27 *Nong-ok* (sixth century BC). She was the wife of Wang Ja-jin, the most renowned of all China's flautists. She learned from him, and when they played together it is said they brought down angel-birds (phoenixes) from the sky to hear them.

these two characters were found engraved upon the flute. They meant "flute harmony."

On a certain day the Emperor took his seat in the Hall of the Fairies, one of the palaces of the Imperial Court, and commanded a eunuch to summon Yang So-yoo. The eunuch went first to the office of the Hallim, but learned there that Yang was out. Then he went post-haste to the home of Justice Cheung and made inquiry, but was told that Yang had not yet returned. So he rushed about here and there but could get no trace of him.

At this time Yang, accompanied by Thirteen, had gone to one of the places of amusement, where he had imbibed so freely that he was very much intoxicated. He was happy and having a hilarious time.

The eunuch hurriedly rushed in and ordered him to report at once to the palace. Thirteen, alarmed by this call, jumped up and went out. But Yang's eyes were heavy with drink and his hair was in disorder. The eunuch addressed him so that he got up and changed his dress and then followed into the inner palace, where he appeared before the Emperor, who commanded him to sit down.

There they discussed the history of the past line of kings, their successes and their failures, and Yang, quick as he was asked, gave answer, his words flowing like running water.

The Emperor, greatly delighted, said: "I should like to ask whom you regard as greatest among the kings of the past, and whom among the ministers."

The Hallim replied: "Among the kings we rank Yo and Soon[28] first, but we need not specially dwell on them. Han Ko-jo wrote an essay called, 'The Great Wind,' while Wee Ta-jo wrote one called, 'The Bright Wind and Shining Stars.' These come first among the kings. Among ministers are Yi Yung of Sa-kyong, Cho Ja of Up-to, To Yon-myong of Nam-cho, and Sa Yom-eum. These are regarded as the first literary masters. Among the kingdoms Tang is first, and among the Tang kings, Hyon-jong. Among ministers is Yi Tai-baik, who is without a peer in all the world."

The Emperor said: "Your opinion is assuredly just what mine is.

---

28   *Yo, Soon.* These are the two most famous rulers of patriarchal China. Their names are associated in Korea with the golden age of the world, and are passed from lip to lip as the ultimate of righteous kingship. Their story is told in the sacred "Book of History."

When I read Yi Tai-baik's 'Chong Pyong-sa' and 'Haing Nak-sa,' I was always very sorry that I did not live at the same time as he did, but now that I have won your lordship to my side, why should I even envy Yi Tai-baik?

"I have," said his Majesty, "in accordance with ancient law, selected ten or more palace women who are specially gifted with the pen and beautiful to see, and put them under a secretary. Now I should like your lordship, following the example of Yi Tai-baik, to write for these women something that they would specially enjoy"; and so he ordered the ink-stone, jade table, and pens to be brought, and placed before the master. The women, delighted that they were to have a sample of his renowned penmanship, brought special paper, silken pocket handkerchiefs, embroidered fans and so forth, on which he was to write.

The Hallim, delighted to show them this attention, wrote with great readiness and rapidity, dashing off his strokes like the wind and clouds or the dazzling lightning. Before the shadows of the evening had begun to fall he had finished the pile of invitations that lay before him. The palace ladies knelt in order, passing writings to His Majesty, who examined them all interestedly. Some were in couplets, some in fours, some again in doubles; all were gems of their kind. There was no limit to the praise the King bestowed upon them. Then he said to the palace maids-in-waiting: "Now that the Hallim has worked so hard and written for you, you must bring him the best wine there is."

Then the ladies brought choice wine in golden platters, in crystal goblets, and in parrot cups, on green stone tables, and arranged various dainties to accompany the wine. Sometimes kneeling, sometimes standing, they vied with each other to serve him.

The Hallim received each with his left hand and raised it to his lips with the right, and when he had had ten glasses or so his face grew rosy like the springtime, while mists beclouded his vision. Then His Majesty ordered the wine to be removed and said to the women: "The Hallim's verses are each worth their weight in gold. What will you give him now in return?"

Some of the women drew forth the golden hairpins that were shot through their hair, some unclasped their jade belt ornaments, some took rings from their fingers. Each tried to outdo the other till their gifts were piled up before him. Then His Majesty said to one of the eunuchs: "Take the ink-stone used by the Master, the pens, and the gifts of the palace-maids, wrap them up, and when he goes take them to his house."

The Hallim thanked His Majesty for his kindness, got up to go but fell over. The Emperor then ordered a eunuch to help him along under the arms as far as the South Gate; where they mounted him on his horse. At last he reached his quarters in the park pavilion. Cloudlet received him, helped him to change his ceremonial dress, and asked in amazement: "Wherever has your lordship been that you have drunk so much?"

Yang, who was very drunk indeed, could only nod his head. Then in a little time there came a servant bearing a great load of gifts from the Emperor – pens, ink-stone, fans, etc., which were piled up at the hall entrance.

Yang laughed and said: "These are all presents that His Majesty has sent to you, Cloudlet. How do my winnings compare with those of Tong Pang-sak?"

The next day the Hallim arose late, and after he had made his toilet the gate-keeper came suddenly to say that Prince Wol had come to call upon him.

Yang gave a start and said: "Prince Wol has come? Something surely must be the matter."

He went hastily out to meet him, showed him in, and asked him to be seated. His age would be about twenty. Very handsome he was, with no traces of the common world on his features.

Yang, humbly kneeling, said to him: "Your Highness has condescended to visit my humble dwelling; what orders have you for me, please?"

The Prince answered: "I am an admirer of specially gifted men, even though I have had no opportunity to get acquainted with your Excellency. Now, however, I come with commands from His Majesty, and to convey his message. The Princess Nan-yang has now reached a marriageable age and we have to choose a husband for her. The Emperor, seeing your superiority, and greatly admiring your gifts, has made you his choice, and has sent me to let you know. In a little the Imperial orders will be issued."

Yang, greatly alarmed, said: "The grace of heaven coming down to so low and humble a subject means 'blessing exceeding bounds,' and where blessing exceeds bounds it becomes disaster. There is no question about it. Your servant is engaged to the daughter of Justice Cheung, and almost a year has gone by since the gifts were exchanged. I beg and beseech your Highness to make this known to His Majesty."

The Prince replied: "I shall certainly report as you say, but I regret it very much, for the Emperor's love of the highly gifted will turn out a disappointment."

The Hallim answered: "This matter is of great concern in my world of affairs, and one I dare not deal lightly with. I shall bow before His Majesty and ask for punishment." The Prince then bade farewell and returned to the palace.

Yang then went to the apartments occupied by Justice Cheung, and reported to him what the Prince had said. Already Cloudlet had told the lady of the house, so that the whole house was upset and in a state of consternation, no one knowing what to do. Clouds of anxiety gathered on the old Justice's face and over his eyebrows, and he had no words to say.

"Do not be anxious," said the Hallim. "The Emperor is good and enlightened and most careful to do exactly what is according to ceremony and good form. He would never set any of the affairs of his minister at naught, and though I am unworthy I would die rather than do the wrong that Song Hong did."

The Empress Dowager had the previous day come into the Hall of the Fairies and had peeped in on Yang So-yoo. She had been greatly taken with him, saying to the Emperor: "He is indeed a fitting mate for Nan-yang (Orchid). I have seen him, and there is no longer any need for consultation." Thus she commanded Prince Wol to report to Yang.

The Emperor himself now desired to make the same proposition. He was seated alone in the Special Hall. He was thinking over the wonderful skill that Yang had displayed in the writing of the character, and desiring once more to see what he had written, ordered one of the eunuchs to have the women bring him their compositions. They had each put the writing very carefully away, but one palace maiden took the fan on which Yang had written, went alone to her room, placed it in her bosom and cried all night over it, refusing to eat. This maiden's family name was Chin, and her given name was Cha-bong. She was a daughter of

Commissioner Chin of Wha-joo. The Commissioner had died a violent death, and Cha-bong had been arrested and made a palace maid-in-waiting. All the women loved and praised Chin See. The Emperor himself summoned her to his presence and desired to make her one of the Imperial wives, but the Empress, fearing Chin See's surpassing beauty, did not consent. "Chin See is indeed very lovable," said she, "but Your Majesty has had to order her father's execution. To have close relations with his daughter would break the saying of the ancients, which runs: 'Enlightened kings of the past put far away women who were related to the households of the punished.'"

The Emperor, recognising that this was true, consented. He had asked Cha-bong if she could read the character, and finding that she could, had appointed her to be one of his literary secretaries and put her in charge of palace documents. Also, the Empress Dowager had made her the literary companion of Princess Orchid, to read to her, and to drill her in the practice of composition. The Princess greatly loved Chin See for her beauty of character and the wonderful knowledge she possessed. She treated her like a near relative and would not let her out of her sight.

On that day she was waiting on the Empress Dowager in the Hall of the Fairies, ready to attend the commands of the Emperor. She was one of the women who received the verses composed by Yang. Yang's face and form were already deeply imprinted upon her heart. How could she mistake him? Waking or sleeping, she had never dropped him from her memory. She knew him at once, but Yang, having no knowledge that she was alive, and being in the presence of the Emperor, did not dare to lift up his eyes. He simply wrote and passed on what he had written.

Now that Cha-bong had seen him, her heart was all afire, but she stifled her feelings and emotions, and her desire to be known, fearing that she might arouse suspicion. After her return to her room, in distress over the hopelessness of trying to piece together the broken threads of her destiny, she had unfolded the fan and read over what he had written. She opened it again and again, not once putting it down. The writing read:

"This silken fan is round as the moon,
As fair and soft as the hand that holds it,
Over the harp strings its zephyrs play
Till it find its way to the Master's keeping.
As round it is as the shining moon,
May the soft fair hand ne'er lay it down,
Nor its silken smile e'en once be hidden,
In all the days of the happy spring."

When Chin See had read the first lines she sighed, saying: "Master Yang does not know my heart. Even though I am in the palace, why should I ever be thought of as the wife of the Emperor?"

She read further and sighed again and said: "Although others have not seen my face, assuredly Master Yang will never forget me in his heart. His verses prove, however, that a foot away may mean a thousand miles. When I think of the willow song that I received when I was in my home I cannot stifle my sorrow."

The tears dropped upon her dress. She now wrote a verse and added it to his upon the border of the fan, read it over, and sighed again. Suddenly she learned that a command had gone forth from the Emperor to collect all the fans and other things upon which Yang had written, Chin See in great alarm, and with terror entering into her very bones, said "I am doomed to die, doomed to die."

CHAPTER VIII
A HOPELESS DILEMMA

THE eunuch said to Chin See: "His Majesty desiring again to see the writing of Master Yang, has commanded me to gather up the fans. May I have yours also?"

Chin See began to cry, saying: "Unhappy being that I am, I thoughtlessly wrote a companion verse under what the Master had written for me, and now it proves my death warrant. If His Majesty sees it there will be no chance of escape. Rather than die under the arm of the law, I would prefer to take my own life. When I am dead, may I trust you for the burial of my body? Please have pity on me, and see that my poor remains are not left to the mercy of the ravens."

The eunuch replied: "Why do you, a literary secretary, say such things as these? The Emperor is kind and ready to take a liberal view of everything. He would never regard this as a serious offence. Even though he should be angry I will use my office to placate him; follow me."

Chin See then followed the eunuch, who left her outside the palace while he went in alone. His Majesty looked at the compositions in order till at last he came to Chin See's fan, where he found someone else's verses just below Master Yang's. He wondered what it could mean and asked the eunuch. The eunuch said in reply: "Chin See told me that, never dreaming of your Majesty's asking to see them again, she had boldly written this just below the poem on her fan, bringing upon herself a sentence of death. Her purpose now is to take her own life, but I urged her not to do so and brought her here."

The Emperor read what was written and it ran as follows:

"The rounded fan, like the shining moon,
Calls me back to the light that was dimmed so soon.
I never had thought through my tears and pain,
That a day would come when we'd meet again."

When his Majesty had read it through, he said: "Chin See must have had some experience in the past that this refers to. She is highly gifted in her writing and worthy of praise." He then told the eunuch to call her.

As she came in she bowed low in the court, and confessed her fault.

His Majesty said: "If you tell me the truth I will forgive your deadly sin. To whom do you refer in this verse?"

Chin See bowed again and said: "How can I dare to hide anything from your Majesty after what I have done? Before my home was destroyed, Master Yang, on his way to the Government examination, passed in front of our house. Unexpectedly we saw each other, and on his writing a love song to me, I composed a reply and sent it by a messenger, proposing marriage. He accepted it and so it was decided upon. The other day in the Hall of the Fairies, while in waiting on your Majesty, I saw him again and knew his face, but he did not see me. Your unworthy servant, thinking of what had passed, foolishly wrote this verse which has found me out. I deserve to die a hundred deaths."

His Majesty, sorry for her sad experience, said: "Can you recall the love song that brought about your engagement of marriage?"

Chin See then wrote it out and presented it to him. He said to her: "Though your fault is a grievous one, still, because you have wonderful ability and are so greatly loved by the Princess Nan-yang, I forgive you. Be thankful for my clemency, and give your whole heart and attention to the service of the Princess." He then gave her back the fan, which she received, and after thanking him again she withdrew.

On the same day Prince Wol returned from the home of Justice Cheung and told the Emperor that Yang's future was decided, and that he had already sent his marriage presents.

At this the Empress Dowager was very much displeased, and said: "Master Yang has already been advanced to the rank of

Minister of State, and must know the laws and traditions of the Government. How can he be so determined to have his own way?"

The Emperor replied: "Yang So-yoo may have sent his marriage gifts, but that is not the same as having completed the marriage ceremony. I am sure that if one reasons with him, he will not fail to listen." So the next day Minister Yang was summoned to the palace, and he at once appeared.

The Emperor said: "I have a sister who is uncommonly gifted, and, apart from yourself, I know of no one who could be a suitable mate for her. Prince Wol has already conveyed to you my wishes, but I hear that you decline and offer as an excuse the fact that you have already sent your marriage gifts to the house of Justice Cheung. Evidently you have not thought the matter over carefully. In olden days when a choice of Imperial daughter-in-law was to be made, sometimes even a wife was chosen, not to speak of one simply betrothed. One ancient king spent a whole life of regret thinking of the women who refused his command. My idea is that we are not just the same as the nation at large. We are the parents of the people, and therefore what binds the people does not necessarily pertain to us. Even though you should break off your engagement with Justice Cheung's daughter, she could easily find another opportunity. As you have not yet celebrated the marriage, in what way can you be said to have broken the law of human deportment?"

Yang humbly bowed and said in reply: "Your Imperial Majesty has not only not punished me, but like a father with his son has kindly and gently admonished me. I thank you most sincerely for this. I have nothing to say further except to add that my circumstances are not like those of others. I am only a poor literatus from a distant part of the country. I had not even a lodging when I first entered the capital. By the kindness of Justice Cheung I escaped the loneliness that beset me. Not only have I sent the marriage gifts, but I have taken the place of son-in-law to Justice Cheung, and also I have already seen his daughter's face, so that we are as good as husband and wife. That the marriage ceremony was not already performed was due simply to the fact that there were so many affairs of State to see to, and that I have had no opportunity to bring my mother up to the city. Now, fortunately, since the outside States are pacified and there are no longer fears

CHIN SEE'S FEAR: CLOUDLET SAYS FAREWELL

for the Government, your humble servant intended to ask a short furlough to return home to bring his mother, choose a day, and have the marriage performed, when unexpectedly your Majesty's commands have come to him and he is alarmed and knows not what to do. I know that if I obeyed out of fear of punishment, Cheung's daughter would guard her honour safe till death, and never marry elsewhere. But if she should lose her place as wife would this not be reckoned a flaw in the reign of your Imperial Majesty?"

The Emperor replied: "Your ideas are most correct and good, and yet, if we speak according to the actual conditions of the case, you and Cheung's daughter are not really husband and wife. Why should she not marry elsewhere? My wish to decide this marriage with you is not only in order to place you as a pillar of the State and so reward you, but also to please the Empress Dowager, who is greatly taken with your bearing and commanding gifts, and does not leave me free to act as I might wish."

Still Yang emphatically declined.

The Emperor said: "Marriage is a very important matter and so cannot be settled by a single conference; let us have a game of go and help to pass the time."

His Majesty then ordered a eunuch to bring a go-board, and they sat down, Emperor and Minister, to try their skill. Only when the day grew late did they cease to play.

Yang returned home, and Justice Cheung met him with a very sorrowful countenance. Wiping his eyes he said: "To-day a command came from the Empress Dowager to send back to you your marriage gifts, so I passed the order on to Cloudlet and they are now in the park pavilion. If we think of it from our side, it puts us two old people in a very pitiful plight. I might bear it, but my old wife is overcome by it and has been rendered ill, and is now unconscious and unable to recognise her friends."

Greatly upset by this, Yang turned pale and was unable for an hour or so to say anything in reply. At last he said: "If they realise the unfairness of this, and if I memorialise the Government against it with all my heart, will they not heed?"

The Justice waved his hand in opposition: "Master Yang, you have already run counter to the Imperial orders. If you petition against it I fear for the results; you may be severely punished.

Your only way is to submit. Besides, too, under the circumstances your living here at the park pavilion will be embarrassing, so if you can find a suitable place elsewhere you had better move."

Yang made no reply but went into the Park Pavilion, and there was Cloudlet with tearful face and broken voice, who offered him the marriage gifts. "As you know," said she, "I was ordered by the young mistress to wait on your lordship. I have been kindly treated and am grateful to you, but the devils have been jealous, and men have looked askance at our happiness, so that all has come to naught; and the marriage expectations of the young lady are hopelessly ended. I, too, must bid you a long farewell, and return to my mistress. Is it God, or Mother Earth, or devils, or men who have done it?" Her sobs and tears were most distressing.

"I intend to petition His Majesty," said Yang, "and I am sure he will listen. But even though he does not, when once a young woman has yielded her consent, her following her husband is one of the first laws of nature. How can you possibly leave me?"

Cloudlet replied: "Though I am only of the lower classes, still I have heard the sayings of the Sages and am not unaware of the Three Relationships[29] that govern a woman's life. My circumstances, however, are peculiar and different from those of others. I played from earliest years with the young lady and was brought up with her. All thoughts of difference in station were dropped, and we swore a solemn oath to live and die together, to accept the fortunes of life with the glory and shame that might come to us. My following the lady is like the shadow following the body. When once the body disappears, how can the shadow play a part alone?"

Yang answered: "Your devotion to your mistress is most commendable, but your lady's person and yours are different. While she goes north, south, east, or west as she chooses, your following her, and at the same time attempting to render service to another, would break all the laws that govern a woman's existence."

Cloudlet said: "Your words prove that you do not know the mind of my mistress. She has already decided to remain with her aged parents. When they die she will preserve her purity, cut off

29   *The Three Relationships.* The subject's duty to his sovereign; the son's duty to his father; the wife's duty to her husband.

her hair, enter a monastery and give herself up in prayer to the Buddha, in the hope that in the life to come she may not be born a woman. I, too, will do just the same as she. If your lordship intends to see me again, your marriage gifts must go back to the rooms of my lady. If not, then to-day marks our parting for life. Since I have waited on your lordship I have been greatly loved and favoured, and I can never repay, even in a hundred years, a thousandth part of all your kindness. It has turned out, however, different from what we had anticipated, and we are come now to this dire extremity. My one wish is, that in the life to come I may be your faithful dog or horse, and may show my devotion to you. Please, noble Master, may all blessing and happiness be yours." She turned away and wept bitterly. A moment later she stepped from the verandah, bowed twice and entered the women's apartments.

The Master's heart was greatly disturbed, and all his thoughts were in confusion. He looked up at the sky and sighed long and deeply; he clasped his hands and drew hopeless gasping breaths, saying: "I must petition His Majesty with all my heart." So he wrote out his memorial, which was full of earnestness, and ran thus:

"The servant of your Imperial Majesty, Yang So-yoo, bows low and prostrates himself in the dust as he offers this memorial. In deepest reverence he would say, The Primary Laws[30] are the foundation stone on which your Imperial Majesty's Government rests, and marriage is the first of these laws. If once we lose its right relation all prosperity for the State ends, confusion and disorder must follow. If we fail to exercise care in regard to this fundamental matter, the house affected by it will not long endure. Matters of State prosperity rest here also. Therefore the Sages, and the specially enlightened ones, thought carefully of this in the governing of a country, and regarded the correct observance of the Primal Laws as the most important thing of all, and considered that in a well-ordered house marriage was of greatest importance.

"Your humble servant had already sent his gifts to the daugh-

---

30   *The Primary Laws.* These are the Five Laws for which special honour is done Confucius, as the great sage who emphasised their importance. They are: duty to the king; duty to a father; duty to an older brother; duty to a husband; duty to a friend.

ter of Justice Cheung, and already had become a member of his household. After this had been accomplished, he is, by your gracious command, unexpectedly and unworthily chosen as the Imperial son-in-law. At first he was in doubt, and finally he was reduced to great distress and fear. He fails to see that the decision of your Imperial Majesty and the approval of the Government is in accord with the established laws of ceremony. Even though your humble subject had not sent the required gifts, still his social position is so inferior and his knowledge so circumscribed, that these alone would disqualify his being chosen as the Imperial son-in-law. Also he is already the son-in-law of Justice Cheung, and though the whole Six Forms[31] are not yet completed it is the same as an accomplished marriage. How can Her Highness the Crown Princess ever bow to one so low as he, and how can your Majesty let pass so improper a proceeding without close investigation; or permit so grave a breach of form without searching inquiry? Alas, a secret order has come forth making null and void that part already accomplished and commanding the return of accepted marriage gifts, a thing that your humble servant could never have dreamed possible. The petitioner fears that on his account the Government of your Majesty may suffer permanent loss, and the laws that rule society will be hopelessly damaged; that in high places truth will be forfeited, and that in low places violence and wrong-doing may result. He earnestly prays that your High Majesty will stand by the rock on which the State rests, reverse the order that has gone forth, and set your humble servant's heart free."

The Emperor read the memorial and showed it to the Empress Dowager. The Empress was very angry, and ordered the arrest of Yang So-yoo, but the various officers of the Government used their united efforts against such a proceeding. The Emperor himself said: "I think it would be going too far to arrest him, but the fact that the Empress Dowager is so angry renders it impossible for me to forgive him out and out."

Several months went by and the Empress did not recognise Yang or show any signs of yielding. Justice Cheung, too, was under a cloud, so that he closed his doors and saw no one.

---

31   *The Six Forms.* These have to do with marriage, and may be defined as: first, the announcement; second, asking the name; third, choosing the day; fourth, making the presents; fifth, settling the various times; sixth, performing the ceremony.

At this time the Tibetans, with an army of a hundred thousand men, made a sudden invasion into China proper, and took possession of certain cities and territory. The advanced outposts had come as far as the Bridge of Wee, so that the capital itself was in great confusion. The Emperor assembled his ministers and conferred with them. They replied: "The soldiers of the capital do not exceed a few thousands, and those of the provinces are far away and out of reach. Your Majesty therefore ought to leave the capital for a time, make a wide circuit eastward, muster all the soldiers from the various districts and set matters right."

The Emperor could not decide, but said: "Among all my retainers Yang So-yoo is the most resourceful in the way of plans and proposals, and has excellent judgment. I have found him the very soul of wisdom heretofore. The three States that we returned to order and submission were brought so by his merit." He then dismissed the assembly and appealed to the Empress Dowager. "Let us forgive So-yoo, call him and ask what plans he would suggest."

So-yoo was called, and said: "In the capital are the tombs of the Imperial ancestors, and the palaces. If your Majesty were to turn your back on them, the people would be greatly disturbed. At such a moment, if a powerful enemy were to enter the city, it would be exceedingly hard ever to dislodge them. In the days of Tai-jong (627–650 AD), the Tibetans, along with the Mohammedan tribes, marshalled a million men or so and attacked the capital. At that time the forces in the city were not equal to the present, but with his cavalry, Prince Kwak Cha-heui drove them off and defeated them. My powers and gifts are not in any sense equal to those of Kwak's, but with a few thousand good soldiers I can settle accounts with these invaders, and so repay a little the great favours accorded me by your Imperial Majesty."

The Emperor at once appointed Yang as Generalissimo, and allowed him to set out from the barracks with thirty thousand troops to attack the Tibetan army.

Yang said the word of farewell, drew up his army and encamped near the Bridge of Wee. He drove back the vanguard of the enemy, and took prisoner Prince Choa-won, so that the enemy were thrown into confusion and many troops hid themselves or ran away. He followed up this advantage at once and fought three battles, beating the enemy badly, killing about thirty thousand men and taking eight thousand horses. From this place he sent a memorial of his victory to the Emperor.

His Majesty was greatly pleased, ordered his return, and appointed for each general gifts according to his merit.

The message sent by His Excellency ran thus: "I have heard it said that the Imperial troops are ever to be depended on. I have heard it also said that troops who always win think lightly of the enemy, and are not anxious to take advantage of special moments of weakness or hunger. This is a mistake. I cannot say that the enemy is not strong, or that they are not well equipped in arms. They have rebelled against their sovereign, and we ought to await only the moment of their greatest disadvantage to make our final attack. Their condition grows less favourable for them daily. It says in the Book of Wars: 'Labour hard to strike the enemy in the moment of his hardest labour.' One who fails to conquer then will fail simply from lack of skill. Already the enemy is broken and on the run. Their weakness is evident. All the districts along the way have abundant provision piled up for us, so that we have no fear. The wide plains and broad valleys are at our service, and the enemy has no place in which to pitch his camp. If we follow them sharply with fast cavalry we can make them completely ours. But if your Majesty rests now with a partial victory our best opportunity will be lost. To cease from the attack is not good policy in your servant's opinion. My wish, with your gracious permission, is to set the troops at once in motion, follow into the enemy's camp, burn them out, and make sure that not another armed man will cross the border, or another arrow be shot at us, and so remove from your Majesty all anxiety."

The Emperor read this memorial and was greatly struck by the wisdom of it. He advanced Yang to the rank of Chief Commissioner and Minister of War. He gave him his own sword, bow and arrows, embroidered belt, white flag and gilded battle-axe, and wrote out a command mustering further troops from north, east, and west.

Yang So-yoo received this, bowed his thanks toward the palace, selected a propitious day, made the necessary sacrifices and then set out. His disposition of the army was according to the ancient Six Laws,[32] and his arrangement of the camp according to the Eight Diagrams.[33] All were under strict discipline. Like rushing water they went forth and straight as the splitting bamboo. In a few months the lost territory was recovered and Yang's main forces had arrived at the foot of the Chok-sol Mountains. A strange sign occurred there. A great whirlwind appeared in front of his horse and broke into the camp and passed by. On this the Master cast the horoscope and learned that the enemy would attack his forces with great vigour, but that in the end he would be victorious.

He pitched his camp under the lee of a mountain, and scattered about it caltrops and "Spanish riders" to keep off the enemy. At this time the General was seated in his tent with a lighted candle before him, reading certain military dispatches, while the guards outside had already announced the third watch of the night. Suddenly a cold wind extinguished the light of the candle and an eerie chill filled the tent. At this moment a maiden stepped in upon him from the upper air, and stood before him with a glittering double-edged sword in her hand. The General, guessing her to be an assassin, did not quail before her, but stood his ground sternly and boldly asked: "What kind of creature are you, and what is your intention coming thus into the camp by night?"

She said in reply: "I am under command of King Chan-bo of Tibet to have thy head."

The General laughed. "The superior man," said he, "never fears to die. Take my head, will you not, and go?"

Then she threw down her sword, bowed low, and said in reply: "My noble lord, do not be anxious, how could your servant ever dare to cause you fear?"

The General then raised her up, saying: "You have come into the camp with a sword girded at your side, and now you say you will not harm me. Pray, what is your meaning?"

---

32   *Six Laws.* These pertain to the art of warfare, and are explained in the famous treatise said to have been written by the Duke Kang-tai, who flourished in the twelfth century BC. The six divisions are marked respectively by the names Dragon, Tiger, Ideograph, Warrior, Leopard, Dog.

33   *Eight Diagrams.* These are sets of lines divided and undivided, arranged in threes, which, when combined in double sets, form the basis of "the Book of Changes," the most famous literary work of Far Eastern Asia.

"I would like to tell you," said she, "all my past history, but I cannot do so in a moment."

Then the General asked her to sit down and inquired of her: "Your ladyship, not fearing the terror of my forces, has come seeking me. There must be some beneficent purpose in your mind; tell me, please."

The lady made reply: "Though I am called an assassin, yet really I have no heart for anything of the kind. I will tell your lordship exactly what my mind meditates." She got up, lit the lamp again, and came close to the general and sat down. He looked at her. Her cloudlike hair was fastened with a golden pin. She wore a narrow-sleeved outer coat with a military jacket underneath, embroidered with stone and bamboo designs. She wore phoenix-tail shoes and at her belt hung a dragon sword. Her face was bright like rose petals with dew upon them. She opened her lips, which were red as the cherry, and spoke slowly in tones like the oriole, saying: "Your servant came originally from Yang-joo county, where for generations we have been subjects of the Tangs. I lost my parents when young, and became a disciple of a woman who was a great master in sword-drill; she taught me her art. My name is Sim Hyo-yon, commonly spoken of as the Swallow. Three years after learning the science of the sword, I learned also that of metamorphosis – to ride the winds, to follow the lightnings, and in an instant to travel a thousand *li*. Several of us were taught, and we were all about alike in our sword skill, but when the teacher had some special enemy to destroy or some wicked person to kill, she invariably sent one of the others to do it. She never sent me. I was angry at this, and asked: 'We all alike have followed our teacher and have been taught the same lessons, yet I alone have made no return to you for your kindness. Is it because my skill is poor and I could not be trusted to carry out the will of my mistress that you fail to send me?'

"The teacher then said: 'You are not of our race. Later you will hear the truth and be made perfect. If I were to send you as I do the others, to kill and to destroy, it would for ever mar your virtue. For this reason I do not send you.'

"I asked again, saying: 'If that be so, then of what use is my practising sword drill?'

"The teacher replied: 'Your appointed mate lives in the Tang kingdom, and he is a great and noted lord. You are in a foreign land and there is no other way by which you can meet him. By means of my teaching you this insignificant craft you may come face to face with your special affinity. In your search you will enter a military camp of a million men, and among the swords and spears you will find him. The Emperor of the Tangs, I know, is to send a great general against the Tibetans, and King Chanbo has issued a proclamation calling for assassins who are ready to destroy this appointed leader. Do not miss the opportunity to descend from the hills. Go at once to Tibet and show your skill with the swordsmen of that country. On the one side you can save them from the danger that the Tangs threaten, and on the other you can meet your Master.'

"I received the commands of my teacher and went at once to Tibet, tore off the notice that I found on the city gate, and carried it to the king. He called me and allowed me to try my skill with others. In a few minutes I had struck off the top-knots of more than ten persons. The king was greatly delighted and chose me, saying: 'When you bring me the head of the general of the Tangs, I will make you my queen.' Now that I have met your Excellency I find that my teacher's words have come true, and my desire is to join those who wait on you and share a part in your life. Will you consent?"

The General, greatly surprised and delighted, answered: "Your ladyship has already spared this head of mine that was doomed, and now you wish to serve me. How shall I repay you? My wish is to bind you to me by the endless contract of marriage."

Thus they plighted their troth. Around the tent the glitter of swords and spears served for candle light, and the sound of cymbals for the festal harp. This marriage hall within the warlike enclosure was a happier one than was ever that of shimmering silks or embroidered screens.

From this day forth the General fell a victim to the fair one and took no account of officers or men. Days passed thus, when Sim the Swallow said: "A military camp is no place for women. I fear that I shall hinder the movement of the troops, so I must go."

The General replied: "But your ladyship is not a common woman; I hope that you will stay and teach me some special craft or science that pertains to war so as to defeat these rebels. Why should you leave me?"

"Your lordship," said Swallow, "does not need me, but with your power will easily destroy the haunts of the rebel. Why should you fear? Though I came forth by order of my superior, yet I have not said my farewell to her, so I shall go back to my teacher in the hills and await your return to the capital. By and by I shall meet you there."

The General asked: "After you are gone, in case Chan-bo sends another assassin, how shall I defend myself?

Swallow said: "Though there are many assassins they are not my equals, and if your lordship accepts me as your devoted one all danger is dispelled." She then felt at her belt, drew forth a jewel, and gave it to him, saying: "The name of this is Myo-ye-wan, a pin that King Chan-bo wore in his headdress. Please send a messenger to him with it saying I shall return no more."

The General inquired further: "Have you no other matters to suggest?"

Swallow said: "On your way ahead you will pass a place called Pan-sa-gok where good drinking-water will fail you. Make all haste to dig wells when there, so that the soldiers may not die of thirst."

He desired to ask further questions, but Swallow gave a leap into the air and was gone. The General then called his officers to him and told them of her coming. With one accord they said: "Your Excellency's luck is like that of the gods, and your power to affright the rebels is by means of angels who come to help you."

CHAPTER IX
AMONG MERMAIDS AND MERMEN

GENERAL YANG at once sent an officer into the camp of the enemy to restore the pin to King Chan-bo. The army was then set in motion and moved forward till it reached Tai-san, where the valley was exceedingly narrow with room only for horsemen to pass in single file. Circling a wall of rock they skirted the high bank of a river. In a long thin line of procession they went like fishes in a stream, till after some hundred *li* they found a fairly roomy place and there pitched their camp and rested. The soldiers were greatly worn by thirst and could find no drinking water. There was beneath the mountain a large lake toward which they struggled. Scarcely had they tasted of it, however, than their bodies turned green and they became dumb. Trembling seized them, and the expression of their faces grew fixed as in death.

The General was greatly distressed and went himself to look at the lake, the water of which was green and the depth of it beyond his power to fathom. A cold, forbidding breath seemed to issue from it like the frosts of autumn. Then he remembered, and said: "This must be the place that Sim Hyo-yon referred to as Pan-sa-gok." He urged those soldiers who were able to do so to dig wells, and though they dug in several hundred places to the depth of ten *kil* and more, not a drop of water was to be found.

The General determined at once to move his camp to another place, when suddenly the sound of drums was heard from behind the mountain. The earth shook and trembled and the valleys echoed. Evidently the enemy had blocked the way in this dangerous defile and had cut off all means of retreat.

Thus were the Imperial forces dying of thirst, and menaced in front and to the rear. The General sat in his tent vainly thinking by what means he might extricate himself from the difficulty. In his distress and weariness he leant on his desk and fell asleep.

THE DRAGON KING DEFEATED: AMONG THE MERMAIDS

Suddenly a sweet fragrance seemed to envelop the camp and two maidens came before him. Their faces were wonderful, and he knew that if they were not fairies they must be of a certainty disembodied spirits.

Said they: "We have a message from our Lady Superior to your Excellency; please condescend to come with us to our lowly place of dwelling."

The General asked: "Pray, who is your mistress, and where does she live?"

They said: "Our mistress is the younger daughter of the Tong-jong Dragon King. She has left the palace for a little and is living here."

The General replied: "But the place of residence of the Dragon King[34] is underneath the water and I am but a man of mortal race. By what possible law can my body descend to your depths?"

The maidens made answer: "We have spirit horses tethered outside the gate. If your Excellency will but mount one of these you will go there without trouble. The Water Palace is not far off, and there is no difficulty connected with the journey."

Yang then followed the maidens to the entrance outside the camp, and found there a score or more of servants of peculiar appearance, wearing strange dresses. They took hold of him and set him upon his horse. The creature went skimming along, its feet never touching the ground, and suddenly they were at the Water Palace. The palace was high, massive, and beautifully built, as a place where a king dwells should be. Guards with fish heads and beards like the whale stood before the entrance. Several waiting-maids came from within, opened the gate and led the general to the throne room. In the hall of audience there was a white marble seat facing south, and the maids persuaded Yang to come forward and be seated there. A silken rug covered the floor and led off toward the inner chambers. In a little, a dozen or so of waiting women accompanied a fair lady from the apartment to the left and conducted her to the centre of the audience hall. Her appearance was very beautiful, and her dress more splendid than

34   *The Dragon King.* He is said to live in the crystal palace, in the bottom of the sea, and to be the giver of rain. As the tiger is regarded as the king of the mountains, so the dragon rules the deep. The chief Dragon King presides over the Four Seas, while the lesser dragon kings hold court in such places as Nam-hai, Tong-jong, etc.

words can describe. One of the ladies came forward and said: "The daughter of the Dragon King desires to meet General Yang."

The General gave a start and attempted to make his escape, but they took him by the arms and held him prisoner, while they made him bow four times before this daughter of the Dragon King. Clinking of gem ornaments made sweet music for the occasion, while the odour of soft perfume greeted the nostrils.

The General invited her up to the throne seat beside him, but the Dragon King's daughter declined and instead caused a small mat to be spread on which she sat. Said he: "I am but a being from among mortal men, while your ladyship is a daughter of the world of spirits. Why should you prepare for me so elaborate and extravagant a reception?"

The Dragon King's daughter said: "I am Pak Neung-pa, the youngest child of the King of Tong-jong. When I was born my father was having an audience with God Almighty, and there he met Chang Jin-in, of whom he inquired concerning my future fortune. Jin-in took my birth characters and unfolded them, saying: 'This daughter, in essence, is one of the fairies, but because of sin that she has committed she has been sent into exile and has become your child. She will later take on human form and be the wife of a famous and gifted man. She will enjoy great riches and honour, and all the delights of eye and ear. In the end she will return to the Buddha and become a priestess of the priestesses. We dragon folk who have merman ancestors and dwell in the midst of the sea count it great glory to be born into human form, or to arrive at the state of the fairy or the Buddha. For this we all long. My eldest sister at first became a daughter-in-law of the Dragon King of Kyong-soo, but because she was unhappy in her marriage the two homes were rendered unfriendly and she married again Prince Yoo-jin, where her relations honoured her and all her attendants reverenced her. As for myself, I expect by and by to meet my appointed lord, and even to surpass my sister in glory and honour.'

"When my father heard what Jin-in said, he loved and prized me more than ever, and all the waiting-women of the palace treated me as an angel visitor from heaven. When I grew up, Oh-hyon, the son of the Dragon King of Nam-hai, who had heard of my history and attainments, asked marriage with me of my father, and because we of Tong-jong are under the authority of Nam-hai, my father dared not refuse but went instead and explained what Jin-in had said, asking permission to withhold his consent. For this the Dragon King on behalf of his proud son told my father that he had deceived him, severely reprimanded him, and became most insistent in the matter of the marriage. I reasoned to myself: 'If I am with my parents I shall not escape dishonour, so there is nothing else for me to do but to make my escape.' This I did, breaking through thorns and briars and taking refuge by myself in this unknown place. Here I am living poorly and in fear while the persecution on the part of the King of Nam-hai lasts. My parents said: 'Our daughter does not wish your son but has run away and hidden herself.' The foolish boy, however, regardless of my sufferings, gathered an army and came and tried to take me prisoner. My cries of despair moved heaven and earth so that the waters of the lake changed and became cold as ice and dark as hell. Thus the troops have not dared to enter it, and I have been preserved and have escaped with my life. To-day I ventured to invite your Excellency to come to this humble home of mine, not only to tell you how I am circumstanced, but also to consider how the Imperial troops have long suffered want and lacked water, no springs appearing in the wells they dig. The work of digging and delving is a great labour, and though you dig through the whole mountain a thousand cubits and more, no water will be forthcoming. Human power is not equal to it. The original name of this lake was Chong-su-tam, Bright Water Lake. It was wonderfully sweet then, but since I have come here to live, the flavour has changed and all who drink of it fall ill, so that the name now is Paik-yong-tam, White Dragon Lake. Since your Excellency has accepted my invitation my soul has found a place of dependence, like spring coming back to the shaded hill. I put myself under your care and my life into your keeping. Your anxieties become my anxieties, so I shall use all my powers to give you aid. From now on the flavour of the water will be sweet as formerly, no harm will come to the soldiers who drink of it, and those who are ill will recover."

The General said: "Now that I have heard your ladyship's words, I realise that people are mated in heaven, that the devils know of it, and that the decision of the Grandmother of the Moon[35] is something for which it is worth casting lots. All your wishes find their complement in mine."

The Dragon King's daughter said: "I have already made promise to you of this humble body, but, in short, there are three reasons why I ought not to be mated to your Excellency. The first is, I have not yet told my parents; the second, that I should accompany you only after I have changed this form of mine. I still have the scales and fishy odours of the mermaid, with fins that would defile my lord's presence. The third reason is that the messengers of the son of Nam-hai are all about spying in every nook and corner. It would be sure to arouse their anger and to cause disaster and no end of trouble. Let your Excellency retire to the camp as soon as possible, destroy the enemy, win great renown, and return to the capital singing your song of victory. Later, your servant will pick up her skirts, emerge from the waters, and follow you to your home in the great city."

The General said: "Though your ladyship's words are most acceptable, it seems to me that your being here is not only to preserve your own honour, but because the Dragon King desired you to await my coming and to please me. Your ladyship was a fairy in your former life, and therefore you have a spiritual nature. Between men and disembodied spirits intercourse may be carried on without wrong being done, then why should I have any special aversion to fins and scales? Though I have no special natural gifts, still I am under orders from His Imperial Majesty with a million of troops at my command, with the wild winds for guide and the spirit of the sea for my protector. If I can but meet this wilful child of the South Sea he will be but an insect for me to crush. If he does not at once repent and cease from his foolishness, I shall unsheathe my sword and finish him. We have met thus happily to-night, why should we miss the opportunity to seal our happy contract?" So they swore the oath of marriage, and found great delight in each other.

35 *Grandmother of the Moon.* There was a man in the time of the Tangs called Wi-go, who greatly desired to get married. Once, while he was going on a journey he saw an old woman sitting in the moonlight reading a book, while she leaned her back against a linen sack. Wi-go asked what book she was reading, and she replied that it was a book of the marriages of all the earth. Again he asked, "What is in the sack?" "Red string," said she. "When once I have tied the feet of those who are destined for each other with this red cord the whole world cannot keep them apart."

Before the day dawned fully a sound of thunder was heard, so that the Crystal Palace shook and trembled. Then the daughter of the Dragon King gave a start and arose, while the palace women in intense excitement came to her and said that a fearful disaster had overtaken them. The Crown Prince of Nam-hai had brought a vast army to the foot of the hills, had pitched his camp, and now demanded that they try the fierce odds of battle.

The General, in anger, said: "Mad creature, how can he dare so to venture?" He shook his sleeves and arose, sprang forth to the shores of the waters, where he found that the Nam-hai soldiers were already encircling the walls of the Paik-yong-tam with a wild clamour of noise, and causing noxious odours to arise on all sides. The so-called Prince Imperial on horseback rode swiftly out of the camp and shouted: "Who are you who would dare to steal another man's wife? I swear I will no longer live on the same earth with you."

The General mounted his charger, laughed, and said: "The daughter of the Dragon King of Tong-jong and I have been mated to one another from a former existence, and it is so recorded in the palace of the great God, as Jin-in well knoweth. I am but carrying out the will of heaven and doing as I have been directed. A contemptible creature of a merman like you to dare to affront me thus!" He commanded his troops to form in order and to advance to the attack.

The Prince Imperial, in fury, called together all the fishes of the sea; a carp, the general of the forces; a turtle, his chief of staff. He aroused them to a pitch of wild enthusiasm so that they advanced with unexampled bravery.

The General met them by a counter sword attack and raised aloft his white stone whip. In a moment, thousands and tens of thousands were crushed beneath the blow. Pulverised scales and fins bedewed the earth. The Prince himself received two or three spear thrusts, so that power to metamorphose departed from him, and finally he was captured, taken prisoner, bound, and brought before the charger of the General. Greatly pleased, Yang sounded a bugle call to his troops to retire, when the gate guards brought him word, saying: "The lady of Paik-yong-tam is now before the camp entrance and wishes to congratulate your Excellency on so great a victory."

Courtiers were sent forth to show her in. She presented her distinguished compliments, and added a thousand measures of wine and ten thousand head of cattle to feast the soldiers. They ate to the full, and were a hundred times more than ever incited to deeds of bravery.

General Yang then sat side by side with the daughter of the Dragon King and ordered that the Prince Imperial of Nam-hai be brought before them. In a commanding voice he addressed him thus: "I am under orders from the Emperor to beat down rebellion in all quarters of the State, and to put far from us devils who disobey Imperial commands. You, however, a little child, ignorant of what is right, desire to oppose the troops and thus to die by suicide. I have a sword called Eui-song-sang, the same sharp knife with which I killed the King of Kyong-hai. With it I ought to cut off your head to prove the truth of my words, but your dwelling in Nam-hai gives rain to a wide world of men and is for that reason deserving of merit. I shall therefore forgive you. Cease from your past evil ways, and do not sin any more against this woman." So he sent him off.

The prince was so overcome that he was unable to draw a long breath. He bowed low and ran for his life like a rat that desires to hide itself.

Suddenly a bright light arose from the south-east and a red cloud shone forth that sparkled with variegated colours. Flags and battle-axe insignia became visible in the upper air, and an angel dressed in scarlet bowed low and said: "The Dragon King of Tong-jong, learning that General Yang had scattered the troops of Nam-hai and saved the princess from dishonour, desired to come himself to the camp and offer his congratulations, but being held by his office and unable to leave of his own free will, he has arranged instead a great feast in honour of the General and now invites him to come. Please will your Excellency condescend to follow me? He commands also that the princess attend us."

General Yang said: "Although the enemy is driven off they still have their camp close by. Tong-jong is thousands of miles from here. It would take many days to go and come. How can one thus in command of troops go so far away?"

The angel said: "The light dragons are hitched to the sky-wagon and are ready. Half a day will be quite sufficient for you to go and return."

CHAPTER X
HUMBLE SUBMISSION

THE General then mounted the dragon-car with the Dragon King's daughter beside him; a wonderful wind blew the wheels and they whirled away up into mid air beyond the clouds. He did not know how close lay the outskirts of heaven, or how many miles from earth they were. A veil of mist like a white umbrella covered all the sphere. Little by little they descended till they came to Tong-jong. The King had come out a long distance to meet his guest with every possible form of ceremony and every evidence of love for him as a son-in-law. He bowed, and after having made Yang mount the highest seat of honour, prepared for him a great feast. The King himself raised his glass and congratulated Yang, saying: "I am a man of few and feeble gifts, with but little means at my disposal, not able even to make my own daughter prosperous and happy. By means of your Excellency's surpassing skill we have taken prisoner this proud upstart, and have saved my daughter's honour. I greatly desire to repay this kindness high as heaven and deep as the nether sea."

The General said: "It was all due to the incomparable strength and prowess of His Imperial Majesty. What cause have you to thank me?"

They drank till their hearts were merry and then the King called for music; and splendid music it was, arranged in mystic harmony, unlike the music of the earth. A thousand giants, each bearing sword and spear, beat monster drums. Six rows of dancing-girls dressed in phoenix garb and wearing bright moon ornaments, gracefully shook their long flowing sleeves and danced in pairs, a thrilling and entrancing sight.

The General asked: "What tune is this to which they dance?"

The Dragon King said: "In ancient days this tune did not exist in the Water Palace. My eldest daughter, as you know, was married to the Prince Imperial of Kyong-ha, and according to the writings of Dr. Yoo in 'The Shepherd and the Sheep,' was found destined to hardship. She fell a victim to oppression and ill-treatment, and my younger brother fought and defeated the King of Kyong-ha and saved her. The musicians of the palace invented this tune, calling it 'The Defeat of the Enemy.' Now, however, that your Excellency has overcome the Prince of Nam-hai and have caused the father to meet his daughter once more, the name of the tune has been changed to 'The Song of the General's Victory.'"

Yang asked again: "Where is Dr. Yoo now, and may I not see him?"

"Dr. Yoo," said the Dragon King, "is an official among the genii and so is at his post and cannot come."

After the various glasses, nine in all, had been passed, the General said good-bye. "I have many things to see to in the camp," he said, "and cannot stay longer, for which I am very sorry. My one desire is that the lady may not forget her marriage vows."

The Dragon King said that he would see that they were kept. He came outside the palace to see the General off.

On looking up Yang saw before him a great and high mountain, with five peaks that reached up to the clouds. At once a desire took possession of him to go and see them, so he asked of the Dragon King: "What mountain is this? I, So-yoo, have seen many famous mountains of the world, but never this one before."

The Dragon King inquired: "Do you not know the name of this mountain? It is Nam-ak, full of spiritual lights, strange and mysterious."

"Where are the approaches?" asked the General.

The Dragon King replied: "The day is not yet late, let us take a hasty look at it before we go."

The General then mounted the chariot and was soon at the base. He took his bamboo staff and entered on the stony way, crossed a hill, passed over a yawning chasm, where the surroundings seemed more and more wonderful, with a thousand views opening out before his vision, impossible to take in at a single glance. The old saying of "A thousand peaks vied with each other and a thousand streams rushed by" was true of this fairy region.

The General rested on his staff and surveyed the wide landscape with an increasing sense of surprise and questioning. He then sighed and said: "I have long been a follower of the camp and engrossed in the fortunes of war, so am tired of the dust of earth. How can the earth-to-earth particles of this body be so important? How can one win lasting merit, and after death attain to eternal life?"

As he said this to himself he heard the sound of bells from among the trees. He pushed forward. "Evidently," said he, "there is a temple of the Buddha somewhere near." He crossed a dangerous pass and ascended a lofty peak, and there stood a temple with the main hall hidden away in a shady recess. Many priests were gathered about. The chief priest sat on an elevated dais, and at the time of Yang's approach was reading the sacred books and discoursing on the same. His eyebrows were long and white and his features thin and transparent. His age must have been very great indeed.

Seeing the General approach, he called all the priests together to meet him. "We dwellers in the hills," said he, "are dull of hearing and so did not know beforehand of the coming of your Excellency, nor have we gone out to meet you beyond the gates as we should have done. Please forgive us. The day of your final coming has not yet arrived. Will you not enter the hall, worship and return?"

The General entered before the Buddha, burnt incense and made his obeisance. Then he returned, and as he stepped down his foot slipped and he awoke with a start, and behold he was leaning on his writing-table in the midst of the camp.

The east began to lighten. In wonder he asked his aides: "Did you gentlemen sleep and dream too?"

They made as one reply: "We accompanied your Excellency and fought an awesome spirit army, defeated it, took captive their commander, and returned. This is assuredly a proof of certain victory."

The General told all that he had seen in his dream, and afterwards they went together to inspect the White Dragon Lake. The ground was covered with scattered scales of fish and blood that flowed like running water. First of all the General raised his cup and took a drink of the fateful potion and then refreshed the sick soldiers. They recovered, and the army came in companies with their horses to the shore and drank freely. Their glad shoutings

shook the earth; the rebels heard it and trembled, desiring forth-
with to make terms.

Yang then wrote a communication announcing victory. The
Emperor was greatly delighted, and in his memorial to the
Empress Dowager he praised Yang So-yoo, saying: "So-yoo is
indeed the greatest general since the days of Kwak Pom-yang; let
us wait for his return to make him First Minister of State and so
reward him for his unparalleled success. If he has fully decided
as to the marriage proposal with the Crown Princess and can
conform to our commands, all is well, but if he still persists in
having his own way, we cannot punish one so meritorious as he
nor compel him by force. It is a question difficult to solve and one
full of deep perplexity."

The Empress Dowager said in reply: "The daughter of Justice
Cheung is truly a very beautiful girl. He and she have met and
seen each other. How can he readily cast her aside? My idea is to
take advantage of So-yoo's absence, issue an order commanding
Justice Cheung to marry off his daughter elsewhere, and so do
away for ever with this desire of So-yoo. How can they fail to do
as we command?"

His Majesty did not reply, but waited for a moment. He then
got up quietly and went out. At this the Crown Princess, who
was seated by the side of her mother, said: "Mother, your honourable decision is indeed quite wrong. The question of Cheung
See's marriage belongs not to us but to her family. How can the
Government undertake to direct a matter of this kind?"

The Empress replied: "This is a matter of exceeding great importance to yourself as well as to the State. I must talk with you about
it. General Yang So-yoo is not only superior to others in looks and
learning, but already by the tune he played on the jade flute he
has proven himself your chosen affinity. You cannot possibly turn
him away and choose another. So-yoo has already established a
special attachment with the house of Justice Cheung, and cannot
cast that off either. This is a most perplexing matter. I think that
after So-yoo's return, if he is married to you, he will not object
to take Cheung's daughter as a secondary wife. I wanted first to
inquire what you thought of this."

The Princess said: "I am not a person given to jealousy. Why
should I dislike Cheung See? But the fact that Yang had already

sent her his wedding presents forbids his making her his secondary wife. An act like this would be contrary to all good form. Justice Cheung's is one of the oldest ministerial families, distinguished from time immemorial for ability and learning. Would it not be high-handed oppression to force her into the place of secondary wife? It would never never do."

The Empress said: "Then what do you propose that we should do?"

The Princess replied: "Ministers of State may have three wives of the first order. When General Yang returns with his high honours, if he attain to the highest he will be made a subject king, if to the lowest he will still be a duke, and it will be no presumption on his part to take two wives. How would it do to have him take Justice Cheung's daughter as his real wife as well as myself?"

"It would never do," said the Empress. "When two women are of the same rank and station there need indeed be no harm or wrong done, but you are the beloved daughter of his late Majesty and the sister of the present monarch. You are therefore of specially high rank and removed from all others. How could you possibly be the wife of the same man with a common woman of the city?"

The Princess said: "I am truly high in rank and station; this I know, but the enlightened kings of the past and those who were sages honoured good men and great scholars regardless of their social position. They loved their virtue, so that even the emperor of a thousand chariots made friends and intimates of such and took them in marriage; why should we talk of high rank or station? I have heard that Cheung's daughter, in beauty and attainments, is not behind any of the famous women of the past. If this be true I should find it no disgrace at all but an honour to make an equal of her. Still, what I have heard of her may not be true, and by rumour alone one cannot be sure of the real or the imaginary. I should like to see her for myself, and if her beauty and talents are superior to mine I shall condescend to serve her, but if they are not as we hear them reported, then we might make her a secondary wife, or even a serving-maid, just as your Majesty may think best."

The Empress sighed, and said: "To be jealous of another's beauty is a natural feeling with women, but this daughter of mine loves the superiority of another as much as if it were her own, and reverences another's virtue as a thirsty soul seeks water; how can the mother of such a one as she fail to be happy? I, too, would like to see Cheung's daughter. I shall send a dispatch to that effect to-morrow."

The Princess replied: "Even though your Majesty should send such a command I am sure Cheung's daughter would feign sickness and not come. If she should decline there would be no way of summoning her by force as she belongs to a minister's household. Let us do it by means of the Taoist priestess and the Buddhist nun. If we knew of Justice Cheung's day of sacrifice in advance, I imagine we should have no difficulty in meeting her."

The Dowager thought well of this and sent a special servant to make inquiry of the various Taoist priestesses who lived in the neighbourhood. The old woman superior of the Chong-se Temple said: "Usually Justice Cheung's family do their sacrificing to the Buddha at our temple, but the daughter does not come herself; she sends her servant, General Yang's secondary wife, Ka Choon-oon. She comes with orders for her mistress and with prayers written out that are placed before the Buddha. You may take this written prayer of hers if you care to show it to Her Majesty the Dowager."

The eunuch accepted it, returned, and told what he had heard and showed Cheung See's written prayer.

The Dowager said: "I am afraid in these circumstances that it will be difficult to see her." With that the Crown Princess and she unfolded the written prayer and they read it together:

"Thy disciple, Cheung Kyong-pai, by means of her servant Cloudlet, who has bathed and made the required offerings, bows low, worships and makes her petition. I, thy disciple, Kyong-pai, have many sins to answer for, sins of a former existence as yet unexpiated. These account for my birth into this life as a desolate girl who never knew the joy of sisterhood. Already had I become the recipient of marriage gifts from General Yang and had expected to live my life in his home, but the choice of Yang as son-in-law to her Majesty the Empress Dowager has reduced all my poor hopes to nothingness. I am cut off from him, and can only regret that the ways of the gods and the ways of men do not harmonise. Such an unlucky person as I have therefore no place of expectation. Though I had not yet given my body, my mind and soul were already given, and for me to change and put my affections elsewhere would not be according to the law of righteousness. I will stay then with my parents during their remaining years. In this moment of sadness and disappointed experience I come to offer my soul to the Buddha, and to speak my heart's desire. Please condescend, ye Holy Ones, to accept this prayer of mine, extend to me pity, and let my parents live long like the endless measure of the sky. Grant that I be free from sickness and trouble so that I may be able to dress neatly, and to please them, and thus play out my little part in life on their behalf. When their appointed span is over I will break with all the bonds of earth, submit my actions to the requirements of the law and give my heart to the reading of the sacred sutras, keep myself pure, worship the Holy One, and make payment for all the unmerited blessings that have come to me. My servant, Ka Choon-oon, who is my chosen companion, brings this to thee. Though in name we are maid and mistress, we are in reality friend and friend. She, in obedience to my orders, became the secondary wife of General Yang, but now that matters have fallen otherwise, and there is no longer hope for the happy affinity that was mine, she too has bade a long farewell to him and come back to me so that we may be one in sorrow as well as in blessing, in death as well as in life. I earnestly pray that the divine Buddha will condescend to read our two hearts, and grant that for all generations and transmigrations to come, we may escape the lot of being born women;[36] that thou wilt put away all our sins of a former existence, give blessing for the future, so that we may transmigrate to some happy place to share endless bliss for ever. Amen."

When the Princess had read this she knit her brows, and said: "By one person's marriage decision two happy people's hopes are broken. I fear that a great wrong may be done to worth and virtue unknown to us."

The Dowager heard this and sat silent.

---

36 *Transmigration of Souls.* This is a teaching that came in with Buddhism, and has had a ruling place in the thought of the East for two thousand years. A righteous life in this present age means a step upward in the next existence, which, if continued, will at last bring one to Nirvana. Sin brings one lower and lower till at last it lands the guilty one in the hells that await the lost.

VISIT TO THE MONASTERY: PICTURES TO SELL

At this time Cheung's daughter waited upon her parents with placid countenance and resigned expression. Not a trace was there of dejection or sorrow. When her mother saw her she felt overcome with a sense of pity and dismay. Cloudlet attended lovingly and compelled Cheung See to engage in writing or games so as to pass the time, her own mind likewise being most desolate and her heart broken. Little by little she became thin and frail, as one overcome by an incurable sickness. Cheung See served her parents on the one hand, and on the other engaged herself on behalf of poor Cloudlet. Thus was her heart hopelessly confused, finding no place of peace, though others would not have guessed it. The daughter, wishing to comfort her mother by means of the servants, sought every variety of music or interesting recreation, and so moment by moment tried to gladden her ears and eyes.

On a certain day a woman came bringing two embroidered pictures to Cheung's house desiring to sell them. When Cloudlet had unrolled and looked at them, one was a picture of a peacock among the flowers, and the other of a partridge in the forest. All the embroidery work was exquisitely done. Greatly admiring them, Cloudlet made the maid wait till she had shown them to the mother and daughter. She said: "My mistress is always praising my embroidery, but look at these pictures, please. What do you think of them for skill?"

The young lady opened them out before her mother, gave a great exclamation of surprise, and said: "No present day embroidery can possibly equal these, and yet the colour and decorations mark them as new and not old. They are wonderful. Who can possess skill such as this?" She bade Cloudlet ask the maid whence they came, and the maid replied: "This embroidery is done by the hand of the young mistress of our home. Just now she is living alone, and finding special need of money wants to sell them regardless of price."

Cloudlet asked: "To what family does your mistress belong, pray, and for what reason is she staying alone?"

The maid replied: "Our mistress is the sister of Yi Tong-pan, who, with his mother, has gone to Chol-dong where he holds office. Because she was unwell and unable to follow, the young lady remained at the home of her maternal uncle, Chang the

Charioteer. Her quarters are occupied by Madam Sa, just over the way, where she is awaiting the return from Chol-dong."

Cloudlet, on hearing this, went in and told it to her mistress. The young lady gave a liberal price in hairpins and other ornaments for the pictures, and had them hung up in the main hall where she sat all day in admiration of them, praising their excellence and expressing her delight. After this the maid who sold the pictures came frequently to Justice Cheung's home and became very friendly with Cheung's servants.

The young lady said to Cloudlet: "The fact that Yi See has such wonderful skill of hand is proof that she is no common citizen. I shall make one of the servants follow her maid and find out what kind of personage she is." She chose a bright waiting-woman and sent her. The servant followed and found the lady's residence to be one of the town houses, very small and very neat, with no outside quarters for men.

When Yi See knew that she was a servant from Justice Cheung's, she treated her to the best of fare and sent her on her way rejoicing. The servant returned and reported, saying: "For beauty and loveliness of face and form, she is a second copy of our own dear lady. They are just alike."

Cloudlet did not believe this. "Her embroidery," said she, "is indeed wonderful, but as for her beauty, why do you tell me such stories? I am sure there is no one in the world so pretty as our own lovely mistress."

The servant replied: "If Madam Ka doubts my word, let her send someone else to see and then she will know the truth of what I say."

Cloudlet then sent another person privately, who also came back saying: "Beautiful, beautiful, the lady is a fairy angel from heaven. What we heard yesterday is true. If my lady Ka still doubts, how would it be if she should go and see for herself?"

"All this talk," said Cloudlet, "is nonsense. How is it that you have no eyes?" And so they laughed together and then separated.

A few days later Madam Sa called at Justice Cheung's to say: "The daughter of Yi Tong-pan has come to live in my house for a little, and her beauty and wonderful ability excel anything I have ever seen. She has heard of your daughter and greatly admires what she hears of her beautiful spirit and behaviour. She would like to meet her once and hear her sweet accents, but they are not acquainted and so she could not readily herself make request. Knowing that I was a friend of yours, she has begged me to come instead and make it for her."

At once Madam Cheung called her daughter and told her what had been said. The daughter replied: "I differ from other people in my freedom and I really do not wish to see anyone, but, learning that the young lady's attainments and beauty are on a par with this wonderful embroidery work, I should like to meet her once to brighten my darkened outlook."

Madam Sa was greatly pleased at this and returned home.

On the day following, the young lady sent her servant in advance to say that she was coming, and a little later she came in a neat curtained chair with two or three attendants who accompanied her to Cheung's mansion. Cheung See met her in her bedroom, and there they sat, hostess and guest, to east and west, just as when the Weaving Damsel[37] was welcomed to the Palace of the Moon, or to the feast of gems in the Paradise of Kwon-loon. The halo of light that attended them illuminated the room, so that they startled each other.

Cheung See said: "From messengers that have come and gone, I learned that you were living in the neighbourhood, but one so unlucky and so unfortunate as I had broken off intercourse with friends and had given up paying visits till now your ladyship has condescended to call on me. Thank you so much. I am unable to express my delight and appreciation."

The visitor replied: "This little sister of yours is a very stupid girl. Early in life I lost my father, and my mother spoiled me so that I really did not learn anything and have nothing to show for the years that have gone by. This I regret as I say to myself: 'A boy is free to go to all points of land and sea, can pick and choose good friends, can learn from another and can correct his faults, while a girl meets no one but the servants of her own household. How can she expect to grow in goodness or to find in any such place

37   *Weaving Damsel.* She is one of the celestial lovers. Her sweetheart, the herdsman, is supposed to be the star Beta in Aquila, while she is the star Alpha in Lyra. They are lovers who, by the abyss of the Milky Way, are separated all the year round, till the seventh night of the seventh Moon, when the magpies of the earth assemble and form a bridge over the chasm and enable them to meet. This is one of the Orient's most famous legends.

answers to the questions of the soul?' I was mourning over the fact that I was a girl shut up in prison, when happily I heard that your knowledge was equal to that of Pan-so's,[38] and your virtue and loveliness on a par with the ancients. Though you do not pass outside your own gateway, yet your name is known abroad even to the Imperial Palace. Because of this, and forgetting my own mean qualifications, I wished to see your excellent face. You have not refused me admittance, and now I have attained my heart's dearest desire."

Cheung See made answer: "Your kind words will ever live in my humble heart. Locked up as I am in these inner quarters, my footsteps are hindered from freedom and my sight and hearing are limited to this small enclosure. I have never seen the waters of the wide sea nor the long stretch of the hills. So limited in experience and knowledge am I that your praise of me is too great altogether." She brought out refreshments and they talked as those long acquainted.

Yi See said smilingly: "It has reached my ears that there is a little Madam Ka in your home. If that be so I should like very much to meet her."

Cheung See replied: "I, too, had just that wish in mind," so she called Cloudlet to come.

When Cloudlet came Yi See arose to greet her. With that Cloudlet gave a sudden start of surprise, and then with a sigh said to herself: "What we were told is true. Divine heaven hath surely created my own dear lady and also this most charming Yi See. Beyond one's expectation I find that Pi-yon[39] and Ok-han are alive at one and the same time upon earth."

The young lady said to herself: "I have often heard of Madam Ka, but she is really prettier than I ever dreamed. How could General Yang fail to love her? Why, also, when mistress and maid are thus gifted and graced, should he give them up willingly?" So

---

38   *Panso.* She is the most noted of ancient literary women. Her brother is one of the first historians of the East, and after his death she, at the command of the Emperor, carried on what he had begun.

39   *Pi-yon* (first century BC). A famous dancing girl who, by her grace and loveliness of form, won the name of Pi-yon, Flying Swallow, and became the first favourite of the Emperor. So gifted was she in the touch of the toe that she could dance on the open palm of the hand.

interested was she in Cloudlet that she spoke to her frankly and familiarly as with the dearest friend. Then she said farewell, and added: "The day is drawing late and I must not stay longer, but I am sorry to go. Your little sister's home is just over the way; when you have a moment of leisure, come, I pray you, and let me hear your dear voice again."

Cheung See said: "All unexpectedly you have come into my life and I have heard your sweet words. In return I should like so much to call on your distinguished home and present my felicitations, but my circumstances are different from those of others, and I dare not set foot out of the main gateway. Please forgive this defect of mine and accept my love."

The two bade each other good-bye with the keenest regret. Not only so, but Cheung See said to Cloudlet: "Although the sword is within the sheath, the glittering light from its blade shoots up to the seven stars of the Dipper; and though the ancient crayfish lies hidden in the depths of the sea, the sphere of it ascends to the pavilion heights. That we have lived in this same city all our lives, she and I, and yet that I have never heard of her before puzzles all my powers of comprehension."

Cloudlet replied: "Your humble servant has one doubt in mind regarding this matter. General Yang has frequently said that he met the daughter of Commissioner Chin first of all by seeing her in the upper storey of her pavilion, and again he received her writing in the city guest-house and made a contract of marriage with her, but Commissioner Chin died a violent death and lost everything. He praised her matchless beauty and sighed over her. I, too, have seen the love-song that she wrote and assuredly she is a gifted girl. It may be that she has changed her name, and by making friends with your ladyship hopes to unite the broken threads of her affinity."

Cheung See replied: "I, too, have heard elsewhere of Chin See's beauty and I think she must be very much like this lady, but after the disaster that overtook her I understood that she became a palace maid-in-waiting. In such circumstances how could she ever come here?" Then she went in to see her mother, and ceased not in her praise of the mysterious visitor.

The lady replied: "I, too must invite her once and see her." A few days later she sent a servant asking that Yi See would condescend to come. To this she gladly assented.

The lady Cheung went out before the main hall to welcome her. Like a near relative, Yi See made a deep obeisance before her. The lady Cheung was highly delighted, and loved her dearly and treated her with the greatest respect. "My young ladyship came the other day so graciously to see my daughter and was so loving and dear to her. Old woman as I am, I thank you most heartily. That day I was unwell and did not see you, a matter of the deepest regret to me now."

Yi See bowed before her and said: "Your humble niece had long desired to see the fairy dweller of your household, but had feared that she might miss her. Meeting her thus and being treated by her as a dear sister, and your ladyship's receiving me as though I were a member of your family, embarrass me so that I do not know how to express my thanks. I desire, as long as I live, to go in and out of your home and serve your ladyship as though you were my mother."

The lady two or three times declared that she could never let that be so.

Cheung See in company with Yi See waited on her mother for the day and then she invited her into her own room, where they sat like the three feet of the incense burner, she, and Yi See, and Cloudlet.

They laughed sweetly and talked in soft and tender accents. Perfect agreement possessed them in thought, and mind, and soul, and they loved each other with infinite delight, talking of all the great masters of the past and of the renowned ladies of ages gone by till the shadows of the night began to cast their lines athwart the silken window.

CHAPTER XI
THE CAPTURE OF CHEUNG SEE

WHEN the young lady had taken her departure, the lady Cheung said to her daughter and to Cloudlet: "The relation of our two families, Choi and Cheung, has always been very close and intimate. Hundreds of times and more they have intermarried, and in these two families, from my earliest years, I have seen many persons of great gifts and beauty, but none just like Yi See. She is indeed your peer. If you two, gifted as you are, could become sworn sisters it would indeed be well."

Cheung See mentioned what Cloudlet had said regarding Chin See, and added: "Cloudlet has her doubts about the lady Yi, but her opinion differs from mine. Besides ability and beauty of face, Yi See has a distinguished manner and a dignity of behaviour that differs entirely from the ordinary young women of the city. Although Chin See be as gifted as she is said to be, how could she ever hope to compare with one so striking? If I were to speak as I have heard rumour say, she has a face and a heart that answers to the Princess Orchid. Her great ability agrees thereto likewise, and her loving tender spirit. I have heard it said, too, that Yi See's face is not unlike that of the Princess Imperial."

To this the lady Cheung made answer: "I have never seen the Princess and so cannot definitely say; but even though she occupies her high place and wears her Imperial name, how could she possibly equal Yi See?"

The daughter's reply was: "I am in doubt, and must send Cloudlet to take note of her surroundings and behaviour."

On the second day Miss Cheung and Cloudlet were talking the matter over when Yi See's servant arrived to say: "Our lady finds a messenger going to Chol-dong, where her brother is, and intends to depart to-morrow. She would like to come to-day and make her farewell salutation to the lady and her daughter."

On hearing this, Cheung See ordered the hall to be specially brightened up and waited breathlessly. Shortly after Yi See
arrived, bowed to the lady and to Cheung See, and spoke her
message of departure. The sincerity with which the two took their
farewell was specially touching. They were like two dear sisters
separating one from the other, or a lover bidding a long good-bye
to his sweetheart.

Yi See said to the lady Cheung: "Your niece's separation from
her mother and brother now measures a whole year, and I long so
much to see them that I cannot wait. My heart, however, is bound
to your ladyship and to my dearest friend with an unbreakable
tie. As I attempt to pull myself away I find that it grows stronger
and stronger. I have one word to say and one wish to express. I
fear, nevertheless, that Cheung See may not grant my wish, so I
mention it to your ladyship." She hesitated, however, so that the
words failed to express themselves.

The lady said: "What is it that you would like to ask?"

Yi See made answer: "I have just finished an embroidered picture of the merciful Buddha that I have worked in memory of my
late father. My brother is now in the county of Chol-dong; I am a
woman and cannot ask a favour of the literati, so I have not found
anyone to write an inscription on it for me. I am most desirous
that my sister Cheung See should write two or three lines of verse.
Because the picture is wide in size and difficult to fold or carry,
and in danger of being damaged by a journey, I would rather not
bring it. The only alternative is that I take her to my home with
me and get her to write or compose something there, so that my
poor effort on behalf of my late father may be made perfect and
my soul find delight. I do not know, however, what Cheung See
may think of it, so I did not dare to ask her directly; therefore I
make my wishes known first to your ladyship."

The lady looked at her daughter and said: "You are not accustomed to go to the homes even of your near relatives, but you have
this invitation now which we cannot but regard. It comes from
Yi See's earnest heart of devotion to her father. Besides her place
of residence is not far away. I think it would be quite right and
proper for you to go and return quickly."

Cheung See's face clouded at first with hesitation, but when she
thought of it she quieted her apprehensions and said: "Yi See's

circumstances are such that her time is very limited, so it would not do to send Cloudlet instead. I shall avail myself of the opportunity to see what her world is like and thus solve the question that is in my mind." This she said to herself, but to her mother she replied: "If Yi See's invitation were an ordinary one I could not accede to it, but her devotion to her father is something that all must commend. How can I refuse? I shall wait, however, till evening, and when night falls I shall go."

Yi See was greatly delighted and thanked her over and over again, saying: "But if it is too dark it will be very difficult for you to write. If you dislike the confusion of the way, my chair, though narrow and uncomfortable, can easily enough accommodate two persons like us. Come with me, will you not, please, and when evening falls you can then return home."

Cheung See made answer: "I am unable to resist your kind words."

With this she bowed to her mother and said her adieu. She gave to Cloudlet a little press of the hand by way of special recognition, and then she and Yi See rode side by side in the same palanquin, with a number of serving-women from Justice Cheung's following behind.

They arrived at Yi See's private room, where the things displayed were not many in number but were of a very excellent quality. The fare, also, while not lavish in quantity, was of the daintiest kind.

Cheung See thought: "I am in greater perplexity than ever."

The day passed and the evening gradually grew near, but Yi See said nothing whatever about the writing.

"Where have you placed the picture of the Merciful Buddha?" inquired Cheung See. "I would like so much to make my bow before it."

Yi See said: "Assuredly, I must ask you to come with me to see it."

Before she had finished speaking, a sound of horses and chariots was heard from before the door and a long succession of flags suddenly lined the street-way.

The servants from Justice Cheung's came rushing in in great fear to say that a company of soldiers had surrounded the house. "Mistress, mistress," said they, "what shall we do?"

THE PRINCESS VISITS CHEUNG SEE:
CHEUNG SEE'S RETURN VISIT

Cheung See, already guessing the nature of the commotion, sat still and unmoved.

Yi See said to her by way of assurance: "Please do not be alarmed in the least. Your little sister is no other than Princess Nan-yang, So-wha. Nan-yang my title and So-wha my given name. My bringing you here was at the command of the Empress Dowager."

Cheung See instantly arose from her seat and made reply: "Though wholly unenlightened myself and unsophisticated, I knew by your Highness's face and form that you were different from the rest of the world. But your visiting me was so far beyond the most extravagant dreams of my fancy that I have been entirely taken off my guard. I have failed in the proper forms and have in a hundred other uncomely ways sinned before you. Please have me punished as I deserve."

The Princess did not have time to reply before a servant came in and said: "The palace maids, Sol, Wang and Wha, have been sent to inquire for your Highness."

The Princess then said to Cheung See: "Wait here for a moment, will you please." She went out to the main hallway where the three women had entered in order and gave the ceremonial bow before her, saying: "It is now several days since your Highness left the palace. The Empress Dowager greatly desires to see you. The Emperor, too, and the Empress have sent maids-in-waiting to make inquiry. To-day is the appointed time of your return, so horses, carriages and other necessaries wait outside the door. His Majesty has ordered the eunuch Cho to attend you."

The three maids added: "The Empress Dowager has commanded that Cheung See ride with you in the royal palanquin and come to the palace."

The Princess told the maids to wait while she went in once more, and said to Cheung See: "I have many things to say to you as soon as we find quiet, but now the Empress Dowager, my mother, wants to see you and has come out to the Ma Pavilion, where she is waiting. Please come with me at once and be presented to her."

Cheung See, knowing that she must not refuse, said in reply: "Your humble servant knows already how tenderly your Highness loves her, but an uncouth country girl who never in her life before was presented at court, fears that she may fail to do the proper thing, and is very much alarmed."

The Princess replied: "The thought that prompts the Dowager to see you is the same thought that makes me love you. Please do not be anxious in the least, but just come."

Cheung See said: "Will your Highness not proceed to the palace first? If you do so I shall return home to tell my mother and then follow."

But the Princess objected. "The Empress has already given commands," she said, "that I ride with you in the same palanquin. Her commands are very pressing. I urge you not to hesitate."

Cheung See then said: "I am only a humble child of a subject; how could I think of riding in the same chair with your Highness?"

"Kan Tai-kong," said the Princess Nan-yang, "was only a fisher by the Wee River, and yet he rode in the same chariot with King Moon. Hoo-yong was only a gatekeeper, and yet he held Prince Sillong's horse. It is our duty to do honour to those who are great and good. Why do you call attention to rank and station? You yourself are of an old family of the nobility. Why should you hesitate to ride in the same chair with your little sister?" So she took her by the hand and they mounted the palanquin together.

Cheung See sent one servant home to tell her mother, while another attended her to the palace.

Thus they went together, the Princess and her charge, entering by the East Gate. They passed the nine pagoda arches to the private entrance, where they dismounted. The Princess said to lady Wang, who was in waiting: "You remain here for a little with my lady Cheung."

Lady Wang replied: "I have, in accordance with the commands of her Majesty the Dowager, prepared a special place for the lady Cheung to stay."

The Princess, greatly pleased at this, bade them wait while she went in and presented herself before the Empress Dowager.

At first the Dowager had had no desire to meet Cheung See, but since the Princess had lived in disguise near her, and had won her friendship by means of the pair of pictures, and had discovered that her character and attainments were lovely, her feelings of interest were kindled likewise. From what had been reported she had learned to appreciate why Yang had not wished to give her up; why her daughter, the Princess, and Cheung See loved each other; why they had made a contract of sisterhood; and why in one home they would serve the same husband.

The Empress Dowager had therefore learnt to understand, and had given consent at last to the Princess and Cheung See both becoming wives of General Yang. She now desired greatly to see her face, and had devised the plan by which she had been brought.

Cheung See waited for a little in the appointed place. Presently two maids came out from the inner palace bearing a box with clothing. They also delivered the commands of the Empress Dowager, which read: "Miss Cheung is a daughter of a minister and should therefore conform to the required ceremonies of the nobility. She is now wearing the dress of an unmarried girl, in which no one can come into my presence. I am sending herewith a ceremonial robe of a lady of high rank."

"We maids-in-waiting have taken Her Majesty's commands," said the attendants. "Please, your ladyship, dress and enter."

Cheung See bowed, and said: "How can anyone so unpractised as I dress in a lady's ceremonial robe? Though my garb is poor, still it is the dress in which I appear before my parents. Her Imperial Highness is the mother of us all, please let me appear in the dress that I wear before my parents while I go into audience before her."

The maids so reported, and Her Majesty was greatly delighted with the answer and called her at once. She followed step by step, and arrived at the dais. On each side the ladies-in-waiting vied in their efforts to see, and said in wondering admiration: "We had thought that all beauty and loveliness belonged exclusively to our Princess. Who would have believed that this little lady Cheung could be so startlingly beautiful?"

She made her deepest obeisance and then was led by the maids up to the dais. There the Empress made her sit down and gently said to her: "The issuing of an Imperial command ordering the return of your marriage gifts to General Yang was an act of the Government, and not of myself personally. My daughter objected to it at that time, and said: 'For any man to break a marriage contract pertains not to the straight and narrow way on which kings should walk.' She desired instead, and proposed in fact, that she should serve General Yang along with you. I counselled with His Majesty, and we have decided to follow the unselfish wish of our daughter. We now await the return of Yang in order to have him once more send his gifts and make you his first and chief wife. Such kind favour was not known before, nor was it ever heard or dreamed of, I am sure. This is what I specially desired to tell you."

Cheung See arose and made reply: "Your Majesty's kindness is exceedingly great, and of such a character as no courtier could ever dream. I, in my lowly station, can make no return for your illimitable favour. I, your humble subject, am only the daughter of a minister and ought never to stand on the same footing as Her Highness the Crown Princess, nor accept a place equal to her in station. Even though I might desire to yield obedience to your commands, it would be impossible for my parents to consent. They would rather die than allow me to do so presumptuous a thing."

The Dowager replied: "Your humility is most becoming, yet members of your family for generations have been marquesses and earls. Your father was a valued minister of my late husband, and received special honour in the court. Difference in rank is not a thing to be troubled about."

But Cheung See said: "A courtier's ready obedience to his king's commands is as natural as the course of nature in the changing seasons. Though you elevate me to the rank of nobility, or degrade me to the place of servant, how dare I offer opposition, and yet how could Yang So-yoo accept it with complacency? Your humble subject has no brothers or sisters, and my parents are already old. My one supreme wish is to serve them with a faithful heart during the remaining years of their life."

The Dowager went on to say: "Your devotion to your parents greatly pleases me, but why should you stay in a place of obscurity where you will never be able to attain to a single wish of the heart? You are born with all possible graces and gifts. How could Yang So-yoo think of casting you off? Also my daughter here has given proof of a destined affinity with him by a tune played upon the flute. What God hath joined together let no man put asunder. Yang So-yoo is a great general of the highest order. He has such genius as has not been seen since the days of the ancients. What offence against society would it be his taking two wives? I had originally two daughters, but Nan-yang's sister died at ten years of age, and I have always much regretted Nan-yang's loneliness. Now that I see you, with your pure heart and beauty, not inferior in the least to hers, it seems as though I had got back my dead child. I shall make you my adopted daughter, and shall get the Emperor to assign you title and rank. In the first place you shall be the sign of my love for my dear departed child; in the second place you shall be my gift to Nan-yang; and in the third place I shall have you along with her come under the protection of Yang So-yoo and so settle all these perplexing questions. What do you say to this?"

The young lady bowed low and said: "Since your Majesty has so decided, this humble girl will, I fear, die under the weight of too great favour. My one desire is that your Majesty will withdraw the command, and let this obscure child fly away in peace."

The Empress said: "I have made known my wishes to His Majesty the Emperor, and he will definitely decide it. You must not be headstrong in the matter."

She called the Princess and made her come forward near to Cheung See.

The Princess, in ceremonial robes, shining in glory, sat by her side.

The Dowager laughed and said: "You have wished to have Cheung See for your sister, and now it has come to pass. No one could tell who is the elder, you or she. Have you no regrets now?" She took Cheung See by the hand to make her her adopted daughter. She then stood her close up to Princess Orchid. The Princess, greatly delighted, thanked her mother, saying: "Your Highness's decision is the dearest in the world. You have brought all my fondest wishes to pass. How can I tell you of the joy that now fills my soul?"

The Dowager gave Cheung See a great and magnificent reception, and as they talked of the old poets she said: "I have heard from the Princess that you are skilful with the pen and at poetic composition. It is all quiet here in the palace, and with the delights of spring about us, will you sing for me once? Do not be backward now, but cheer me, my child. Among the noted ancients there was one famous scholar who could write a verse before the quick of foot could go seven courses; can you do that, my child?"

Cheung See made reply: "Now that I have heard your gracious command, I must try with all the skill I have to please your Majesty."

The Empress picked out from the palace maids those most nimble, made them stand in a row in front of the main hall, gave out the subject and made ready a signal.

But Princess Orchid called to her and said: "Mother, you must not have Cheung See write all alone; I'll join her and try also."

The Dowager, pleased with this, gave permission. She said: "Daughter, your wish is a proper one." She then thought of a subject. It was late spring. The peaches were in bloom outside the pavilion railing, and the happy jay-birds were calling as they sat upon the branches. The Dowager pointed to these and said: "I have decided upon your marriage, and yonder jay upon the high tree-tops announces his delight. He is a lucky omen. Let us make this the subject, The Peach Flower and the Happy Jay-bird." They were to write a verse before the seven courses could be run, and each verse was to contain some reference to their happy marriage.

She told the maids-in-waiting to have everything in order, pen, ink, and so on, for the Princess and Cheung See. At the given signal the women in front of the main hall started on their way, but fearing that the two would not be able to finish while the seven courses were being run, they looked back at them and took their steps slowly. The two pens flew like swift wind or a sudden squall of rain. Off the lines were dashed, and they were done before the women had completed five of the courses.

The Dowager read what Cheung See had written, and it ran thus:

> "The swift wind rocks the tipsy peach
> 　　Before the Palace Hall,
> While from the height, far out of reach,
> 　　There sounds the mavis' call.
> The dancer's swing and silken fold
> 　　Awake the happy day,
> While in the group a magpie bold
> 　　Has found her wondering way."

The Princess's verses ran thus:

> *"In the court of the Palace a hundred buds blow,*
> *As the jay-bird sweeps in with his spirit aglow.*
> *He bends his strong back o'er the wide Milky Way,*
> *To bear two small dots who are coming to stay."*

The Dowager read these and sighed, saying: "These two are the spirits of Yi Tai-baik and Cho Cha-gon. If we could mark women as literary graduates, we should rate them first and second in the contest of the year." So she exchanged the two compositions, giving one to each, and each admired and praised the other.

The Princess said to Her Majesty: "I have managed to fill out my couplets, but the sentiment is one that might be easily expressed by anyone. Cheung See's, however, are beautifully done. I cannot attain to such excellence."

"That is so," said the Empress; "but yours too, dear, is very well done, and everyone would admire it."

TWO IN ONE PALANQUIN: THE POETRY CONTEST

CHAPTER XII
YANG'S SUPREME REGRET

A T this time the Emperor came in to make his salutations before the Empress Dowager, and the Empress bade the Princess and Cheung See make their escape into a neighbouring room. She spoke to the Emperor, saying: "In reference to the Princess's marriage, you know I made the Cheung family return the gifts that had been sent, and this has caused damage to the Imperial prestige. To make Cheung's daughter a wife along with the Princess would be refused by the Cheungs themselves; to make her a mistress would seem cruel and hard. To-day I have called her, and she is indeed lovely and gifted with great ability, a fitting sister for the Princess. Because of this I have adopted her and have decided to wed them both to Yang So-yoo. What do you think of it?"

The Emperor was greatly pleased and congratulated her, saying: "This is a right and noble decision, and wide as the sky in its justice. In such generous treatment and bountiful favour as this no one has ever equalled my mother."

Then the Empress called Cheung See so that she might meet the Emperor, as she was now his sister. He made her come up and sit upon the dais, while he said to the Dowager: "Since Cheung See has now become a sister of the Emperor, why should she still wear the dress of the common people?"

The Empress replied: "As there is no command of the Emperor to that effect she declined to put on ceremonial robes."

Then the Emperor said to the chief of the palace ladies-in-waiting: "Bring a roll of figured silken paper." This Chin See, the phoenix, brought. The Emperor raised the pen and made as if to write. Then he said to the Empress Dowager: "Since you have already made Cheung See a princess, you must, of course, give her the family name of our house."

The Dowager replied: "I thought at first to do so, but learning that Justice Cheung and his wife are old people, and that they have no other children, I felt desirous on their behalf that she should carry on their family name, and so I decided to leave her surname as it is."

Then the Emperor wrote the following in large characters with his own hand. "I approve of the divine wish of Her Majesty the Empress Dowager, and record Cheung See to be her adopted daughter. Her name is Princess Yong-yang, or Blossom." When he had written this he stamped it with a pair of palace seals and gave it to Cheung See, and he ordered the palace maids to dress her in royal robes.

Cheung See descended from the dais and expressed her thanks.

The Emperor then decided the order of precedence between Princess Orchid and Princess Blossom. Blossom was a year the senior of Nan-yang, but she would not have thought of taking precedence of her.

The Empress said: "Princess Blossom is now my daughter, and for the elder to be first and the younger second is the proper order. There is no re-adjusting of the place between brothers and sisters."

Blossom bowed low, and touching her brow to the ground, said: "The order appointed pertains only to the future, why should we not ignore it to-day?"

The Dowager said: "In the time of the Spring and Autumn Classic, the wife of Cho-chi, although the daughter of Prince Chin-moon, gave up her place to the first wife who was chosen. Much more should my daughter, as you are her elder sister, give up without a question."

Still Blossom persisted long in declining the place. Then the Dowager settled it: "We have decided, and it is settled according to seniority." And from that time forth all in the palace called her Princess Blossom. The Empress showed the verses that the two had written to the Emperor, and he praised them, saying: "They are both very pretty, but Blossom's verse has followed the order of the Book of Poetry and places all the credit with Orchid. She has observed the highest refinements of good form."

"True," replied the Dowager.

The Emperor again said: "Since you love Blossom so greatly,

for truly nothing was ever before seen equal to it, I too have a favour to ask of you." He then told of the palace-maid Phoenix, and of what had taken place in regard to her affair. Said he: "Her case is indeed a very pitiful one. Though her father died from his own fault, her forefathers were all faithful ministers of state. If we take all the circumstances into account and make her a secondary wife to Yang, would it not be a kindness on your part? I pray you so to do."

The Dowager then looked toward the two princesses, and Orchid said: "The palace-maid Phoenix told me her story some time ago. She and I are now fast friends and never wish to part. Even though you should not consent to order it, my wish would already be recorded thus."

Then the Empress Dowager called Phoenix and said to her: "The Princess desires that you should keep each other company through life and unto death. I therefore appoint you a secondary wife to General Yang, so that your wishes may come to pass. In future let all your heart go into repaying the Princess for her kindness to you."

Chin See, overcome with gratitude, shed tears and spoke her thanks.

The Empress went on: "The marriage of the two Princesses is now happily decided upon, and a jay bird of good omen comes to confirm it. I have already had the Princesses write for me, and now that you, too, have found a place of refuge and have the same happy prospect in view, you must write for me as well."

At once Chin See wrote and handed her verse to the Empress. It read:

> *"The happy jay that shouts his mirth*
> *Athwart the Palace halls,*
> *Has seen the spring on gilded wing,*
> *Step forth within his walls.*
> *So, too, the humble phoenix bird*
> *Will long no more to roam,*
> *But with the four, she'll meet once more,*
> *And join the happy home."*

The Empress along with the Emperor read the verses and in delight said: "Even Sa Do-on who wrote concerning the willow catkins could not surpass this. The verse also follows the Book of Poetry and draws a clear distinction between the first and second wife, most sweet and becoming."

Princess Orchid said: "The subject and material from which this verse is drawn are limited, and we two sisters had already written all that was to be said about it. Poor Chin See had nothing left on which to place her hand, and yet how pretty it is."

The Dowager replied: "Since ancient times the most noted writers among women were Pan Heui, Chai Nyo, Princess Tak-moon and Sa Do-on, these four only. Now three girls of unsurpassed ability meet in one and the same dwelling-place. It is surely a marvellous sign."

Orchid replied: "Princess Blossom's waiting-maid, Cloudlet, is also greatly gifted with the pen."

At this point the day began to draw late and the Emperor withdrew to the outer palace. The two Princesses retired and slept in their rooms, and when at the earliest dawn the cocks crew, Blossom went in and made her salutation to the mother, and asked permission to withdraw, saying: "When your child came into the Palace, my parents must certainly have been anxious and full of wonder. May I please withdraw for a little, see them, and make my boast to all my kin of the grace of your High Majesty and the loving kindness and beauty of my sister Orchid? Kindly grant me this favour."

The Empress said: "My child, how can you think of leaving me so easily? I have something to consult about with your mother, and so shall make request that she come here in audience instead."

The Cheungs, when they heard what the servant had come to tell, were somewhat relieved from their fears, and a feeling of thankfulness took possession of them. Suddenly the command came for the lady Cheung to report in the palace.

The Empress met her, took her by the hand, and said: "My taking possession of your daughter is not only because I love her beauty, but for the sake of Princess Orchid's marriage. Once having seen her lovely face I can never let her go again, so I have made her my adopted daughter and the elder sister of Orchid.

My thought is that in a former existence she may have been my daughter, and that she has now come to be yours. Since Blossom is a Princess, one ought really to give her the name of the Imperial household, but I have thought of your having no son, and so have not changed her name. You will know by this how deeply I love you."

The lady Cheung could not express the thanks that filled her soul. She bowed low and said: "I, your humble subject, had a daughter born to me late in life whom I loved as one loves only gems and pearls. Her marriage proposals failed of fulfilment and we sent back the bridegroom's presents. My soul lost all its sense of life, and my bones seemed broken within me. My one wish was to die quickly and no longer see her sad and desolate plight. Unexpectedly the dear Princess came to our home and bent her lovely form to our low conditions, making friends with my humble daughter. Then she took her with her to the Palace and made her the recipient of undreamed of honours. This is indeed making green leaves to sprout forth on the dry tree, and waters to flow afresh along the parched bed of the stream. All my heart and soul and strength would go forth to requite, if possible, one of the thousand favours and kindnesses of your Majesty, but my husband is an old man and has many ailments of body. While his heart would desire it, still he is too old to enter upon the duties of office, and so make some small return. I, too, am feeble and am already a neighbour of the spirit world, so that I could not serve as palace-woman even to do menial labour. What can we possibly do to show our gratitude for the kindness heaped upon us by your Imperial Majesty? The only way I know is to let the grateful tears fall as rain." She arose and bowed again, and then prostrated herself and wept till her sleeves were soiled with tear-drops.

The Empress, moved with pity, sighed and said: "Since Blossom is now my daughter your ladyship must never take her away."

The lady Cheung replied: "How could I think of taking her away from you? But the fact that we cannot meet together and speak the praises of all your Majesty's worth is my only disappointment."

Here the Dowager laughed and said: "Before the marriage ceremony she may not go out, but after that, of course, she may go. Do not be anxious about that. After the wedding Princess Orchid shall be put into your care, too, and you must look upon her just I do upon Blossom." She called Orchid that she and lady Cheung should meet again. The lady Cheung several times spoke of her regrets at the way in which she had received the Princess when she came to call at her home.

The Empress said: "I have heard that you have among your waiting-maids a little one called Cloudlet; I should like very much to see her."

The lady then summoned Cloudlet, who came in and made her bow before her Majesty.

The Empress said to herself: "Beautiful she is!" She made her come up close beside her, and then said to her: "I have heard Orchid say that you are very skilful with the pen. Will you not write something for me?"

Cloudlet said: "How could so ignorant a person as I dare to write before your High Majesty? But I shall try to do my best as you command me."

The Empress opened up the four verses that had already been written and said: "Can you equal these?"

Cloudlet then brought her ink and pens and with one swift dash wrote her verse and handed it to the Empress Dowager. It read:

"This magpie heart of mine
  Awakes to joys untold,
Shall join the circle superfine,
  And both its wings unfold.
Ye pretty flowers of Chin,
  Behold the wondrous sight,
A group of fairies gathering in
  From all their scattered flight."

The Empress read it, showed it to the two Princesses, and said: "I heard before that the lady Ka had great skill, but who would have dreamed of this?"

Princess Orchid remarked: "In this verse she likens herself to the magpie and us to the 'circle superfine.' She has caught the spirit of the old masters and reminds one of the songs of the Book of Poetry. Her thought is pretty but she has stolen it from the ancients. They say 'The birds of heaven find rest with man, and man is naturally sorry for the birds,' and this suggests Cloudlet."

The Princess again said: "The chief of the waiting-maids is Chin See from Wha-eum, the one who decided to live and die with Cloudlet."

Cloudlet replied: "Is this not Chin See who wrote the willow-song?"

Chin See gave a start and asked: "From whom did you ever hear of my willow-song?"

Cloudlet made answer: "General Yang has ever had you in his thoughts, and once when he repeated this verse I overheard him."

Chin See, with a sorrowful countenance, said: "And so General Yang has not forgotten me?"

Cloudlet replied: "How can you suggest such a thing? The General carried hidden away with him these verses of yours, and when he read them the tears used to flow. When he sang them he sighed. How is it that you alone fail to know his loving heart?"

Chin See said: "If the General has the same love that he used to have, then this humble person, though she never see him again, can die happy." Then she told of his verse that had been written on her silken fan, and Cloudlet said: "The hairpins and rings that I wear were won for me on that day."

Then the maids-in-waiting gathered and reported, saying: "The lady Cheung is about to take her departure."

The two Princesses went in and waited upon her, while the Empress Dowager said to the lady Cheung: "In a little time Yang the Wanderer will make his return and the former marriage gifts will naturally be sent once again; but to receive the gifts again that were once sent back would seem poor and mean. On the other hand, Princess Blossom having become my daughter, I want to have the two of them send theirs at one and the same time. Will your ladyship give consent? "

Then the lady Cheung bowed low to the earth and said: "How can your humble subject dare to do otherwise? Let it be as your Imperial Majesty suggests."

The Dowager laughed: "General Yang has for the sake of Blossom more than three times refused to do my bidding, and now I want to play a practical joke on him. They say in common speech: 'The unpropitious word turns out to be propitious.' You shall wait till he returns and then say that Cheung See has suddenly fallen ill and died. I saw in the General's letter that he had met her in a dream. On the first day of the ceremony I shall be amused to see if he will know her or not."

The lady Cheung received the command, took her departure, and returned. The daughter saw her beyond the first palace entrance, and then bowed and spoke her farewell. She called Cloudlet and told her secretly of the plan to deceive the General. Cloudlet replied: "I have been a fairy and I have been an evil spirit to deceive him, and that is surely enough. Would it not be mean of me to attempt anything more?"

Cheung See replied: "This is not our plan, or our affair, but the Empress Dowager's."

Cloudlet smothered her laughter and went away smiling.

At this time General Yang had made his soldiers drink the waters of the White Dragon Lake till their health returned and they longed for battle. The General then summoned his aides, gave them their orders and made them march forth at the sound of the drum. Just at this moment Chan-bo received the gem sent by the dancer Swallow, and knowing that General Yang's troops had passed Pan-sa valley, he approached the General's headquarters in a state of great fear and talked of surrender. The various leaders of the Tibetan forces took Chan-bo, bound him, entered General Yang's camp and there surrendered.

Once again Yang drew his troops up in order and marched into the capital, stopped the plundering of the city, and quieted the people. He then went up into the Kolyoon Mountains and put up a memorial tablet with a record of the power and goodness of the kingdom of the Tangs. Then he faced about with his army, sang his songs of victory, and returned home. When he reached Chin-joo it was already autumn; the mountains were bare and the earth dry and sear. All the flowers had been baptised in death and sorrow. The wild geese piped out their sad notes, reminding him that he was far away from home.

The General spent the night in a guest house. His mind seemed unrested and the hours long. Sleep failed him. He thought in his heart: "It is already three years since I left home and my mother's health cannot be as it has always been. To whom can she turn for protection and care in sickness? To what time shall I put off my morning and evening salutations to her? To-day the land is quiet, war has ceased, but my desire to wait on and serve my mother is not yet satisfied. I have failed in the serious part of life's duty and man's first requirement. For several years I have been busy with State affairs, have not married, and have found it difficult to hold my engagement with Cheung See. The various matters in which I have been disappointed proved the truth of the old saying: 'Eight or nine times out of ten comes disappointment.' Now I have quieted five thousand *li* of territory, and have received the surrender of a million rebels, so that my name will be heralded abroad as great. His Majesty will doubtless appoint me to some high office as a reward for my many labours. If I decline office and ask instead that my request to marry Cheung See be granted, I wonder if consent will be forth-coming?"

Sad were his thoughts, and thus did his mind seek relief, so he laid his head upon his pillow and fell asleep. In a dream his body took wing and flew up to heaven. From the Palace of the Seven Precious Things,[40] that shone with glittering splendour and was encircled with clouds of glory, two waiting-maids came out to meet him and said: "Cheung See is calling for your Excellency."

So the General followed them and entered. In the wide court the flowers were in bloom. Three fairies were seen seated in an upper pavilion of white marble. Their dresses were like those of the waiting-maids of the palace and their eyebrows lined off with soft touches of the fairy's wand. Their eyes were luminous and a halo of light encircled their forms. They leaned upon the railing and dallied playfully with each other, having in their hands buds of fragrant flowers. When the General entered they rose from their seats, made way for him, and when he was seated the leading fairy asked:

"Since your Excellency said good-bye have you been well all the time?"

The General rubbed his eyes and looked peeringly, and lo! it was the lady who had talked to him about the tunes on the harp, Cheung See. In fear and gladness he tried to speak, but the words refused to come. The fairy then said: "Since I have departed

---

40   *Seven Precious Things.* First, the full moon; second, lovely ladies; third, horses; fourth, elephants; fifth, the guardians of the treasury; sixth, great generals; seventh, wonder-working pearls.

from the world of men and have come to dwell in heaven with its delights, I find that all that has happened belongs to my former existence. Though your Excellency meet and see my parents you will find no news from me awaiting you." And she pointed to the two fairies at her side, saying: "This is the Weaving Damsel and the other is the Incense Angel. They are united to you by the affinity of the world life. Please do not think of me any more but think only of them. If you are joined first to them by the happy contract, I, too, will find a place of consolation."

The General looked at the two fairies, and the one who sat on the lower seat was known to him, but he could not recall her name. Suddenly the drum sounded and he awoke, and it was only a dream.

He thought over what he had seen, and he realised that it was not a happy omen, so he sighed and said: "Cheung See is surely dead; if not why should I have had so unpropitious a dream?" Again he thought: "On the other hand, if we think specially of a thing we dream of it; perhaps, because of my thinking so much of her, I have so dreamed. Moonlight's recommendation, and the priestess Too-ryon's serving as go-between, were, I am sure, according to the leading of the Mother of the Moon. If our pre-destined affinity be not attained to, and if the living and the dead are thus to contradict each other, then surely God must be uncertain and ignorant of the laws that rule. It is said that the unlucky omen becomes the lucky. I wonder if that will find fulfilment in this dream of mine?"

After a prolonged march the leading forces reached the capital and the Emperor came out as far as the River Wee to meet and welcome him. The General, wearing a green helmet with phoenix plume ornaments, and gilded armour, rode a Persian war-horse, and there were banners and battle-axes in front, behind, and extending out on each side of him. King Chan-bo was drawn along in a cage in advance of him, while thirty-six princes of Tibet, each bearing his tribute, followed in the rear. The majesty of the sight was something never before seen. Onlookers lined each side of the road for a hundred *li*, and within the walls of the capital there was a deserted city.

The General dismounted from his horse and bowed low, while the Emperor took him by the hand, raised him up, and spoke kindly to him concerning all his hard labours; praised him for his great success, and for the merit he had won. He then had an order issued similar to that which related to Kwak Poon-yang, of ancient times, appointing to him a certain district of territory and making him a king with great and rich rewards.

These the General emphatically and sincerely declined. Finally the Emperor yielded and issued a special order making Yang the Wanderer Generalissimo, and creating him Prince of Wee. The remaining gifts and presents were so many that it is impossible to record them.

General Yang then followed the Imperial car, entered the palace and gave thanks for all the favours and rewards showered upon him.

The Emperor, in response, gave command that a great feast celebrating peace should be prepared, and that the gifts and prizes should be displayed before those assembled. He ordered, also, that Yang's portrait should be given a place in the Temple of Famous Men.

The General then withdrew from the palace and betook himself to the home of Justice Cheung. There he found all the family and relatives gathered in the outer rooms. They met him, bowed before him, and offered him their congratulations. When he had inquired for the Justice and her ladyship, Thirteen made reply: "Uncle and aunt were holding out well until after my cousin's death. They were so heart-broken and distressed over that that they have fallen ill, and their strength is not what it used to be. That is the reason they do not come out to the outer court to greet you. My wish is that you let me go in with you to the inner quarters."

The General, when he heard this, behaved as if he were mad or drunk and could make no intelligent inquiry. After the lapse of some time he returned to consciousness and inquired: "Who is dead?"

Thirteen made answer: "My uncle never had a son; he had one daughter only, and God's way with him has been very hard indeed. Thus has he arrived at this condition. Is it not pitiful? When you go in please do not say anything about it."

Then Yang gave a great shudder, and overcome by untold distress could scarcely get his breath or utter a syllable. Tears streamed from his eyes.

Thirteen comforted him, saying: "Even though your marriage contract was made firm as rocks and tempered steel, still the luck of this house is so unpropitious and bad that it has turned out otherwise. I hope that you will do the right thing and exercise yourself to comfort the old people."

Yang wiped away his tears, thanked him, and they went in together to the Justice and the lady Cheung. They were seemingly happy over the congratulations poured out upon Yang, and made no reference to the fact that their daughter was dead.

Yang said to them: "Your humble son-in-law, by good fortune and with the prestige of the State behind him, has fallen heir to great gifts from his Imperial Majesty. I had just declined these with the one earnest request that his Majesty should change his mind and let me fulfil the marriage contract that I had entered upon, but already the dew of the morning has dried up and the colours of the springtime have faded. How can life and death overtake one thus without breaking the heart?"

The Justice said in reply: "Life and death are wrapped in destiny; gladness and sorrow, too, aid destiny and are the appointments of God. What is the use of talking about or discussing them? To-day the whole household has met for a great celebration; let us not talk of anything that grieves or is sad." Thirteen frequently made signs and winks in the direction of Yang so that he ceased to say anything more about the matter, but went out into the park.

Cloudlet came down the steps to meet him, and when he saw her it was like seeing the daughter. Grief overcame him once more and his tears began to fall.

Cloudlet knelt down and comforted him, saying: "Why should your Highness be sad to-day? I humbly beg of you to set your mind free, dry your tears and hear what I have to say. Our maiden was originally a fairy from heaven, who was sent to earth for a little period of exile, and the day she returned home to heaven she said to your humble servant: 'You, too, must cut yourself off from General Yang and follow me. Since I have already departed from the world of men, if you were to go back to General Yang it would mean leaving me. One of these days he will return home, and should he think lovingly of me or sorrow at my loss you must give him this message: "The sending back of the wedding gifts indicated my departure. How much more the resentment that I felt over the hearing of the harp. Do not be too sad or anxious. If you sorrow overmuch for me it will mean opposition on your part to the Emperor's command, and a desire to do your own will. It will mean damage to the one who is dead. Besides, if you should pour out a libation at my grave or go there to wail it would proclaim me as a girl whose life had not been correct and would distress my soul in hades. This too I will add: his Majesty will await your return and will again make proposals of your marriage with the Princess. I have heard it said that Kwan-jo's dignity and virtue were a fitting mate for the superior man. My hope is that you will willingly accede to the command of the Emperor, and not fall into rebellion." Tell him this, will you.' This is what she said," added Cloudlet.

The General on hearing it was greatly overcome and said: "Even though the dear girl's wishes were such, how can I be without sorrow? To know that she thought thus of me at the last moment makes me feel that though I die ten times I can never repay so great a devotion as hers."

Then he told the dream he had had in the camp and Cloudlet wept and said: "Doubtless she dwells with God before the altar of Incense, and, when your Excellency has lived out your years on earth, you will meet again and fulfil your happy contract. Do not sorrow, please, or injure your health."

Yang asked: "Did she say anything beyond this?" Cloudlet made answer: "She did say something to herself, but I dare not repeat it with my lips."

"What you heard," said the General, "you must tell me now and make no concealment."

Then Cloudlet said: "The young lady said finally to me, 'You, Cloudlet, and I, are one and the same person. If his Excellency does not forget me and desires you as he desires me, and does not throw you away even though I descend into the earth, it will be as though I were blessed and loved of him.'"

Yang was greatly moved by this, and said: "How could I ever think of putting you away, my Cloudlet? How much the more now with the dear one's wishes so expressed. Though I should marry with the Weaving Damsel or be wedded to the Water Fairy, I would never, never put you away."

THE CLOUDY DREAM LAND: CLOUDLET'S SORROW

CHAPTER XIII
THE AWAKENING

THE day following, the Emperor called General Yang and said to him: "In regard to the marriage of the Princess, the Empress Dowager issued a very urgent command that at first quite distressed me, but learning later that the daughter of Justice Cheung was dead, and that the Princess's wedding had waited long for your return, I feel that, even though your thoughts be with Cheung See, the dead are the dead, and no power on earth can restore them. You are a young man and belong to the highest rank and therefore need a wife. How can you yourself see to such matters as food and dress? A minister, too, of your standing while he holds office ought not to remain unmarried. You are also Lord and Prince of Wee, and at the ancestral grave need your wife to pour out the second libation which ought not to be lacking from the sacrifice. I have already made the necessary preparations within the Palace and am now awaiting the decision. Do you still oppose the request, and refuse to marry the Princess?"

Yang bowed low and said: "My sins of rebellion merit that I fall under the headsman's axe, but your Majesty has granted me a second opportunity and has so kindly dealt with me, that I am moved to accede and act as though I were fearless of all presumption. My repeated refusals, heretofore, were because of my regard for the laws of honour, and I could not help myself; but now that Cheung See is dead, why should I offer any objection, except to say this, that my social standing is insufficient for it, my gifts are mediocre, and I am in no way suited to be the Imperial son-in-law."

His Majesty, highly delighted, at once issued an order to the Master of Ceremonies to have a lucky day selected and reported, and later the Chief Geomancer announced the fifteenth day of the ninth moon as the day agreed upon.

The Emperor said to General Yang: "The other day, when we had not fully decided about the wedding, I did not tell you all, but now that this is settled I want to say that I have two sisters, both refined and highly gifted, and since we can never possibly find such another one as thee, I have been commanded by the Dowager to have my two sisters put under your care."

Suddenly General Yang remembered the dream that he had had in the guest-room of the camp, and his mind was greatly disturbed when he thought how unearthly it was. He bowed low and said:

"Since you have chosen me as the Imperial son-in-law, I have tried to make my escape by all possible means, but could find no way; I have endeavoured to run off but the road has been blocked. I did not know what to do, and now your proposition that two Princesses should serve this one man is something never dreamed of since the world began. How can I venture to accept any such proposal?"

The Emperor replied: "Your service for the State is of the very highest order, and there is no possible way open to reward you as you deserve. That is why I propose that my two sisters should serve you together. Also the love of these two for one another is a born instinct with them. When they rise each follows the other; when they are seated each finds support in the other; and their one wish is never, never to part, so that their being given in marriage to the same man is not only their own desire, but the wish of her Majesty the Dowager as well. Please do not refuse it. Also there is the palace-maid, Chin See, a daughter of a house that has been for generations high in office. She has beauty, too, and ability, and is specially gifted with the pen, while the Princess regards her as her good right hand, and treats her as her very own. On the day of the wedding she desires to make her her married maid-in-waiting, and this too I am to inform you of."

The General again rose and expressed his thanks.

Cheung See had already been a Princess in the palace for several days. Her service on the Empress's behalf had been performed with all her heart. She, along with Princess Orchid and Chin See, were like born sisters, and in return the Dowager loved her dearly.

The time for the marriage being now at hand she said quietly to the Empress: "At first when you decided the place of precedence

THE WEDDING: WILDGOOSE AND MOONLIGHT

for Orchid and me, you made me sit in the upper seat, which was a very presumptuous thing on my part, and yet to refuse it I feared might wound the love and tenderness of my dearest Orchid. So I yielded, and did as your Majesty commanded me; but this was never my wish or desire. Now when we are united to General Yang, it will never do for Orchid to decline the first place. My desire is that your Majesty and the Emperor will kindly think of the proper form and arrange it so that I shall be happy according to my station, and not be a cause of confusion in the home."

At this Orchid replied: "Blossom's accomplishments and ability make her my superior, my teacher, and though it be a 'gate of honour' in question, I shall, just as the wife of Cho Che-wee resigned her place, resign mine. Since we have already become elder and younger sisters, how can we again raise the question of rank? Though I become the second wife I shall still not lose the reality that I am the Emperor's daughter, but if I am pushed up to the first place, wherein, mother dear, will lie the purpose of your adopting Blossom? If my sister declines in my favour, I shall not wish then to become a member of General Yang's household."

Then the Empress said to the Emperor: "How shall we decide the matter?"

The Emperor's reply was: "Orchid's wish, as she expresses it, is from the heart; and yet from ancient days till the present time, I never heard of such a thing. Please take note, however, of her humble and beautiful spirit and yield to her on the matter."

The Empress replied: "You are right." At once she issued a command making Princess Blossom[41] the left hand wife of Prince Wee, while Princess Orchid was made the right hand wife, and because Chin See was the daughter of a high official she was made the highest wife of second grade.

Since ancient times the marriage of a Princess had always been celebrated outside of the palace, but on this occasion the Dowager decided that it should be held within the Imperial precincts.

When the happy day came, General Yang, dressed in Imperial robes and jewelled belt, went through the ceremony with the two Princesses. The splendour and magnificence of the scene are

41   *The left hand.* While in the East the right hand is really the place of honour if we judge by evidences of antiquity, still in ordinary usage the left comes first. In the marriage here mentioned, Princess Blossom takes precedence of Princess Orchid.

impossible to describe. When all the rites were completed they sat themselves down on the embroidered cushions, and Chin See appeared, made her bow and was led before the Princesses. When they were seated, lo! they were like three fairies gathered before him. The colours that bedecked them reflected the brilliance of the clouds; and lights and shades were seen in a thousand shimmering patterns. The General was dazed by the brilliance of it, and uncertain of his own consciousness. He wondered if he were amid realities or in a dream.

That night he shared the room of the Princess Blossom and arose early in the morning and made his obeisance to the Empress.

She had a great feast spread, at which both the Emperor and the reigning Empress were present, and the whole day was spent in rejoicing. The second night he spent with Princess Orchid, and on the third he went to Chin See's room.

When Chin See saw him she began to weep.

Yang in wonder asked what she meant: "To-day we should laugh and be glad, why do you weep? What do these tears mean?"

Chin See made answer: "You do not know me, and so I know you have forgotten who I am."

Then he suddenly recollected, took her white hand in his, and said: "You are Chin See from Wha-eum, are you not?"

Chin See choked up with tears and could make no reply.

The General said: "I thought that you had left us, and that you were buried beneath the sod, but here you are in the Palace. We parted in far off Wha-eum, and your dear home was broken up so that no one dared to speak of it. Since my flight from that inn, not a day has passed that I have not thought of you. But I thought you were dead and never imagined that we should meet again. To-day comes the fulfilment of our contract, which I never dreamed could come to pass."

Here he drew from his pocket the verses that Chin See had written, while Chin See drew from her bosom what he had sent her, and they were the same as they had despatched to each other on that day of first acquaintance. Each unwrapped the piece of paper, and their hearts melted at the sight of it and beat a tattoo in their bosoms.

Chin See said: "The Willow song seals the contract that we

made so long ago. I did not know that a little silken fan, too, was to be evidence of the union that is consummated to-day." Then she opened a lacquer box and took out the fan, showed it to General Yang, and told him about it, saying: "It is due entirely to the kindness and favour of her Imperial Majesty, the Empress Dowager, his Majesty the Emperor, and Princess Orchid."

General Yang said: "At that time I made my escape to the South Mountain and when I came back I asked of your whereabouts. Some said you were attached to the palace; some that you had been removed to a distant county as a *yamen* slave; others that you had not escaped from the general destruction. I did not know the exact truth, but I had no hope and so was compelled to seek marriage elsewhere. Always when I passed Wha-eum or crossed the waters of the Wee I was like the wild bird that had lost its mate. Now, however, through the Imperial kindness, we meet again. My one sorrow of heart is that the contract we made by the way in the inn should have turned out the contract for a sub-ordinate wife. To think also that you should have condescended to take so humble a place fills me with shame."

Chin See said: "I was not unaware of my ill-starred home and its prospects when I sent the old nurse to the inn, and it was with the thought that if you took me it might be even as a subordinate wife. Now that I have won a place, second only to my revered Princesses, I am crowned with glory and blessed with the highest of good fortune. If I should complain or be ungrateful, God would be displeased with me."

The joy of meeting Chin See with old faith and new love was very great.

The day following, the Master and Princess Orchid met in Blossom's room, and as they sat together the wine glass was passed. Suddenly Princess Blossom gently summoned a waiting-maid to call Chin See. When the Master heard her voice there was awakened in his heart a sense of loss and sorrow that at once showed itself in his face. On the occasion when he visited Justice Cheung's and played the harp before the maiden he had heard her comments on the tunes, and he remembered her face distinctly, and now to-day the Princess's accents seemed as though they were a voice that came from Cheung See. He had heard the voice and now that he glanced up to see the face, the voice was not only Cheung See's but the face was Cheung See's as well.

He thought to himself: "In this world it happens sometimes that those who are not sisters, and in no way related, look exactly alike. When I made a contract of marriage with Cheung See I decided in my heart that it was for life and death, and now here am I enjoying the delights of home felicity while poor Cheung See's lonely spirit is wandering I know not where. To avoid making myself conspicuous, I have not poured out even a single glass as an offering at her grave; nor have I once even wept in the little hut by her tomb. I have indeed treated dear Cheung See very, very unkindly."

The thoughts in his heart showed themselves in his face, and the tears were ready to come. Cheung See, with her clear and quick perception, guessed the sorrow that possessed him, and so caught her skirts neatly about her and knelt to ask: "I have heard that if the king is dishonoured, the courtiers should die; and that if the king is anxious it is a discredit to his ministers. My service to my lord is like that of a courtier to his king. I notice with anxiety that even now when the glass is passed a hidden shade of disappointment crosses my master's face. May I ask the reason?"

The Master thanked her and said: "There is no reason why I should conceal from your Highness the thoughts that trouble my soul. I, So-yoo, once went to Justice Cheung's home and there I saw his beautiful daughter. Her voice was your Highness's voice, and her face was your Highness's face, and so my eyes, spellbound by you, call up these recollections and fill my soul with sorrow. I regret that I have given you cause for anxiety. Please do not be troubled or disappointed with me."

When Blossom heard this her cheeks suddenly blushed crimson. She arose and hurried into the inner chamber and did not come out again.

The Master sent a waiting-maid to invite her, but still she did not come.

Princess Orchid said: "My sister is so greatly loved of our mother, that her head has been turned and her heart has grown proud over it. She is not lowly in her disposition as I am, so that the Master's comparing Cheung's daughter with her has made her very indignant."

Yang then asked Chin See to beg forgiveness for him and say to
Princess Blossom that he was intoxicated at the time and so said
what he regretted. "If she will please come out I will do as Prince
Chin Moon did and request that she put me in prison."

After a long time Chin See returned but had nothing to say.

The Master asked again: "What does her Highness say?"

Chin See replied: "Her Highness is very angry. What she says
is too dreadful to be repeated."

The Master said: "Her Highness's dreadful words are her own,
and no fault of yours; tell me exactly what she said."

Chin See then made reply: "Princess Blossom says, 'Even
though I am contemptible and mean, I am the Dowager's much-
loved child. This girl, Cheung See, even though she be so wonderful, is only a common village maid. It says in the Book of
Ceremony that men even bow before the King's horse. That does
not mean that they reverence horses in general, but that they reverence what his Majesty rides. If they reverence even the King's
horse, should they not reverence the daughter whom her Majesty
loves? If the Master truly reverences the King and reveres the
court he can hardly compare me with the daughter of a plebe-
ian. Moreover this daughter of Cheung, forgetful of common
modesty, and presuming on her knowledge, met the Master face
to face and talked with him, yes and argued with him over the
tunes he played. She can hardly be called superior. One can read
from this the sort of character she was. She worried herself, too,
over the delay in her wedding till she brought on "impatient"
sickness, and died in her youth. When her fortunes have turned
out so unhappily, why should the Master compare her with me?

"'In ancient days in the Kingdom of No, Chin Ho, by means
of gold, tried to tempt an honest woman who was picking mul-
berries, and she, rather than yield her honour to him, jumped
into the stream and took her own life. Why should I be obliged
to look upon the Master with a shamed face? I do not wish to be
the wife of a man who has no respect for me. Besides, the Master
remembers her face after she is dead and long departed. He thinks
he still recognises her voice in mine. I am outraged by it, and
though I have not the courage to follow the woman of antiquity
and jump into the water, I shall indeed from now on never go
outside the middle gateway, but stay here till I die. As Orchid is

so very meek in her disposition she will suit you. Be pleased to live your life with Orchid, pray.'"

The Master grew very angry at this, and said: "In all the world who ever saw a girl pride herself so on her rank and station and act as Blossom does? You may judge of what this son-in-law is destined to suffer."

He said to Orchid: "My meeting with Cheung's daughter has caused this misunderstanding, and Blossom tries to put upon me some wretched wrong or other. I am not anxious about this myself, but the disgrace of it affects even the dead with shame."

Orchid said: "I will go in and see my sister and explain it to her so that she will understand." And she turned and went in; but to the close of day she did not come out again. Already the lights were trimmed and shining in the rooms.

Orchid sent a waiting-maid to say: "Though I have explained the mistake in every possible way, my sister will not change her mind, and I have been compelled to do as she has done, and decide to live and die with her and share her joy and sorrow. Thus have we sworn to heaven and earth and all the gods. If my sister means to shut herself away alone in the inner palace, I too will do the same and shut myself away. If my sister does not mean to live with the Master, I too cannot live with him. Please let my lord go to his dear wife Chin See and be at peace."

At this Yang's anger flamed up, but still he controlled himself and did not let it show in his words or countenance. The empty curtains and coldly embroidered screens seemed very comfortless to him. He leaned on his reclining bed and looked at Chin See. Chin See took a light and led the way for him to her room, where she cast some dragon incense into the golden brazier. On the ivory couch she arranged the embroidered quilts and pillows and then said to him: "Though I am very dull and stupid still I have read of the Superior Man, and it says in the Book of Ceremony: 'The secondary wife may not appropriate the early hours of the evening.' The two Princesses have retired to the inner palace, but even so I cannot think of being the one to wait upon your Excellency at this time of the night, so shall now retire. May you sleep in peace." And with this she quietly withdrew.

The Master, hating all this disagreeable fuss, let her go for the sake of quiet. The prospect seemed a hopeless one, so he drew the curtains and lay down upon his pillow. Uneasy in heart, he said to himself: "This company forms itself into a league and plays all manner of tricks to befool its lord and master; how can I find any pleasure in praying or supplicating them? When I lived in the park pavilion at Justice Cheung's, Thirteen and I enjoyed ourselves during the happy hours of the day, and Cloudlet and I sat in peace before the lights and passed the glass. Every day was happy, not one failed us; but now that I have come to be the son-in-law of the Imperial Family, three days have scarcely gone by before I am lorded over and my life made miserable."

He drew aside the curtains, opened the windows, and the Milky Way was seen athwart the sky. The light of the moon flooded the open court. He took his shoes and went out, and following the shadow of the eaves, stepped across the square to where he saw in the distance Princess Blossom's room with the lights burning brilliantly behind the illumined blinds.

The Master whispered to himself: "The night is already late; why are they not sleeping I wonder? Blossom is angry with me and has sent me off; I would like to know if she herself has retired."

Fearing lest his shoes might make a noise he stepped lightly and carefully, and at last reached the outside of the window. The two Princesses were talking and laughing together, and the sound of dice was heard within. He peeped in through the chink of the blind, and there was Chin See seated before the two Princesses with another person in front of the dice table who was calling out the numbers. When she turned to trim the candle, behold it was Cloudlet. Cloudlet, desirous of seeing the Princesses' wedding, had already been several days in the palace, but she had concealed her whereabouts so as not to let the Master know.

He gave a sudden start of surprise as he said to himself: "How in the world has Cloudlet come to be here? Evidently the Princesses must have invited her."

Once again Chin See arranged the dice board and said: "You have put down no wager, and so evidently you are not interested in the game. I will make a bet with you, Cloudlet."

Cloudlet said: "Cloudlet is only a poor low-class girl; one dish of sweets would be a fortune for her. But Chin See has for ages been at the side of the Princess; she would look on silks and satins as rough sackcloth and would regard the daintiest fare as common seaweed. How can you propose to me to make a wager?"

Then Chin See said: "If I do not win I'll give whatever you select from the gems at my waist-belt, or from the pins in my hair; but if you don't win then you must give me what I ask. Truly it will only be very little and something that will cost you nothing."

Cloudlet said in reply: "What will you ask, pray, and what would you like to have?"

Chin See said: "I have heard the two Princesses talking together, and I understand from them that you, Cloudlet, once became a fairy, and again became a disembodied spirit, and so befooled the Master. I have never heard about it definitely, so if you lose you must tell me the story."

Cloudlet then pushed away the dice board from her and said to Princess Blossom: "Sister, sister, sister, you told me the other day that you loved me dearly. Why have you reported this ridiculous story to the Princess? Chin See has also heard about it. Everybody in the palace who has ears to hear will know of it. With what face can I meet people?"

Chin See said: "Cloudlet, in what way is the Princess your sister? Blossom is the wife of our lord and Master, and Princess of Wee, and though she is still young, her rank is exceedingly high. How can she possibly be a sister of yours?"

In reply, Cloudlet said: "The lips that have been trained for years cannot change their ways in a single morning. Our happy contests together with flowers and sprigs of green are as yesterday. I am not afraid of her Highness the Princess." And they all laughed together.

Princess Orchid asked of Blossom: "Your sister never fully heard about Cloudlet either. Did she really deceive the Master?"

Blossom said: "The Master has been many times deceived by Cloudlet. How can smoke come from a chimney where there is no fire? She only wanted to see the frightened look in his face, but he was too dense for that and did not know what fear was. It reads in the Book of Ceremony, 'The man who greatly loves women is possessed of a spirit that has died of starvation.' Evidently this is true of the Master. Why should a spirit that has died thus fear another spirit?" And they all burst out laughing.

At last Yang recognised to his amazement that Princess

Blossom was none other than Cheung See. Like meeting one from the dead, and with his startled soul in his mouth, he was about to throw open the window and go violently into the room, when he thought again and said to himself: "Their desire is to play all manner of jokes upon me, so I'll befool them instead." Then he went quietly to Chin See's room and slept soundly.

Early the next morning Chin See came and asked of the waiting-women: "Is the Master up yet?" They replied: "Not yet."

She waited for a long time outside the window till daylight filled the court. Breakfast too was ready, but still the Master slept.

Chin See then went in and asked: "Is your Excellency unwell?"

Suddenly he opened his eyes, stared blankly as though he did not see anyone, but went on talking to himself in a wandering way, so that Chin See asked again: "Master, why do you act so?"

Yang then seemed to hear but made no reply. After a little he asked: "Who are you?"

Chin See answered: "Does the Master not know his wife? I am Chin See."

Yang replied: "Chin See? Who is Chin See?"

She made no further answer but stroked his brow and said: "Your head is very hot, and I am sure you are unwell. What trouble is it that has overtaken you, I wonder?"

The Master replied: "All night long I saw Cheung See in a dream and talked with her. How can I be well?"

Chin See asked him to tell her more fully, but he made no reply and simply turned as if to sleep again.

In a state of great distress, Chin See told a palace-maid to wait on the Princesses and say that the Master was ailing and to please come at once.

When the message was given, Blossom remarked: "One who ate and drank so freely yesterday could hardly be seriously ill to-day. It is only a trick on his part to get us to go to see him."

But Chin See came herself in great anxiety: "The Master is dazed seemingly and unconscious, and does not know anyone, but talks in a wandering way. Would it not be well to inform his Majesty and let the chief physician of the Court be sent for?"

The Dowager overheard them at this point, called the Princesses, and reprimanded them, saying: "You have gone too far in your jesting, you naughty girls. You hear that he is very unwell and yet have not even gone to see him. What kind of treatment is that? Go at once and make inquiry, and if he is very ill, get the most experienced and skilful Court physician called and see that he is cared for."

Blossom now finding that there was no help for it, went with Orchid to the room where the Master slept and waited for a little at the threshold of the door. She made Orchid and Chin See go in first.

The Master looked at Orchid, waved his two hands, and gazed into space as though he did not know her. Then he whispered: "My life is going and I want to take a long farewell of Blossom. Where is Blossom that she does not come?"

Orchid replied: "Why does the Master say such things?"

He answered: "Last night, in a vision, Cheung See came to me and said, 'Master, why have you broken your vow?' and then in great anger she up-braided me and gave me a handful of pearls. I took and swallowed them. Assuredly this was a dreadful omen, for when I shut my eyes Cheung See seems to hold my body down, and when I open them she stands before me. Life is but a moment at best, and that is my reason for desiring to see Blossom."

Before he had finished speaking an apparent faintness came over him, and he turned his face to the wall and talked at random.

When Orchid saw this she was alarmed and came out and said to Blossom: "I am afraid that the Master's illness is due to worry and anxiety. Without you there is no hope of his recovery." And she told just how he seemed.

Blossom, half inclined to believe, and half inclined to doubt, hesitated to go in, but Orchid took her by the hand and they went in together. They found Yang talking incoherently in a conversation that he seemed to be having with Cheung See.

Then Orchid in a loud voice said: "Master, Master, Blossom has come; please look at her."

He raised his head for an instant, waved his hand about several times as though he wished to get up, then Chin See took hold and helped him. He sat on the side of the couch and speaking to the two Princesses said: "I, So-yoo, have abused the grace of God and have been married to you two Princesses. I have sworn my vow that for all time to come I will live and grow old with you, but there is one whose purpose it is to arrest and bear me away, so I cannot long remain."

Blossom said in reply: "Master, you are a gentleman of intelligence and reason. Why do you talk such nonsense? Even though Cheung See's frail soul and dead spirit do exist, this inner palace is so closely guarded by a hundred angels, who serve as its protecting force, that she could never enter here."

The Master replied: "Cheung See was just now at my side; how can you say that she could not enter?"

Then Orchid answered: "The ancients saw in the wine glass the shadow of a bow, and fell ill of fear. I am sure that the Master's illness is because he has mistaken the archer's bow for a serpent."

But the Master made no reply, simply waving his hands. Blossom, seeing that the matter grew gradually worse and worse, did not longer dare to keep up the deception. She went forward, knelt down, and said: "Master, do you want to see only the dead Cheung See and not the living?"

Yang, pretending that he did not understand, replied: "What do you mean? Justice Cheung had one daughter only, and she has been dead for a long time. Since the dead Cheung See visited me, what living Cheung See can there be beside her? If she is not dead, why she is alive? If she is not alive, why she is dead? Anybody knows that. To say sometimes of anyone, 'Why they are dead?' and again sometimes 'Why they are alive?' is nonsense. One must inquire whether the dead person is really Cheung See, or whether the living person is really Cheung See. If it is true that she is really alive then it is false that she is dead; and if it is true that she is really dead then it is false to say that she is alive. I cannot understand what your Highness says."

Orchid then broke in: "Her Majesty the Dowager adopted Cheung See as her daughter and made her Princess Blossom, and put her and me together in the Master's service. Princess Blossom is indeed the same Cheung See who listened when you played the harp. If not so, why should she be in every look and feature the exact image of Cheung See?"

The Master made no reply but gave a little moan and then suddenly raised his head and said: "When I lived at Cheung See's home, Cheung See's maid Cloudlet waited upon me. I have something that I want to ask of Cloudlet. Where is she now? I want to see her."

Orchid said: "Cloudlet just now came into the palace to see

Blossom, and learning that the Master was unwell, she is anxiously waiting outside and wants to make her salutations."

The door opened and Cloudlet entered. She went up to the Master and said: "Are you better, my lord? I certainly hope so."

Yang replied: "Let Cloudlet stay by me alone, and let all the others go out." And so the Princesses and Chin See withdrew and stood at the head of the open porch.

Then the Master arose, washed, arranged his dress and told Cloudlet to call the other three.

Then Cloudlet, bottling up her smiles, came out and said to the two Princesses and to Chin See: "The Master wants to see you," and so the four went in.

Yang now wore a ceremonial robe and special hat, and held in his hand a white stone chatelaine. His face was fresh as the spring breezes, and his mind as clear as the autumn stream. Not a vestige was there of anything that would mark him as ill. Blossom suddenly realised that she had been fooled, laughed and bowed low, making no further inquiries as to his health.

Orchid asked: "How is your lordship feeling now?"

The Master, with a serious countenance, said: "Truly we have fallen on peculiar days when the women of a household band together to play practical jokes upon the husband. I am a man of high rank, of the dignity of a first minister, and I have sought high and low for some way by which to correct this disorder in my family but have not succeeded. In my anxiety I fell ill, but I am quite recovered now, so do not be anxious, please."

Orchid and Chin See laughed with all their might but made no reply, and then Cheung See said:

"This was not our doing, please. If the Master would find full recovery from his sickness let him look up to the Empress Mother and tell her."

Yang could no longer restrain his pent-up feelings, but broke out laughing and said: "I had expected to meet you only in the next world and had so planned, but to-day you were in my dream. Is it not truly a beautiful dream?"

Cheung See said: "It is all due to her Gracious Majesty's kindness to me her child, and to the unbounded favour of his Majesty the Emperor, and the love and tenderness of Princess Orchid. It is written on my bones and engraved deep in my heart. Never can my life be able to speak all my remembered gratitude." Then she told him everything that had come to pass, and he thanked her, saying: "The equal of your dear-heartedness has never been recorded since time immemorial. I have no way to make any return for this highest favour. My sincerest regards and tenderest love shall all be yours while we live our happy life together."

The Princess then spoke her thanks, saying:

"This is all due to my dearest sister's plans, and it is her heart of love that has moved heaven to bless us. It was no work of mine."

At this time the Empress Dowager summoned some of the palace-maids to inquire concerning the Master's health, and when she knew the reason for it she laughed heartily and said: "I was indeed in doubt regarding it." So she summoned Yang to her presence and the two Princesses came as well and sat together with him.

The Empress said: "I hear that the Master has united again the happy bonds that bound him to his dead Cheung See."

Yang bowed and made answer: "Your Majesty's kindness is great as high heaven; though I wear down my body and offer up the vitals of my soul I can never pay the hundredth part of all the favours you have shown me."

The Empress said: "That is all a joke; why do you talk of such nonsense?"

On this day the Emperor received audience of the ministers in the Grand Hall of the palace. Certain of them said: "We learn that a great star has arisen; that sweetened dew has fallen; that the waters of the Whang-ho have become clear; that the crops have grown to abundance. Three subject kings have offered their land as tribute; the fierce Tibetan rebels have changed in heart, and now bow in grateful submission. This is due to the virtues of your Majesty."

The Emperor graciously disclaimed merit and put it all to the credit of his ministers.

But they made reply, saying: "General Yang So-yoo remains these days long within the palace and affairs of State are heaped up and need looking after."

His Majesty laughed and said: "The Empress Dowager has held him fast these days and so the General is not free to go. I shall tell him myself, however, and see that he gets to work."

The day following the Master went to the home of Justice Cheung to look after some business, and from there he wrote a memorial asking that he be permitted to bring his mother. His memorial read:

"General the Prince of Wee, son-in-law of her Majesty, bows in humble salutation, and presents to his Majesty this memorial. Of humble origin from the land of Cho, I had but two or three fields on which to live. My scholarship embraced only a single set of the Classics. My old mother still lives, but I have not cared for her as I should have liked. I thought of the measures of grain that I would have given her, and of the delicacies that I would have prepared. When it came to parting, my mother said to me, 'Our literatus home has fallen to decay, and the fortunes of the family run low. You are responsible for the future, and the lives of the past are in your keeping. Be diligent and learn; win the examination and let your mother share your renown. This is my hope. But if office or reward come too quickly there is danger in it. Think well of this.'

"I took my mother's word, wrote it in my heart, and never have I forgotten it. Great and good fortune have fallen on me, for only after a few years at Court my rank has risen by leaps and bounds. By Imperial decree I passed others by and made the knees of the rebel to tremble. I received orders to go west and to bind the hands of the fierce Tibetan. To begin with I was but an inexperienced son of the literatus; how could I have ever imagined plans to attain to such as this? It is all due to the prestige of your Majesty. The officers gladly risked their lives and your Majesty so generously encouraged the little efforts that we made, and rewarded them so liberally, that my heart is rendered uneasy and ashamed and I would rather not speak of it. All my mother's wishes on my behalf have come to pass, and I am chosen as the Imperial son-in-law with fortune unheard of. The Imperial command has been so pressing that I could not resist it, and ashamed as I am that the State should be dishonoured by one so mean, I still have had to accede. My aged mother's hopes did not pass at first the peck measure, and my own, too, did not go beyond a humble office of the literati. Behold me now in the highest seat of the land and first among my peers. In the rush and business of the day I have never yet had an opportunity to escort my mother to the capital. I have lived in my beautiful home while she has occupied a thatched hut; I have eaten of dainty fare while she has eaten only of the meanest. Thus am I living in luxury and leaving my mother to poverty and disgrace, disregardful of the fundamental laws and failing in the duty of a son. My mother, too, is old; she has no other child but me, and the distance separating us is great, with messengers few and far between. If I go up to the hills and call on the clouds to bear my greetings they heed not, and so my heart is sore. Now that matters are quiet in the State and affairs are fallen into repose, I humbly pray that your Majesty will kindly consider and grant my request, giving me two or three months so that I may go and replace the sod on my ancestors' graves, and bring my mother here that we may both together praise your Majesty's high and exalted virtue. If you graciously grant me this, I shall in my turn do my best to repay the Imperial kindness. I humbly bow and make this petition, and may your High Majesty please to grant me a favourable answer."

The Emperor read it and sighed, saying: "You are a filial son, Yang So-yoo."

He gave him rich rewards, gold a thousand pieces, eight hundred rolls of silk to be presented to his mother, and the word of command to bring her quickly.

The Master then entered the inner palace and bade farewell to the Empress Dowager. She also gave gold and silk in abundance, twice as much as the Emperor.

Yang then withdrew and bade farewell to the two Princesses, to Chin See and to Cloudlet, and set out on his way. When he reached the Chon-jin Bridge, the two dancing-girls, Moonlight and Wildgoose, having been informed by the Governor, awaited him at the guest-house.

The Master greeted them smilingly and said "This journey of mine is a private one and has no relation to the King's commands; how did you two know of my coming?"

Moonlight and Wildgoose replied: "The Master, Prince of Wee, son-in-law of the Empress, could hardly set out on a journey without its being known to us. From the secluded valleys we hurried forth to meet you. Even though we were in the deep recesses of the hills still we had our ears and eyes; how much the more when the Governor regards us as second only to your Excellency? Last year when you went by in your official capacity we won lasting glory, but now with still higher office, and with honour still greater, our glory will be a hundred-fold enhanced. We have heard that you are married to the two Princesses, and are wondering if they will tolerate us."

The Master replied: "Of the two Princesses, one is sister of the Emperor and one is a daughter of Justice Cheung, who, at the request of the younger Princess, became an adopted daughter of the Empress Dowager. We have Cheung See and her sister's kindly and loving dispositions and liberal spirit to trust; will they not be glad at your happiness?"

At this Wildgoose and Moonlight looked at each other and spoke their thanks and congratulations.

The Master spent the night and then started for his native place. He had left his mother and begun life's journey as a boy of eighteen. Now he was returning, riding in the chair of a Minister of State, wearing the insignia of the Prince of Wee, and having upon him the honours of the Imperial son-in-law. All this had taken place in four short years. Was it not a wonder?

He appeared before his mother, and in her joy she took him by the hands and lovingly patting him said: "Are you truly my boy, So-yoo? I really cannot believe it. When you repeated your cycle years so long ago and began your first lessons in the character, who would have thought that such glory awaited you?"

Her joy passed all limits and her tears flowed.

The Master then told her how he had won his fame, of his marriage, and of the secondary wives that he had.

She replied: "Your father always said of you that you were to bring glory to our home. I am so sorry that he did not live to see it for himself."

Yang visited the ancestral graves on the near hills. The gold and silk that came from the Palace were made ready, and then, on a great feast being given in honour of his mother, he presented these. All the friends and relatives were called, and the rejoicing lasted for ten days. On its completion, in company with his mother, he set out on his return. The officials along the route, with the governors and the magistrates, made their salutations and helped to do honour to his progress. His way glittered with splendour.

When the Master passed Nak-yang he sent word to the magistrate to have Wildgoose and Moonlight called, but the answer came back that they had already left for the capital. Disappointed to miss them, he went on his way and at last reached the Imperial City. Here he led his mother into his home and into the Palace, where she made her deep obeisance. She was commanded to audience and they gave her gold, silver, silks and satins. The ministers and courtiers were invited and for three days a feast was celebrated amid joy and rejoicing.

The Master selected a lucky day and led her to her new home that he had prepared as a gift. It was like a palace with towers, pavilions and parks. Cheung See and Orchid performed the ceremony of the bride before the mother-in-law, and Chin See and Cloudlet also made ceremonial salutations. By abundance of gifts and in gentleness of deportment they showed themselves such that the mother's face shone with joy and her soul was filled with delight.

When the Master came to give all the gifts that he had received for his mother he had three days of feasting again, on which occasion the palace band of music was sent for and tables of food were brought from the Imperial halls that the officials shared.

The Master, dressed in coloured robes and with the two Princesses by his side, raised high his glass, made way for his mother, and then all joined in the chorus. Before the feast broke up the gate guard came in to say that just before the entrance were two girls who had passed in their names for the ladies and the Master.

"Doubtless Moonlight and Wildgoose," said he. He told his mother of them, and she invited them in. They bowed before the step way, and all the guests remarked that Wildgoose from Nak-yang and Moonlight from Ha-book had long been famous, beautiful women, surpassing others.

If the Master had not been a magician how could he have brought all this to pass?

He commanded the two dancing-girls to entertain the guests with special selections, and at once they both arose, put on their dancing shoes, waved their soft silken sleeves and made the bright-coloured folds fly like fluttering birds as they danced together. Their songs were like falling flowers, like the passing of leaves on the spring breezes, like the shadows of clouds rolling across the eave-tops of the city.

The mother and the two Princesses treated the two dancing-girls to the most bounteous gifts; and, as Chin See had been formerly acquainted with Moonlight, they talked of the past with overflowing joy.

Cheung See took up the glass and specially offered it to Moonlight to thank her for her recommendation. But the mother said: "Do you thank Moonlight only and forget my cousin? You will overlook the source of it all if you are not careful."

The Master said: "My joy to-day is due to the priestess Too-ryon, and now, mother, that you have come to the capital, even though no special command is issued, she too must be specially invited to join us. Messengers have been sent to the office to say: 'It is three years since the teacher Too-ryon went to the land of Chok, and the lady Yoo is greatly concerned about her.'"

IN THE FAIRY LISTS: SWALLOW AND WHITE-CAP ENTER

CHAPTER XIV

IN THE FAIRY LISTS

AFTER the arrival of Wildgoose and Moonlight at the Master's home his maids and attendants daily grew greater in number. He appointed to each their particular place of residence. Palaces, halls, galleries and pagodas were called into requisition.

In the palace enclosure there were eight hundred musicians, the most beautiful in the Empire. They were divided into two divisions to east and west. To the east were four hundred of whom Moonlight had charge; and to the east a like number with Wildgoose for overseer. These were taught singing and dancing and were given lessons in music. Each month they all met in the Chong-wha Pavilion and engaged in contests of skill.

The Master, along with his mother, the two Princesses accompanying, would act as judge, give prizes or require forfeits. Each winner would get three glasses of wine and a wreath of flowers for her brow crowning her with glory. The loser was given a glass of cold water and a dot of ink was imprinted on her forehead. This mark was such a disgrace and shame that they laboured to escape it and advanced in skill day by day, so that the musicians of Prince Wee and Prince Wol were the finest in the world.

One day the two Princesses and the other women were in attendance on the mother, when the Master brought a letter to where they were seated and gave it to Princess Orchid, saying: "This is a letter from your brother, Prince Wol."

The Princess opened it and read: "The spring weather is so beautiful, may all blessing and happiness be yours. Heretofore so many affairs of State have engaged you that you have had no leisure. No horsemen have been seen on the Festal Grounds, and no boats have been moored at the head of Kong-myong Lake. The fathers of the city talk of the splendour and life that accompanied the days of Cho and weep over the departed glory of the past with tearful faces. By the grace of the Emperor, and your Excellency's skill, we are at peace on every hand and the people are well content. This is the time to recall the happy days of the past. Spring is not yet too far advanced, the weather is agreeable and the flowers and willow catkins make a man's heart glad. No time is more suitable for an agreeable outing or for sights to see than now. I suggest that we meet on the Festal Grounds and try a spell at the chase and at music, and help the world a little toward the perfection of its joy. If your Excellency will kindly consent to choose a day and let me know, I shall avail myself of the privilege of joining you."

When the Princess had read it she said to the Master: "Do you know what lies behind Prince Wol's thought?"

The Master said: "Why, has he some deep thought or other hidden underneath this? Nothing more, I should think, than an ordinary outing among the flowers and willows. It is the proposal of one who enjoys pleasure."

The Princess answered: "Your Excellency does not understand it fully. Prince Wol likes pretty girls and good music. The prettiest girls in the world are not all in the Palace. Recently one arrived at Prince Wol's, a special favourite, a noted dancing-girl from Mu-chang whose name is Ok-yon. The maids-in-waiting have seen her and lost their hearts to her. They are almost beside themselves, feeling that they are mere nothings and nobodies in comparison. Ok-yon's skill and beauty are without a parallel, and now my brother, Prince Wol, hearing that there are many beautiful women in our home, wants to do as did Wang-kai and Sok-soong in days of yore and have a trial of skill."

"I read it indifferently," said the Master; "your Highness knows his thought better than I do."

Cheung See said: "Even though this is to be a trial of skill entered on but once, let us see to it that our side wins." She nodded to Wildgoose and Moonlight and added: "Though you train soldiers for ten years, yet the trial you put them to may be only for a morning. Our success rests altogether on the skill of you two leaders. Do your best I pray you."

Moonlight made reply: "I am afraid we cannot beat them. Prince Wol's band has the highest reputation in the world; and Ok-yon from Mu-chang is echoed from mouth to mouth through all the Nine Provinces. Prince Wol has already got such an orchestra in hand, and such a skilful performer as she to assist, that I fear that he will be a very difficult opponent to face. With our one-sided small force, unacquainted with the rules that govern a performance like this, I am afraid that before ever the battle begins our people may decide to run off and make their escape. Our own shame is not to be specially thought of, but our family would be put to eternal disgrace."

The Master said: "When I first met Moonlight in the Chong pavilion of Nak-yang, they said that she was the prettiest girl by far, and Ok-yon was there as well. It must be the same person referred to here. When I have Che Kal-yang[42] on my side, why should I fear to meet Hang-oo or Han Pom-jing?"

The Princess said: "In the palace of Prince Wol Ok-yon is not alone the special beauty."

Moonlight added: "In Prince Wol's palace the number of those who paint their faces and put on rouge is like the blades of grass on Pal-kang Mountain. There is no help for it but quickly to make our escape. How can we ever hope to meet them? Please, your Highness, ask Wildgoose to take charge of it; I am a person of such small courage that when I hear anything like this my throat closes up, and I am not able to utter a word."

Wildgoose apparently grew very angry and said: "What do you mean, Moonlight? Is this true? We two have travelled over seventy counties of Kwan-dong and not a noted player was there that we did not hear, and not a single singer that we did not listen to. My knees have never yet bowed to another, why should they yield the first place to Ok-yon? If the ladies of Han were there who upset cities and kingdoms by their beauty, or the fairy maids of Cho, who could at will become clouds and rain, I might possibly be startled, but with only this Ok-yon to face, why should I be anxious?"

Moonlight said: "Wildgoose, you talk as if it were so easy a matter. True, when we were together in Kwan-dong, we took part on many great occasions at which there were magistrates, governors, and nobles present; at lesser ones, too, where there were literati

---

42   *Che Kal-yang.* He is the great Napoleonic leader of China 200 BC. Hang-oo and Pom-jing, who lived shortly before the beginning of the Christian era, were lesser lights in the world of the warrior.

and scholars, but we never once met any capable opponents. Now, however, it is a question of Prince Wol with a critical eye, who has grown up among gems and jewels. He regards great mountains and wide seas as nothing. How can one mistake a small hill the size of the hand or the little stream like a thread of silk for one of these? This is like combating Son-o, or like trying one's strength with Poon-yok. A great general cannot be opposed by a little child; how much less Prince Wol's household by this poor weakling? To beat him lies beyond a hundred miles of probability. How can you look at it so lightly? I see in Wildgoose's boastful word that she has spoken like Cho-kwal, foretelling her own defeat." Then she added, speaking to the Master: "Wildgoose has a boastful spirit; I should like to tell you some of her defects. When she first followed your Excellency she stole one of the fine steeds of the King of Yon, rode it, calling herself a young man from Ha-book, and then from the side of the Hai-tan roadway, along which you were to pass, she greeted you. If Wildgoose be really so graceful and pretty, how was it that your Excellency mistook her for a man? On the first night, too, that she was with you, taking advantage of the darkness, she usurped my place. Yet after all this she says these boastful words."

Wildgoose laughed as she replied: "Truly there's no knowing people's minds. Before I followed your Excellency, Moonlight praised my beauty and looked upon me as Hang-a of the moon, and now she regards me as more worthless than a cash piece. It must mean that you love me better than you love her and she wants to have all your love to herself."

Then Moonlight and the others laughed, and Blossom said: "Since Wildgoose's refinement and delicacy are such, the fact that the Master took her for a boy must be due to his defective eyesight. It is nothing to Wildgoose's credit to be so regarded, for Moonlight's words are true. It is not ladylike to assume the guise of a boy and wear men's clothes; neither would a man's putting on women's clothing to deceive another be considered manly. Because of their weakness and defects in each case they assume a disguise."

The Master laughed and said: "Your ladyship has evidently pointed this joke at me, but I may say in reply that your dear eyes were not bright, for though you could distinguish the different tunes you did not know a man from a woman. This was due to the fact that though you have ears to hear, your eyes are defective in seeing. If one set of faculties is defective, would you call the person perfect? Though you make light of me, still the people who see my picture in the Neung-yoo Pavilion all praise the majesty of its proportions, its strength and its dignity."

Those assembled laughed delightedly when Moonlight went on: "Just now it is a question of falling in and marching out to meet a powerful enemy; why do we sit idly by and waste time? We two alone cannot be fully trusted to win the day. Suppose we have Cloudlet to help us. Since Prince Wol is not an outsider, Cloudlet could have no special objection to seeing him."

Then Chin See said: "If the two, Moonlight and Wildgoose, are to go alone into the arena, I should like to help, but when it comes to singing and dancing what use would I be? If I go I fear Moonlight will never win."

Cloudlet said: "Although I do not excel in dancing and singing, still if the question pertain only to my own person, why should I not have a view of such a gathering as this? But if I should go the people will assuredly point me out and say with smiles: 'Yonder is Prince Wee's wife, second to the Princesses Blossom and Orchid.' Such would mean contempt for the Master, and would prove a source of anxiety to the ladies. I certainly cannot go."

The Princess said: "In what possible way could the Master be dishonoured by Cloudlet's going, or what anxiety could that be for us?"

Then Cloudlet answered: "If we pitch the wide silken awning and the sky-coloured tent, the people will naturally say: 'The General's beloved wife Cloudlet is coming,' and they will rub shoulders and crowd heels, and strive to see and push up for a place, and after all will behold only my ill-starred face and frowzy head, and they will say with amazement: 'General Yang must have disease of the eyes to have chosen such as she for wife'; and will this not be a cause of disgrace to the Master? Prince Wol has never yet set eyes upon a contemptible performer, and if he should see me he would undoubtedly be filled with nausea and be made ill. Will not the two ladies be disgraced likewise?"

The Princess said: "Cloudlet, really your modesty is amazing. Once upon a time you changed from a girl into a spirit; now you want to change from a peerless beauty into a perfect fright. I cannot trust you, Cloudlet, at all." So she referred the matter to the Master, saying: "In your reply what day have you decided upon?"

The Master replied: "We have decided upon to-morrow."

Wildgoose and Moonlight gave a start of dismay, saying: "No orders have as yet been issued to the two divisions of dancing-girls. How can you possibly have it in as short a time?" They then called their leaders together and said: "The Master has appointed a general gathering for to-morrow with Prince Wol at the Festal Grounds, when all the dancing girls of the two divisions are to gather in their best outfits, setting forth at earliest dawn."

Eight hundred dancers heard this command, drew long faces and lifted their eyebrows. But they took their instruments in hand and began to tune up in preparation.

On the next day the Master arose early, dressed in ceremonial robe, took bow and arrows, and mounted his snow-white charger. With three thousand chosen huntsmen to attend him, he passed through the South Gate of the city. Moonlight and Wildgoose, specially dressed and bedecked in gold ornaments and chiselled green stones, and wearing flower embroideries, were in command of the dancers. They rode mounted on beautifully caparisoned horses, seated in gilded saddles, with silver stirrups hanging by the side, and jewelled bridle reins in hand. They raised their coral whips and followed close behind the Master, while eight hundred dancers mounted on beautiful horses brought up the rear.

On the main roadway they met Prince Wol, and lo! he had hunters and musicians enough to equal those of Master Yang.

Thus they rode side by side, when Prince Wol asked of General Yang: "What breed of horse is that you ride, sir?"

The Master. replied: "A Persian horse. It seems to me that the one your Highness rides is the same."

Prince Wol made answer: "Yes, that is so. This horse's name is 'Thousand Mile Cloud Breed.' Last year, in the autumn, while out hunting along with the Emperor, there were over ten thousand horses from the Imperial stables present. There were perfect wild wind flyers among them, but none of them could equal this one. Now Nephew Chang's fast horses and General Yi's black steeds are both said to be specially fine, but compared with mine they could hardly be dignified by the name of horse."

The Master said: "Last year when I led the attack on Tibet over deep and dangerous waters and by precipitous cliffs where a man could not go, this horse walked as freely as if he were on level ground, and never once missed his footing. Any success I had was largely due to this good steed's efficiency. You know Toojami says: 'One in heart with man and equal to him in merit.' He refers to the horse.

"After I had brought back the forces my rank was raised and I laid down office, so that I rode lazily in a palanquin and went softly along the easy way of life till both horse and man were ready to fall ill. Please let us lay on the whip and have a race and see which of these two steeds will win. Let us show the ancients what we can do in the daring field of courage."

Prince Wol was greatly delighted and said: "Those are my sentiments exactly."

Then they ordered the leaders who followed them with the two companies of guests and dancers to wait in the tent pavilion. They were about to lay on the whip when suddenly a huge stag that had been awakened by the hunters dashed past Prince Wol. The Prince called to the two keepers of the seal to shoot. Several let fly their arrows simultaneously, but they all missed, and the Prince, disgusted, dashed forth on his horse and with one shot in the side felled the huge beast. The soldiers shouted: "Long live the Prince."

The Master said: "Your marvellous bow outdoes King Yo-yang."

But the Prince said in reply: "What is there to praise in a little thing like that? I would like to see your Excellency shoot; won't you give me a sample?"

Before he had done speaking, a pair of swans came sailing along in the rifts of the cloud, and the soldiers shouted: "These birds are hardest of all to hit; we must use a Hadong falcon."

The Master said: "Don't disturb them," but carefully fitted an arrow to his bow and let fly, hitting a bird and driving the shaft straight through its head so that it fell before the horses.

The Prince gave a shout of applause and remarked: "Your Excellency's skill is equal to that of Yang-yoo."

Then the two suddenly raised their whips and away they dashed on horseback, like shooting stars, or like devils of the night, with demon flashes of fire accompanying. In an instant they had crossed the wide plain and had scudded up the hill.

The two riders drew rein exactly even. For a time they stood gazing out over the wide expanse and talked of music and archery. Little by little the servants began to approach them, bringing the deer and the swan on bearers, which they offered to the Prince and to the Master.

The two dismounted, sat on the grass, drew the sword that was in the hilt and cut some of the meat, which was cooked and eaten. They passed the glass in mutual congratulation. As they gazed into the distance they saw two red-coated *yamen* servants running towards them at great speed with a host of people following.

One rushed forward to say: "The Emperor and the Empress have sent out refreshments."

The Prince and the Master then returned, went into the pavilion and waited. Two officers of the Court poured out the Imperial wine and ordered two others to bring specially decorated writing paper.

They each took one in hand, knelt down, opened the roll and the subject suggested was "The Hunt," and the command was given to write.

What the Master wrote ran as follows:

> *"In early morning, with all the combatants, off we go,*
> *With glittering swords and arrows like shooting stars.*
> *The tent is filled with the prettiest faces in the land.*
> *In pairs, before the horses, are the keen-eyed falcons.*
> *We unite to taste with grateful hearts the sweet wine of the king,*
> *We draw the glittering sword and cut from the high roast before*
> > *us.*
> *I think of last year, and the wild western hordes,*
> *While I go forth on this happy hunt to-day."*

Prince Wol wrote:

> *"Flying dragons go by us like the lightning,*
> *Fitted to the saddle, and accompanied by the rattling drum.*
> *Swift like shooting stars, like arrows that strike the deer,*
> *Round as the moon, flash the bows and the falling wildgoose*
> > *answers.*

The joy of the hunter rises in the keen zest of the play,
While all faces shine from the royal wines that flow.
Let's no more talk of the fine shots of Yo-yang;
How could he ever equal the feats of this happy day?"

The officials received the compositions, bade farewell and returned within the city, while the two companies of guests sat each in rows and the stewards passed refreshments. Who can tell of the delightful flavour of wine mixed with milk and of the tender lips of the monkey? Fruit was there from Wol, and potatoes from Yong piled high on the green stone platters, and such a banquet none had ever seen even at the Lake of Gems with the Western Queen Mother presiding. One need not speak of gatherings under Moo-jee of Han or of such delicacies or delights ever having been seen before.

Behold the dancers ready, a thousand strong, in ranks three deep with the broad silk awning shading them. The sound of gems and ornaments was like rippling thunder; the slender waists of the dancers were more lithe than the willow; the hundred pretty faces vied with the flowers in freshness and beauty; the sound of harps and flutes surpassed the music of many waters; the singing made the whole South Mountain to tremble.

When the glass was passed Prince Wol said to the Master: "I, your humble servant, have been the recipient of your abundant favour, and there is no way by which I can return my lively appreciation. I want once to make you glad through the maids-of-honour that I have brought with me, so, if you please, I will call them and make them sing and dance before your Excellency."

The Master thanked him and said: "How should your humble servant look upon the ladies of my lord's household, but since we are brothers, bound together by your sister's gracious favour, I shall venture to be so bold. I, too, have my household here who desire to see the celebration, and I shall call upon them to accompany the ladies of your palace, each following the music according to her own special skill, and so add cheer to the occasion."

The Prince replied: "Good, how happy your suggestion is."

Then Moonlight and Wildgoose and four dancers of Prince Wol came forth, and made their obeisance before the dais.

The Master said: "In ancient times King Yong had one famous

dancing-girl whose name was Lotus Bud. Yi Tai-baik earnestly requested King Yong that he might hear her sing, but he never dreamed of asking to see her face. Now I, your humble servant, see all these pretty dancers and behold their beauty, and am therefore blessed many times beyond Yi Tai-baik. What are the names of these four, please?"

The four then advanced and gave answer for themselves, saying: "I am the Cloud Fairy of Keum-neung; I am Hair Pin of Chin-joo; I am Ok-yon of Moo-chang; I am Soft Whinny of Chang-an."

Then the Master remarked to Prince Wol: "When I was a young scholar and travelled from place to place, I heard the famous name of Ok-yon. Now that I see her face to face she far surpasses in beauty the renown that preceded her."

Prince Wol hearing the names of Moonlight and Wildgoose, and recognising them, said: "These two famous women are noted the world over, and now they have become attached to your Excellency's household. They certainly have been very fortunate in the master they have chosen. I wonder where you first met them?"

The Master replied: "Moonlight I met on my way to examination. When I reached Nak-yang she came to me of her own accord. Wildgoose was originally attached to the palace of the King of Yon, but when I went there as envoy she made her escape and followed me."

The Prince clapped his hands, laughed, and said: "Wildgoose had courage indeed."

The Master went on: "When I think of those days, really it is amusing. A poor scholar like me, riding a mean little donkey, with but a boy to accompany me, started out on my way. I was overtaken with thirst, and drank overmuch fragrant wine, and when crossing Chon-jin Bridge found several score of the literati youth enjoying themselves with music and dancing. I took courage and went in. My poor clothes and headgear were put to shame by the dresses of the slaves that served. But I took a seat and there was Moonlight. In the exhilaration of the moment I never thought of making a laughing-stock of myself but wrote a verse or two. I do not know now what I wrote or what it was like, but Moonlight chose it before all the others and sang it. There had been an agreement in the first place that Moonlight should be given to the one whose verse she chose to sing, so there was no question that she was mine; besides it was a predestined affinity that settled the matter between us."

Prince Wol laughed and said: "You are winner in more than one field. Certainly to win her was more marvellous and delightful than being crowned with laurel. I am sure what you wrote must be very fine indeed. Might I hear it?"

The Master replied: "How can I possibly recall what I wrote then?"

Then the Prince said to Moonlight: "The Master has forgotten the verse that he wrote when he first met you. Can you not recite it for me?"

Moonlight said: "I remember it well; shall I write it out and hand it to your Highness, or shall I sing it?"

The Prince, pleased with the reply, said: "If you would sing it, as well as give it to me, I should be delighted."

Then Moonlight advanced and sang, so that the assembled guests were transfigured with joy. The Prince, overcome with a sense of wonder and awe, praised her, saying: "Your Excellency's gift in writing and Moonlight's soft compelling song are nowhere to be equalled. The bouquets of flowers that bloom forth from that song of yours rival the pretty girl's soft robes and ornaments. It would make even Yi Tai-baik take a second place. How can those who make a pretence at writing nowadays ever venture to look at such?"

Wine was then passed in a golden goblet filled to the brim, and thus were Moonlight and Wildgoose rewarded.

The four dancers from Prince Wol's palace and these two sang together the tune of "Long Life," and the assembled guests announced them angels from heaven. Ok-yon's name was rated with that of Moonlight and Wildgoose. The three others, while not equal to Ok-yon, were yet wonderfully skilful.

The Prince, congratulating himself on the occasion, and highly pleased, now asked all the guests to step forth from the tent to see the military master's sword exercise, spear drill and charging in the lists.

He said: "The women's horsemanship and shooting with the bow are worth seeing. Several among my palace maids are adepts. Your Excellency has among yours, no doubt, women from the north, who would, if you gave command, shoot a rabbit or pheasant for the amusement of the assembled company."

The Master was pleased at this and gave the order for a score or more to be chosen who were practised with the bow and in dashing horsemanship. These, with the maids from the palace of Prince Wol, laid wagers. Suddenly Wildgoose stepped forward and said: "Though I am not trained with the bow, still I have seen a great deal of riding and shooting and to-day I should like to try."

The Master gave ready assent, unfastened the bow from his own belt and handed it to her. Wildgoose took it and said to the combatants: "Even though I do not hit the mark you girls must not laugh at me." At once she mounted as if by wing one of the fast horses and sped away from before the tent. Just then a pheasant came flying from the copse. Wildgoose instantly straightened her slender back, grasped the bow, and the arrow went singing through the air, when a bunch of feathers in all the five colours fell before the horse's head.

The Master and the Prince clapped their hands and gave a ringing outburst of applause.

Wildgoose turned rapidly, rode back and alighted before the tent. She walked slowly to her place and sat down while all the girls congratulated her, saying: "We have trained for ten years and all to no purpose."

But Moonlight turned to her and said: "Though we two have not been beaten by the dancers from Prince Wol's palace, still there are four of them and we only two. This is hard work. Our not bringing Cloudlet was a great mistake. Though dancing and singing are not Cloudlet's speciality, her beauty and grace are such as would hold their own with Ok-yon's company." She gave a sigh. Suddenly two women were seen coming from the farther side of the grounds in a swift palanquin across the blooming green sward. They reached the entrance of the pavilion, when the gate-keeper said: "Do you come from Prince Wol's palace, or from the home of the Prince of Wee?"

The charioteer replied: "These two ladies are from the household of General Yang. They have been delayed, and so did not get here at first with the others."

The soldier guards then went in and reported the matter.

Master Yang said: "It is evidently Cloudlet who has come to see, but why has she come in this unaccountable way? Call her in."

The two ladies wearing embroidered shoes alighted from the

palanquin. In front was Swallow, and behind was the maiden seen so clearly in the dream, the daughter of the Tong-jong Dragon King. The two came forward before the Master and bowed.

Then Yang pointed towards Prince Wol and said: "This is his Highness Prince Wol; go and make your obeisance to him."

When they had done so, the Master gave orders that they should be placed beside Wildgoose and Moonlight. Then he said to Prince Wol: "These two maidens I met first on my campaign against the Tibetan. I have been so busy recently that I did not have opportunity to bring them before. They have come in order that they might enjoy the music and see the sights of the day."

When the Prince had looked at them again he saw that they were beautiful, like sisters to Moonlight and Wildgoose, with their grace of form even enhanced if that were possible.

The Prince was astonished, and all the faces of the galaxy from his palace turned pale as ashes.

He asked: "What are the names of these two ladies and where are they from, please?"

One of them replied, saying: "I am Sim, the Swallow. I come from west Yang-joo." And the other replied, saying: "I am White-cap, who came originally from the neighbourhood of the So-sang River. Unfortunately I met with trouble and made my escape from home and have taken refuge with the Master."

The Prince said: "These two maidens are not mortals, I am sure. Do they know how to play the harp?"

Swallow replied: "I am a humble person from a distant part and never heard the harp in my early days. By what possibility could I entertain your Highness? In my childhood I learned the sword dance, but this is an entertainment of the camp and not of the drawing-room."

The Prince was now all excitement and said to the Master: "In the days of Hyon-jong, the great dancer, Kong-son was renowned the world over for her skill in sword-dancing. Later generations lost the art and I have always felt sorry that I have not seen it. Now that you say the maid is skilled in sword-dancing I am more delighted than ever."

Then the Prince and the Master each drew from their belt the sword that they carried and gave it; Swallow fastened up her sleeves, put off her belt ornaments and stepped forth to dance.

At once from top to floor came the flashing of the blades, and the swift fierce passings from side to side. The red cheeks and bright sword blades melted into one, like the snows of the third moon that fall on the red buds of the springtime. Suddenly the speed of the sleevelets increased, and the whirling edges went faster and fiercer, till a blaze of white light filled the tent and Swallow's form was lost entirely to view. Mysteriously a rainbow halo suddenly appeared and a cool wind was felt to pass between the cups and glasses of the feast board. All the assembled company felt a shuddering in their bones and their locks stood on end.

Swallow intended to give an exhibition of the various forms she had learned, but fearing that it would cause alarm to the Prince, stopped, threw down the sword, bowed and retired.

The Prince was some time in recovering his senses; then he said: "How could any mortal attain to such skill as that? I have heard that many fairies are skilled in the sword-dance. Tell me are you not a fairy?"

Swallow said in reply: "The custom of the west is to practise feats of skill with military weapons, so I learned this when I was a child. Why should you think me a fairy?"

The Prince said: "When I go back to my palace, the best dancers among my maids shall be chosen and sent to you in the hope that you will kindly teach them."

Swallow bowed and gladly assented.

The Prince then asked White-cap: "What special skill have you, young lady?

White-cap replied: "My home overlooked the So-sang River, the place where A-whang[43] and Yo-yong played together, where the skies seem so far away, and the nights are so quiet, with soft breezes and a clear moon. From between the gentle rifts of the clouds I have heard again and again the strains of the harp, and these from earliest childhood I set myself to imitate. I used to play there alone and was so happy. I am afraid your Highness would not care for it, however."

The Prince said: "In the writings of the ancients we read that

43   *A-whang; Yo-yong.* These were two sisters, daughters of the Emperor Yo (2288 BC), who, like Leah and Rachel, were given to his successor as his faithful wives. Tradition relates that they journeyed south with him till they reached Chang-o, where he died. They wept, and their tears, falling on the leaves, caused to come into being the spotted bamboo.

A-whang and Yo-yong played upon the harp, but I have never heard that their tunes were passed on to mortal generations. If you have learned and know them let us hear them. Why should we compare them with the common music of the day?"

Then White-cap drew from her sleeve a small harp and played in tones indescribably tender, clear and persuasive, like waters hurrying through the mountain passes, or like the wildgeese clamouring the long length of heaven. All the guests were deeply moved, and tears began to flow. Suddenly the petals of the flowers trembled and the rustlings of autumn broke in upon the scene.

The Prince, mystified, said: "I never heard before that music could move the seasons in their course. If you are only a mortal, how is it that you can turn spring to autumn, or cause the leaves to fall? Could any mere human being ever learn a tune such as this?"

White-cap replied: "I have passed on merely the dregs of what I have heard, and have shown no special skill in the little that I have played for you."

Ok-yon here interrupted and addressed the Prince, saying: "Though I have no special skill of my own, yet there is one tune that I should like to play to your Highness. It is called the Song of the White Lotus. Shall I play it?"

She took up a harp such as was used in Chon-king's time, went forward and began to twang the strings. Across the twenty-five of them that lined the board, passed her hands in sweet and lovely music, well worth the hearing. The Master as well as the two dancers, Moonlight and Wildgoose, praised its beauty and the Prince was greatly delighted.

CHAPTER XV
THE WINE PUNISHMENT

ON this day of the happy festival Swallow and White-cap came in at the last and added the final touch of delight. The Master and the Prince, while desiring to stay longer, were compelled by the falling shadows of the evening to break up the feast and return. They gave to each performer rich presents of gold, silver and silk. Grain measures of gems were scattered about and rolls of costly materials were piled up like hillocks. The Master and the Prince, taking advantage of the moonlight, returned home to the city amid the ringing of bells. All the dancers and musicians jostled each other along the way, each desiring to be first to return. The sound of gems and tinkling ornaments was like falling water; and perfume filled the atmosphere. Straying hairpins and jewelled ornaments were crushed by the horses' hoofs and the passing of countless feet. The crowd in the city, desiring to see, stood like a wall on each side of the way. Old men of ninety and a hundred wept tears of joy, saying: "In my younger days I saw his Majesty Hyon-jong out on procession, and his splendour alone could be compared with this. Beyond all my expectations I have lived till to-day and now see this happy gathering."

The two Princesses with Chin See and Cloudlet were with the mother awaiting the return of the Master. In a little he came, bringing in his train Swallow and White-cap, who at once appeared before the mother and the two Princesses and made their salutations.

Cheung See said: "Your Excellency has spoken very often, saying that by the help of these two maidens you had brought into subjection whole districts of rebels. I was always sorry that I had never met them. Why is it, girls, that you have come so late?"

Swallow and White-cap made answer: "We are unknown peo-

ple from a distant province, and though the Master has kindly
looked upon us, we feared that the two ladies would not be willing
to accord us a place with them so we hesitated to come. But now
having entered the gates and having heard the people say that
the two Princesses were blessed with the happy hearts of Kwa-jo
and Kyoo-mok, and that their kindly virtues moved high and low
alike, we have come boldly in to make our obeisance. Just at the
time of our entrance into the city we learned that the Master was
engaged in the Festal Grounds; so we hurried out and joined in
the happy gathering. Now that your kind words are spoken to us
how delighted indeed we are."

The Princess laughed and said to the Master: "To-day we have
a garden of flowers gathered in the palace. Without doubt your
Excellency will boast of it. It all pertains to our merits, however,
and is due to us two. You must not think it due to yourself."

The Master laughed heartily and said: "The saying runs, 'Folks
in high places like praise.' It seems to be true. These two come
for the first time to the palace, and are afraid of the dignity
of your Highnesses, so they have resorted to flattery. Do you
take what they say as real and so pride yourselves on your own
merit?" And all those present laughed. Then Chin See and
Cloudlet asked of Moonlight and Wildgoose: "Who won to-day
in the lists?"

Wildgoose made answer: "Moonlight laughed at my boasting,
and yet with one word I took all the courage out of Prince Wol.
Che Kal-yang on a little boat like the leaf of a tree entered Kang-
dong, and with a few diminutive words made clear where right
and wrong lay, so that Chu Kong-geum and No Ja-kyong could
not utter a syllable for shame. Prince Pyong-won went to the
kingdom of Cho to make a contract of peace and amity, while
the nineteen who accompanied him had no occasion for a word,
and nothing whatever to do. It is because my heart is large that
my lips at times are boastful; but in my boastful words there lay
victory. You may ask Moonlight; she knows what I say is true."

Moonlight said: "Wildgoose's skill of bow and horseback riding
is indeed wonderful and suited to the Festal Ground, but if arrows
and stones were raining round her on the battlefield she would
not dare to ride a pace or draw a bow. The taking all the courage
out of Prince Wol was due to the arrival of the two fairy maids,

with their beauty and skill; how could she think of its being due to herself? I have just one word to say to Wildgoose, and I will say it now. In the days of the Spring and Autumn Classic, Minister Ka had a very dirty, unwashed face, so that people who passed by, in contempt, spat upon him. He was married for three years without his wife once having smiled. On a certain day he went with her into the fields when he chanced to shoot a pheasant that was flying by. His wife laughed for the first time. Wildgoose's shooting the pheasant was just like Minister Ka. He was no good and yet he shot a pheasant."

Wildgoose made answer: "Minister Ka, in spite of his dirty face, by means of skill at the bow and horsemanship, made his wife to smile; how much more would one with skill and beauty besides when they shoot a pheasant, make the world to smile and sing their praises."

Moonlight laughed and said in reply: "Your boastfulness, Wildgoose, grows apace. It is because the Master loves you over-much that you are vain and proud."

The Master laughed and said: "I knew long ago that Moonlight was greatly gifted, but I never knew that she was up in the Classics as well. Now I find that she is acquainted with the Spring and Autumn Book."

Moonlight's answer was: "In my leisure I used to study the Classics and history, but how could you say that I was acquainted with them?"

On the following day the Master went into audience before his Imperial Majesty. His Majesty summoned the Empress Dowager and Prince Wol. The two Princesses had already come in and were seated with them.

The Empress Dowager said to Prince Wol: "You and the General had a contest of pretty girls yesterday; tell me who won?"

The Prince replied: "I was altogether defeated; no one can hope to equal General Yang in the blessings of life and good luck. But how do blessings like these," pointing to the secondary wives, "appeal to your daughters, I wonder? Please, your Majesty, ask this of his Excellency, will you?"

The Master broke in: "His Highness's statement that he was defeated by me is quite aside of the mark. It is like Yi Tai-baik turning pale when he saw the writing of Choi-ho. Whether this is a happiness to the Princesses or not, how can I answer? Please ask their Highnesses themselves."

The Dowager laughed and looked toward the Princesses, who replied, saying: "Husband and wife are one, whether it be for gladness or for sorrow. There can be no difference in their lives. If our husband wins glory we win it too, but if failure falls to his lot, we too must share it. Whatever makes him glad makes us glad also."

Prince Wol said: "My sisters' words are all very sweet to listen to, yet they are not from the heart. Since ancient times there never was such an extravagant son-in-law as this General. It would indicate that the good old laws that once prevailed are losing ground. Please have his Excellency sent to the Chief Justice, and his contempt of court and disregard of the laws of State looked into."

The Dowager laughed and said: "Our son-in-law is doubtless somewhat of a sinner in this respect, but if you desire to judge him according to the law you will plunge an old woman like me and my two daughters into a whirl of anxiety. Let's dispense with the State laws and deal with him privately."

Prince Wol then said: "Though it might cause a measure of anxiety you cannot lightly overlook such a sin as his. Please let us inquire into his case before your Majesty, determine the nature of his offence, and deal with him accordingly." (He then wrote as though dictated to by the Empress.)

The Empress laughed while Prince Wol hastened to write out his statement:

"Since ancient times the son-in-law of the Empress has never taken to himself secondary wives. This is not due to the fact that he might not desire to do so, nor to the fact that he lacked sufficient food and clothes to give them, but only from a desire to do reverence to the Emperor and honour to the State. Now, however, if we regard the lofty station of the two Princesses, they are daughters of my own, and in their bringing-up and attainment they are not inferior to Im-sa.[44] But you, Yang So-yoo, have not been appreciative of this or of your bounden duty. Instead you have possessed yourself of a spirit of lawlessness and wild

---

44   *Im, Sa.* Two famous women of China, who lived 1122 BC.

excess, and have lost your heart over every painted cheek and powdered head, and have given your thought to dainty silks and gaudy dresses. You have gathered a host of pretty girls together in an astoundingly greedy manner, seeking them in the east by morning light, and in the west at evening time. You have let the light and the lands of Cho and Yon to blind your eyes, and you have allowed your ears to be filled with the songs of the Cheung Kingdom, condescending to look on groups who gather like ants in the music halls, or like bees in swarms to talk and chatter together. Though the Princesses in their spirit of liberality show no jealousy, how about your duty and your behaviour in the matter? One cannot but punish a sin of pride and excess. Now let us have no dissimulation, but a straightforward confession and an acceptance of the sentence."

The Master then descended from the dais, put off his headgear and awaited sentence. Prince Wol went to the end of the railed enclosure, and in a loud voice read out what had been written, and after the Master had heard it he said by way of confession: "Your Majesty's humble subject, Yang So-yoo, has presumptuously accepted of favours accorded by your two Excellent Majesties and has been crowned with the greatest possible glory, having the two Princesses made his very own with all their true and matchless graces. I had already won more than all that heart could wish. Still I was ungrateful, and my soul did not cherish the delight of the modest and the beautiful, but loved music excessively, as well as dancing and singing. This was indeed excess beyond what one already so greatly blessed should have shown. Still, as I humbly read the laws of the State, the son-in-law of her Majesty may have secondary wives, that is if they be taken before his marriage with the first Princess. Though I have secondary wives, my wife Chin See is mine by reason of the command of your Excellent Majesty, concerning which there can be no question. My wife Cloudlet was my attendant while I lived in the home of Justice Cheung. My wives Moonlight, Wildgoose, Swallow and White-cap were taken in the days before my marriage with the Princesses. Their being here in this place is also by command and with the permission of the Princesses themselves, and not by reason of any act of mine. If we speak of State laws or your Majesty's expressed will,

THE WINE PUNISHMENT: GREEN MOUNTAIN CASTLE

I feel that there is no sin in this that deserves punishment. These are your humble subject's statements and he offers them in fear and reverence."

The Empress Dowager on hearing this laughed and said: "The taking to himself of several wives does not in any way impair the dignity of the Superior Man. This I can forgive, but excess in the matter of drink causes me anxiety. Be careful!"

Prince Wol, however, went on to say: "It is not right that the son-in-law should take so many wives. So-yoo, too, blames the Princesses, forgetting that he has his own responsibility to answer for. I should like to have him properly disciplined for this. Please, your Majesty, ask concerning this again."

Then Yang in a state of embarrassment bowed his head and asked forgiveness, while the Dowager laughed and said: "So-yoo, while my son-in-law, is indeed a Minister of State. Why should I treat him as a son-in-law?" and she bade him put on his headgear and come up before the dais.

Prince Wol said: "Though his Excellency's merit is very great, and it is difficult to punish him, still the laws of the State are strict and he ought not to go without some mark of reprimand. You might try the wine punishment upon him."

The Dowager laughed and gave consent.

The palace maids then brought out a little white stone goblet, but Prince Wol said: "The General has the capacity of a whale, and his offence is so great that you must use a larger dish than this." So they brought a huge ornamented gold goblet and poured it full to the brim. Although the Master's capacity was large still this could not fail to make him drunk. He nodded his head and said: "The Herdsman loved the Weaving Damsel very, very much, and was scolded by his father-in-law. I, too, for taking too many wives, am punished by my mother-in-law. It is indeed difficult to fill the place of son-in-law of the Empress. This wine has gone to my head and I ask permission to retire, please."

The Dowager laughed and ordered the palace maids to help him away. She said also to the two Princesses: "The Master is upset and feeling ill, you must go and look after him."

The two Princesses obeyed orders and followed.

At this time Madame Yoo had lit the lamps in the main hall and was waiting her son's return. Seeing him drunk she said in amazement: "What is this? Drink? I have seen you drink before but never saw you drunk. What does it mean?"

The Master, with intoxicated look, at first made no reply, but after a time, pointing to the Princesses, he said: "The Princesses' brother, Prince Wol, has prevaricated to the Empress Dowager and brought me into judgment. I pleaded my own cause with skill and really cleared myself, but the Prince, by force, has put an imaginary fault upon me, and has caused me to under-go the wine punishment. If I had not been accustomed to wine I should have died. It is nothing but the result of his mortification of having been beaten in the lists yesterday. He wants to settle accounts with me, I see, and Orchid is jealous of my having so many wives. She has joined her brother in this scheme, no doubt. Her generous heart of former days seems to have gone. I pray you, mother, to give Orchid a glass of punishment as well and so make amends for this disgrace of mine."

The mother said: "It is not at all clear that Orchid is guilty as you say, and she has never tasted wine in all her life. If you desire that I should punish her, let it be with a cup of tea instead."

The Master said: "No, that will not do, it must be wine."

The mother laughed and said to Orchid: "If your Highness does not drink of it, this wretched fellow will not be satisfied," so she called a maid and ordered her to give to Orchid a glass of punishment.

While the Princess attempted to drink it, the Master suddenly expressed a doubt and tried to take the glass by force to taste it, but Orchid quickly threw it on to the matting. The Master then dipped his finger in the dregs, tasted it, and found that it was only sweetened water.

He said: "If her Majesty, the Empress, had punished me with sweetened water, my mother's giving sweetened water to Orchid would have been all right, but I have had to drink strong wine, so Orchid must have strong wine too and not sweetened water." He called a maid and bade her bring a glass and he himself poured it full and sent it. The Princess, having no alternative, drank it all.

Then he said again to his mother: "The one who urged the Empress to give me wine punishment was Orchid, but Blossom was in the scheme, too, you may be sure. She sat before the Empress and saw all my confusion, but she only laughed and nodded to Orchid. There is no fathoming her. My desire is that you punish Blossom too."

The mother laughed and sent the glass to Cheung See. Cheung See retired from her place and drank it.

The mother then said: "The Empress's punishment of the Master was on account of his having taken so many wives. The two Princesses have both had to drink of it, how can you girls escape?"

The Master said: "Prince Wol's meeting me on the Festal Field was simply to find about our singers and dancers, and there, in spite of all his great company, he was defeated by Wildgoose, Moonlight, Swallow and White-cap. Our weak numbers put his whole palace to shame. In the contest we won the day, and this is why Prince Wol has vented his resentment on me and caused my discomfiture. These four must certainly be punished as well."

The mother asked: "Do you punish those who win in the contest? Yours are the ridiculous words of a drunken man." But she called the four and gave them each a glass; and when all had drunk, Wildgoose and Moonlight knelt before the mother and said: "The Empress's punishment of the Master was assuredly on account of his many wives, and not because of his having won the day on the Festal Field. Swallow and White-cap have not shared the Master's home and yet they have been punished also. Will this not be a source of resentment later? Cloudlet has for a long time been with him, and has been greatly favoured, but she did not share the sports on the Festal Field, and so has escaped the punishment altogether. The rest of us humble folk feel that this is not fair."

"You are perfectly right," said the mother. Then she gave a large glass to Cloudlet, who smothered her laughter and drank it, so all were made to share alike in the glass of punishment and all were put to confusion.

Princess Orchid was overcome and in great distress; but Chin See sat in a corner in a manner wholly unconcerned, saying nothing and without a smile.

The Master said: "Chin See alone is not moved by it, and regards all the rest of us with contempt. She shall be punished once more." So he poured out another glass to the full and gave it to Chin See, who took it with a laugh and drank it.

213

The mother asked of the Princess: "Your Highness has never tasted of this before, how are you feeling?

She replied: "My head aches terribly."

The mother told Chin See to help the Princess to her room, and bade Cloudlet pour out another glass and bring it. She took the glass and said: "Our two daughters are Princesses of the Palace and I feel that I am wholly unworthy of them. Now you in your intoxication have caused them much discomfort. If her Majesty the Empress hears of this she will be very much disturbed. I have failed to bring you up properly, so we have had this disgraceful scene to-day. I cannot say that I am without sin in the matter, so I shall have to take a glass myself." She drank it all.

The Master, alarmed, knelt and said: "Mother, on account of my misdeeds, you have yourself shared in the glass of punishment. A beating, such as you give a child, would not be enough for me." Then he made Wildgoose bring still another big glass. He took it and, kneeling, said: "I have not lived up to the teaching of my mother, but have caused her pain and anxiety, so I drink this extra glass for shame." He drank it all and was so overcome that he could not sit up. He desired to go to his room and made signs accordingly. The mother asked Cloudlet to help him away, but she said she could not because Wildgoose and Moonlight would be jealous, so she told Moonlight and Wildgoose to do so instead.

Moonlight remarked: "Cloudlet does not wish to do it on account of what I said; I shall not either."

Wildgoose laughed, arose and helped the Master away, and so they each and all retired.

Swallow and White-cap were great lovers of the open hills and streams. This the Master knew, and had made for them a beautiful lake in the middle of the Imperial park. There he erected a special home which he called "Butterfly Pavilion." Here White-cap lived. On the other side of the lake was a hill whose top was ornamented with great rocks that were piled one above the other. There the shadows of the ancient pines screened the light and the spare graceful bamboo cast its grateful shade. Here also was a house built which he called "The Hall of Ice and Snow" in which Swallow took up her abode. When they all came out to have a happy time in the garden, Swallow and White-cap acted as hostesses of the sylvan halls.

The several sisters asked quietly of White-cap:
"Could you explain to us the wonderful law of metamorphosis through which you have passed."
White-cap replied: "That is something that belongs to a former existence. Taking advantage of the divine wheel of change, and by means of the powers of nature, I put off my former body and changed my appearance. The scales and discarded features were very gruesome to behold. I am like the sparrow changed into a clam. How can you expect me still to have wings with which to fly?"
The ladies all said: "Surely the principles and laws governing such a thing are wonderful."
Though Swallow, to please them, sometimes gave an exhibition of sword-dancing before the mother, the Master and the Princesses, she did not care to give it often, saying: "Though I met the Master because of my skill of hand with the sword, still the suggestion of death that goes with it does not make it a pleasant exercise nor one that should be often indulged."
From this time on the two ladies and the six subsidiary wives were all gladness and joy together, like fishes in the stream, or birds that flit among the clouds. They were ever united in heart and ever dependent one on the other like real sisters, while the Master regarded them with love all alike. Though it was due to the goodness of the two ladies that the whole house was so happy, still it was specially due to the fact that the nine had all been once together on Nam-ak Mountain and thus their wishes were fulfilled.
On a certain day the two Princesses said to each other: "In olden days sisters were known to marry into one and the same family, some becoming wives of the first order, and some becoming wives of the second order. Now we two wives and our six attendant sisters love each other more than those born of the same house; and among us are some who have come from distant regions. How could this be otherwise than by the ordinance of God? Our persons and our names differ one from the other; our social conditions, too, were widely separated, and yet here we are to-day with no incongruity to mar our gathering. We are indeed older and younger sisters and love so to be called."
Thus they spoke to the six sisters, when these, with great ear-

nestness, disclaimed any such possibility, maintaining that they were wholly unworthy, especially Cloudlet, Wildgoose, and Moonlight.

Cheung See said: "Yoo Hyon-tok, Kwan On-jang, and Chang Ik-tok were all courtiers of the king, and yet they preserved to the last the bond of brotherhood. How much more should I be a loved and trusted sister to Cloudlet who was my dear friend in days gone by? The wife of Sokamoni and the wife of their next-door neighbour were worlds apart in social standing, and also in virtue and chastity. Still they each became disciples of the Buddha, and they became one in heart. One rises to the place of illumination and rectitude."

The two Princesses said to the six:

"Let us go to the Merciful Buddha who sits within the palace chapel and there burn incense and offer prayer."

They wrote out a solemn oath which read thus: "Such a year, such a day, the disciples Cheung called Blossom, Yi called Orchid, Chin called the Phoenix, Ka called Cloudlet, Kay called Moonlight, Chok called Wildgoose, Sim called Swallow, Pak called White-cap, having bathed and cleansed their hearts, come now with all reverence before the great Buddha of the Southern Sea.

"People of the world oftentimes reckon all within the Four Seas as brothers because they are similar in thought and desire. Even those born by appointment of God as brothers in the same family sometimes view each other as strangers and unknown passers by. This is due to the fact that they fail in love and have no common interest. We, eight disciples, though we have been born at different places, and have been separated wide as the four corners of the earth, now serve one husband, live in one place, and are one in thought and life. Our love is perfect and flows out to each other. If one were to make comparison we are surely like a group of flowers that grew on one twig and fared alike in wind and weather, till at last one fell into the palace, one into a home of the gentry, one on the bank by the way, one was swept into the mountains, one borne down the stream and out to sea, but if we seek the origin it will be found that we are all from one root and finally shall all return at last to one place. So it is with men when born of a similar blood though separated widely by the vicissitudes of time; they all come home to abide together in the end.

"The past has far receded from us. But in it we eight were born at one and the same time, and though we have been separated by this wide expanse of empire yet here we are gathered together and living in the same home. This is truly an affinity that has come down to us from a former existence and explains the joy and gladness of our present life.

"So we eight disciples make a solemn vow and swear an oath of sisterhood to receive together the blessings or the reverses of life; to live together and die together and never, never to part. If among us there be any otherwise minded and forgetful of this oath, may God strike them dead and may the invisible spirits regard them with abhorrence.

"We humbly pray that the great Buddha may give us blessing here and remove from us all sorrow, and help us so that when life is over we may enter the regions of the blessed."

The two ladies hereafter called the six their younger sisters, but they, out of regard for their humble station, did not call the Princesses older sisters though they truly loved them as such in heart.

They each were blessed with children. The two Princesses, Cloudlet, Moonlight, Swallow and Wildgoose had each a son, while Phoenix and White-cap had each a daughter. Not once did any of them see a little child die in the home, which is an experience that differs from the common world of mortals.

At this time the whole world was at peace, with people dwelling safely and enjoying years of plentiful harvest. Little was there for the Government to do.

When the Emperor went on hunting expeditions the Master accompanied him, and on his return he would retire to his mother and family, where, with music and dancing, he passed happy days. Their joy and gladness accompanied the changing seasons. With years of office, the Master enjoyed great reward and prosperity. But in the providence of God when peace recedes unrest comes in its place, and, when joy has reached its full, sorrow falls.

Unexpectedly the lady Yoo fell ill and died at the advanced age of over ninety. The Master mourned deeply and sorrowed, so that both their Majesties were anxious and sent a eunuch to comfort him and attend his needs. He buried his mother with all the honours of a queen. Justice Cheung and his wife also passed away at a great age, and he mourned for them with no less sorrow than Cheung See herself.

The Master's six sons and two daughters were all blessed with the beauty and comeliness of their parents, like jade-stones and orchid flowers. The eldest son's name was Great Honour, child of Cheung See, and he rose to the office of Minister of Foreign Affairs; the second son's name was Lesser Honour, a son of Wildgoose, and he rose to the rank of Mayor of the Capital; the third was Lightsome Honour, a son of Cloudlet, who became Chief Justice; the fourth was Latest Honour, son of Princess Orchid, who became Minister of War; the fifth was called Fifth Honour, Moonlight's son, who rose to the rank of Chief of the Literati; the sixth was Final Honour, a son of Swallow. At fifteen he was stronger than any grown man, and was like the genii in his wisdom. The Master greatly loved him, and made him general-issimo of the forces. He commanded the forty thousand soldiers who served as guard for the Imperial Palace.

The eldest daughter's name was Tinted Rose, a child of Chin See. She married, later, Prince Wol's son. The second daughter was called Eternal Joy, born of White-cap. She became a second wife of the Prince Imperial.

The Master, who originally was but a common literatus, had met a King who knew his worth and took advantage of his mighty talents. He it was who brought a great war to a glad conclusion, and in merit and renown equalled Kwak Poon-yang.

The Master said: "If we are too prosperous misfortune easily follows, and if our cup of joy be too full a danger exists of running over. I shall now make request to retire from office." And so he wrote, "I bow a hundred times and make my humble petition to his Majesty. My desire for riches and long life has been realised, and no longer does anything remain to be fulfilled. Parents ask for their children only riches and honour, thinking that if they attain to these nothing is left beyond. Is it not the glory of long life with fame and wealth that the world struggles and contends for? They are indeed the things that the human heart constantly craves. Men do not know the wisdom that says 'Enough,' but desire ever more and more till at last they plunge themselves into the sea of destruction that follows. Though long life and honour have their attractive sides, still they cannot equal a contented mind, or dying peacefully in one's native land. Though these are things we rejoice over, how can they equal a happy home? My abilities were of a mediocre kind and my powers limited, yet I have come to the highest estate possible and have held the most important offices in the land. I have had every honour and glory extended to me. My earliest ambitions did not reach a thousandth part of what has come to pass. Who would have guessed that such lay wrapped away in the future? Notwithstanding my humble station, I became the Imperial son-in-law, superior to all the other courtiers of the Palace; and the gifts of your Majesty have been showered upon me beyond measure. From a child who lived on herbs I have come to dine on the richest fare; and from the lowest origin I have come to be a dweller among kings. I fear that it will prove a blot on your Majesty's record and a wrong that I have permitted. How can I be happy in view of it? In my early days I desired to hide my origin, to retire from the world, to close my gates, to refuse all favour and to confess my presumption to Heaven, to Earth, and to the invisible spirits. But your Majesty's favours were so great that I could not resist them; and since I was strong and well in physique, I accepted, desiring to repay if possible some single part of what you had bestowed upon me. I guarded my ancestral graves, and so lived out my life. But old age is coming on and my hair is growing grey. My form is like the decaying tree and shows the approach of the autumn season and signs of the yellow leaf. My heart is like an unused well, which though never drawn from still runs dry. Although I take to myself as my model the dog and the horse and set my strength in an effort to requite the many favours that have been accorded me, there is no way open by which to do it.

"May your Gracious Majesty, seeing that all is quiet in the outlying regions of the empire, that there is no need longer for military force; that the people are at peace and that the sound of the drum has ceased from the land, grant me my request. God's blessing is upon you and the harvest is rich and plentiful as it was in the happiest days of the Three Kingdoms. Even though you hold me still to office, and make me carry on affairs of State, it means only the expenditure of public money and the hearing of Kyok-yang songs. What special profit will it be, or what new reform can you expect?

"The King and his officer are like father and son. Now a father loves even an ungrateful son because he is his child and he thinks of him when he goes beyond the gate. I pray your Majesty to look upon me as aged and past service. I desire to act my part as a child does towards a parent, and know that you will think of me as the best parent thinks concerning his son. My load of Imperial favour is on my back. How can I go far away or say a long farewell to so good a King? Since you cannot fill fuller the glass already full, and since a broken cart can no more be ridden, my prayer is that your Majesty will behold how I can no longer bear the burden of State and let me go back to my native land to fill out my span of life and sing for ever the Imperial praises."

The Emperor read this memorial and wrote the reply with his own hand: "Your Excellency's great office and influence have been a blessing to all the people. Your experience has been of immense service to the State. Your prestige and weight have held the empire steady. In olden days Ta-kong and So-kong aided the kingdom of Cho till they were nearly a hundred, and helped in the minutest affairs of government. Your Excellency has not yet reached the limit of age when office is laid down, and though you excuse yourself and desire to retire I cannot grant it. The pines and the firs of the forest look with contempt upon the snow and are strong in spirit, while the willows have their leaves stripped from them when they meet the cold winds, because they are not courageous in soul. Your Excellency is of the nature of the pine and the fir, how can you be anxious concerning a fate similar to that of the willow and the poplar?

"As I behold you, you seem as young as ever; your strength has not diminished since the day you first took office. It is as vigorous as it was when you crossed the Wee Bridge to fight against the rebels. Though you say you are old I do not accept it. By all means change your attitude from that of So-boo[45] and aid me in my government. This is my decision."

The Master, when a disciple of the Buddha, had received the mysteries of the doctrine from the teacher on Nam-chon hills.

---

45 *So-boo* (Nest-Father). He is a legendary being said to have lived 2357 BC, and to have made his home in a tree; hence his name. He was a man of singular uprightness, who greatly influenced his age for good. Once, when offered the rule of the empire by the great Yo, he went and washed his ears in the brook to rid them of the taint of worldly ambition.

He had there tasted its refining influence, so that now, though his age was far advanced, he still showed no signs of decay, and the people referred to him as one of the immortals. This is why the Emperor so worded his reply.

But the Master again memorialised the Throne so earnestly that his Majesty called him and said: "Your Excellency has so persuasively made request to retire, that though my desire is on no account to accede to you, still I find I must. If you should go far away to your own state and reside there, there would be no one to whom I could refer the more pressing affairs of the kingdom. Now, also, that the Empress Dowager has taken her departure to the distant regions, how can I bear to part for so long from Blossom and Orchid? To the south of the city, forty *li* distant, there is a special palace called the Green Mountain Castle where King Hyon-jong used to go to escape the hot season. It is quiet and retired and is just such a place as old age could enjoy and delight itself in. I give this to you."

So he issued a proclamation making the Master the honorary Chief of the Literati, and appointing to him five thousand extra homes to exalt his rank, while he relieved him of all the arduous duties of active office.

YANG LOOKS AWAY FROM THE WORLD:
BACK TO RELIGION

CHAPTER XVI
THE ANSWER: BACK TO THE BUDDHA

THE Master was exceedingly grateful for this Imperial favour and bowed low and gave thanks. He then removed his whole household to Green Mountain Castle, which was among the hills to the south of the city. The towers were all in good repair and the views from their tops, beautiful beyond comparison, were like the fairy vistas of the Pong-nai Hills.

The main hall was empty and there he placed the Imperial rescripts and orders. In the inner pavilion he made the two Princesses live and the six sisters. Day by day in company with his household he visited the groves and streams, enjoyed the light of the moon, or went into the valleys to seek cherry blossoms. There they wrote verses as they sat under the shade of the pines, or played on the harp, so that all who knew of it spoke with admiration of their happy old age.

Desiring quiet, the Master no longer saw guests or callers.

On the 16th of the 8th Moon, which was his birthday, a great feast was held at which all the members of his clan were present. It lasted for ten days, during which time the whole place was astir. When it was over and quiet had returned, the retired mode of life was resumed.

A little later came the 9th Moon, when the buds of the chrysanthemum began to open and the so-yoo berries bloomed red on the high peaks and ledges of the hills.

To the west of Green Mountain Castle was a high tower from which a view of the Chin River was to be had, stretching a hundred miles, silvery and clear in its long expanse of water. The Master greatly enjoyed this view, and one day he took the two Princesses and the six ladies with him to the top. Each had a wreath of chrysanthemum flowers encircling her brow, and as they looked off over the autumn valleys they passed the glass together. Suddenly the descending sun cast a shadow from the neighbouring peak that ran a shaft of darkness over the wide stretch of plain. The Master drew forth his green stone flute and began to play. The tune was one plaintive beyond expression, as though heaped-up sorrows and hidden tears had broken forth upon them. The ladies' hearts were overcome with sadness, joy departed, and deep, long shadows closed down upon the soul.

The two Princesses asked "Your Excellency has won everything in the way of honour and fame. You are rich in goods that you have long enjoyed, with which the world blesses you – something but rarely seen. When you are so happily circumstanced, with a beautiful world outstretched before you, and the golden flowers dropping their petals at your feet, why should you suggest sadness and sorrow? With our loving hearts around you, too, what more could you have of what the world calls happiness? The notes of your flute break our hearts and cause our tears to flow. You never did this before; what does it mean, pray?"

Then the Master threw away the flute, drew aside, and resting on the railing of the balcony, pointed to the darkening landscape and said: "When I look north a stretch of level country greets me as far as the eye can see; one dismantled hilltop only breaks the view. The falling light of the evening permits me to see indistinctly amid the long grass the ruined A-bang Palace where dwelt the Emperor Chin-see. When I look west the lonely winds rustle the dry reeds of the evening as the mists crown the hill over the deserted tomb of Moo-jee of Han, As I look east, a white wall encircles a hill, and a red-tiled palace rises skyward over which the moon now casts its beams. The marble railings show no one resting on them, for it is the long-vacated palace of Hyon-jong, where he dallied his days away with the famous woman Yang Kwi-pee. Alas, these were all kings of great renown, who made their gates of the surrounding sea, and their court of the far-stretching world. All the people were their subjects, and were at their service as courtiers or mistresses. Their mighty powers and talents were enlisted in search of the eternal Pong-nai Hills where they might enjoy unending bliss for ever.

"I, So-yoo, in my boyhood was a poor scholar, but I have been blessed with enduring favours from his Majesty, and elevated to the highest rank. The members of my household have lived together in sweetness and accord till this time of old age. If it had not been for the affinity of a former existence, how could this have been? By reason of this mysterious bond it has all come to pass. When the term fixed for this mortal life is completed, we must part; and when once death has swept us away, even this lofty tower shall fall and the fair lake beneath us shall be dried up. This palace hall, where to-day is music and dancing, will be overgrown with grass and the mists will cover it. Children who gather wood or feed their cattle on the hillside will sing their songs and tell our mournful story, saying: 'This is where Master Yang made merry with his wives and family. All his honours and delights, all the pretty faces of his ladies, are gone for ever.'

"The boy who gathers wood and the lad who cares for the cattle will look upon this place of ours just as I look upon the palace and tomb of the kings that have gone before us. When I think of it, a man's life is only the span of a moment after all.

"There are three religions on earth, Confucianism, Taoism, and Buddhism. Among the three, Buddhism is the most spiritual; Confucianism deals with terrestrial matters and has to do with the duties of man to man. It helps to pass on names to posterity. Taoism is related to the misty and unknown, and though it has many followers there is no proof of its verity.

"Since I gave up office I have dreamed of meditation before the Buddha. This is proof of my affinity with the God. Just as Chang Cha-pang[46] followed Chok Song-ja, the fairy, I, too, must say farewell to my home and go to the distant shore, there to seek the Merciful Buddha, ascend the Sacred Hall, and bow low before his image. The Way that has no birth and no death beckons to me and puts off all the sorrows of life. To you with whom I have spent so many happy days I must say a long farewell, and so my sorrow and loss is expressed by the sad notes of the green stone flute."

The ladies in their former existence had been the eight fairies who lived on Nam-ak Mountain. Now they had fulfilled their human affinity, and hearing the Master's word they were moved by it and said each to the other: "In the midst of all his affluence

---

46   *Chang Cha-pang.* One of the founders of the Han Dynasty (206 BC) and one of China's three great heroes. Mayers says: "At the close of his official career he renounced the use of food and prosecuted the search for the elixir of life under the guidance of a supernatural being, but failed to attain immortality."

the Master's speech is evidently at the command of God, We eight sisters who have lived our life in these inner quarters and have bowed night and morning before the Buddha shall await the departure of our lord. When he goes he will assuredly meet the Enlightened One and the righteous friends who have gone before him and will hear the words of life. Our humble wish is that after he has attained he may be pleased to teach us the way."

The Master, greatly delighted, said: "Since your hearts are one with mine in this you need have no fear. I start to-morrow."

The ladies all said: "We shall each raise the glass that wishes you great peace on the eternal way."

Just at the moment when they had given orders to the serving maids to bring the glasses, the fall of a staff was heard on the stone pavement beyond the open balcony. They exclaimed: "Who has come, I wonder?"

Immediately an old priest appeared before them with eyebrows an *ell* long and eyes like the waves of the blue sea. His appearance and his behaviour were mysterious and wonderful. He ascended the tower, sat down before the Master, and said: "A dweller from the hills seeks audience with your Excellency."

Already the Master knew that he was no common man, so he arose quickly and made a respectful obeisance as he replied: "Whence comes the honoured teacher?"

The old priest made answer: "Do you not know an old friend? I have heard before that you had a gift for forgetfulness, and now I find that it is true."

The Master looked carefully and then he thought he recognised the face, but he was not sure. Suddenly he recollected, and turning to the ladies said: "When I went into Tibet against the rebels, in my dream after I had shared the feast of the Dragon King and was on my way home, I went for a little up the Nam-ak Hills and saw an aged priest sitting in the seat of the Master reciting with his disciples the sacred sutras of the Buddha. The priest whom I saw there is the same who greets me now."

The priest clapped his hands, laughed and said: "You are right, right. You remember, however, seeing me in your dream only; the ten years that we spent together you have forgotten all about. Who would say that the Master Yang was an enlightened man?"

Yang, not knowing what he meant, replied: "When I was sixteen

I was still with my parents. I then passed my examinations and from that time entered office, and did not again leave the capital till I went south as envoy. My next journey was to put down the Tibetans. There is no place that my feet have travelled over that I do not recall. When did I spend ten years with you, sir?"

The priest looked sad and said: "Your Excellency has not yet awakened from your dark dream."

"Have you, great teacher, any means of awakening me?" asked Yang.

"That is not difficult," said the priest. He raised his stone staff and struck the railing, when suddenly a white cloud arose all about them that came forth from the recesses of the hills till it enclosed the tower and made all dark and indistinct so that no one could see.

The Master, bewildered as in a dream, called loudly: "Will the Teacher not teach me the true way, instead of applying to me the terrors of magic?" He did not finish what he was about to say, for suddenly the clouds moved off and everybody had disappeared, including the priest and the eight ladies. He was greatly alarmed and mystified, and looked with wonder to find the tower with its ornamented curtains, but it also had passed from view. He turned his eyes upon himself to find his body, and there he was sitting cross-legged on a little round mat in a silent temple. There was an incense brazier before him from which the fires had died out. The moon was descending towards the west. He felt his head and it had just been shaved, with only the prickly roots noticeable. A string of a hundred and eight beads was round his neck, and there he was a poor insignificant priest with all the glory of General Yang departed from him. His mind and soul were hopelessly confused and his heart beat with trepidation. He suddenly awakened and said: "I am Song-jin, a priest of Yon-wha Monastery."

As he thought over the past he remembered how he had been reprimanded and what had followed. He recalled his flight to Hades and how he had transmigrated into human life; how he had become a clansman of the Yang family; his passing the examination and becoming a high Hallim; his promotion to the rank of General, and later to be the head of the entire official service; how he had memorialised the Emperor to resign his office; his retirement with the two Princesses and the six ladies how he had enjoyed music and dancing and the notes of the harp and lute; how he had drunk wine and played at go, and had lived his days in pleasure. Now it was all as a passing dream.

Then he said: "The Teacher indeed, knowing my great sin, sent me forth to dream this dream of life so that I might learn the fleeting character and instability of all earthly things and the vain loves of human kind."

So he hastened to the stream of water rushing by and washed his face, put on his priest's cassock and hat and went to take his place among the disciples before the Teacher. When they were arranged in order the Teacher called with a loud voice and said "Song-jin, how did you find the joys of mortal life?"

Song-jin bowed, shed tears, and said: "I have at last come to realise what life means. My life has been very impure and my sins I can lay at no one's door but my own. I have loved in a lost and fallen world, where for endless *kalpas* I should have suffered sorrow and misery had not the honoured Teacher by a dream of the night awakened my soul to see. In the ages to come I can never, never sufficiently thank Thee for what Thou hast done for me."

The Teacher said: "You have gone abroad on the wings of worldly delight and have seen and known for yourself. What part have I had in it, pray? You say that you have dreamed a dream of mortal life upon the wheel and that now you think the two to be different, the world and the dream itself; but that is not so. If you think it so it will show that you are not yet awakened from your sleep. Master Chang became a butterfly, and the butterfly became Master Chang. Was Chang's becoming a butterfly a dream, or was the butterfly's becoming Chang a dream? You, Song-jin, now think yourself reality, and your past life a dream only; you do not reckon yourself one and the same as the dream. Which shall I label the dream, you Song-jin, or you So-yoo?"

Song-jin replied: "I am a darkened soul and so cannot distinguish which is the dream and which is the actual reality. Please, Teacher, open to me the truth and let me know."

The Teacher said: "I shall explain to you the Diamond Sutra to awaken your soul, but there are other and new disciples whom I am shortly expecting. I await their coming."

Before he had ended speaking the gate-keeper came in to say: "The eight fairies of Lady Wee who called yesterday have again arrived before the gate and desire to see the Great Teacher."

They were invited in, and as they entered they joined hands and bowed, saying: "We maids, though we wait upon Lady Wee, are untaught and unlearned and have never known how to repress the lawless workings of the soul. Our earthly desires have gone forth after sin and evil in the dream of mortal life and there is no one to save us but the Great Teacher, who in love and mercy Himself came to call us.

"We went yesterday to Lady Wee, confessed our sins and wrongdoings and asked forgiveness. Now we have bade a long farewell to her, and have come home to the Buddha. We humbly pray that the Great Teacher will forgive our many shortcomings and tell us the way to the blessed life."

He answered: "Though your desire is one greatly to be praised, the law of the Buddha is deep and hard to attain. It cannot be learned in a moment of time. Unless there be great earnestness and a deep heart of longing it can never be attained. I ask that you fairy maidens think well over it before you decide."

The eight fairies then withdrew, washed the rouge and colour from their faces and put aside the silks and satins in which they were bedecked. They took scissors and cut away their clouds of floating hair, and again entered to say: "We have made the necessary changes in our persons and will take the teaching of the Master with sincere and faithful hearts."

The Teacher answered: "Good, good. Since you eight have thus shown your true and earnest purpose, why should I longer withhold the Truth from you?"

Then he led them to their places in the Hall of the Buddha and made them recite the Sacred Sutras and the Chin-on. Thus did Song-jin and the eight priestesses awaken to the truths of religion and become partakers of the Buddha.

The Great Teacher, seeing the faithfulness and devotion of Song-jin, called his disciples to him and said: "I came from a far distant world to the Empire of the Tangs in order to preach the Truth. At last I have found one who can take my place and the time has come for me to go."

He took his cassock, his alms-dish, water-bottle, his ornamented staff, his Diamond Sutra, gave them to Song-jin, bade farewell, and took his departure to the west.

From this time Song-jin became chief of the disciples on the heights of Yon-wha and taught the Doctrine, so that fairies, dragons, demons and men all revered him as they did the late Great Teacher. The eight priestesses, too, served him as their master, drank deeply of the Doctrine, and at last they all reached the blissful heights of the Paradise to come.

APPENDIX
INTRODUCTION TO THE 1912 EDITION

THE BOOK

THE reader must lay aside all Western notions of morality if he would thoroughly enjoy this book. The scene of the amazing "Cloud Dream of the Nine," the most moving romance of polygamy ever written, is laid about 849 AD in the period of the great Chinese dynasty of the Tangs. By its simple directness this hitherto unknown Korean classic makes an ineffaceable impression.

But the story of the devotion of Master Yang to eight women and of their devotion to him and to each other is more than a naive tale of the relations of men and women under a social code so far removed from our own as to be almost incredible. It is a record of emotions, aspirations and ideas which enables us to look into the innermost chambers of the Chinese soul. "The Cloud Dream of the Nine" is a revelation of what the Oriental thinks and feels not only about things of the earth but about the hidden things of the Universe. It helps us towards a comprehensible knowledge of the Far East.

THE TRANSLATOR

But first a word on the medium through which this extraordinary book reaches us.

Travellers, artists, students, archæologists and history writers, journalists and literary folk, officials and diplomatic dignitaries who wend their way to China by way of Seoul, carry in their wallets letters of introduction to Dr. James Gale.*

For more than thirty years Dr. Gale has been clearing and hewing in a virgin forest, the literature of Korea. He is the foremost literary interpreter to the West of the Korean mind. This is how he regards that mind – the words are taken from an address to a group of Japanese officials who sought Gale's counsel on a memorable occasion:

"The Korean lives apart in a world of wonder, something quite unlike our modern civilisation, in a beautiful world of the mind. I have studied for thirty years to enter sympathetically into this world of the Korean mind and I am still an outsider. Yet the more I penetrate this ancient Korean civilisation the more I respect it."

No man knows more of Korea or more deeply loves her people, and is loved by them, than Dr. Gale. Japanese officials have also a sincere regard for Dr. Gale. They have been accustomed to carry to him their perplexity over Korean problems, just as the Korean has come to Gale in his troubles with the Japanese. It is because of a combination of social qualities with scholarship that Dr. Gale has been able so convincingly to translate Far Eastern romance and character study.

All the literary interpretative work that Gale has done before the present book – from the fascinating diary of a Korean general of a thousand years ago, who wrote his impressions as he travelled through Manchuria to pay his devoirs at the great court of China, to that literary gem preserved in Gale's translation of the brief Petition of two aged Korean Viscounts, who pleaded in terms of archaic simplicity with the Japanese Governor-General Hasegawa to listen to the plaint of their people for freedom – is so sincere, lucid, and impersonal, that the reader knows that he is being given reality and not an adaptation.

Dr. Gale is the unhurried man who has time for every public behest. Much of the hard literary work of his full day is done in the hours of morning calm before the world has breakfasted. The chief native helper of this quiet-eyed missionary in the work of translation has been with him for thirty years. The unsought, almost unconscious influence of a man like Gale justifies the hopes of the most old-fashioned believers in Christian missions and lends romance to work that too often seems to lead nowhere. Here is the real ambassador in a foreign land: that rare thing the idealist and scholar who has an understanding of the small things of life; the judicially-minded man who makes such deep demands on principle that he draws all men to him.

THE AUTHOR

Writing somewhere of the Korean love of literature, Dr. Gale says: "Literature has been everything in Korea. The literati were the only men privileged to ride the dragon up into the highest heaven. The scholar might not only look at the King, he could talk with him. Could you but read, intone or expound the classics, you might materially be dropping to tatters but still the world would wait on you and listen regardfully to show you honour. Many an unkempt son of the literati has the writer looked on with surprise to see him receive the respectful and profound salutations of the better laundered classes. Korea is not commercial, not military, not industrial, but she is a devotee of letters. She exalts books."

I hear some traveller say: "What! Do you mean to suggest that those funny chaps I saw in the streets of Seoul wearing baggy white trousers and queer little Welsh hats, who sat around in lazy groups smoking long pipes and looking into nowhere, have a literature? I always understood that the Japanese had an awful time cleaning up their country and getting them to bury their dead. I've always heard that if it weren't for Japanese money and hustle the Koreans would be nothing but walking hosts of small-pox and plague germs."

And the traveller would be wrong.

"The Cloud Dream of the Nine" lures the reader into mysterious vales and vistas of remotest Asia and opens to him some of the sealed gateways of the East.

The seventeenth-century author, Kim Man-Choong, mourned all his life that he should have been born after his father had died. So remarkable was his filial piety that his fame as a son spread far and wide.

In his devotion to his mother, Yoon See, he never left her side except on Court duty. He would entertain her as did those of ancient days who "played with birds before their parents, or dressed and acted like little children." In his efforts to entertain his mother Kim Man-Choong would read to her interesting stories, novels and old histories. He would read far into the night to give her pleasure, and his reward was to hear her laugh of joyful appreciation.

But there came a day when Kim Man-Choong was sent into exile. His mother's words were: "All the great ones of the earth, sooner or later, have gone thus to distant outlying sea coasts or to the hills. Have a care for your health and do not grieve on my account." But those who heard these brave words wept on the mother's behalf.

Kim Man-Choong wrote "The Cloud Dream of the Nine" while

he was an exile, and his aim in writing it was to cheer and comfort his mother. The thought underlying the story is that earth's best attainments are fleeting vanity and that without religion nothing avails. The book became a favourite among the virtuous women of the day and for long afterwards.

Kim Man-Choong matriculated in 1665 and was made later a famous Doctor of Literature and President of the Confucian College. He was exiled in 1689. On his death the State erected a Gate of Honour calling attention to his filial piety and marking his title, Moon-hyo Kong, Prince Moon-hyo. So says "Korea's Famous Men," Vol. III, page 205.

THE TALE

Far off in the glorious mountains of Eastern Asia, whose peaks "block the clouds in their course and startle the world with the wonder of their formation," there is an innermost group that is "charged with divine influences." Since the days of the Chinese Deluge (BC 2205–2197) holy men and women and genii have been wont to dwell in these mountain fastnesses, and no pen can ever record all the strange and wonderful things that have happened there.

Here in the days of the Tang dynasty a priest from India who was a "Master of the Six Temptations" was so moved by the marvellous beauty of the hills that he built a monastery on Lotus Peak and there preached the doctrines of the Buddha. Among his six hundred disciples the youngest, Song-jin, barely twenty, who was without guile and most beautiful in face and form, had greater wisdom and goodness than all the other followers, so that the Master chose him to be his successor when he should "take his departure to the West."

But temptation befel Song-jin.

He was sent by the Master with a greeting to the Dragon King, who feasted him and deceived him with wine. Although Song-jin refused many times, saying, "Wine is a drink that upsets and maddens the soul and is therefore strictly forbidden by the Buddha," he finally drank three glasses and a "dizzy indistinctness possessed him." On his way back to the monastery he sat by the bank of a stream to bathe his hot face in the limpid water and reprimand himself for his sinfulness. He thought also of the chiding he would receive from the Master.

But a strange and novel fragrance was wafted towards him. It was "neither the perfume of orchid nor of musk," but of "something wholly new and not experienced before." It seemed to "dissipate the soul of passion and uncleanliness." Song-jin decided to follow the course of the stream until he should find the wonderful flowers.

He found, instead of flowers, eight fairy maidens seated on a stone bridge.

These maidens were messengers sent by a Queen of the genii who had become a Taoist by divine command and had settled on one of the mountain peaks with a company of angelic boys and fairy girls. While Song-jin was at the palace of the Dragon King, these eight fairy girls were calling on the Master of the monastery with greetings and offerings from their heavenly Queen. They had rested on the bridge to admire the scenery and had dallied there fascinated by their own reflections in the stream below.

Song-jin greeted them ceremoniously and told them that he was a humble priest returning to his home in the monastery. "This stone bridge is very narrow," he said, "and you goddesses being seated upon it block the way. Will you not kindly take your lotus footsteps hence and let me pass?" The fairies bowed in return and teased the young man. They quoted the Book of Ceremony to the effect that "man goes to the left and woman to the right," but they refused to budge and recommended that Song-jin cross by some other way. They laughingly challenged him: if he were a disciple of the Teacher Yook-kwan he could follow the example of the great Talma who "crossed the ocean on a leaf." At this Song-jin also laughed, and answered their challenge by throwing before them a peach blossom that he carried in his hand. The blossom immediately became four couplets of red flowers and these again were transformed into eight jewels. The fairies each picked up a jewel, then they looked towards Song-jin, laughed delightedly and "mounted on the winds and sailed through the air."

There followed a period of darkness and misery for Song-jin. He tried to justify himself to the Master for his long tarrying, but though he tried to rein in his thoughts when he retired to his cell the lure of earth was strong. "If one study diligently the

Confucian classics," said the tempter to him, "one may become a General or a Minister of State, one may dress in silk and bow before the King and dispense favours among the people. One can look on beautiful things with the eyes and hear delightful sounds with the ears, whereas we Buddhists have only our little dish of rice and spare flask of water, many dry books to learn and our beads to say over till we are old and grey. The vacant longings that are never satisfied are too deep to express. When once the spirit and soul dissipate into smoke and nothingness, who will ever know that a person called Song-jin lived upon this earth?"

The young priest was tormented by visions of the eight fairy maidens, his ears ringing with sweet voices until he became like one "half insane or intoxicated." He burnt incense, knelt, called in all his thoughts, counted his beads, and recalled to his consciousness the thousand Buddhas who could help him. But in the middle of the night the Master called him and, refusing all excuse, condemned him to Hell.

The young Song-jin pleaded with tears and many eloquent words, saying: "I came to you when only twelve. Our love is as between an only son and a father. My hopes are all here. Where shall I go?"

To Song-jin's appeal for mercy the Master said: "While your mind remains unpurified, even though you are here in the mountains, you cannot attain to the Truth. But if you never forget it and hold fast, you may mix with the dust and impurities of the way and your return is sure. If you ever desire to come back here I will go to bring you. You desire to go; that is what makes me send you off. You ask, 'Where shall I go?' I answer, 'To the place where you desire to go.'"

Song-jin descended into Hell, and the King of that region was so surprised and perplexed by his coming that he sent to the Buddhist God of the Earth for advice about punishing him. At the same time the eight fairy maidens arrived in Hell, and the King after hearing their story commanded nine of his messengers, "in a low voice," to "take these nine and get them back as soon as possible to the world of the living."

So a great wind arose, tossed and carried the nine through space, and after whirling them to the four ends of the earth, finally landed them on solid ground. They were all born into different families, and as human beings knew nothing of their former existence nor guessed that their present experience was an expiation.

Song-jin was born again as the only child of a hermit and his wife. They loved him greatly, for they saw that he was a heavenly visitor. The father, who was originally of another world, when he recognised his son to be a "Superior Man," said good-bye to his wife whom he had faithfully loved, content now to leave her in the care of their son, and he returned to his friends the genii on a famous mountain.

There follows the story of Song-jin's earthly life and his eight-fold love story. Each fairy maiden having an affinity with Song-jin was destined to serve him as wife or mistress. Song-jin bore the name of his hermit father, Yang, and the name given him at birth.

Master Yang, as we shall now know him, was a child of such beauty and a youth of such wisdom that the governor of his county called him the "Marvellous Lad" and offered to recommend him to the Court. His physical strength, learning and ability in the Classics and composition, his marvellous knowledge of astronomy and geomancy, his military prowess – he was a wonder of skill in tossing the spear and fencing with the short sword – were only equalled by his filial piety. He "deftly solved the mysteries of life as one would split the bamboo."

While still in his teens Yang expressed his desire to go forth to compete at the Government Examination so that he should "for ever establish the reputation and honour" of his family. His faithful mother stifled her fears for the long journey, for she saw that his "spirit was awake and anxious." By selling her few treasures she was able to supply means for his travels. Master Yang set out on his adventure accompanied by a little serving-lad and a limping donkey. As he had a long and leisured way before him he was able to linger over the beauties of the scenery through which he passed.

The story unfolds with fascinating perplexity the love drama of nine. The maidens are all peerless in beauty, virtue, talent, goodness and charm. So generous is the flame of Master Yang's affection that he enshrines each love with apparently equal and unabated warmth. Of the eight maidens, seven openly declared their choice of Yang as their master and one was sought deliberately by him. No shade of jealousy mars the perfect affinity of the nine.

Yang easily won the highest place in the Government Competitive Examination and became a master of literary rank. This raised him from obscurity to fame and from poverty to wealth. "His name shook the city. All the nobility and peers who had marriageable daughters strove together in their applications through go-betweens."

But Yang had already decided to offer marriage to the only daughter of a certain Justice Cheung. Disguised as a Taoist priestess, he had gained entry into the inner court of the Cheung household some days before the examination. In the presence of the ladies of the family he had played on his harp and had sung with a voice of unearthly sweetness certain songs that had been taught to him by genii.

The young lady sat attentively listening while she identified in turn each song, "Feathery Robes," "The Garden of Green Gems and Trees," "The Distant Barbarian" and others. She defined one as "the supreme expression of all music," the thought of which ran, she said, "He travelled through all the nine provinces and found no place in which to rest his heart." The young lady so amazed Yang by her accuracy and skill in divining and revealing the nature and history of the rare music that finally, "kneeling, he cast more incense on the fire and played the famous 'Nam-hoon Palace of King Soon.'" On which she quoted, "The south wind is warm and sweet and bears away on its wings the sorrows of the world." "This is lovely," the young lady said, "and fills one's heart to overflowing. Even though you know others I have no desire to hear them."

She would have left the apartment, but the disguised Yang humbly begged permission to play and sing one other. He straightened the bridge of his harp and "the music seemed far distant at first, awakening a sense of delight and calling the soul to a fast and lively way. The flowers of the court opened out at the sound of it; the swallows in pairs swung through their delightful danings; the orioles sang in chorus to each other. The young mistress dropped her head, closed her eyes and sat silent for a moment till the part was reached which tells how the phoenix came back to his native land gliding across the wide expanse of sea looking for his mate.

She looked at the pretended priestess, the red blushes mounted to her cheeks and drove even the pale colour from her brow. She quietly arose and went into her own apartment."

Neither her mother nor any of the attendants understood why the young mistress had retired, nor could they persuade her to return. But in the privacy of her chamber, Jewel, for that was the name of the young lady, spoke to her adopted sister, Cloudlet.

"Cloudlet, my dear, you know I have been careful of my behaviour as the Book of Rites requires, guarding my thoughts as pearls and jewels, and that my feet have never ventured outside the middle gates.... I, an unmarried girl of the inner quarters, have sat for two full hours face to face with a strange man unblushingly talking to him. When I heard the song of the phoenix seeking her mate I looked closely into the priestess's face. Assuredly it was not a girl's face at all. Did anyone ever hear such a thing in the world before? I cannot tell this even to my mother."

Cloudlet pleaded for the young man whose beauty and powers were so unusual. But Jewel was not to be moved, and when later Master Yang formally called on Justice Cheung and proposed marriage and the Justice was honoured by his proposal and delighted to accept it, Jewel's scruples were hard to overcome. She felt that the young man must be punished, and to "save her face" determined to carry out a scheme of revenge on her affianced. Her plan needed the help of her beloved adopted sister Cloudlet, who, as we have seen, had conceived a partiality for the bold lover Yang. According to custom Yang was invited to stay at a guest house in the grounds of the Cheung residence, and was treated as a loved son by the Justice and his lady. The lady Cheung herself supervised his food and clothing. Jewel proposed to her mother that Cloudlet, who was skilful as well as beautiful, should be appointed to oversee Master Yang's comfort so as to save her mother. The mother protested. "Your father desires," said the lady Cheung, "that a special husband should be chosen for Cloudlet that she may have a home of her own. When you are married Cloudlet could not go with you as a servant; her station and attainments are superior to that. The only way open to you in accord with ancient rites would be to have her attend as the Master's secondary wife."

Jewel's answer to her mother was: "Master Yang is now eighteen.

He is a scholar of daring spirit who even ventured into the inner quarters of a Minister's home and made sport with his unmarried daughter. How can you expect such a man to be satisfied with only one wife? Later when he becomes a Minister of State and gets ten thousand rice bags as salary, how many Cloudlets will he not have to bear him company?"

But Jewel's mother was not satisfied, and when the Justice was appealed to, she said " To appoint a secondary wife before the first marriage is something I am quite opposed to." The mother was overborne, however, and the Justice entered with amusement into his beloved daughter's plan of revenge.

Jewel then put the matter to her beloved Cloudlet thus: "Cloudlet, I have been with you ever since the hair grew on our brows together. We have loved each other since the days we fought with flower buds. Now that I have my wedding gifts sent me, I wonder who you have thought of for a husband." Cloudlet answered: "I have specially loved you, dear mistress. If I could but hold your dressing mirror for ever I should be satisfied." Jewel continued: "You know that Master Yang made a ninny of me when he played the harp in the inner compound. Only by you, Cloudlet, can I ever hope to wipe out the disgrace. We have a summer pavilion in a secluded part of South Mountain. We could prepare a marriage chamber there. The views are beautiful, like a world of the fairies. I am only desirous that you, Cloudlet, will not mind taking your part in it." Cloudlet laughed and said: "Though I die I will go through with it and do just as you say."

Master Yang was lured to South Mountain with the help of a male cousin and left in a lonely but beautiful place. Here Cloudlet appeared in the guise of a fairy and enticed him into the pavilion. So skilful was Cloudlet's wooing that Yang "loved her from the depths of his heart and his love was reciprocated." A most intricate practical joke was played on Yang for many weeks. Cloudlet pretended to vanish and reappear as a disembodied spirit, and the love-making was then continued in the house given to Yang in the Cheung compound. Then Cloudlet disappeared again, and Yang's "sleep failed him and his desire for food fell away."

The whole household was in the secret, and the Justice, who was watching the affair with amusement, obtained Yang's confidence and hinted that it was a mistake to let a disembodied spirit make love to him. "Even though you say she is a disembodied spirit," said the distressed young man, "this girl is firm and substantial in form and by no means a piece of nothingness." When the Justice felt that the joke had gone far enough he revealed the deception to Yang. The male cousin "rolled in fits of merriment" and "the servants were convulsed with laughter." The old people quietly enjoyed what the Justice said was "a laughable enough joke in its way." Cloudlet gained the desirable position of secondary wife before the consummation of the first marriage and proved her loyalty and love for Mistress Jewel, while Yang had the joy of Cloudlet's constant care and attention.

But before the consummation of Yang's marriage with Jewel many stirring events were to happen. He was sent to far regions to quell rebellions against the State and, after many victories, rose to the highest military command in the land. Meanwhile, the other six love affairs were unfolded. Two of these had been started on his first journey from his native village before passing the Government Examination. The first was the meeting with the maiden, Chin See.

"At a certain place he saw a beautiful grove of willow trees. A blue line of smoke, like silken rolls unwinding, rose skyward. In a retired part of the enclosure he saw a picturesque pavilion with a perfectly kept approach. He slowed up his beast and went near to enjoy the prospect. He sighed and said: In our world of Chok there are many pretty groves, but none that I ever saw so lovely as this. He rapidly composed a poem which ran:

"Willows hung with woven green
Veiling all the view between;
Planted by some fairy free,
Sheltering her and calling me.
Willows, greenest of the green,
Brushing by her silken screen,
Speak by every waving wand,
Of an unseen fairy hand.

"He sang it out with a rich clear voice. It was heard in the top storey of the pavilion, where a beautiful maiden was having a siesta. She opened the embroidered shade and looked out through the painted railing. Her hair, like a tumbled cloud, rested soft

and warm upon her temples. The long jade pin that held the
plaits together had been pushed aside till it showed slantwise
through her tresses. Her sleepy eyelids were as if she had just
emerged from dreamland. Rouge and cosmetics had vanished
under the unceremonious hand of sleep and her natural beauty
was unveiled, a beauty such as no painter has ever portrayed. The
two looked at each other with a fixed and startled expression but
said not a word. The maiden suddenly recollected herself, closed
the blind and disappeared from view. A suggestion of sweet fragrance was borne to Yang on the breeze."

The maiden, Chin See, said to her old nurse: "A woman's lot in
life is to follow her husband. Her glory or her shame, her experiences for the span of life are wrapped up in her lord and master.
I am an unmarried girl and dislike dreadfully to become my own
go-between and propose marriage, but it is said that in ancient
times courtiers chose their own king, so I shall make inquiry concerning this gentleman. I cannot wait for my father's return, for
who knows whither he has gone or where I shall look for him in
the four quarters of the earth?" She then unclasped a roll of satin
paper and wrote a verse or two which she gave to her nurse, telling
her to find "a gentleman handsome as the gods, with eyebrows
like the loftiest touches of a picture, and his form among common
men like the phoenix among feathered fowls." The practical old
nurse replied, "What shall I do if the gentleman is already married or engaged?" The maiden thought for a moment and then
said, "If that unfortunately be so, I shall not object to become his
secondary wife." Her message was:

> "Willows waving by the way,
> Bade my lord his course to stay,
> He, alas, has failed to ken,
> Draws his whip and rides again."

Yang's response was prompt and unmistakably reassuring:

> "Willow catkins soft and dear,
> Bid thy soul to have no fears
> Ever may they bind us true,
> You to me, and me to you."

But Yang's love affair with Chin See of the willow grove came nearer tragedy than any of the eight experiences. Many vicissitudes prevented their speedy union. Meanwhile the love dramas in which two peerless dancing girls, Moonlight and Wildgoose, played their part saved Master Yang from grieving too much over the temporary loss of Chin See.

Moonlight was the next love. She it was who foretold Yang's future greatness and his certain victory at the Competitive Examination. Moonlight chose Yang from among a group of youths who were competing for her favour. When Yang, at Moonlight's invitation, was entertained by her privately, she made her feelings known to him with entire frankness. "I am yours from to-day," she said, "and shall tell you my whole heart." She told the story of the death of her father and the sale of herself by her stepmother for one hundred yang. "I stifled my resentful soul and did my best to be faithful," said Moonlight, "praying to God, who has had pity on me. To-day I have met my lord and look again on the light of sun and moon. I have had opportunity to study thousands of passers by, yet never has one passed who is equal to my master. Unworthy as I am I would gladly become your serving-maid." Yang was as yet without experience and Moonlight became his wise counsellor, giving him hope for the future and confidence in his powers. As he was too poor to marry her, they agreed that he would always come to visit her when he passed that way.

Moonlight's prophecy was speedily fulfilled, and when Yang next visited her he had become a famous general and was on the road with "all the insignia of power – flags, drums and battle axes." Their meeting was full of joy. "Yang, with pent-up heart longings and desire to see her face to face, caught her lovely expression, which took fresh grip of him.... Moonlight saw him dismount and bowed low. She accompanied him into the guest room, where in her joy of soul she took hold of the border of his robes. Her tears flowed faster than her words. She congratulated Yang on his engagement to the daughter of Justice Cheung, and told him how she had had at one time to cut off her hair to escape dishonour so that she might remain true to him. "They renewed their former happy acquaintance and he tarried for several days."

Then follows an account of Moonlight's ruse to let Wildgoose become acquainted with Master Yang without his knowledge: "That night he talked over the past with Moonlight and said how they had indeed been destined for each other. They drank and were happy till the hours grew late. Then they put out the lights and slept. When the east began to lighten he awoke and saw Moonlight dressing her hair before the mirror. He looked at her with tenderest interest and then gave a start and looked again. The delicate eyebrows, the bright eyes, the wavy hair like a cloud over the temples, the rosy-tinted cheeks, the lithe graceful form, the white complexion – all were Moonlight's, and yet it was not she."

Wildgoose made an eloquent plea for her presence. "How could I ever have ventured to do such a thing," she said, "were it not that I have had born in me one great indomitable longing that has possessed me all my life – to attach myself to some renowned hero or superior lord. When the King of Yon learned my name and bought me for a heaped-up bag of jewels, he fed me on the daintiest fare and dressed me in rarest silk. Yet I had no delight in it but was in distress. When the King of Yon invited you to a feast I spied on you through the screen chinks and you were the one man that my heart bounded forth to follow. The palace has nine gateways of approach, but when you had been gone ten days I secretly took one of the King's fast horses and sped forth on my way. What I did last night was at the request of Moonlight. If you will permit me to find shelter under your wide-spreading tree, where I may build my little nest, Moonlight and I will live together, and after the Master is married to some noble lady, she and I will come and speak our good wishes and congratulations."

Yang replied with generous words, and Moonlight also appeared and said: "Now that Wildgoose has waited on my lord as well as I, I thank thee on her behalf." And they bowed repeatedly.

The most startling of Yang's love stories is his meeting with Swallow. It happened during a military campaign. The General was seated in his tent with a lighted candle before him reading despatches during the third watch of the night. Suddenly a cold wind extinguished the light of the candle, an eerie chill filled the tent, and a maiden stepped in upon him from the upper air holding a glittering double-edged sword in her hand. The General, "guessing her to be an assassin," did not quail but stood his ground sternly and asked who she was. "I am under the command of the King of Tibet," she said, "to have thy head." The General laughed. "The Superior Man," he replied, " never fears to die. Take my head, if you please, and go." At this the maiden disclosed her real intent. She had entered the camp at the bidding of the King of Tibet for the ostensible purpose of carrying back to that monarch the head of the great General, but her real object was to reveal her love for Yang and to save his life and help him to victory. "Her face was bright like rose petals with dew on them. She wore phoenix-tail shoes, and her tones were like the oriole." The Teacher who had helped her to become a "master of the sword drill" and had taught her how to "ride the winds, follow the lightnings, and in an instant travel 3,000 *li*," had also revealed to Swallow that Yang was her destined master and her true affinity.

Yang was naturally as delighted as he had been surprised, so "they plighted their troth, the glitter of swords and spears serving for candle light" and the "sound of cymbals for the festal harp." After many days of pleasure Swallow said to Yang, "A military camp is no place for women; I fear that I shall hinder the movements of the troops, so I must go." In vain Yang tried to persuade her that she was not as other women. The Swallow gave him a parting talisman and some sound advice and then "sprang into the air and was gone."

As astounding also was General Yang's love affair with White-cap, the daughter of the Dragon King. This lady helped Yang in his military career by means of magic. Her love-making took place in a grotto under a mountain lake, where she was in hiding in the form of a mermaid. "I am Pak Neung-pa," said White-cap, giving her full name. "When I was born my father was having an audience with God Almighty."

She then explained how she had been dowered from birth with superhuman abilities and had incurred the hatred of a neighbouring King because she refused to listen to the wooing of his undesirable son. She had sought Yang because her affinity with him had been divinely disclosed. White-cap went on: "I have already made promise to you of this humble body, but there are three reasons why I ought not to be mated to your Excellency. First, I have not told my parents; second, I can accompany you only after changing this mermaid form of mine. I still have scales and fishy odours with fins that would defile my lord's presence. Third, there are spies of my unwelcome royal suitor all around us. Our meeting will arouse their anger and cause disaster." The General waived all the objections. "Your ladyship was a fairy in a former life," he said, "and you therefore have a spiritual nature. Between men and disembodied spirits intercourse may be carried on without wrong, then why should I have aversion to scales and fins? Why should we miss this opportunity to seal our happy contract?" So they "swore the oath of marriage and found great delight in each other." After this encounter Yang's military victories were more glorious than ever and he returned home the greatest man of the age.

On Yang's return to the capital the highest honour had been prepared for him that can fall to the lot of an Imperial subject. A marriage had been arranged between him and the lovely Princess of the Imperial family, Princess Orchid, and he became a Prince in rank. How this marriage was arranged, and Yang's marriage with Justice Cheung's daughter, Jewel, who was raised to Imperial rank by adoption, was consummated, and how the reunion took place with Cloudlet and Chin See, the reader is told with many thrilling and humorous details.

Yang's aged mother was brought with great ceremony to the capital. Honours and gifts were showered upon her. The two Princesses bowed before her as dutiful daughters-in-law, and the six secondary wives also delighted in giving her honour. Yang's princely household was so great that palaces, halls, galleries and pagodas were requisitioned. His life with his eight wives, their children and his aged mother, was a revelation of earthly bliss and wondrous grandeur. The Emperor's reign was also a notable time of peace and prosperity. Even in old age Yang and his ladies had beauty and the power of enjoyment.

But a day came when the Master heard "faint voices calling from another world." "Slowly his spirit withdraws from earthly delights."

One day, while sitting in a high tower from which there was a view of Chin River stretching in silvery reaches for a hundred miles, he drew forth his green stone flute and played for his ladies a "plaintive air as though heaped-up sorrows and tears had broken forth upon them." The two Princesses asked why he should suggest such sorrow in the midst of their exceeding happiness with "golden flowers dropping petals" at his feet, and "our loving hearts around you?" The Master pointed to distant ruins of palaces that had held famous men and their women folk. He spoke of his boyhood as a poor scholar and the wonderful triumphs of his career and their nine rare affinities. "Children who gather wood or feed their cattle on the hillside," he said, "will sing their songs and tell our mournful story, saying, 'This is where Master Yang made merry with his wives and family. All his honours and delights, all the pretty faces of his ladies are gone for ever.'" Hearing the Master's words the ladies were moved and knew that he "was about to meet the Enlightened One."

Then there appeared an old man leaning upon a staff. His "eyebrows were an *ell* long and his eyes were like the blue waves of the sea." He was the aged priest of Lotus Peak who had come to summon Yang. He conversed with Yang, who did not at first recognise him – and in a little while Yang woke to find himself in a small cell in a monastery on a mountain side. He looked at himself and at his dress. He was again Song-jin the acolyte. His earthly power and his eight wives had vanished as a dream that is gone. The Teacher came to him and said: "You have soared on the wings of worldly delight and have seen and known for yourself. You say that you have dreamed a dream of mortal life upon the wheel and now you think the world and the dream itself to be different. But this is not so. If you think it so, this shows that you are not awakened from your sleep." Song-jin replied: "I am a darkened soul and so cannot distinguish which is the dream and which is the actual reality. Please open to me the truth."

Before the Teacher had time to explain, the eight fairies of the Queen of the genii appeared at the monastery gate. They said to the Teacher: "Our earthly desires have gone forth after sin and evil in the dream of mortal life, and there is none to save us but the Great Teacher who in love and mercy himself came to call us."

The Great Teacher appointed the eight fairies their places in the Hall of the Buddha. Then he took "his cassock, his alms-dish, water-bottle and his ornamented staff, his Diamond Sutra, gave them to Song-jin, bade them all farewell and took his departure to the West." Song-jin became chief of the disciples on that height and taught the Doctrine, and the eight fairies, as priestesses, served him as their master and drank deeply of the Doctrine.

And at last they all reached the blissful heights of Paradise.

WOMAN'S VOICE IN POLYGAMY

Polygamy is the chief bulwark of the Chinese and Korean family system, and when its basic claim is accepted by a community its practicableness, if not its justice, is undoubted. The men of the Tang era had everything to gain by such a system. The women meekly accepted their place because they believed that they were expiating the faults of a former existence by enduring the shame of being women. But in this tale, which honours the mating of one man and eight women, we find some of the women giving voice to an inward discontent.

The Princess Orchid, Jewel and Cloudlet, we read, sat "like the three feet of the incense burner," so perfectly were they matched in beauty, grace and learning. "They laughed sweetly and talked in soft and tender accents. Perfect agreement possessed them in thought and mind and soul, and they loved each other with an infinite delight. They talked of all the great masters of the past and of the renowned ladies of ages gone by till the shadows of the night began to cast their lines athwart the silken window."

There is nothing more convincing in the whole story than the impression that the writer unconsciously gives of the strenuous intellectual and artistic pastimes of these women of the Tang era. Their physical charms are dwelt on poetically and fancifully but never sensuously; their accomplishments are so varied that they not only embroider and paint, study music, dancing and sword drill, and write poems so that their "pens flew like swift wind or a sudden squall of rain," but in classical allusion and metaphor they hold their own in conversation with literary men.

The Princess said to Jewel: "A boy is free to go to all points of the land and sea, he can pick and choose good friends, can learn from another and can correct his faults, while a girl meets no one but the servants of her own household. How can she expect to grow in goodness or to find in any such place answers to the questions of the soul? I was mourning over the fact that I was a girl shut up in prison when I heard that your knowledge was equal to that of Pang-So and your virtue and loveliness like that of the ancients. Though you do not pass outside your own gateway, yet your name is known abroad even to the Imperial Palace. You have not refused me admittance and now I have attained my heart's dearest desire."

Jewel made answer: "Your kind words will live for ever in my humble heart. Locked up as I am in these inner quarters, my footsteps are hindered from freedom and my sight and hearing are limited to this small enclosure. I have never seen the waters of the wide sea nor the long stretches of the hills. So limited in experience and knowledge am I that your praise of me is too great altogether."

And Jewel's real inner heart is expressed in her prayer to Buddha when she believed that she would have to give up Yang, who was under royal command to wed the Imperial Princess. She prayed:

"Thy disciple, Kyong-pai, by means of her servant, Cloudlet, who has bathed and made the required offerings, bows low, worships and makes her petition.

"Thy disciple has many sins to answer for, sins of a former existence as yet unexpiated. These account for her birth into this life as a desolate girl who never knew the joy of sisterhood. Condescend, ye Holy Ones, to accept this prayer of mine, extend to me pity and let my parents live long like the endless measure of the sky. Grant that I be free from sickness and trouble so that I may be able to dress neatly and to please them, and thus play out my little part in life on their behalf. When their appointed span is over I will break with all the bonds of earth, submit my actions to the requirements of the law and give my heart to the reading of the sacred sutras, keep myself pure, worship the Holy One and make payment for all the unmerited blessings that have come to me.

"My servant, Cloudlet, who is my chosen companion, brings this to thee. Though in name we two are maid and mistress we are in reality friend and friend. She in obedience to my orders became the secondary wife of General Yang, but now that matters have fallen otherwise and there is no longer hope for the happy affinity that was ours, she too has bade a long farewell to him and has come back to me so that we may be one in sorrow as well as in blessing, in death as well as in life. I earnestly pray that the divine

Buddha will condescend to read our two hearts and grant that for all generations and transmigrations to come we may escape the lot of being born women, that thou wilt put away all our sins of a former existence, give blessing for the future so that we may transmigrate to some happy place to share endless bliss for ever."

Cloudlet's good-bye to Master Yang proves that Jewel's belief in her devotion and loyalty was well founded. Yang had tried to persuade Cloudlet that she might remain with him. He said: "Your devotion to your mistress is most commendable. Still your lady's person and yours are different. While she goes north, south, east or west as she chooses, your following her and at the same time attempting to render service to another, would break all the laws that govern a woman's existence."

Cloudlet replied: "Your words prove that you do not know the mind of my mistress. She has already decided to remain with her aged parents. When they die she will preserve her purity, cut off her hair, enter a monastery and give herself up in prayer to the Buddha, in the hope that in the life to come she may not be born a woman. I, too, will do just the same as she. If your lordship intends to see me again your marriage gifts must go back to the rooms of my lady. If not, then to-day marks our parting for life. Since I have waited on your lordship I have been greatly loved and favoured and I can never repay even in a hundred years a thousandth part of all your kindness. My one wish is that in the life to come I may be your faithful dog or horse...." She then blessed him and turned away weeping bitterly.

HEAVEN ON EARTH

Confucian, Buddhist and Taoist ideas are mingled throughout the story, but everyone speaks with confidence of Heaven as a place. While the Buddhist conception of Heaven is so pure that no earthly desire can exist there, Yang is carried in dreamland to a very different Heaven. He is being entertained by the Dragon King, who desires to do him all honour and to express gratitude for Yang's deliverance of the Dragon King's daughter from her enemy. After being borne on the wind to a spot "close to the outskirts of Heaven," they arrive at the palace, where a gorgeous feast is spread for them.

"They" (the Dragon King, Yang and the Dragon King's daughter) "drank till their hearts were merry and then the King called for music. Splendid music it was, arranged in mystic harmony unlike the music of the earth. A thousand giants, each bearing sword and spear, beat monster drums. Six rows of dancing girls dressed in phoenix garb and wearing bright moon ornaments, gracefully shook their long flowing sleeves and danced in pairs, a thrilling and enchanting sight."

Yang seems to have touched the height of satiety also at a festival in his earthly paradise. We read:

"The Master (Yang) and the Prince were compelled by the falling shadows of the evening to break up the feast and return. They gave each performer rich presents of gold, silver and silk. Grain measures of gems were scattered about, and rolls of costly materials were piled up like hillocks. The Master and the Prince, taking advantage of the moonlight, returned home to the city amid the ringing of bells. All the dancers and musicians jostled each other along the way. The sound of gems and tinkling ornaments was like falling water, and perfume filled the atmosphere. Straying hairpins and jewelled ornaments were crushed by the horses' hoofs and the passing of countless feet. The crowd in the city, desiring to see, stood like a wall on each side of the way. Old men of ninety and a hundred wept tears of joy, saying: 'In my younger days I saw his Majesty Hyon-jong (AD 713–736) out on procession and his splendour alone could be compared with this.'"

We smile at such an absurd conception of life. But it is to this strange ideal of a commingling of earthly paradises and fairy heavens that the world owes the exquisite perfection of so much Chinese craftsmanship. The artists of that bygone day moulded the drinking vessels, embroidered the robes, fashioned the jade flutes and made all the other lovely things worshipfully. A more sophisticated age looks almost with despair on the remnants of the loveliness they created.

THE PRESENT TRANSLATION

On the literary presentation of this work a word may be said. Dr. Gale is a scholar and a broad-minded and intensely sympathetic student of Oriental life. His first aim, his compelling aim, is, in his own words to the writer, "to contribute towards some more correct knowledge of the Far East." His thoughts are on a faithful interpretation of the Far Eastern mind and Far Eastern manners rather than on those felicities of word and phrase with which literary reputations are sought. We have had of late a piece of Far Eastern translation in which too much was sacrificed to literary form. Dr. Gale makes no claim whatever to literary graces. Only those whose knowledge of the Korean language, life and character approaches the learning of Dr. Gale may safely criticise his phrasings. It is clear that, in executing the immense task he set himself, his wish has been to write down the simplest possible renderings. Some may wish that more time had been spared for niceties; no reader will fail to feel the self-suppression of the translator and the absence of linguistic or other affectations. Because there is no labouring after the literary, because the translator's heart is set first on sincerity, the artless happy word and phrase constantly occur. The way in which this version carries us through the mazes of a story on a plan so foreign to that of Western fiction is marvellous. The work must enhance, if that be possible, the reputation of Dr. Gale as an interpreter of the Korean mind and increase that sense of obligation which every man and woman who wishes to grasp something of Far Eastern thought and sentiment already feels towards this unusual man.

Elspet Keith Robertson Scott[†]

†Elspet Keith Robertson Scott was the younger sister of British artist Elizabeth Keith. The daughter of a civil service family, she was raised in England, and in 1906 married the journalist, author, and publisher J.W. Robertson Scott. They moved to Japan in 1914, where J.W. Robertson Scott established a monthly magazine and toured the country studying Japanese rural life and people. During their time in Japan, Elspet Keith Robertson Scott came to be acquainted with many of the leading literary and cultural figures of the day, both in Japan and Korea. She and her sister – who came to Japan in 1915 – travelled widely, and together they produced the classic *Old Korea: The Land of Morning Calm* (Hutchinson, 1946): Elspet contributing the text, and Elizabeth the illustrations. James Gale, the translator of the present book, contributed to the notes. Starting in 1923, she supported J.W. Robertson Scott in his role as founder-editor of *The Countryman* magazine, and in his activities in English local government. She died in 1956.